AN IGNOBLE DESIRE?

Jasmine scrambled back, pressing against the hardwood headboard. Unsmiling, Thomas regarded her as he stripped off his shirt. His chest was sprinkled with dark hair, his stomach flat and rippling with muscle.

Her gaze traveled downward. A tiny gasp fled her as she glimpsed the bulge in his trousers. Jasmine was innocent, but she'd once seen the stable hand coupling with the downstairs maid in the hay. She knew what that bulge meant: He wanted her, as a man wanted. Not as an earl's heir, or an aristocrat, but as a man.

Thomas reached the bed and leaned over, bracketing her body with his powerful arms. A hank of dark hair hung down on his forehead. She felt an absurd, tender urge to brush it back. He smelled of leather and bayberry. The scent intoxicated her. The green of his eyes was brilliant emerald.

"I must have you," he said.

Other *Leisure* books by Bonnie Vanak:

THE SWORD & THE SHEATH
THE PANTHER & THE PYRAMID
THE COBRA & THE CONCUBINE
THE TIGER & THE TOMB
THE FALCON & THE DOVE

The Scorpion & the Seducer

Bonnie Vanak

LEISURE BOOKS NEW YORK CITY

For Frank, my hero. Forever and always.

A LEISURE BOOK®

May 2008

Published by

Dorchester Publishing Co., Inc.
200 Madison Avenue
New York, NY 10016

ISBN 10: 0-8439-5975-4
ISBN 13: 978-0-8439-5975-8

Printed in the United States of America.

10 9 8 7 6 5 4 3 2 1

Visit us on the web at www.dorchesterpub.com.

The Scorpion
& the Seducer

Chapter One

His mouth was bloodied. A long scratch ran down his cheek, as if a cat had clawed him. Grass strains marred his clothing.

All these were possible to conceal, if Nigel didn't tell, and Thomas prayed his brother wouldn't. Please God, he silently beseeched, for once let his brother keep quiet. Please. He didn't know if he could stand another beating.

The townhouse was quiet when he crept inside, the gleaming staircase smelling of beeswax, the floors clean and bright. Father couldn't tolerate mess. Thomas glanced down at his ripped clothing. He was a mess. Perhaps the downstairs maid could polish him, too.

Barely had he started up the stairs, filled with dim hope, when a stern voice called out behind him, "Where do you think you're going?"

Fear clawed up his spine. Thomas bit his lip and tried to hold back his terror.

"I, um, Father—"

"Come down here."

Slowly, he turned. Turned and saw him: the Earl of Claradon glowering at him with his beet-red face, the starched white collar at his fleshy throat looking to choke him. Beside the earl, Nigel smiled. A knowing, evil smile.

Thomas swallowed hard. He must be brave. But he couldn't help shaking a little as he made his way downstairs. Nigel, the precious, good son. Nigel could do nothing wrong. Nigel was perfect. Perfect, as Thomas was not.

His father hissed in disgust as Thomas descended to the bottom stair. "A girl. A damn girl, and not just any girl. That brown heathen belonging to that Egyptian woman. Where is your spine, that you'd allow an inferior to best you? You're twelve years old. You're soft, boy. Be like your brother. You're a Wallenford."

The earl's voice was low, which indicated his fury. Courage welled inside Thomas. He looked directly at his father.

"I could never be like Nigel, Father. No matter how hard you try to make us the same."

Blood infused the earl's face. "Watch your tongue, boy."

"I think Thomas should invite Jasmine to the party next week just so everyone can see exactly who thrashed him," Nigel spoke up."

Thomas dared lift his hostile gaze to his brother. "I would, just to avoid looking at your ugly face. Jasmine is a sight prettier."

"My ugly face? Look in the mirror." Nigel sneered, then began singing, "Thomas likes Jasmine, Thomas likes Jasmine. He's in love with the little brown scorpion."

Pain lanced Thomas. Why didn't his brother like him anymore? Once they had laughed together, played together, hunted frogs and gotten in scrapes. They'd stood up for each other like best mates. Then, four winters ago, Nigel fell seriously ill. Thomas had been sent away with his aunt and uncle to visit warm, sunny Egypt. When he'd come home, terrified that Nigel had died, he found his brother alive.

But Nigel had changed. He was no longer a friend, but an enemy. Thomas had quietly forced himself to accept the fact that Nigel would always detest him, and that his father would always sigh and shake his head and compare them unfavorably.

Nigel loathed both Thomas and eight-year-old Amanda. Time and again he'd stated to them in private how he wished he were an only child. Last week he'd locked Mandy in the hay bin, telling her he was tired of her incessant chattering.

Thomas had found her an hour later, silent tears streaking cheeks. He'd vowed to protect her from his brother's cruelties.

Thomas glanced now at the stairs. Crouched at the top, her blue eyes wide, Mandy stared down at him from between the rods of the stairway railing. She mustn't be seen, lest Father draw her into this as well. Thomas gave his head a barely perceptible shake, entreating her escape back upstairs. Mandy vanished quietly as a mouse. Thomas released the breath he'd held.

The Earl of Claradon looked with disgust at him. "You're more useless than the stable boy. Nigel is right. You will invite that heathen girl. Your mother will then show this Jasmine her proper place. She'll never dare to show her face among her betters again."

Dread filled Thomas. They'd humiliate Jasmine terribly. Jasmine, whom he teased and mocked, whom he secretly admired for daring to ride a horse the Bedouin style. Jasmine, from that exotic land of Egypt, which always fascinated him. Jasmine, with her wild snapping eyes and spirit. When he'd insulted her, she didn't cry and run away like a girl; she punched him.

Now he'd pay the price. And so would she.

"Come along, boy." His father took him by the ear, while Nigel walked alongside with a smug look. They went to the stables Thomas loved so much. The pungent scent of horses and manure was comforting. His father barked an order to the stable hands. Thankfully, they left. Thomas felt a dim gratitude they would not witness his humiliation.

The earl picked up a riding crop, rapped it against his thigh. Each blow made Thomas tremble. He knew what was coming.

This time, it would be bad, very bad indeed.

"Six strokes this time—double the usual amount because you humiliated our family. Take off your shirt."

With shaking hands, Thomas did so. Wanting to defy him. To run away. But Wallenfords did not run away. They took their punishment. They were perfect, like Nigel; remote in public, and reserved. Thomas thought of Jasmine, who fought back.

The earl raised the crop. Thomas did something he'd never before had the courage to do. He grabbed the crop, held on tight.

For once, he faced the earl. "No, Father."

Red infused the earl's face. "No," he repeated, his voice rising. "No?"

Even Nigel backed off, fear flickering in his eyes.

His father yanked the crop from Thomas's hand, tossed it aside. He picked up a horsewhip hanging from a nail. "I'll show you *no*. You'll learn obedience, boy. I'll beat it into you."

Nigel looked at the earl with horror. Then he said words Thomas could scarcely believe. "Father, don't do this to him—please," he begged.

Disgust twisted the earl's face. "Are you turning soft as well? Get out."

Nigel stared at Thomas, something akin to grief shadowing his face. "I'm sorry I told on you," he whispered.

Thomas's throat closed with emotion. He watched his brother run off, filled with dim hope that Nigel did care. Then the terror returned.

The horsewhip whistled through the air. It held a volatile fury of its own, snapping, stinging the flesh on Thomas's left hand.

Thomas bit back a cry. He turned and exposed his back. He tried to be brave, but the pain made him gasp and double over with each hard lash. Over and over. Six blows. Seven. Eight. Warmth he knew was blood ran down his back. Despite his resolve, tears dripped down his cheeks.

"Remember, boy." His father's voice became a drone accompanying each stroke. "You will never, ever again, let your inferiors best you. Let this be a lesson you'll never forget."

As he clenched his jaw to avoid screaming, Thomas promised himself: He wouldn't forget. Ever.

Chapter Two

They hadn't invited her to the ball again. She sneaked in anyway.

Hidden in the shadows, Jasmine Tristan lurked in the stately gardens of the Earl of Claradon's London townhouse. A faint scent of roses filled the air. Jasmine reached out, stroked a bloodred petal. These plants: beautiful, trimmed daily with ferocious care. No cow parsley or straggling primroses were permitted to ruin this very orderly setting. Lady Claradon pruned the garden as carefully as the guest lists for her annual masquerade ball.

Snapping off a blossom, Jasmine inhaled its fragrance. Heavy, cloying. But very much admired by the English. She waved the flower like a magic wand at the ballroom's tightly closed French doors.

"Open sesame," she whispered, remembering her favorite *Arabian Nights* tale.

Dewy grass sloshed beneath Jasmine's feet as she raced for a stately oak and hid behind it. Shadows swallowed her as she crept toward the terrace. The haunting strains of music by violin and flute drifted outside the ballroom.

She peered around a square-cut boxwood hedge. Graceful as windspun feathers, couples in elaborate costumes twirled past the windows. Muted light from the crystal chandeliers gilded the golden silk wallpaper of the ballroom. It looked like a glittering fairy tale, complete with handsome princes, princesses and fawning courtiers.

She felt like an invading ogre.

Jasmine smoothed her gown with a shaky hand. The Renaissance dress with its emerald overskirt and gold brocade underskirt draped over her full hips and breasts. It fell in elegant lines in a sweep of velvet. The long, puff sleeves adorned with pearls and gold braid concealed her slender arms. A gold snood swept back her waist-length ebony corkscrew curls. Rice powder applied over a heavy coat of white theatrical greasepaint coated her neck and face. It turned her honey-gold skin pale as an English lady's. No one could tell she was dark as the Egyptian parents who birthed her.

For years, she'd tried to pry open the doors to English society's upper crust. Nothing succeeded. Not learning English speech and English ways and English dress. Not cloaking her Egyptian accent or learning to sit properly at tea parties. Not even her adopted father's viscount title helped. Jasmine's family wasn't wealthy enough to kick that particular door down.

Only her uncle, the Duke of Caldwell, had managed to gain her a very limited Season after presenting her at Court. But at her coming out, when Uncle Graham's back was turned, some remarked how Jasmine resembled a brown wren in her white gown.

Her attention whipped back to the terrace. The brief, sharp whistle came as planned. Time to attend the masquerade.

Silhouetted by the ballroom light, her best friend walked down the stone steps. Chloe's plain, round face, plump figure and modest dowry failed to attract many suitors. But she had a sweet disposition, and tiger claws for anyone who mocked Jasmine's heritage. Unfortunately those people were plentiful, which meant Chloe was left out of society events nearly as frequently as Jasmine. Chloe didn't care. Jasmine loved her like a sister.

The Earl of Claradon's annual masquerade ball attracted society's cream. More the sediment, Chloe had been invited to honor her friendship with Lady Amanda. Thin as a river reed, Amanda probably reasoned the plain, plump Chloe would provide a striking contrast.

"Jasmine?" Dressed as a milkmaid, Chloe pushed her half-mask up on her forehead.

"No wild jasmine here, just a very prim English rose," she quipped, tapping her friend's nose with the bloom.

Chloe grinned, settled the mask back on her face. "We'll pretend we were strolling in the gardens, gossiping. Then just come inside with me. No one will notice you. You'll blend perfectly." Her friend's gaze swept over Jasmine and she sighed. "You look beautiful. Surely you'll attract many eager to dance."

Fierce loyalty rose in Jasmine. "You will as well, Chloe."

A head shake. "No one so far, but Thomas, and he was just being nice. He did introduce me to his friend, Simon, who seemed interested, but—" Her voice trailed off. She leaned close to Jasmine, dropped her voice. "Then again, if I freely gave out what Amanda does."

Jasmine raised her brows. "Treats?"

"Of a certain nature. Last year, after Amanda's dinner party. Everyone had long since left, but I remained, talking a while with Thomas. After he excused himself for another engagement, I went into the garden to take in the air and admire Lady Claradon's roses. There were moans coming from behind the bushes. I saw Amanda with the gardener. He was quite clearly plucking a flower—but not the garden variety."

Shocked, Jasmine reeled back on her heels. Amanda, the prim daughter who just became engaged to Lord Ridley?

"Amanda? Are you certain?"

Chloe shrugged. "It was dark, and the gardener was obscuring, er, her face, but I'm fairly certain. Besides, I recognized the shoes. She always boasted about those shoes; they were her favorites."

This household did have its black sheep, even if they were white. The thought amused Jasmine.

"I'm certain Lady Claradon would be horrified to know her prize bud has lost its bloom, and to a mere servant," she whispered, snickering.

"He snipped her right and good." Chloe made a low-pitched squealing sound of pleasure, giggled. She pointed toward the ballroom. "Are you ready to go inside?"

"Ready." Setting the rose aside, Jasmine slipped on her emerald satin half-mask outlined with sparkling paste jewels.

Bending their heads together, the women walked on the stone path leading to the limestone terrace. Chloe climbed the steps, looked over her shoulder. Jasmine hung back, one hand gripping the heavy folds of her dress.

"Come on!" Chloe whispered.

A shudder raced down Jasmine's spine. Setting foot inside the ballroom presented a personal challenge. Ever since that horrific night in the park, she had avoided any contact with the earl's family. She swallowed hard. She'd already made one dreadful mistake. Was she risking another? If discovered, she'd surely be thrown out—or worse, mocked. Lady Claradon, who reputedly called Jasmine "that ugly brown Egyptian scorpion" behind her back, would do it to her face.

Jasmine glanced down at her hands, covered by prim white gloves. For once she'd prove to them, and herself, she could fit in. Even if only for five minutes.

"The hell with it," she said aloud. "Chloe, go on. I'm not sneaking in. I'm making my own damn entrance."

Grayish moonlight showed the stark surprise on her friend's face. Then Chloe grinned, gave a brief nod and vanished inside the door, closing it firmly behind her.

Jasmine drew a steadying breath as she climbed the steps. She waited a heartbeat or two, then reached for the brass door handle. Head back, chin tilted skyward, she swept inside the ballroom, confident as a queen entering her court.

She saw a blur of costumes. Jasmine steeled herself as she recognized Lady Amanda dressed as Alice in Wonderland, Mozart by her side. Others murmured. Watched. Scrutinized.

Lady Amanda tossed Jasmine a censuring look, as if to silently abrade her guest for strolling the gardens. For a moment, Jasmine faltered. Then she remembered what Chloe had told her. Smothering a knowing grin, she squared her shoulders.

Chin up—no slouching, no lowering of one's gaze like a servant. She picked up her skirts and sailed forward, leaving no hesitation in her wake. Here was the H.M.S. Jasmine, journeying to victory over the snobbish English *ton*.

Heart racing, she headed for a quieter corner, settled in to observe. Waited. After a moment she realized no one approached, questioned or stared. Strains from a waltz began. Couples floated onto the floor.

Safe. For now. Jasmine's heart beat with hopeful joy. She relaxed the grip on her skirts, gazed about her with interest. Musicians played on a raised dais near one silk-paneled wall. Jewels dripped from the thin, wrinkled necks of older women supervising their younger charges.

Jasmine caught sight of a pirate waltzing with a petite, dark-haired woman dressed as a princess. She went still as the pirate turned, revealing the chiseled features of the Earl of Claradon's only son and heir.

Thomas Wallenford.

When she was nine and he was twelve, she'd punched him in the face for calling her an ugly mare. His mother would call her far worse, and had she known him better, she might have saved that blow for another day.

Shortly afterward, Tommy invited her to his birthday party. She'd attended out of pure curiosity. But he'd actually talked with her of horses and even grinned when she called him Caesar, the nickname she'd given him, "Because you think you're as important as a Roman emperor."

Then his mother spilled an entire pot of tea on Jasmine and sent her home to change. When she'd returned with her governess, the butler told them to use the servant's entrance. Humiliated, her governess took her home.

Thomas. Handsome, unreachable. Nigel, his brother had

died two years ago riding the Arabian mare Uncle Graham had just sold to Thomas.

Customary guilt pinched Jasmine, and memories: that night. Nigel's mocking, drunken laughter echoing through the park. Her anger and shame. The sound of hooves pounding wildly into the grass as he rode off. The dreadful scream that followed.

She shook off thoughts of Nigel, concentrated on watching Thomas. Uncle Graham admired his sharpened eye for commerce. Business acquaintances called him ruthless. Women called him the Seducer. They whispered he was a skillful, generous lover, taking time to learn a woman's pleasures, and taking even greater delight in delivering them.

Her breath hitched as the waltz ended and Thomas left his partner. Immediately, a gaggle of ladies flocked to him. So handsome. So dangerous.

He resembled an English Lucifer with jade-green eyes. His dark chestnut hair waved over a high forehead and curled rebelliously at the edges. She liked the dashing look it gave him. His angular cheeks were clean-shaven. Thick dark brows settled rakishly over impossibly large eyes—eyes tipped with crescents of long black lashes that would make him appear feminine but for his aquiline nose, chiseled jaw and the implacable set of a full, sensual mouth.

Thomas was dressed as a pirate, in snug black breeches molded to muscular thighs, knee-high jackboots and a crisp white linen shirt, open at the throat. A wooden cutlass hung from his leather belt. Instead of a mask, he wore an eye patch. He looked powerful and rakish. A slight shiver skated down Jasmine's spine.

Inching closer for a look, she pressed through the crush. Hands hooked behind his back, Thomas smiled. He appeared raptly interested as one gushing woman illustrated her story with flapping white arms. What could be so fascinating? Intrigued, Jasmine drew closer, a moth beating close to his flame.

Not too close, should her wings singe, she warned herself.

Snippets of conversation drifted over. Jasmine strained to hear.

"Lord Thomas, you should take in the stupendous delights of *my* gardens. My English roses are impeccably trimmed by no less than ten gardeners. Your time would be well consumed in inspecting roses. The pink color is spectacular, and the blooms are very fleshy."

Thomas, enchanted by roses? Jasmine rolled her eyes. When had he become so girlish? Whatever happened to the boy who bragged how he'd ridden the earl's high-spirited stallion? Those long eyelashes flickered, and in his eyes she caught a flash of honest emotion: Boredom. Jasmine grinned. Not girlish. Just very well trained.

Thomas gave a brief nod. His gaze flicked over to his companion's three whey-faced giggling daughters, filling their pink satin gowns like overstuffed sausages. "Mrs. Hadden, I'm certain I'd find your English roses very . . . pink and fleshy."

The deep timbre of his voice sent another shiver coursing down Jasmine's spine. She waited, interested. Had Mrs. Hadden more sense than a peahen, she'd realize Thomas obliquely insulted her. Silent applause rang in her head, knowing what a boor the woman was. *Good show, Thomas.*

A hint of vulnerability crossed his face. Thomas looked as lonely as Jasmine felt. But what rubbish. He had everything: money, an imminent title, scads of adoring women at his feet.

Riveted, she continued staring as a beanpole-thin woman dressed as the Queen of Hearts appeared at his side. Jasmine reeled in a shocked gasp. Lady Claradon. Wouldn't the harridan enjoy playing that role if she spotted Jasmine? *Off with her head!* she'd snap in a trice.

The women flocking about Thomas drifted away, disappointed looks etching their faces. The earl's wife rapped her son's arm with her heart-shaped scepter, gestured to someone. Flick, the scepter went. Flick, flick.

Jasmine picked up her skirts, ready to find safer ground. She was scanning the crowd for Chloe when Thomas glanced her way. Her heart raced as their gazes caught, held. Lifting his piratic eyepatch, he studied her. Dread coursed through Jasmine. This was a terrible mistake. How could she have assumed she'd waltz inside and never come into contact with him? She had to avoid him. The earl's son could do something worse than his mother and break her dignity: he could very likely break her heart.

Thomas snapped the eyepatch back, detached himself from his mother.

"Thomas, where are you going?" Lady Claradon demanded.

Ignoring his mother's protest, he began to push his way toward Jasmine. Being a sensible type, Jasmine did the only thing one could in such a predicament.

She fled.

How was it possible to be lonely while surrounded by hundreds of people?

Lord Thomas Wallenford pondered the question as he waltzed his mistress about the parquet floor, his sharpened gaze studying the ballroom occupants. In their masks, they could be anyone. They were not. Like him, they were society's elite. And yet they were replicas of each other, as unremarkable as the room's gilded wallpaper. But that wallpaper veiled ugliness; behind the façade of elegance, rot had begun sinking into the townhouse walls. How appropriate the analogy.

His thoughts drifted to a meeting with the Duke of Caldwell, his new business partner. He and Graham had discussed commerce while the duke sprawled on the floor of his drawing room, playing "bear" with his two adorable daughters. They squealed and plucked at Graham's jacket as he growled at them. Sitting in a chair nearby, the duchess, his wife, smiled.

The adoring looks the duke and duchess cast each other made Thomas feel empty. Could he ever find the same?

"You're looking rather pensive tonight. What is it?" Charlotte asked.

Instantly on guard, he offered a charming smile. "I was admiring the scenery," he murmured. *And thinking how pretentious everything is.*

The Duke of Caldwell was not pretentious. But neither was he accepted. Thomas's social equals distrusted the duke and excluded him from most soirees. Raised in Egypt, Graham was cause for speculation. Some hinted at ancient scandal.

Thomas avoided scandal. Except for business, he associated only with the right sort of people, whose adherance to the strict social codes was as rigid as their proper British spines. If loneliness was the price he paid, then it was worth the cost, he reflected ruefully. He was the future Earl of Claradon.

"Thomas, you're not looking at me again. I wore this just for you." Charlotte pouted.

He studied the woman in his arms. Her low-cut Empire gown showed the delicious, dark valley between her ample breasts. He considered the possibilities. Dance her about the ballroom, then a much more private dance in her bedchamber later.

"You look splendid, Charlotte. That gown is fetching."

"Perhaps you should visit me later and see my other attire. It is equally fetching."

God, he adored women. Especially deliciously widowed, deliciously endowed, deliciously sensual women. Dangling from the end of a fine chain was his latest gift to her: a gold ankh charm. She fingered it and cast him a seductive look from beneath her long lashes.

"You promised me a present, Thomas. What will it be? Another of your Egyptian charms? They fascinate me," she pressed.

"I thought you had little interest in Egypt."

"I have interest in you. And you say some bestow good fortune—such as that scorpion amulet you showed me that's a good luck charm. I need good luck . . . as much as I need you." Her cheeks dimpled again, and she stroked his arm.

"Perhaps." Thomas arched like a purring cat at her light touch, feeling his body harden.

Her voice dropped to a sultry whisper: "You know, you're not like your brother. Nigel could never equal you in bed, try as he might."

His smile, and everything else, drooped. Charlotte's whispered words were like a douse of icy water on his private parts.

"Dear Charlotte," he murmured back, "I must decline your invitation. I've made it a habit to avoid ménage a trois."

Bemusement shadowed her lovely face. Thomas suppressed a sigh. Lovely, but a dull wit. The waltz ended and he escorted her off the dance floor.

"Thomas, will I see you later? I must," she wheedled.

Thomas made an excuse, citing a prior engagement. Ignoring her annoyed pout, he walked off.

As his critical gaze swept the dance floor, it softened as he spotted Amanda, beaming as she danced with her fiancé. His sister's love match was rare, with the soon-to-be-groom's rigid family approving of Mandy's spotless reputation; Thomas vaguely recalled a broken engagement when the baron discovered his previous fiancée had indulged in an affair with an American industrialist.

Seeing his sister and Richard together amplified his inner loneliness. Would he ever find someone to love? He must marry for duty, either way. But at least Mandy's joy was assured. Her happiness was crucial.

Thomas walked. He felt restless tonight, riddled with a yearning he couldn't define. Life was splendid and filled with pampered extravagance. Mandy's engagement was secured and his own future was as sparkling as the champagne served in crystal glasses. Why then did he feel so damn unhappy?

Friends were the solution. Thomas signaled to William Oakley. Oakley lifted his mask, nodded and vanished into the crush. The club—a few rounds of drinks, some laughs. This boring evening would resolve itself predictably.

He'd started planning a quiet exit when his mother appeared. She chased away the toadies briskly, as a broom sweeping out dust. Unfortunately, she had an agenda. She nodded at a young girl in an indigo silk gown frothed with ivory lace. A sharp rap of his mother's scepter indicated approval.

"Thomas, I am going to introduce you to The Honorable Alice Randall, the viscount's daughter. The family's financially solid. She's only eighteen and just had her come-out ball, but has good bloodlines and will make you an excellent wife. And she's extremely robust about the hips. Healthy. Will breed you fine sons."

Breeding. Bloodlines. He felt like a reluctant stud, his cock bound by duty as much as he was.

"Mother, I'm only twenty-five. I have plenty of time for siring a multitude of heirs."

Tears filled his mother's rheumy eyes. She grasped the lace handkerchief hidden in her long sleeve. "Your dear brother was unmarried and childless when he died. It's all the fault of that wild Arabian!"

Emotion clogged his throat. Nigel, the brother who'd hated him and then became his friend again. Nigel, the perfect son who became perfectly determined to ruin himself. Thomas had tried to stop him. The result of his failure lay six feet below the earth in a mouldering coffin. Thomas would not fail his family again.

Nigel, ah Nigel! Why the hell did you ride my mare, damn you? You knew you couldn't handle her. She was too spirited and you were too intoxicated. It's my fault. I should have known, should have stopped you. And now you're gone.

His mother dabbed at her eyes. "Thomas, you cannot marry soon enough. If you die without issue, the title will pass on to your father's dreadful cousin. Do you want to see us lose everything?"

Masking his feelings, he swept a scrutinizing gaze over the corpulent Lady Alice, duly noting the dour look she returned.

Marriage and production of the coveted heir would fulfill his duty to the title, a duty he felt more pressure to perform each day. And while Thomas was determined to marry a wealthy woman of status who engaged his passion in bed and his intellect out of it, one might as well coax a brilliant star to descend to the earth. Still, if he could not have such, then he wanted an attractive bride to enjoy conceiving the heir. Lady Alice Randall did not fit the part. He liked large women, but this one looked appallingly dim-witted. Lady Alice's bulbous nose twitched, as if scenting something unpleasant.

"No, Mother, she's not for me," he said.

Her thin lips twitched with displeasure as she stuffed the handkerchief back into her sleeve. "I saw you waltzing earlier with that Miss Sanders. Thomas, do not waste your time. She's the daughter of a butcher—not our sort at all. I only invited her because Amanda insisted."

"I like Chloe. And no one else asked her to dance. I want to make all our guests feel welcome and comfortable—even those without social standing," he shot back.

His mother sniffed. "Well, I suppose it did show you as gallant and charitable to those less fortunate than us."

"It wasn't for show. She's interesting and intelligent."

"You don't need an intelligent wife. You need one of fine breeding, who can give you healthy sons."

Movement caught his eye as the crowd parted and flowed around a figure in emerald green. Thomas glanced her way. Then he lifted his eyepatch for a better look, and glanced again.

Now *there* was a woman. Rose-red mouth, pert nose, an exotic heart-shaped face. His hungry gaze devoured what he could view of her figure. Ah yes, those breasts—that conservative emerald velvet couldn't disguise her generous curves. A surge of heat slammed into him as he imagined cupping their heavy weight in his hands, stroking over the pearling nipples, enjoying her little cries of excitement.

But what drew him the most was her dignified nonchalance; as if she did not belong here and yet didn't give a damn.

He wanted her, for at least a dance.

As he started forward, she fled. He pursued her like prey.

She had nearly reached the doors when he skirted her side, blocked her way. The lady drew back, but instead of alarm, indignation flashed in her eyes.

"Do you mind?"

Her melodious voice was English, but threaded with exotic undertones. Puzzled, he studied her. Eyes dark as a midnight sky narrowed at him. Not frightened, but angry.

Intrigued, he stepped closer.

"I wasn't blocking your way. Not really. Will you dance with me?"

"No."

No? No one had ever turned him down.

"Why not?" he pursued.

"Because I don't feel like it."

"That's not a reason."

"It is for me. Now, do you mind stepping aside?"

Thomas's shock evaporated. A surge of heat slammed into him like a powerful fist. He would not let her go. This one had fire. No meek, mincing debutante here. Who *was* she?

He would discover her identity or renounce his title.

Chapter Three

Thomas used his cutlass tip to slightly lift the woman's skirt hem. Very nice ankles beneath snow white stockings. Trim, shapely. The lady pulled back.

"What the hell are you doing?"

Thomas chuckled, delighted by her indignation and even more by her vulgarity. "I'm inspecting your ankles. I never dance with a lady willingly before first examining her."

She snatched her skirts back. "You must have limited dance partners. Keep your sword to yourself."

He took heart that she had not repeated her lack of desire to dance with him. "I said 'willingly' dance. Many dances are reluctant on my part," he sallied, studying her. She was so familiar. Where had he met her before?

He searched her pale face. It was too white, as if she'd spent odious amounts of time indoors, doing embroidery or other dull pursuits. Thomas felt a stab of disappointment. Here was another wilting flower, disinclined to ride or partake in the outdoor sports he enjoyed.

Still, he decided to pursue the banter, test the waters and see how she'd respond.

"Alas, keeping my sword to myself is not always possible. Some women insist on seeing it displayed. Just as I enjoy inspecting their ankles, they like inspecting my weapon to ensure its length can . . . strike to the core."

Humor flashed in her dark eyes, then mischief. "Be careful, sir, lest you cut yourself on your own boastings. It's not the size of one's sword that matters but how one thrusts and parries."

Thomas felt his eyes widen and his desire grow. This here was no fainting chit who'd scurry behind her mama's skirts at bold overtures. This conversation was the liveliest exchange he'd had all night.

"I am quite skilled at most aspects of swordplay," he said. Damn, how he wanted to know her identity. "I'm also a fair hand at dancing. And I must insist you waltz with me."

He held out his bare hand. She peered at it.

"No dancing gloves? This could be a very good sign that you are a pirate at heart, sir—or a very bad dancer."

Thomas laughed. "A buccaneer," he admitted, "and one who *must* plunder the pleasure of your name, now that I've glimpsed your fine feet and ankles." He swept her an elegant bow from the waist. "Lord Thomas Wallenford. And you are?"

Her expression became suddenly troubled, and he straightened. Her fingers tightened around her skirts. Interesting. Did she truly wish to remain anonymous? He'd not let her. He had to know her identity.

"You may address me as Lady J," she said.

His desire to solve the mystery deepened. And he was ruthless when it came to pursuing what he desired.

"Where are you from? I don't recall seeing you at any previous assemblies or balls."

Her little chin lifted further. "I'm visiting from Europe. Scandinavia, to be precise. My father, the king of Scandinavia, sent me here because I was grieving him with my wild behavior. So he sent me out of the country to mold me into a lady by attending this Season's fetes."

Catching the impish flash in her dark eyes, Thomas asked, "And has it worked? Or do you still cling to your hellion ways?"

"No, I'm afraid it's failed miserably." She heaved a tiny, delicate sigh. "There would have been some hope of him succeeding, if not for the only son and heir of my host family. I placed a gooseberry tart on his chair."

Thomas laughed. Damn, but she reminded him of someone. Who? "What precipitated such an unladylike action?"

"I was merely demonstrating to him what a gooseberry tart really felt like when applied to one's bottom, since he claimed that cook's gooseberry tarts were sticking to mine, that my bottom was growing abnormally large."

Thomas slid an admiring glance at the body part in question. Her bottom was nicely rounded.

"You exhibited very improper behavior for a royal princess of Scandinavia," he agreed. "However, your actions were quite justified in that the gentleman was insulting. He deserved a good gooseberry tarting."

"Indeed. I'm quite glad you can see my point, and will judge you a reasonable man."

"Then, being called so, will you do me the honor of a dance?"

Thomas held out his hand again. A Strauss waltz began. Lady J took his palm. He noticed the delicacy of her fine-boned fingers, the sharp whiteness of her satin gloves.

Her gaze darted about like a hummingbird; then, to his immense satisfaction, settled only on him. He pulled her into his arms and they took to the floor. Lady J was tiny, barely clearing his chin. She looked delicate, yet he sensed a wiry, tensile strength like the tempered steel of his sword.

As she stared over his shoulder, concentrating on her steps, Thomas pulled her closer, determined to coax her out of silence. A delicate fragrance drifted from her. Something wild, fascinating. Like her.

"Lady J," he murmured. "Mysterious Lady J, a Scandinavian princess. The enchanting Lady J. Who are you?"

"A Renaissance princess wandered into a pirate's lair by mistake, a dashing pirate who waltzes skillfully. Your crew of cutthroats have trained you well."

Thomas laughed, and saw several heads turn in their direction. He bent his own, enjoying the chance to whisper into her shell-like ear. "One or two particular cutthroats. My dancing instructor when I was younger, and my mother. And your trainer? You dance exquisitely."

"Certainly not your mother," she murmured. "I learned the hard way, by treading on the toes of several victims."

"And they were?"

"Look for men who limp. A great deal."

Thomas laughed again. "Do you ride?" he asked on impulse. "I have a fine stable—the best in London—if you lack your own mount. Meet me tomorrow at dawn at the park. I recently acquired a steed I'm quite anxious to try before anyone has the chance to see him toss me."

She raised her gaze to his, and he glimpsed a flash of amusement. "You ride well, and I doubt Ulysses could toss you so easily."

Thomas was taken aback. "How do you know his name?"

Small, even white teeth nibbled at her full lower lip. Thomas wanted to do a little nibbling himself. "Er, I believe I overheard mention of your Arabian while chatting with others here tonight."

Only close friends knew of his recent purchase; Thomas had yet to ride his mount in public. Still, he let her remark slide. *She's someone I know, someone playing a game. Very well.* Smothering his delighted grin, he felt the evening suddenly brighten.

Thomas seldom acted on impulse. Yet tonight he yearned to break free of routine and expectations. He waltzed Lady J over toward the French doors, then pulled her off the dance floor. He guided her outside.

Lady J tilted her delicate chin up as he closed the door with a firm *snick*. "And why did you waltz me outside? Was it fear of having your toes tromped, or do you have other motives in mind?"

He released her hand and walked to the balustrade. Breathing in the night and its promise, he gazed at the sky. "Have you ever truly regarded how beautiful the stars are? So close, yet so far away. They take my breath away. One can only stand quietly and admire them."

"Like many things in life, they make me feel wistful. Sometimes I feel they are free and I am not."

Startled by her mournful sigh, he whirled and regarded her. She was lovely and brilliant herself, and he felt an odd kinship with her.

"Freedom is a relative word. What freedom can one ever have? One always has obligations to meet and duties that cannot be ignored."

"Like marriage, you mean, Sir Pirate? When will you choose to stop sailing the seas and settle into the respectability of a wife and family?" Her smile reminded him of someone, and he racked his brain to remember. She tilted her chin upwards to regard him and added, "Choosing well is even more advisable for a woman than a man, because marriage for my gender is life, whereas for a man it is a duty. Rather like this novel I'm reading. *The Egoist*."

Thomas gaped in delighted disbelief. "I am reading the very same book."

With tremendous enthusiasm, they began an animated discourse. After a few minutes, Lady J gave a heartfelt sigh. "I much admire Clara for being a rebel, attempting to extricate herself from the odious Sir Willoughby. She's so daring." She tipped her head up at him. "Do you admire daring women, Sir Pirate? Women who assert their own needs? Women who might be forward enough to steal a kiss in the moonlight?"

Thomas hungered as his gaze swept over her lovely body. An enticingly packaged exterior and an intelligent and witty interior. He felt alive and intoxicated. One kiss. Bold, yet safe. And as shadows covered them, no one would witness the impropriety. He must taste the mouth that delivered such delicious wit.

"What are you going to do, Sir Pirate?"

"You are playing a dangerous game, Lady J," he said softly.

"Pirates require more than a mere kiss. I should ravish you." Thomas found the idea very appealing.

His prisoner of desire put gloved hands on her hips. "You can't. I haven't the time. It's nearly midnight and I must leave. I turn into a pumpkin after midnight. You can't ravish a pumpkin. It's not proper."

"Oh bother, come on, stay," he coaxed. "I promise it will be a quick ravishment."

"Typical pirate. Ravishment, then it's off to sea. No, I don't want it quick."

Blood thrummed in his veins. How would she like it? Slow, very slow. He could make it as slow as she wanted.

"Then I shall settle for one kiss," he shot back, feeling heady and reckless and oddly free. "One kiss, then you're free to leave."

Alarm flickered in her eyes, then they darkened. She moistened her red mouth. Thomas felt his body respond. One kiss. It wouldn't satisfy him, but he'd settle for that tonight. Afterward . . .

His bed? Perhaps. He held on to the thought as he watched her lush mouth part in anticipation.

"Only one kiss?" Lady J whispered.

"One is a good start," he murmured. "But then I shall require more. Many more."

Thomas started to cup her cheek. She pulled back. Perplexed, he shot her an inquiring look.

"No, Sir Pirate, we will do this *my* way."

She reached up, slid her gloved hands behind his neck and pressed her lips against his.

The kiss caught him off guard, with its innocence twined with carnal need. Bold and eager yet clearly inexperienced, she kissed him, her luscious mouth sliding against his. Thomas stood utterly still, letting her take control. His body hummed, grew taut with desire.

Not enough. Thomas pushed her against the wall for better support, needing the friction of their bodies rubbing against each other. He felt his erection grow. He pulled her close, ground his mouth against hers. His tongue boldly thrust into her mouth, flicked, explored. He plunged, plundered, ravished her mouth, pirate that he was.

Damn it, he wanted more, needed more. Not a single kiss, but a shower of them. Her skin, naked against his. Bodies pressed against each other, flesh to flesh, nothing in between.

Thomas grappled for control, fought to even his ragged breaths. He couldn't. One kiss and his blood had ignited. He felt it, that heady, dizzy feeling as if the world spun madly on its axis, threatening to tip him.

His groin ached unmercifully. Damn it, he couldn't have her. Not immediately. Thomas stepped back. Lady J stared, panting. He touched her cheek, a light touch. "My brilliant star has descended to earth," he whispered.

Oh, how he wanted more. Not a quick ravishment. A full, brazen courtship. Flowers, chaperoned strolls in the park, meeting her parents and talking over crumpets and tea. He wanted it all. A ring on her finger? Was he mad?

Perhaps not. Providing Lady J had money and the right credentials (she was no more a princess than he was a chimneysweep). Her intellect and ready knowledge of books proved she was someone of his class, someone educated. And every woman here tonight was his social equal except poor Chloe.

Thomas glanced into the ballroom and was delighted to see Chloe waltz by in the secure arms of his old boyhood chum, Simon. Her face glowed as she chattered away. The usually quiet Simon was smiling and responding. Good. Thomas's earlier dance with Chloe then subsequent introduction to his shy, bookish friend had had the desired results. They'd make a good match, too.

Yes, a good match. There were no undesirables here. His mysterious lady, whom he held prisoner, would make a fine partner, even if she wasn't wealthy.

Yes, he must have more of her. He could not wait. He'd take her inside right now, introduce her to his parents. It wasn't as if Lady J was a servant. She fit into society. Just like him.

Jasmine gulped down a quivering breath. First, the lovely, fascinating discussion, then that kiss. Thomas's kiss left her boneless, breathless and afraid. Never had she felt anything like it. One innocent kiss turned into a raging sandstorm of passion. What the hell had she started? Hadn't she learned anything since that night in the park? One foolish mistake, thinking a shared love of horses and a midnight adventure would lead to something more meaningful. Instead, it had nearly ruined her. Socially, Thomas was as far away from her as Egypt was to England.

"Lady J," the hoarse whisper came.

His knuckles brushed her cheek, lingered there for the barest second. Her trembling breath hitched as all of her senses focused on that singular point of touch. Their gazes caught and met. Dark turmoil reflected in his. Then his eyes shuttered, shielding all emotion as neatly as a curtain dropping on a stage performance. He looked brisk, businesslike. He stepped back, breaking off the intimacy. Jasmine stared at his outstretched palm.

"Let's return inside. I want you to meet someone," he said in formal tones.

Her limbs turned to water, and Jasmine sagged against the stone wall. Someone? His parents, most likely. Suddenly the ballroom seemed bigger than the sands of Egypt her mother always mentioned in stories—hot, deadly, menacing.

Playing the part of a pampered princess had been amusing. She'd caught the twinkle in Thomas's eyes and knew he had discerned her jest. Yet he'd continued playing the game. It had been delicious fun.

Now the fun was over, snipped by the ominous vision of his mother discovering her ruse.

Jasmine shivered. Lady Claradon was the wind that would rip her to pieces, as a Khamsin wind tore apart a desert rose.

"I cannot," she whispered.

He gave an encouraging smile and pulled her with him.

Ahead in the crowd, Thomas's mother spotted him, wrinkles lacing her forehead. She squinted, an unbecoming habit of late, as if trying to peer into the future. Spectacles were beneath her.

Thomas glanced at Lady J. Her breathing was fast, like one of his thoroughbreds after a good gallop. He reasoned it was the kiss. He felt rather lightheaded himself.

Reaching the countess, he gave Lady J a reassuring smile. "Lady J, allow me to introduce you to my mother, Lady Claradon, hostess of this fair event. Mother, Lady J."

His mother scrutinized his companion with a frown. "Lady J?"

That little chin thrust into the air with haughty arrogance. "My chosen name for this masquerade. In other circles I am known as a princess."

"Of Scandinavia," Thomas put in, resisting the impulse to chuckle.

Lady J shot him an imperious look fraught with royal hauteur. "That is correct," she agreed with a nod.

The change in his mother was remarkable, like watching heavy drapes flung open to greet the morning sun. "*Princess* J?"

"The J is short for my real name, which remains a secret for this event. It is, after all, a masque, and does not a masque cover secrets and identities?"

The countess's eyes rounded to the size of poached eggs,

while Thomas's suspicions mounted. He suddenly noticed the lilt of Lady J's voice, a melodious exotic inflection as if she'd traveled through foreign lands. Like . . . Arabia.

Sudden awareness slammed into him. The accent, the impertinent lift of the chin, the saucy sparkle in her eyes.

Deliberately he edged closer. From this new angle, the chandelier shed light upon her delicate features and heart-shaped face. He focused on her eyes. Her very dark eyes, rich as brown velvet. Exotic, intriguing.

Yes. It must be her. But good God, how had she gotten here? Surely his mother hadn't relented in her venomous attitude toward foreigners.

She hadn't. She never would.

Bloody hell. His guts lurched. He had to whisk Jasmine away, get her free, out of his mother's sight. If she knew, his mother would publicly rip her to shreds. A fierce protective urge he'd never felt before overwhelmed him in a cresting wave.

"Lady J," he said urgently, "Would you care to accompany me in another waltz?"

"Oh, Thomas, you've plenty of time to dance with this delightful young lady. Let me spend some time getting to know her." His mother patted Jasmine's hand. Thomas nearly groaned. Damn it, he had to get her free.

"A royal princess of Scandinavia! We're so honored, your highness." His mother curtseyed low, and Lady J blinked. She recovered her aplomb and gave a slight nod.

"I have heard much of your annual masquerade ball, and desired to observe for myself. I do hope my lack of an invitation isn't a problem."

The countess looked aghast. "Of course not! Had I known you were visiting, why, I know we'd have issued an invitation. I apologize for my oversight."

Jasmine inclined her head in a slight, gracious nod. "Apology accepted."

Thomas saw the sparkle in Jasmine's eyes. His mother, apologizing? This was quite the show. Lady J could apparently handle herself. He found himself oddly attracted to her daring. She had wit and spirit.

Of course, while his brilliant star had descended to earth, he could not have it. Jasmine lacked breeding. Alas, she was not a proper bride.

Regret pierced him, but Thomas swept it aside. Such feelings would be examined and studied later. Now was not the time.

Now was the time to get Jasmine away, and fast, before anyone discovered who she was.

Chapter Four

I can do this.

Confidence filled Jasmine as she nodded gravely at something Lady Claradon said. The woman pressed close, gushing in excitement.

"I am so flattered, your Highness, that you deigned to attend my humble affair. Perhaps you would honor us by attending a special tea I will arrange in your honor? It will give you the opportunity to become more acquainted with my son. We are quite eager for Thomas to find a suitable bride. It's time for him to marry, and you make a lovely couple—just as my Amanda does with Lord Ridley, her intended. We are planning a delightful June wedding next year, and perhaps you could even return—"

Amusement filled Jasmine. Amazing, how playing the part of a fair-skinned princess caused doors to open instead of slam shut. "A tea in my honor would be most agreeable," she replied.

Then Jasmine caught a warning flicker in Thomas's green eyes. Had he caught her ruse?

"Lady J," he began, his lips thinning to a narrow line. "I must insist on accompanying you outside immediately. You expressed interest in my new steed, remember? The Arabian stallion that came from the Duke of Caldwell's stables. As I recall, you are close to his family. *Relatively* close."

Jasmine's jaw fell. Oh bother, Thomas knew! She gave another regal nod, went to take his hand, and spotted trouble scurrying over, Mozart in her wake. Lady Amanda.

Thomas's sister pushed her way forward with a bewildered look. "Mother, why is everyone whispering about a visiting princess? I don't recall issuing invitations to European royalty."

Lady Claradon beamed. "Your Highness, please allow me

to introduce you to my daughter, Lady Amanda. Amanda, Lady J, a princess of Scandinavia."

Jasmine's regal nod felt wobbly and her voice sounded shaky as she said hello. Thomas's sister cocked her head, then reached out and lifted the mask from Jasmine's face. Gurgling laughter followed. "Oh, Mother! What fun. A very clever mask, Jasmine. I thought you didn't invite her, Mother."

Jasmine recoiled as her features were bared.

But her shocked gasp wasn't half as loud as Lady Claradon's. Blood infused the woman's face, turning it scarlet.

"Amanda," Thomas said.

His sister blanched as she took in her mother's expression. "Oh dear. You didn't invite her, did you?"

But it was too late. All knew Jasmine's identity now.

"I can't believe it. Why—" Thomas's mother sputtered. Then her eyes narrowed as she gave Jasmine a scathing look. "How *dare* you trespass where you are not invited?"

Jasmine's stomach clenched, but she gathered her courage. Now was the time when she could prove she did belong. But her prepared speech to prove her worthiness fled. Instead, sarcasm arrowed out of her mouth.

"I apologize, Lady Claradon. I thought you desired to have royalty attend your soiree, and I desired to fulfill your dearest wish by playing the part—since King Edward could not make it." She sketched an elegant curtsy.

Thomas made a sound suspiciously like a laugh, and Jasmine gulped. Each year Lady Claradon invited King Edward to attend her ball, and each year he declined. She'd just unintentionally drawn attention to that fact. Why couldn't she learn to keep her mouth shut? Would Thomas's mother shout for the footmen and have her thrown out on her unroyal bottom?

"Impersonating a member of Scandinavia's royal family is cause for arrest! The authorities will hear of this. I always knew you'd come to a bad end," Lady Claradon fumed.

Thomas lowered his voice. "Actually Mother, there is no such thing as the Scandinavian royal family. Scandinavia is simply the Nordic countries of Europe, such as Norway and Sweden."

Jasmine relaxed. How could she be frightened of a woman with no more brains than a pea pod? Instinct warned that now was the time to leave, while Lady Claradon stood in slacked-jawed embarrassment. But too many years of snubs had taken their toll; Jasmine could not resist hammering at the noblewoman's shattered composure.

"Yes, he's right. You were all too eager to warmly welcome an uninvited princess, whereas someone else would understand my title was but a jest for your masque."

Thomas's jaw tightened in apparent disapproval. A few people tittered. Lady Claradon reddened further. Then fury sparked her eyes. She reached over, yanked on Jasmine's dress, exposing one shoulder. Jasmine gasped, tried to cover herself, but heard the shocked murmurs ripple through the crowd. Thomas's eyes widened. Even Lady Amanda looked startled. Brown skin showed clearly against the white grease paint and rice powder—a dividing line between her world and Thomas's.

"You will never blend in, you hideous brown scorpion. How dare you try to rise above your station. You are an imposter and a wicked devil, and will always be our social inferior. Know your place, girl, and crawl back home." The countess straightened, triumphant.

Jasmine shot Thomas a pleading look. He said her name hoarsely, his hand reaching out as if to touch her.

The countess turned to him. "We do not want her sort here. She's a rude boor who trespassed where she clearly does not belong, and has succeeded in making a fool of you, Thomas."

Jasmine shuddered. She would leave, now, before the sordid display worsened. She'd find no champion in this corner, not in Thomas or anyone else. Everyone in this family was a sword against her flesh. They only knew how to cut, and cut deep.

Murmurs rippled through the crowd, accompanied by sly whispers of her name. Jasmine whipped her head around, saw several looks of disdain. Stupid the woman might be, but Lady Claradon had won again.

A lump rose in Jasmine's throat. She swallowed past it, bit her lip so hard she tasted the coppery taint of blood. Head high, she gathered her torn bodice and marched away in royal dignity. She was an Arabic princess, as in the Arabian Nights, and these peasants would watch in admiration as she made her grand exit.

Head held high, she failed to see the sly foot outthrust in her path. Jasmine stumbled, nearly falling. Behind her she heard Thomas shout her name. Raucous laughter swallowed his voice.

Do not let them see you cry. Jasmine thought of Uncle Graham, who told her to always keep her dignity even when others tried to wrest it away, and somehow she made it outside, marched onto the street, and turned toward home.

When she was fairly certain no one could see, she bolted like a runaway horse, ran past the stern row of regal townhouses sheltering the titled and wealthy. Mist dampened her painted face and hair. When she reached her destination, Jasmine flung open the heavy oak door. She startled a sleepy footman, who murmured a greeting. Ignoring him, she ran up the sweeping staircase, dimly grateful for the late hour: No one was awake to witness her shame.

In her room upstairs, she tore off the tapes securing her gown and pulled it down, stepping out of the rich folds of fabric. The gold snood came off with a vicious yank. Pins rained to the floor as she unbound her hair.

Jasmine went into the water closet adjoining her bedroom. In her corset and chemise, with the hateful twist of foreign-looking black curls tumbling past her shoulders, she stared into the looking-glass. A bowl with sliced fresh lemons sat on the marble countertop. She picked one up and began scrubbing her left arm. Juice ran down her skin, dribbled onto the counter.

"Out, out," she pleaded. "Oh, please, it's got to work this time. Make me pale, like them."

The fruit finally fell from her outstretched fingers. Lemons scented the air. Pulp smeared her exposed arm. A cut on her wrist burned like fire. Jasmine ran water in the basin, rinsing off; then she patted her arm dry and lifted off the towel. But, nothing. Her skin remained dark. Not peaches and cream, a delicate English rose, but a hard walnut.

Jasmine lifted her watery gaze to the looking-glass. "Mirror, mirror on the wall, who's the darkest, ugliest of all?" she whispered.

She threw the lemon rind against the mirror. Juice streaked the glass.

With an angry fist, she scrubbed away the moisture spilling down her cheeks. *I will not cry*, she swore.

But she did anyway.

Thomas struggled to leash his temper as all around him laughed at Jasmine's expense.

"What a show. Did you hire her for the entertainment, Tommy?" his good friend Oakley asked between chuckles.

"Shut up. All of you, just shut up," he snapped.

He firmly grasped his mother's elbow, swept the slack-jawed crowd with a disdainful glare, and escorted her outside. He turned on the countess, ripping off his eyepatch.

Her smug look faded, replaced by the familiar martyred expression she wore so well. The floodgates of his full fury opened.

"Damn it Mother! That was uncivilized, and astoundingly rude."

"Thomas, please, refrain from creating a scene."

"You already did. You, who taught me the importance of deportment and displaying good manners in society. It's a pity you don't follow your own teachings."

Her blue eyes rounded with surprise. "Why, Thomas, I meant every word I said. It matters to your own social set. Miss Tristan is not one of us. She's Egyptian."

"Jasmine is the niece of the Duke of Caldwell, the very man with whom I am partnering in business. You act like her social rank is lower than a London chimneysweep's," he snapped.

"At least a chimneysweep is English."

"You wish to ostracize her simply because of a birthplace? And her family? Your prejudice against them must stop. Now."

"I have no prejudice against Viscount Arndale's family," his mother protested. "His *real* family."

His real family. Not Jasmine, who was Lord Arndale's daughter by adoption. Though the viscount had claimed her, polite society raised inquiring brows. Jasmine, with her arresting features, dark skin and snapping sloe brown eyes, bore no resemblance to the fair-skinned, blue-eyed viscount.

His mother continued. "I even invited Viscount Arndale's daughter, Lydia, to Hope's birthday celebration next week. So you see, Thomas, I am very willing to include the viscount's children in our social circle. Lydia is a sweet child. She looks so much like her father."

"Her English father."

"Yes, of course. Poor Lydia would have quite a time being accepted if she resembled her mother." The countess sniffed. "That Egyptian woman. Thank goodness she seldom entertains."

Thomas paced back and forth, as if the terrace were the deck of a sloop. This ship wasn't sailing anywhere but familiar waters. How many times had his mother and father recited the same rhetoric?

Only, now he was angry enough to challenge it.

"Jasmine may not have been invited, Mother, but your treatment of her was abominable. She deserves respect."

The countess sniffed. "I respect those who deserve my respect. Egyptians are intellectually and morally deficient. That woman is wicked, Thomas. Remember the day I went out of my way to be kind and invite her to your birthday party? She was telling stories about the disgusting ways women dance in Egypt, and she did those horrid gyrating movements she called belly dancing! Scandalous!"

Thomas rubbed his pounding temples. "She was a child, Mother. And it *is* how some women dance in Egypt."

"Women of a baser nature," she agreed darkly. "And don't forget when she did that despicable act at Miss Farnsworth's. Miss Farnsworth invited Jasmine to her afternoon tea, even though no one wanted her there. Why, all Miss Farnsworth did was mention the faces she'd seen in Egypt and speculate they never washed them. That horrid creature put mud in Miss Farnsworth's napkin and the poor dear's face was covered in it."

"She was retaliating for a crude insult, Mother," he said tightly.

"Jasmine wasn't raised in England, Thomas. She lived in that heathen country where children run wild. Who knows who her real father is? Probably some heathen. She's evil."

Evil? Jasmine? Thomas drew in a deep breath. "I remember, Mother, at my birthday party, how Jasmine comforted Amanda because she'd lost her calico kitten. Remember how Amanda cried? Jasmine promised to give Amanda her own kitten, a very special pet to her. And she sent a kitten the next day, though you'd made it clear she was not welcome back to our house. Jasmine is not evil. She has a kind heart, Mother. You conveniently forget that."

"She was currying favor, Thomas. Mark my words. It's but

a matter of time until she commits a crime. It's in their nature. They're sly devils. Wild and uncivilized, like the horse that threw your brother. Oh, my poor Nigel, lost to us forever—and it's all the fault of that *Arabian!*"

The last word, uttered on a shrill note, sank into Thomas like a knife. Any hope of an end to her prejudice lay six feet below the cold earth.

"Blaming an Arabian horse for Nigel's death won't bring him back, Mother," he said quietly, as tears misted her eyes. "Arabians enabled us to recoup part of our fortunes. Selling them to my contacts in Europe has allowed you to host soirees like this."

And I was the one who insisted on keeping that mare from the Khamsim tribe after hearing Jasmine boast of their bloodlines, he thought, his throat tightening. It was my horse that killed my brother.

The countess swiped at her eyes. "Stay away from that trollop. She is a plague to all around her."

"She's not a trollop. Regardless of your feelings, I'm paying a visit to the viscount's home tomorrow and apologizing to Jasmine on behalf of our family. All our family," he growled.

"You wouldn't dare!"

"I will not sit idly by and allow her to think I condone your behavior tonight. You call the people of Arabia uncivilized, but what you did to her was nothing less."

The countess's mouth trembled. "She's wicked, Thomas. I know it. Stay away from her, I beg you. I could not bear it if something ill befell you like your brother. You're all I have, Thomas. Please." Then, dabbing at her eyes, she threw back her shoulders, pasted a bright smile on her face and strode back inside.

Thomas's anger softened. She would never show her distress in public, would pull herself together. Just as she had never wept at Nigel's funeral.

Thomas winced, remembering the sobs drifting from his mother's room that night, long after everyone else had retired.

He leaned against the balustrade, staring at the stars struggling to peek through the gathering clouds. Like Jasmine, they glittered with brilliance then vanished from view. No one questioned it. No one thought his mother was wrong, for this was accepted. Jasmine was Egyptian and an outcast.

"Jasmine," he whispered to the hidden stars. "Jasmine. My brilliant star. Why did you descend into my life, when I cannot touch you? Why?"

The door creaked open. Thomas half turned. Amanda, her half mask pushed up on her forehead, looked distraught.

"Thomas, please. Papa is drinking and smoking again, and the doctor expressly said his heart can't take it." She gave him a beseeching look.

Without him, his family would fall to pieces. He could not ignore the heavy burdens they placed on his shoulders.

Thomas straightened and cast one last glance at the stars swallowed by clouds scudding across the sky. Stars like Jasmine. Distant, glittering. Free. One brief dance, one enchanting kiss of a woman who called to him like a siren song. Forbidden. Dangerous. Exotic. Not for him. Never. Ever.

Ignoring the leaden feel in his chest, he turned and went to fetch his father. Save the family, again? It was, after all, his duty.

Chapter Five

He came to her later that night.

Silver moonlight silhouetted his tall, athletic body. Dressed in dark trousers that hugged muscular legs, and a loose white shirt rolled up to his elbows, he stood at the threshold of the open French doors. Wind combed through his thick, dark hair like a lover. Her name upon his lips was husky with a longing she'd never heard before.

Jasmine sat up, clutching the sheet to her throat. "Thomas? What are you doing here?"

"Looking for you. I had to see you. I can't stop thinking about you."

Curling her legs, she regarded him with a frown. "Your mother drove me off and you didn't even utter a protest. Now you're coming to my room at night where no one can see you? Very brave, Sir Pirate. Get out."

"No." He kept advancing. "I can't." He took a deep breath. "I need you. If I were a pirate, I'd spirit you away, toss you across my shoulder and take you to my ship."

Heart pounding, she stared. "Then what?" she whispered.

"Then I'd lock you away in my cabin and ravish you."

Heat curled low in her belly. Jasmine moistened her mouth. "You wouldn't."

"Yes, I would," he murmured, his voice deep and mesmerizing. "I want you, Jasmine. Only you. And I will have you. I will finish what we started tonight on the terrace."

She could not look away, couldn't think straight.

His stride was determined as he approached. Thomas took the sheet and ripped it back, exposing her. Her white lawn nightgown shone like a beacon in the dark room.

Jasmine scrambled back, pressing against the hardwood headboard. Unsmiling, he regarded her as he stripped off his shirt. His chest was sprinkled with dark hair, his stomach flat and rippling with muscle.

Her gaze traveled downward. A tiny gasp fled her as she glimpsed the bulge in his trousers. Jasmine was innocent, but once she'd seen the stable hand coupling with the downstairs maid in the hay. She knew what that bulge meant. He wanted her, as a man wanted. Not as an earl's heir, or an aristocrat, but as a man.

Thomas reached the bed and leaned over, bracketing her body with his powerful arms. A hank of dark hair hung down on his forehead. She felt an absurd, tender urge to brush it back. He smelled of leather and bayberry. The scent intoxicated her. The green of his eyes was brilliant emerald.

"I must have you," he said.

Sense returned. Jasmine inched back. His lips brushed against hers, lightly. She tried to control the wild feelings, the raw heat leaving her wanton and wanting.

He offered a gentle smile. "You're untouched. A girl still. Tonight, I will make you a woman, Jasmine. My woman."

"No," she whispered.

"Yes."

He pushed her gown up, exposing her thighs. Pushing them open, he stared with avid hunger at her. His expression filled with desire, and fierce possession.

"I'll take you away from all this. You're mine. You have always been and tonight you'll be mine forever. My Jasmine. I'll throttle anyone who dares to come between us."

Words she longed to hear. But still, she was afraid. Giving herself to Thomas meant turning her back on everything she'd longed to obtain. Respect. Acceptance. His friends would see her as a whore, baser than the lowest scullery maid.

"Throttle your mother. That would be lovely," she managed to say, struggling to breathe as his hand stroked her thigh.

"Anyone. No one will come between us. No one."

"Thomas—" Jasmine pushed at his chest, suddenly afraid. He was dark, powerful, overwhelming, and she knew she shouldn't do this.

"Jasmine," he breathed.

She knew then that she had no choice. Her desire was as urgent as his.

He kissed her, the kiss hard and urgent, his hard body pressed against hers. A low moan rose in her throat and she relaxed beneath him. Her thoughts were only of Thomas, his steely body rubbing against her, the two of them in her bed. He planned to claim her now, ravish her like the pirate he'd dressed as, and she couldn't stop him. *Didn't want* to stop him, for he was right—she wanted this, and nothing and no one would ever come between them ever again—

With a startled gasp, Jasmine awoke. Moonlight speared the carpeting. Just a dream. But what a dream . . .

She sat up with a very unladylike snort and wiped her perspiring forehead with the edge of the sheet. The little romance stories she loved to read were playing havoc with her imagination. In the deepest recesses of her heart, she was yearning for something she could never have. Thomas would never sweep her away and fill the emptiness. But wouldn't it be nice if dreams could come true?

Awash in wistful thought, Jasmine lay back down, tried to resume sleep. But it did not come for a long, long time.

In the morning, she rose long before everyone else, crept downstairs to fetch a spot of tea, then retreated to her room. She needed privacy. If Jasmine could not be an English rose, then perhaps an Egyptian princess would suit her.

Fetching the clothing she never touched, she laid it carefully upon her bed. Her mother had given her the garments long ago. Jasmine picked up the rose veil and draped it across her face. Large, dark eyes stared back at her in the gilded looking-glass. She was exotic and enticing.

If I were a real princess, Lady Claradon wouldn't have tossed me out, she thought bitterly.

Swaying her hips to the beat of imagined music, she gyrated in the ancient dance of her mother's people. Egypt, land of hot sunshine and barren desert, where blood surged thickly with the passion that stirred its people. Not cold, blue-blooded English society with its pale bodies and stiff manners. Not English society, where she did not belong.

Tearing away the veil, she studied her mouth, remembering it soft and swollen beneath the urgent, heated press of Thomas's lips. His kiss stirred her blood, awakened desire never experienced before.

Thomas was as out of her reach as if he lived on a distant shore. She was but a tiny grain of sand rubbing against the heel of his snobbish, nasty family's foot. She had to remember that.

Jasmine tossed the veil aside, hot shame pouring through her anew at the memory of last night. From her opened casement windows, a breeze caught the sheer fabric like a feather and nudged it over to rest upon her four-poster.

Her snowy white bedroom was fit for a princess, her stepfather had declared. He'd indulged her fantasy of creating a room where she'd be surrounded by English elegance. The ecru carpeting accented the eggshell white and powder blue walls. Above the white marble fireplace hung a painting of the English countryside, the fertile greens and deep brown hues adding a touch of brilliant color. A cream armoire held her clothing. The white settee before the fireplace and vase of summer roses looked inviting. The four-poster's lacy white canopy was dreamy and romantic. A pretty enameled dressing table held an assortment of cosmetics and a silver hairbrush with her initials on it.

It was all very English.

But it didn't make her feel English. Rather, Jasmine felt like a bird trying to roost on an uncomfortable perch.

Her morning attire of pale yellow made her honey-gold skin look sallow. *Bright, brilliant colors are what your daughter needs to bring out her beauty,* the dressmaker had cried out to her mother. But no one in high society wore such. Jasmine only wanted to belong.

It's not like I'm the only one Lady Claradon loathes, she thought with sudden hope. It's my whole family. Not me. I don't care about her silly fetes, anyway. I just wanted to prove . . .

Prove what? That you enjoy humiliation before the beau monde?

With a philosophical shrug, she touched the glass. Her appearance would never change. And she doubted she could ever change the stubborn minds of some of the beau monde. But maybe, just maybe, she could join those lower in rank. The ones who courted favor because her uncle was a duke.

No. She didn't fit there, either.

What do you want? Who do you belong to? Jasmine stared into the mirror. "I don't know," she whispered.

Her father was Egyptian. Her adopted father, Kenneth, and her mother, never talked of him, even when Jasmine plied them with questions. It was best forgotten, they said.

She didn't remember much of her childhood in Egypt, only the beautiful, gilded cage where she'd lived for seven years. Lovely ladies with painted faces but sad smiles had been her companions; they'd spoiled and fussed over her. Tall, scowling men with swords guarded them. She'd played with her best friend, Nadia, who was two years older. The place was like a harem in Arabian Nights, special and magical, Nadia told her. Then one day the mistress of the harem came and took Nadia away. The mistress with her stern face told Jasmine that one day she, too, would be painted and learn what the others learned.

Eager and curious, Jasmine had followed Nadia that day; she'd crept down the hallway and went to the room where a tall, cruel-looking man went with her. The room inside was dark, lit only by the dull glow of a single candle. Bells on the girdle Nadia wore at her waist jingled with her footsteps. The door closed firmly. Instinctively Jasmine knew she must keep hidden. She had hovered outside, wanting to help her friend, who didn't seem like she wanted to be there. And then she'd heard Nadia's frightened wails of pain and the crude, heavy panting—

Jasmine gulped down the memory. Nadia had afterward turned into a silent wraith, walking the hallways like a ghost. Then another man came and Nadia went away for good. Jasmine had never seen her again.

Shortly afterward, Jasmine's long-lost mother Badra arrived. She brought Jasmine to live with her and the man who loved her, to England, this cold place with its richly-dressed people. Jasmine had never wanted to return to Egypt. Dark doorways, the silent promise of bad things happened there. She'd vowed to herself that she'd fit into this new home, this new land, and become just like them. She'd never become one of those painted ladies with the sad smiles. She'd fit in so well no one would think of returning her to that evil place where little girls screamed. . . .

"You didn't come to breakfast. We had raspberry tarts, too."

Gathering her composure, Jasmine turned to see her little sister entering the room. A smile replaced her harsh frown. "Pigeon, not everyone in this household enjoys raspberry tarts."

"Uncle Graham does. He's downstairs, with Father." Lydia crossed the room, her pretty green skirts flouncing with each un-ladylike movement. Then again, she was seven. Time enough to learn to become a lady.

Time enough to learn disappointment when she, too, was rejected by the English.

Jasmine smiled fondly at her younger sister and picked up a

brush. Lydia bounced up and down on the feather bed, fingered the delicate rose veil. "I hope Hope has raspberry and treacle tarts at her birthday party next week. Lady Claradon promised lots of treats."

Jasmine went very still, staring over her shoulder. "Hope . . . The party Lady Claradon is hosting for her niece—you were invited?"

Her younger sister draped the veil over her light brown corkscrew curls, a product of torturous nighttime rags. She shrugged. "Hope is a bore, but her aunt gives fabulous parties and there'll be lots of sweets and even truffles."

For once, Lydia's self-professed sweet tooth failed to cause Jasmine to tease her sister. She was too shocked.

"Lady Claradon . . . when was this?"

"Last week. She sent the invitation to Mother on parchment in a velvet case." Lydia jumped off the bed and flounced about the room, draping Jasmine's veil over her head and pulling it across her lower face. She admired herself in the looking-glass. "Look, don't I seem exotic, like Mama? Papa says I have her nose and his eyes."

His eyes. Her stepfather's eyes—bright, acceptable English blue. Not dark Egyptian brown. Her Egyptian mother's petite nose. Jasmine's stunned gaze swept over her pretty sister's paler, creamier complexion.

It wasn't her family shunned, after all. Just her. Just Jasmine.

Pain squeezed her insides like an iron band. Jasmine turned back to the gilded mirror at her dressing table, forcing a smile. *Never show emotion.* No one in her family must know how deeply Lady Claradon's snubs hurt.

"You look silly in that. Take it off," Jasmine managed, patting rice powder on her nose. Her brown nose.

"I do not." Lydia pouted. She pivoted and pulled the veil off. "I think I look interesting. Maybe I should wear this. Everyone would turn their heads and say, 'Look, there goes

Miss Lydia Tristan, the daughter of Viscount Arndale, niece of the Duke of Caldwell. Isn't she fascinating in her veil?'"

Jasmine stared at her mirror, the reflection blurring. She couldn't be English. No matter what she did, no matter how many coats of rice powder she applied or how pleasing she tried to be, she'd never fit in, but stand out like a . . .

Brown scorpion.

Like the rest her family, Lydia was blissfully ignorant of Jasmine's ostracism from society's ranks. Never would she find out, either. *It is only you, after all.*

Bitterness as sour as the lemon she'd used on her skin surfaced. If not for Lady Amanda, she'd have made it through the ball last night. Amanda, with her pretty, pale complexion and smug engaged status. It was her fault. Fury boiled inside Jasmine. She tried to clap a lid on her temper but failed. She would not be quietly subjected to such vile humiliation; Amanda's mother would know the error of her ways, and the penalty for daring to cross her.

The plan, Jasmine decided, must be one that challenged the woman's sense of importance, and what was dearest to her. Feeling wicked, she stared into the mirror. Of course! Amanda. Dear Amanda. Wanton Amanda. Should not the rest of the world discover how truly immoral the angelic, virginal Amanda was? Lady Claradon's prize bloom, whom she boasted was making such a fine catch.

A fine catch, indeed. In the garden. With the gardener. Oh, the story was simply too rich. Wouldn't it be smashing to see the fine lady humiliated like Jasmine?

A slow smile spread over Jasmine's face. She pushed back from the dressing table, ignoring the rice powder scattered on the polished surface.

"Lydia, leave me. I have work to do."

Humming a happy tune, Jasmine went to her desk as Lydia flounced out. She reached into a drawer and pulled out a piece of cream stationery and her pen. Worn at the end from her nibbling as she secretly wrote stories, it had sat unused for weeks while she plotted last night's masque. No longer. Now it would be put to use.

The Daily Call was a newspaper filled with gossip about the ton's activities. London's commoners loved reading it. Even the gentry did. Jasmine imagined the publisher needed material, and would welcome her story.

Yes, Lady Claradon would know the same stinging humiliation she'd heaped upon Jasmine. She would know and never forget.

Chapter Six

Duty. Honor. Responsibility. The words were Thomas's litany.

In silence, the Earl of Claradon's heir stood in the formal downstairs drawing room, with its piano, heavy green velvet draperies and ornamoul clock ticking softly on the mantel. Light filtered through the thick Belgian lace curtains. The room was oppressive and dark. Stuffed with furniture, all were good pieces boasting a fortune now dwindling. He leaned an elbow on the mantel, surveying, went to the piano, plinked a few notes that sounded discordant and lonely.

Footsteps drew his attention to the door. He compressed his lips as his father entered the room. The less said, the better. The other night he'd said enough while dragging him from alcohol. The earl was tall and stout, but Thomas's six-foot-three-inches of muscle easily matched him. He was no longer a short, skinny boy to be thrashed.

Today, his father's proud shoulders were slightly stooped, his air less arrogant. He walked to a side table, removed two cigars from a box.

"You shouldn't smoke. The doctor said your heart is too weak," Thomas warned.

"My heart can take one more cigar. Sit with me and tell me about your trip."

They sat and lit the cigars. Blue smoke wreathed his father's face. Thomas talked about his visit to their ancestral home near Manchester. It was the earl's mention of selling land to replenish their diminishing coffers that had spurred Thomas to find alternative sources of income. He vowed never to release the lands, and to take care of his tenants.

"I'm hiring workers to repair the cottages," Thomas admitted.

"Can't afford it. Not in our budget. It'll have to wait until next year."

Thomas's jaw tightened. "They can't wait until next year. The living conditions are miserable. I'll find a way to finance the repairs."

"Don't spend too much. Take care of those you're responsible for, especially the lower classes, but never spoil them. They're like children—mentally deficient, need to be told what to do. Never forget you're superior to them."

"How could I forget? You beat it into me," he growled. *When I am earl, I will make changes. Things will be different.*

"Had to. It toughened you," his father said. "Look at you now—ruthless in business, calculating. Smarter than I ever was with finances. I had to be hard because what you will face when I'm gone is hard. You'll have challenges I never had to endure." His father gave him a somber look. "I'm proud of you, Thomas. You turned out perfect. You'll make a fine earl when I'm gone."

The rare praise surprised Thomas. The earl gestured to the framed portraits on the wall.

"Look at them, son. Your ancestors. Our past. The title goes back to Tudor times. You are the future of England. I'm counting on you to marry well and produce sons of your own. You have a business sense that will lead this family in a new direction. Forge ahead to the new, but never forget where you came from, and who you are."

The earl crushed out his cigar with a loud cough. Thomas watched him leave.

Remember your origins. Remember your place. Never let your inferiors best you.

Troubled, he stubbed out his own cigar, went into the room storing his Egyptian artifacts. After his aunt and uncle died, they'd left him their entire collection. Thomas removed a key from his waistcoat, but to his shock, the door swung open at his touch. He entered and opened the brocade drapes. Dust motes danced in stray sunbeams.

Always, he locked the room. However, the spare key was downstairs and the housekeeper was meticulous. Everything looked in place. Artifacts stood on tables or were crammed into corners. Thomas chose a few pieces the Duke of Caldwell liked. Graham would pay good money, enough for him to repair the cottages.

He halted before a waist-high oil painting propped against a table. A John Singer Sargent. *The Egyptian Girl*, a naked and nubile dark-skinned Arabian. Its soft sensuality and charm had drawn vast praise from the public and mesmerized Thomas when he'd seen the six-foot original. He had contacted the artist and privately commissioned a copy on a much smaller canvas, at a very hefty fee.

His parents were impressed with the artist's celebrity. Nigel had merely cocked an eyebrow and drawled a remark about how the subject possessed a "nice bum." Thinking of that remark brought a smile to Thomas's face.

The smile faded. His mother had insisted on hanging the painting in the drawing room so she could impress guests. When Thomas asked about the ethnicity of the subject, his mother said, "Everyone knows those Arabic women are loose." Thomas had quietly tucked the painting out of sight.

At night he'd dreamed of the Egyptian girl, and she became Jasmine. The little pointed chin and sharp profile with the dreamy, downcast look were Jasmine's. Her tawny form was supple and her breasts heavy and hips rounded. The shy smile held a promise of enticement, and natural sensuality twined with touching innocence. Thomas had such hopeless longing, he sought in dreams that which he could not in life.

The dreams were fleeting. He'd awaken and stretch, feel

the pull of old scar tissue. Feel the heavy weight of duty on his shoulders.

Thomas dug into his trouser pocket and withdrew a brown jasper charm in the shape of a scorpion. Nigel's. It sat snugly in his palm, a fake.

The winter when he was eight, Nigel had contracted measles. Their aunt and uncle had taken Thomas away to Egypt to keep him from falling ill. He'd purchased the amulet in a Cairo market from an old man with skin like leather. The seller said it brought good luck, so Thomas gave it to Nigel upon his return to England.

On the night of Nigel's accident, the doctor had found the scorpion in Nigel's pocket. Thomas locked it away in this room. It remained hidden until last week, when he showed it to Charlotte, who had expressed curiosity about his treasures.

Emotion tightened his throat as he turned it over in his hand like a worry stone. "Ah, Nigel, it didn't bring you much luck, did it?" he murmured.

With a heavy sigh, he pocketed the scorpion. His brother was dead. Thomas had a duty to his family to find a proper bride. If only . . .

Not Jasmine. Jasmine did not fit into his world. Nothing could gain her entrance. It would be indiscreet of him to even pay her a call. Tongues would wag among his social set.

Suddenly, he didn't give a damn. He had to see her again. Had to hear that soft, slightly exotic lilt of her melodious voice, a voice that could deliver caustic barbs in honeyed tones.

For what? To pretend they could ever have anything between them? She ignited his desire, made him laugh, filled him with life. But it was a life not meant for him.

And yet, he did owe her an apology.

Thomas ran a finger around his starched, high collar. Many women in his circle cared only about balls, fashion and gossip:

they bored him. Not Jasmine. She fascinated him. From the first time they'd met, her heart-shaped, dark-skinned face enchanted him. So different from his childhood peers, the prim little girls who cringed at dirtying their pinafores, Jasmine was a tough little fighter who didn't hesitate to blacken his eye in exchange for his taunts. She'd stood out like a beautiful wild blossom struggling to grow among delicate hothouse flowers.

Jasmine's dark eyes and thick ebony hair acted like a siren calling a sailor to dash himself upon dangerous rocks. He knew she was different. Until the day she'd punched him, he'd joined in with others in mocking her. Because, on a level deep inside that he didn't understand, she frightened him.

He still didn't quite understand it. Or her.

And that was what intrigued him so much, Thomas ruefully reflected. Unlike the whey-faced chits whom he could dissect with a mere glance, Jasmine evaded such treatment. She was strong-willed, independent and exotic, quickening his blood like a rare, sparkling wine. He wanted to taste her, lick the droplets spilling over the crystal goblet that was she and absorb everything she was.

He needed to forget her, the forbidden fruit dangling on the unreachable vine.

Thomas gripped the table, remembering last night's debacle, last night's magic, as he'd kissed Jasmine. Passion had heated his blood as she'd turned soft and willing in his embrace. Damn and hellfire; he couldn't stop thinking about the woman. She was a breath of warm desert air blowing into his cold, stale world. She stood up to him and crossed him. Engaged his weary, sexually jaded self. And Thomas adored a challenge.

Yes, he owed her a formal apology for the vile way she'd been treated. True, she had trespassed, but his mother had shown more rudeness in exposing her—literally. He'd pay her a call, offer his family's apology. He could do no less; and also, no more.

But first . . . he pocketed the scorpion amulet and glanced at the painting. Today the footman would hang it in Thomas's bedroom prominently above the fireplace mantel. No more hiding away in a dark room for this Egyptian Girl.

Much later, Thomas stood on the doorstep of Jasmine's father's townhouse. Clutching a bouquet of violets, he ignored curious passers-by (Lord Thomas was calling upon the only eligible lady of the house, Miss Tristan?).

The door sported a brass knocker in the shape of the Sphinx—another "oddity" of the viscount about which his peers whispered. Thomas thought it quite appropriate. Using the ring in the Sphinx's mouth to give a firm rap, he waited. The door opened to a jowled footman.

"Lord Thomas Wallenford to call upon Miss Jasmine Tristan." Thomas handed the servant his crisp white card engraved with black ink.

The footman escorted Thomas inside with a dour look, took his card and vanished into the home's depths.

Thomas studied the gleaming, polished furniture, the spotless floors. The only sign of Egypt was a small statue on a table: Ramses, the warrior pharaoh. The polished stone gleamed.

Thomas's thoughts drifted to Jasmine. Had his mother succeeded in driving the spirit from her? Was she even now upstairs, weeping over last night's debacle? The thought of seeing her red-rimmed eyes and Jasmine turning into a dull ghost of herself filled him with regretful anger. Why couldn't his mother have simply escorted her out without causing a scene?

Moments later, the footman returned, his eyes refusing to meet Thomas's. "Lord Thomas, Miss Tristan is not receiving callers. Specifically you."

Thomas's suspicions rose. "What were her exact words?"

"My lord, I'd rather not say."

"I'd rather you did," he replied firmly.

"Well, Miss Jasmine said . . . she said . . ." The man's gaze dropped to the floor. "Tell that insufferable snob to go to hell."

Thomas bit back a smile, glad his mother hadn't drained Jasmine's spirit. This rejection was no matter. He'd find another way.

"Please give Miss Tristan this bouquet, and advise her I shall be seeing her again. Quite soon."

The servant shook his head. "She won't take them. Trust me, my lord, when she gets 'er dander up like this—"

"I insist on leaving them here."

Thomas dropped the flowers on the polished side table next to Ramses. They lay there in defiance, a fitting gift for the lady, as he turned and left.

Lifting the lace curtain upstairs in her room, Jasmine watched Thomas walk away. Hands laced behind back, pace steady, determined.

With a slight sniff, she dropped the curtain. "Insufferable ass," she mused. "Did you privately call on me when publicly you would not defend me?"

She contemplated the possibility for future social success. With abject disappointment, she realized she'd never again receive such a chance. If not for Lady Amanda, surely she'd have waltzed in Thomas's arms once more, then swiftly waltzed out the door, secretly delighting in having pulled off the ruse. Instead, she had been made a mockery yet again.

No matter. By tomorrow, all of London would be laughing, and not at her.

Minutes later, dressed in her riding habit, a bottle-green top hat and half veil tilted at a saucy angle atop her head, she headed downstairs. Pausing at the door of the upstairs drawing room, she peeked inside. "Mother, I'm going for a ride."

Lady Arndale glanced up from her needlepoint. Her honey-gold face as dark as Jasmine's own, Jasmine's Egyptian-born mother had never broken into England's tight social circles. But Badra remained content with her husband and raising her children; she had never desired to be a raging social success.

Jasmine did. She thirsted for inclusion like a parched traveler trudging across the hot Sahara desired water. Success and acceptance.

Her mother's sloe eyes, as exotic as Jasmine's own, regarded her. "Isn't it late for your ride? I thought you preferred the morning."

Not today. Still stung from last night's debacle, Jasmine needed to show the world they had not succeeded in defeating her. Today, on the track, she would blend in. Just another excellent horsewoman.

"I fancy some afternoon exercise," Jasmine explained, tugging at the hem of one glove.

Interest flared on her mother's face. "Have they invited you to parade with them on the Row?"

A dull flush heated Jasmine's cheeks. "I don't know what you mean, Mother."

"Your little charade, honey. Attending the masque at Lady Claradon's with Chloe." Badra's serene smile rattled Jasmine's self-confidence. "I was tempted to wait up for you, but your father advised against it."

"I honestly have no idea what you're talking about, Mother."

Badra's face fell. "Oh, honey—no, they didn't snub you again? Can't you make friends elsewhere?"

Pride stiffened Jasmine's shoulders and sharpened her response. "Don't wait tea for me." She smoothed down the skirts of her green riding habit, brushed off the black velvet collar and, picking up her crop from the side table, strode downstairs.

Seeing a friendly face, she halted on the bottom step.

Distinguished as ever, in his somber charcoal suit and with a sparkle in his dark eyes, her uncle held out his hands, and gave her palms an affectionate squeeze.

"Jasmine! You look lovely. When will you come for a visit? Your Aunt Jillian is pining for your company." She perked up at this news, until he added, "Her Arabic is suffering, and she expressed a desire for more lessons from you. She much admires how you mastered both languages."

Jasmine's shoulders dropped. Arabic. Of course. Nothing English. Still, she managed a smile. "I've been preoccupied, Uncle Graham. And surely Aunt Jillian is busy with my cousins."

"Busy enough," the duke agreed wryly. "I think I should stop making her quite so busy."

Jasmine dropped her disappointment and shared a grin with her uncle, who had celebrated the birth of another daughter six months ago.

"Only three girls, Uncle. Aunt Jillian is still young, surely you want to try for a boy."

"I have your brother as my heir, and I'm quite content with my girls." Graham smiled, tiny lines crinkling at the corner of his eyes. "But now, enough of me. Are you off to the Row? Your favorite pastime, of course."

"One I do best."

"You were born to sit a horse—either astride or on that preposterous sidesaddle. You are adept at both, Jasmine. Just as in judging horseflesh." Graham leaned against the banister, gave her a thoughtful look. "That black you urged me to sell after putting him to stud, excellent move. He's fathered quite a few foals, and is now giving Lord Thomas Wallenford quite a challenge. Though I suspect Thomas can handle him—unlike others."

Her heart skipped at beat. "Thomas is quite the horseman himself, Uncle."

"You two have that in common. Though I venture to say

your facer is better than his. At least it was when you were younger."

Uncle Graham touched her nose, causing a hot flush to race across Jasmine's cheeks. She scurried away, before he reminisced about her other less admirable actions of the past.

"Jasmine?" he called. She turned, and the duke studied her. "Better take a groom with you in case you run into trouble."

"I can handle myself."

"The groom's not for you, sweet. It's to protect the others." Graham winked. Whistling, he strode off. Jasmine rolled her eyes and thumped her crop against her heavy skirts.

Minutes later, she galloped down the track. She let her mare have its head, ignoring all the others. But the park was quite crowded, and as she pulled Persephone back to a trot, she noticed a few people pointing and staring at her.

Heat raced across her cheeks. So, the word was out. All were talking about her, and about last night's spectacle.

Head held high, Jasmine walked her mare off the sandy track. She kept her gaze forward, until a young nobleman with a spirited thoroughbred caught her attention. The horse was a fine Arabian, its blue-black coat gleaming in the sunlight, its carriage proud and noble. Its spirit was unbroken, much like her own.

To Jasmine's horrified shock, he suddenly began beating the beautiful creature with a riding crop, and the horse reared and kicked in squealing protest. Jasmine dropped her reins, letting her mare crop grass, and ran forward. Without a word, she yanked the crop from the man's hands and grasped the horse's bit. Slowly, soothingly, she spoke to the stallion in a calm, soothing tone—words of reassurance, her voice a lilting melody. As if her voice were magic, the stallion calmed. Jasmine stroked its velvety nose and ignored the outraged rider.

"Miss, are you quite mad? Give me my mount, for I am his master," the owner demanded.

Jasmine shot him a scathing look. "When you learn to treat your horse kindly, and that gentleness earns you a far better ride, you can *then* call yourself a master."

Deliberately, she let the reins drop. The stallion bolted. Jasmine grinned as she watched the indignant and surly nobleman barely keep his seat. Hah! Good riddance. The man did not deserve to own such beauty, let alone try to tame it.

Returning to her own mount, she led her mare toward a small copse. Here, when she was barely nine, she'd punched Thomas Wallenford for calling her an ugly old mare. How she'd wished now she'd given his mother a facer as well.

The park, this damn park. Site of so many miseries. The horse Nigel could not control, his drunken laughter, his horrible screams of pain . . .

Nigel. That night. She clenched her fists, resisted the urge to either laugh or scream. How she detested Thomas's family. His whole family.

But him as well? Was he as wicked as his brother? Could he ever care about her as a person? He believed she did not belong with his set—as his mother had clearly demonstrated it.

The scent of horseflesh, grass and earth swam in Jasmine's nostrils. Late summer sunshine filtered through the thick green canopy. The area felt enchanted. Jasmine leaned against an oak, closing her eyes. She was weary of trying to adapt, wondering where she fit in. And at twenty-two, she was sliding onto the shelf. Did the fates doom her to become a spinster, growing more cantankerous and bitter as the years passed? Envying her younger sister silly birthday invitations?

"And in the park grows a rare jasmine flower among the ordinary thorny roses, infusing a dreary world with her fragrant beauty. A rare flower who can tame the most spirited of horses with her melodious voice and soothing touch. Such is the beauty that walks among us."

Her eyes flew open at that deep, resonant voice. Oh bother, what was *he* doing here?

Thomas stood a few feet away. Resplendent in dark trousers, jacket, starched collar and a brilliant blue tie, he was bareheaded. His piercing gaze regarded her thoughtfully.

"I saw how you handled that beastly incident of the man beating his mount. Good show, I might add. I was about to reprimand him when you strode up. Such a soothing touch you have with horses. You've always had it, Jasmine."

Dread and secret delight made her pulse race. Memories assaulted her. The time in the park. Nigel. Thomas is not his brother, she reminded herself, quelling the tiny fear.

Jasmine detached herself from the oak and stood straight, slightly embarrassed to be caught lounging like a weary char-woman. She sought for dignity and hauteur, but again, when her mouth opened, the wrong words spilled out.

"Your poetic words are nothing more than vacuous eloquence. Much like your mother."

His brow wrinkled as he considered her with a long, thoughtful gaze. Thomas had always had the habit of study-ing her as if she were a hothouse flower on display.

"Ah yes, my mother, she indeed can be the very definition of vacuousness. Or vapidness. Many other terms apply to her, too. Indeed, she's a walking dictionary."

His teasing words coaxed a reluctant smile from Jasmine. "Yes, other adjectives come to mind. Odious and recalci-trant."

"Recalcitrant. Now there's a term that fits better a certain flower I know. A delicious flower, I might add. Always defy-ing those around her and being herself, unlike other flowers, who are dull and lifeless in comparison." Thomas advanced, thrusting his hands into his pockets. "Recalcitrant. A flower who orders me, by instruction of her footman, to the depths of Hades. I've been ordered there by various male peers, but never a female one."

His brows arched upward in an impish expression, which widened her smile further. Jasmine tried to ignore the rapid beating of her pulse. He'd called her a peer. Was it more empty flattery? Mistrust filled her.

"I misspoke to my footman. I should have told him to tell your mother to visit that particular region."

His expression changed, his full mouth flattening in clear disapproval. "Of all the terms my mother calls to mind, there's only one to describe her behavior last night, and I'm far too much a gentleman to say it in the presence of a lady. Instead, Jasmine, will you listen a minute and allow me to make amends?"

She arched her neck to study him. He towered over her, his prodigious height and muscled breadth posing a vague threat. In childhood, she'd punched him; to attempt so now would prove foolhardy.

She rapped her riding crop across her skirts. "I fear your sentiments are expressed too late. I've dismissed the incident—and those associated with it."

A sigh rumbled from his chest. "Jas, don't be that way with me. I'm appalled at how my mother treated you, and wish to make amends. On behalf of my family, I formally apologize."

Considering, she continued beating the crop against her thigh. Thomas reached out, grabbed the instrument. "If you must thrash someone over last night's debacle, thrash me. You've already done so once before. In this very place, remember? And I deserved it, for what I said."

Her gaze lifted to meet his, her amusement fading and replaced by a flash of genuine regret. Jasmine stared at the long, lean fingers masterfully wrapped about her crop. "You called me an ugly old mare," she mused.

"When I should have termed you a most delightful, spirited filly. My metaphor was inappropriate."

Her mouth fell open in dawning anger. Thomas chuckled, and tipped it shut with her crop.

Jasmine allowed her features to relax and grow expressionless. Too many times she'd worn her emotions on her face. Gradually she'd learned to control her errant, wild feelings, learned to school her features. It had been a valuable education.

She removed the crop from his grasp. "Your metaphors don't concern me, Lord Thomas. However, tell me; would you issue your apology in an arena as public as the one last night?"

"If you wanted me to, I would, but I'd suggest against it, to avoid causing you further attention and distress," he said quietly. "I'm not excusing my mother, but understand this: You ventured into a territory she protects with the ferocity of a tiger. Her social functions are as beloved to her as breathing. And she is shortsighted. She blames my brother's death on all Arabians. Though the cause was a steed, she harbors hatred of all who remind her of that event."

"She doesn't hate all Arabs, just full-blooded ones," Jasmine whispered, remembering Lydia's invitation to the party.

Thomas looked stricken. "Jas, I'm sorry. Sorry for every bloody thing she's put you through, now and back then. Will you accept my apology? Please?"

He looked so sincere, so concerned, that a little of the ice around her heart thawed. Jasmine hesitated. Forgiveness marked a lady, as well as her deportment. She thrust out a gloved hand. "Oh, bother. Let's shake and forget it."

He did not shake. Instead, he took and cradled her hand like a precious jewel. He looked at the exposed skin between her brown glove and sleeve. He touched it with one finger.

"What a rare, beautiful flower you are, Jas. Such lovely skin, like rich honey. When I see you, I think of exotic lands and hot desert sun, not the coldness of England."

His voice was thick with emotion. Thomas brought her hand to his mouth and laid a very brief, tender kiss upon her exposed wrist. He pulled back, letting her hand drop. Mischief flashed once more in his eyes.

"Now, Jas. This park brings back memories. You punched

me all those years ago. I always demand payment for a rude
turn, and since I never hit a lady . . . I shall take a kiss instead." He tapped his smooth-shaven cheek with a finger.

"Oh, how I could have throttled you."

"Trust me, little flower, my pride took a more severe bat-
tering than you could ever have provided."

The bitter note in his tone caused her to wonder, but Jasmine dismissed all thought as he pressed closer. He leaned
near enough for his delicious masculine smell of leather and
bayberry to envelop her in a tantalizing cloud. "Come, then.
One kiss and I shall forget the debt. Kiss my cheek and make
it feel better. It's been sore for years now."

"And if I am disinclined to display such affection?" she
asked.

She expected a laugh, or equally light banter in return, but
instead Thomas studied her with such longing that her breath
caught. This was not a matter of mere affection, or of impropriety in the park. Not like that other time. Why, oh why,
couldn't it have been you that night, she thought in abject
misery. Perhaps destiny would have been changed. But regrets were useless.

His look was hungry, and in the startling green depths of
his eyes she saw flashes of wistfulness and equal loneliness.
Was that possible? Or was her imagination conjuring things
again?

Impulsively, she tugged off her right glove and touched his
cheek. The dark skin of her hand contrasted against his pale
face, an illustration of the demarcation between their worlds.
Dark against light. Egypt touching England. A simple caress,
but a dip into the dangerous waters they had treaded last
night.

Thomas stared at her. His knuckles grazed her cheek and
his lips parted. "You are so beautiful, Jasmine. So different,"
he said hoarsely.

Trembling inside, she lowered her lashes, not daring to

speak. When she spoke it always came out muddled. She dared not speak what she felt.

But her body ached. Her body recognized him, thrilled to the husky invitation in his voice, the dark heat in his eyes. The flesh between her thighs tingled. Heat suffused her face, as if a fire ignited within. Like in last night's dream.

Jasmine's heart raced as it did after a long, hearty gallop on the track. Horses. Her mind conjured a stallion in its prime, pawing the ground in impatience as a mare in heat was brought for stud. Her face reddened. She tried to dispel the image of the snorting stallion covering the mare. Dominating her.

Her sly mind shifted the image to Thomas rearing over her, covering her naked, trembling body with his strong, muscled one. Pressing himself against her aching breasts, parting her legs as he dominated her. . . .

A kiss could not hurt. Her hands slid around his neck. Thomas pulled her into his arms and crushed his mouth to hers. His lips pressed hers open, urgent and demanding. It felt like everything poured from his mouth into her—all his emotions, his heat, his very soul. A thrill raced through her as he thrust his tongue into her mouth. She tasted him, licked him as he invaded her mouth. Her fingers combed through his hair as she anchored herself to him.

He tore himself away, staring down at her. Jasmine quivered, uncertain and hungry. Wanting more. Needing more.

"I have to touch you," he muttered, pulling off his right glove with his teeth. He caressed her cheek, his eyes wild and tormented. "So precious and lovely. Why do you tear at me so, Jas? What cruel fate waltzed you into my world when you'll only waltz out again?"

She started to protest. He laid a finger across her lip, stroking gently. "No. If we have only this moment, then damn it, give me this moment and everything in it."

He kissed her again, one gloved hand and one naked hand

tenderly cupping her face, his mouth soft this time. He kissed her as if she were as precious as gold. Her emotions tumbled over each other in a cascading torment. Desire and longing, wonder and awe, and feathering through it all, the sorrow that the fleeting moment would vanish all too soon. Just like her dream.

Dreams and reality clashed. This time, she pulled away. Torment swirled in his eyes, darker now, his breathing ragged. He touched her face again, clearly struggling for words. But with abject horror she remembered her earlier visit to the newspaper, the promise evoked from the publisher. Words penned on paper. Words she could not take back. Words that would hurt Thomas equally as they hurt his mother and sister.

"Thomas, oh no, listen to me . . . I must tell you . . ."

Raucous shouts of laughter stopped her. Alarmed, she recognized the voices: Thomas's set, the men and women who always clustered around him like bees to the hive. They were not within sight, but would be soon enough.

Now, she cried out inside. *Tell them, show them that I belong. That I am one of you. Show them I fit in. Make the dream come true. Make nothing stand between us. Tell them I belong.*

But Thomas smoothed down the hair she'd ruffled in passion. Pulling on his glove, he assumed the expression she remembered from last night. Complete, absolute, impervious boredom.

She put her hands on her heated cheeks, pulled her little half-veil over her face. The voices were coming closer. Thomas stepped away as the crowd entered the copse. Jasmine spotted many of the same faces that laughed at her last night. Among them were the lovely, widowed Charlotte Harrison and Miss Francine Waters. The latter was engaged to one of Thomas's friends, Jasmine recalled. Charlotte was—her mind raced frantically, and Jasmine's polite smile wilted as she remembered the gossip—Thomas's mistress.

He glanced at her with seeming indifference. "Miss Tristan, I bid you good day. Your mare is indeed a fine specimen of the Arabian pedigree I seek. I trust you will tell your uncle I'm interested in acquiring such a mare to increase my stables."

That impervious, regal tone, as if nothing had transpired between them. He did not introduce her. As spots of color increased on her cheeks, Jasmine checked her ire and played along with the ruse.

"Arabic horseflesh is prized throughout Europe, and I'm glad you recognize the merits. I'm happy to convey your wishes to the Duke of Caldwell."

Saying the title was meant as a reminder to all that her uncle was a duke. No one looked impressed. Still, dignity draped about her, Jasmine turned to leave.

Someone laughed—William Oakley, the worst of Thomas's toadies. He elbowed Thomas with a nod. "Tommy, are you considering mares from Egypt? I hear they stray where they aren't supposed to go. And they're usually ugly and not worth a ride." He gave Jasmine a sly look. "Mares named Jasmine, for example."

Jasmine blanched. Others laughed at her discomposure, and Miss Waters blushed. But Charlotte Harrison frowned.

"Really, William, don't be such a boor," she admonished.

Thomas looked outraged. "How dare you insult this lady?" He said. His low, commanding tone was more threatening than if he'd shouted.

"W-what lady?" Oakley stuttered.

Fury burned in Thomas's eyes. "Apologize to Miss Tristan," he demanded.

"For what, when your own family regards her as nothing more than a rude trespasser? Surely you are jesting, Tommy. She's not our sort." Oakley looked outraged.

Jasmine lifted her chin, her insides knotting. They would not see her upset.

Thomas advanced, grabbed his friend's lapels and shook him like a dog. "Apologize," he ordered.

"Sorry," Oakley muttered, his glare a contradiction to the words.

"Miss Tristan, you should leave now," Thomas said quietly, releasing the other man.

Jasmine picked up her abandoned riding crop, fighting the anger that compelled her to strike at Oakley with it. To strike at the whole lot of them. She held her head high and went for her mare.

As she galloped away, she did not look back.

Thomas watched Jasmine go with quiet resignation. When he turned back to his friends, the women, Oakley, Charles Benton, and Lord Bryan Hodges all stared at him as if they didn't quite know him. Perhaps they did not.

Thomas gave the women a polite smile. "Ladies, if you don't mind, a word alone with my mates is required."

Charlotte pouted. "Come along then, Francine. I fancy some shopping before tea."

He waited until they'd strolled out of earshot. Seeing Charlotte take up friendship with Benton's fiancé disturbed him a trifle; he preferred his liaisons discreet, and his bed companions out of sight. But for now . . . he turned to his friends with a grave expression.

"Are you quite mad, Tommy? Why are you defending *her*?" Oakley exclaimed.

"Jasmine's father is a viscount," he replied through clenched teeth.

"Her whole family—well, they're a bit daft," Hodges put in. "Even the duke. All that time in Egypt, and now, always keeping to themselves, never entertaining . . . Don't care if they are peers, they're an odd sort. My father told me there were rumors about the duke and some tragedy in Egypt, how he used to run wild with a Bedouin tribe."

"A Bedouin tribe raising pedigreed Arabian horses that I broker here in Europe. The duke and I have done excellent business together," Thomas grated out.

"You shouldn't associate with them for other than business. I mean, money is money, but socializing? Why, god, man, the viscount had the gall to marry that Egyptian woman and bring her here like royalty, expecting everyone to be all chummy. And Jasmine, well, she's just foreign and without any background. Entertaining, she's always been, like she belongs on stage, but you wouldn't associate with an actress. And a dark-skinned one?" Benton shook his blond head.

For the first time, Thomas looked at his friends with a truly critical eye. They saw only the superficial. How could he convince them Jasmine was worthy of so much more?

"Jasmine Tristan is hardly common like an actress. She is an excellent horsewoman and very intelligent. I daresay she could hold her own in any setting."

"Such as your mother's ballroom, last night?" Oakley gave a bitter laugh. "I think she's bewitched you. Listen to me, Tommy. I won't see you ruin yourself over a piece of skirt. And if I can't make you see reason, then I'll find another way to stop this nonsense. Because if you don't stop it, you'll find yourself just like her—no one will want you in their homes."

Thomas went still at the veiled threat. He gave his friend a dark look. "What exactly do you mean by that, Oakley?"

The trio shifted their feet. Hodges gave a nervous laugh. "Tommy, he didn't mean anything by it. He just wants the old you back; that's it. Let's drop it, shall we?"

They were his friends, who knew him from the time he'd been in short pants. Hodges was right; Oakley just wanted what was best for him. Thomas slowly nodded.

"Come on, then, off to the club for brandy, eh? And tonight, the theater. I hear there's a pretty actress who's looking for a new protector." Benton laughed as the others made sly suggestions.

As he drifted behind them, Thomas realized they were right. He had to stop this mad obsession with Jasmine. It would not work, and it would ruin him in the process. He actually found himself eagerly anticipating a snifter of the amber liquid, a good cigar and a few laughs.

But an hour later at the club, the brandy did not taste as tangy and the cigars were not as sweet. He found nothing to laugh about.

Nothing at all.

Their brief time shared in the park only made Jasmine aware of how very much she was besotted over Thomas. She couldn't help thinking of it the following day as she sat in the garden reading The Egoist. She was about to go inside when Chloe arrived to visit.

Her friend beamed as she clutched her hands. "Oh, Jasmine, I've got the most splendid news. Simon and I—we're in love! He's invited me to visit with his family in Bath. My aunt is taking me later today, but I had to visit first and tell you."

Jasmine's heart twisted, even as she felt overjoyed for her friend. Chloe had found the right man. Would she herself ever do the same?

They talked briefly, then Chloe stood to leave. "By the by, there was a letter delivered for you just as I arrived." Mischief flashed in her eyes. "Perhaps it's a secret admirer."

"Go on," Jasmine said dryly. She hugged Chloe, waited until her friend left, then tore open the envelope with eager fingers. Surely it was from Thomas. Perhaps he had given more thought to their little sojourn in the park. But while hope flared inside her, she didn't dare give it wing, this something inside her breast fluttering and struggling to soar.

"I've had a secret crush on you for years, Thomas, and yet you will never, ever, reciprocate. It's silly, isn't it?" she whispered.

Happiness finally found its way to her best friend's

door. Surely the same must follow her. Didn't she deserve love as well?

With trembling fingers, Jasmine unfolded the letter, quivering inside with eager anticipation.

Her anticipation turned into bitter shock. It wasn't from Thomas. There was no happiness. No love. The paper fluttered to the graveled ground and lay there, the edge pointing upward at her like an accusing finger.

The words screamed in her mind. Fear crested through her in crashing waves.

"YOU KILLED ONE OF LORD CLARADON'S SONS THAT NIGHT IN THE PARK. STAY AWAY FROM THOMAS OR YOU WILL BE THE ONE MEETING WITH AN ACCIDENT. THE BROWN SCORPION WILL DIE."

Chapter Seven

Resplendent in blinding white, his mother and sister sat on the terrace. They chatted about nothing in particular. Nothing important. Nothing like what was going through Thomas's mind.

His high, stiff white collar contrasted with the cocoa-brown cravat knotted at his throat. He tipped up his broad-brimmed hat. Though he pretended absorption in the correspondence before him, he could not stop thinking about Jasmine: the stamp of hurt on her lovely face as she'd left the park, the cruel snickers of his friends. With her soft, kiss-swollen mouth and flushed cheeks, it had been quite obvious what they'd been doing. His curt words had been a guise to cloak their activity, but it had mattered not, for witless Oakley made a jest anyway.

It made little sense to him. Like his mother, his friends too regarded Jasmine as inferior, an insect one might catch and put on a pin to examine and then discard. Jasmine was a kind-hearted and high-spirited woman. Had she been white, she'd be welcomed at social gatherings. She sparkled in conversation and glowed in intellect. Why couldn't anyone else see her like he could?

"Lemonade?" His mother offered a glass from the maple table the maids had set outside. His sister snapped her parasol shut.

"Amanda, do shade your face. You'll turn brown and freckle," the countess advised.

"Perhaps I design to develop a different color," Amanda said airily. "To test Richard's love. For should he not feel the same, be I white, brown or with freckles dotting my face like a leopard's black spots?" She tilted her hat at a saucy angle.

"Amanda, do not trifle with me. Put up your parasol before you ruin your complexion. Before you are married, you must maintain your looks. Proper gentlemen like the baron want creamy English skin, not tough, leathery brown faces."

"Richard is marrying me for love, not for my looks," Amanda pouted.

"Pray do not test that theory."

"Don't say so, Mother. I am assured of his love, and if I chose to freckle, I shall!"

"Let's not have a row," Thomas remonstrated, feeling his temples pound. He suddenly thirsted for his club and the delights of his mistress. Yet even those things didn't appeal as strongly as before. He glanced again at the letter and its promise of escape. Freedom, if only for a few months.

"What does your friend say, Thomas? Is he truly going to Egypt this winter to explore?" Amanda's eyes were bright with interest.

"Indeed." Thomas folded the letter from Edward Ayrton and tucked it away. The Egyptologist, whom he'd befriended recently, knew of Thomas's fascination with excavations. He regarded both of his family members. "Theodore Davis is once more financing a dig in the Valley of the Kings this winter. He's hired Edward to excavate. Edward invited me to visit."

Both his mother and Amanda looked impressed.

"Davis is certain he'll find Tutankamun's tomb this time. He did find KV55 last season—a spectacular discovery, I must say, even if the American has a most destructive means of excavating. Rather like a child digging for treasure instead of scientific exploration. He ruined a mummy. Most disturbing. Still, he has the concession in the Valley, and this is an opportunity I shan't miss," Thomas explained.

Amanda clapped her hands, admiration shining in her eyes. His mother put her hand to her chest. "Really? They say if he finds the tomb, it will be the discovery of the century. Everyone is talking about it, how he's certain to do so. And you were invited to attend? How very prestigious, Thomas!"

"Oh, Thomas, how wonderful! When will you leave?" Amanda asked.

"Straight after Christmas, after the season begins. The Duke of Caldwell invited me to Egypt to look over the last Arabian steeds a Bedouin tribe is selling. The excavation will dovetail quite nicely with the visit."

His mother's enthusiasm drained away. "Surely you do not need more horses, Thomas—especially from the Duke."

"Surely I do," he corrected. "*Shoofi mafi?*"

"Thomas, heavens, what are you talking about?"

"I was merely asking you what's wrong in Arabic, Mother. Arabic, the language the duke taught me. It came in quite handy in our last business deal." He gave her a pointed look. "The transaction that enabled you to host your ball."

Lady Claradon brightened, her thin face looking younger and less strained. "Yes, that was nice. You have a good business sense, Thomas."

"This is an extraordinary opportunity. The al-Hajid have claim to the purebred Majd al Din line, among the finest Arabians in Egypt. No outsiders have been permitted to breed with this particular strain. Now, thanks to the duke, I'll be purchasing their mares. The duke is purchasing Al Safi, the great stallion descended from the Majd al Din line. He is selling me breeding rights. I already have a waiting list of those eager to purchase Al Safi's offspring."

"Thomas, this talk of breeding is not fit for polite company."

"Why, mother, I should think such a topic should prove pleasing, especially since I'm discussing purebloods fit for bluebloods. We of this family are concerned with breeding, are we not?"

She gave him a pained look. "Discretion, Thomas. Such language may be acceptable to the heathens, but not at our table."

"Don't fret, Mother. I shan't be anything but a proper

English example to the heathens where I go. I may even bring one back for training."

Incredulous horror shone in his mother's eyes. Thomas laughed and sipped his lemonade. A heavy tread upon the terrace indicated his father's approach.

A tight frown puckered the earl's face, and he glared at his wife. "Did you see this, madam? What does this mean?" He threw a newspaper upon the table. His finger thrust accusingly at the page's lower half. Dread pooled in Thomas's stomach. His father never cared for gossip. Why then was he disturbed over this?

Thin silence descended, broken by his mother's quavering gasps. Blood drained from her face as she scanned the sheet. "How dare they!"

Thomas picked up the paper and read. His guts twisted in sudden sickness, his mother's caterwauling filling his ears. He clutched the vicious little paper in his fingers, this paper that was delivered to the doorsteps of London's gentry and commoners alike.

" 'The Blue Bloods,' " he read aloud. " 'Adventures of aristocratic highbrows knocked low. By the All-Seeing Eye.' "

What followed was a sly story mocking a wealthy, titled family and the ball they had held recently, and a certain countess's vain attempts to invite King Edward. The king had not appeared because he had "a most pressing engagement in his water closet," and that other activity held for him "more fascination than the hostess's dreary babblings and that of her dull-witted daughter."

The piece was skillfully written, giving details to whet the appetites of the lower classes hungry for delicious gossip. And the reference was cleverly oblique, so that any who knew of the ball would assume it was Thomas's family. The writer went on to mock several other aristocrats, including a few young ladies seen at the ball. At column end, what promised to follow was a bi-weekly series of stories featuring this titled family and other gentry. The series would conclude on St. Valentine's Day, when the author promised to reveal a very real "scandal of love" and the aristocrat involved: "Someone of importance, a marriageable and very eligible fresh bud with very fashionable soles." The delicate flower had been snipped in the garden among the roses last year by a servant.

Enraged, Thomas glanced up. He went very still as he saw Amanda's expression. Horror filled her eyes. It filled him, too.

He dimly heard his father's shouts, his mother joining in the hysteria. His eyes were focused on his sister, on the terror shining on her face.

Thomas thought fast. "It's nothing. Pure balderdash. Stop this caterwauling, Mother."

"But, this person mocked my party," the countess said, wringing her hands.

"Mocked any peer who tried to invite Edward, who did not attend." Thomas tossed the sheet aside. "You give this matter any significance? It deserves not a whit."

His father snorted and strode away. Thomas jerked his head toward his mother. "Perhaps you'd better calm him. Assure him this is nothing but poppycock."

He was pleased to see her chase after the earl. Thomas next dismissed the maids waiting nearby. Then he turned his attention to Amanda, who toyed with her parasol.

"Mandy, come now, out with the truth." He'd gentled his voice, filled with worry about his sister.

She raised a tear-filled gaze to him. "How could anyone have found out? He . . . joined the military shortly after. No one knew," she whispered in a broken voice.

His heart dropped into his stomach. "When, Mandy? Tell me everything."

The story came out in strangled gulps and several swipes at her eyes. Last summer, her beau had broken off his courtship with Amanda and then had the gall to arrive at her dinner party the day after on the arm of his new fiancée. Broken-hearted, her casual friendship with the gardener had turned into desire, which she impetuously indulged among the roses. Desire had turned to regret, and then relief when the man left shortly afterward to enlist in the British Navy.

No one knew, she'd thought.

Someone did.

Thomas withdrew his white linen handkerchief from his jacket, dabbed at her streaming eyes. "Hush now, poppet, all will be well. No one will find out. This is conjecture, nothing more. I daresay if Richard finds out, he will dismiss it for what it is, nothing more than crude insinuations that lack proof."

Mandy grasped the cloth tightly. "Thomas, the author promised to reveal the persons involved. Someone must have been in the garden that day. I was so careful, I even gave that dress and shoes to my maid afterward, should anyone have seen them and recall the fashion. I always give Alice my things, so she thought nothing of it. But that reference . . . If Richard finds out—his family frowns upon scandal. He'll break off our engagement. I'll be ruined!"

Thomas shook his head, shocked. He wasn't sure what to do.

"Please, Thomas, I was absurdly foolish, I know it now. Please don't think ill of me. How I wish I'd done otherwise!"

Thomas squeezed his sister's hand. He was filled with anger at anyone daring to hurt his little sister, and by piercing grief for her lost innocence. "Mandy—I could never think ill of you, poppet, but this is dreadfully tricky. Promise me you'll hold your head high as you always do, and I'll think of a way to stop this."

"Promise?" she whispered.

He steeled himself. "I swear upon it. Whatever it takes, I will stop it." Her tremulous, grateful smile renewed his resolve as she dried her eyes, and he patted her hand. "Why don't you take a small stroll, compose yourself, and pretend as if nothing is wrong?"

She nodded. Standing with abject dignity, she opened her parasol and headed for the flagstone path bordering the shrubs.

Thomas took the paper and read it again, filled with loathing and rage. Damnation! He could understand someone targeting him—perhaps a jealous member of the demimonde. But Amanda? Who would want to hurt his sister? Perhaps other marriageable females harbored jealousy over her very eligible, fawning beau, yet none of them struck Thomas as being so spiteful as to want to hurt her, or his family, like this, No one but . . .

He glanced at the vile piece again, and its proclaimed author. "The All-Seeing Eye."

Eye? Such as from Egyptology and the Wedjat; the eye of Horus? It was an Egyptian eye, belonging to a woman driven away from his mother's ball.

The paper crumbled beneath his powerful fists. *Jasmine.* Why? He knew she'd been hurt, but damn it, why this attack on Amanda? If anyone was to blame, it was him, for standing silent in idle, helpless shock.

His fingers curled into fists. Belief in Jasmine's goodness shattered like glass. His desire, his respect? No more. Bitter disappointment twined with growing fury arrowed through him.

You'll pay, Jasmine. Oh, you shall pay for this.

She was the enemy now, the one holding the sword thrust into Amanda's heart. Long ago he'd promised his sister he'd always look after her.

He'd always kept that promise. Now Jasmine stepped on the crystal cocoon he'd built for Amanda and threatened to smash it beneath her spooned-heeled shoes. She would not.

Thomas felt as if a pretty flower had been moved aside, revealing a writhing brown scorpion hidden beneath. Jasmine, the betrayer. His family was his life. He would protect his sister's reputation and see her marry Richard. And so he had a call to make. . . .

"Upon my word, she *will* see me."

"Beg your pardon, my lord, but the family is not home, and Miss Tristan is not receiving. If perhaps you'd return to-morrow—"

Thomas ignored him. Pushing the startled footman aside, he started for the stairs.

"Did you wish to see me, Lord Thomas?" came a voice.

Jasmine drifted down the stairs, an ivory cameo at her throat. Her white shirtwaist and bottle-green skirt were elegant. Her stunning black curls were twisted at the back of her neck. Tendrils escaped and played about her head like errant children. She stopped at the bottom stair, her hand resting on the railing, and regarded him.

Thomas tried leashing his temper, but it frothed like a wild beast, mingling with the desire she always aroused in him. He met her halfway up the stairs. His fingers encircled her slim wrist, a wrist he'd kissed only yesterday.

"Let's take a stroll—in the garden, the area of your literary expertise," he said.

"An area certain members of your family seem to have an affinity for as well," she replied.

That little slip convinced him. Thomas led her outdoors to a small flagstone footpath. He marched her to a secluded area with a small bench flanked by jasmine bushes. Appropriate. But while the flowers smelled sweet, he was in no mood to enjoy their fragrance.

Releasing her, he silently pointed to the bench. Chin thrust out, she remained standing, arms folded beneath her breasts. Thomas took a deep, controlling breath.

"How dare you mock my family in newsprint, Jasmine? If your quarrel is with me or my mother, be bold enough to strike us. And do so in the open." Thomas removed the crumbled broadsheet from his jacket pocket and threw it down. It landed at her feet. Her dark, exotic eyes regarded him evenly. "This trash is beneath you. Or so I thought."

"You're most eager to accuse me of its authorship, my lord. On what basis?" she asked.

"The 'All-Seeing Eye.' A subtle reference to the eye of Horus, Jasmine? I'm not a fool." He advanced on her, watching her retreat. "You will cease this nonsense now, and snip it in the bud."

"It appears something else has already been snipped," she observed. "Woefully so, I might add. In the garden, by a gardener? And so the sinner loses her soul. Or was it her soles the witness saw?" Her smile grew. "The author, it appears, heard it was your precious Amanda."

Thomas steeled himself to defend his sister's honor. "Preposterous! Shoes, Jasmine? I gave you credit for more intelligence than trusting such sordid gossip. Who did your witness see? My sister frequently gives her shoes to her maid. A kindness Mandy bestows."

Surprise widened Jasmine's eyes. Thomas remained too angry to be satisfied by the reaction.

Then Jasmine's gaze sharpened. "Oh, no," she said softly. "That will hardly do, Lord Thomas. Such an excuse? This rumor is the truth, and we know it. Why would Amanda give away her clothing? Certainly your mother would never teach her such charity."

"She learned it from *you*," he snapped. "After you gave her that kitten at her party, remember? Mandy began giving her things away after that. Clothing, a bit of jewelry her maid admired, shoes. She told me that sharing with those who went without was a good thing, for she had missed her kitten dreadfully, and when you donated yours as comfort, it made a lasting impression. Unfortunately, you seemed to forget your own damn lesson."

Color suffused her cheeks. "Well, you have to understand my surprise. Amanda would never learn to be kind in your household. Your mother runs drier than the Sahara when it comes to the milk of human kindness."

"And you are angry at her, so you take your vengeance out on my sister? A cowardly act from someone I thought had sophistication and courage. Your blow hit the wrong target. Mandy is my family. I protect my own, and your cruel act will not bear fruit."

Thomas struggled to control his temper. "I can understand your anger against my mother for her slight, but how can you rationalize maligning my sister? It's absurd, Jasmine."

"Perhaps the writer of the column knows that such a scandal will be worse for the mother, who sees her position in society as much more precious. And perhaps the daughter herself deserves such as well, for she is equally as guilty of snobbery and causing hurt."

Thomas softened his voice. "Perhaps the author of the column should reconsider her position and show she is the better person by ceasing such gossip."

A brief flash of regret entered Jasmine's eyes. He pressed his case.

"You *will* stop this," he warned.

"Stop what? You'll have to do better than this, Thomas, assuming even that I am the author."

"You will ruin her, Jasmine."

"Yes, public humiliation can be awful," she agreed. She looked deeply thoughtful, as if remembering her own humiliation at his mother's ball. Thomas girded himself against the attack.

"I had such higher expectations of you than—"

"Than your mother?" she taunted.

"Yes. I thought you a better person than she. One able to move past a grievous insult."

Jasmine swallowed hard. She looked away. "It's difficult to forget the sting of the lash which cuts so deep."

Thomas closed his eyes, knowing too well the truth of her words. Still, that didn't justify her actions. "Such injuries aren't healed by lashing out at someone else," he said quietly. "Can you not see this, Jas? I held you to a higher standard than to strike out in petty retaliation."

Her mouth pulled downward. She looked like a lost child. "Lashing out is a natural reaction for a horse who has been kicked, and sometimes I think horses are better than people. Tell me, why did you not introduce me to your friends yesterday in the park?"

His brows knit together. "What?"

"You were ashamed to be seen with me. Admit it. You were as cold as your ice-blooded friends. That's why you deliberately dismissed me in the park. And after you *kissed* me." A becoming flush tinted her cheeks, whether from aroused remembrance or anger, he couldn't tell. Thomas began to understand, and his expression softened.

"You thought I was."

"Ashamed to be seen with me. After what happened at your mother's ball." She tilted her chin up and boldly looked at him. "Is that so wrong to assume?"

"No. I was *protecting* you, Jas. Protecting your reputation by defusing the situation." Despite his steely resolve, Thomas felt his anger dissolve. Damn, this was a bloody difficult situation. Why did their paths cross that night at the ball? It would have been better if they had never seen each other at all. Ever again.

"It was obvious you had been kissed. They would have taken you as my paramour, and your reputation would have been irrevocably tarnished. I could not see you ruined. I had to make a reasonable excuse. Better to suffer my indifference," he explained.

"You were considering my reputation?"

"Of course," he said softly, drawing closer to her, as if pulled by an invisible magnet. "I don't wish to see you hurt, and there are those in my circle who would hurt you even more than my mother."

Her mouth parted as if to speak; and he hungered, knowing the exquisite taste of her lips. Knowing he couldn't have her. Ever. He burned for her. A fire he must douse, and quickly.

"You are a lady, and I always protect a lady's reputation," he said more formally. Never could he allow Jasmine to know there was more. Would always be more. It was impossible. One might as well try reaching for a shining star.

"Thank you, Thomas," she said. She stepped forward, breaching the distance between them. The desire on her face mirrored his own. She wanted to kiss him. His blood stirred. He forced himself to look elsewhere, anywhere but that delectable mouth of hers. If he kissed her, there'd be no turning back. And they could not move forward.

Thomas shook his head and gazed down at her. "Please understand, Jasmine, yesterday was a mistake. I'm sorry for allowing it to proceed that far and leading you down a false trail. It was a kiss, nothing more."

Jasmine bit her lower lip. Thomas stared in hunger, remembering its sweetness beneath the press of his own mouth. He'd never taste it again. The shining light faded in her eyes.

"There never will be anything between us, will there?" she asked.

Regret stabbed him. "No. It's not possible."

Something in her expression reminded him of a wounded puppy. Then a shutter dropped over her features. She gave a little shrug.

"No bother. It was a romp, kissing you in the park. A good experiment. I'm certain other men kiss equally well."

Her casual remark stung, but he retreated to his purpose:

Amanda's joy, not his. "I trust you will find one who makes you very happy," he said stiffly, cloaking his feelings. "So, let us return to the pressing business at hand. Will you then stop writing these stories? For your sake, Jasmine. Trust me. It will haunt you if you continue."

For a minute, he half believed they'd connected and she felt contrite. Then virulent anger entered her gaze again.

"I'm no one's lackey, and certainly not yours, my lord. You can't order me about or tell me what to write. If I want to take down the whole lot of you, I will. Watch me."

"Then you admit you're the author," he grated out.

Dismay touched her features. Then she laughed. "Yes, I admit it. Tell anyone and I'll deny it. There's nothing you can do. How does your mother feel to be in such a position? The high and mighty, smote by others' opinions. More powerful than a sword, words are—something your mother should consider next time she insults her so-called inferiors."

Her slow smile filled Thomas with bitter anger and remorse. Remorse for how embittered she'd become from his mother's taunts, losing the very core of her goodness. Anger because she had him, and had him well.

Leashing his temper, he kept his voice calm. "Jasmine, humiliating my family in print will not improve your own situation. Accusing anyone of impropriety won't make you feel better."

"But I'm not accusing anyone of anything, Lord Thomas. People will draw their own conclusions. Who is the real sinner—that will be decided by others. Is it the weak woman in the garden, seeking the pleasures of the flesh?"

"Don't sneer at such pleasures until you've experienced them yourself, Jasmine," he said softly.

"I'm sure you're an expert," she shot back.

"I could give you lessons. Trust me, I *could* teach you, and teach you well." His gaze swept her, his meaning apparent.

Her eyes grew wide and she lifted her chin. "You never

will, my lord. I'm not weak. But someone in your circle is, and we both know it. And you're powerless to save her."

She was right. But for a moment he wished wildly that he could hold her in his power. "One day you'll find out exactly what it feels like to be powerless," he promised tightly.

He fisted his hands to keep from touching her, fearing he was losing control. Damn it, he wanted to make her realize how repulsive her actions were. He wanted the old Jasmine back, the spirited woman who didn't give a damn about the world, not this remote woman who was growing cold and bitter as an English winter.

And yet, he still wanted her.

He had it all. A title, power, a life many envied. He needed only to snap his fingers and servants scurried like bugs to obey his orders. Friends admired him. Women cast him coy glances and matrons wanted to hand over their virginal daughters for his marriage bed. Why then did he want the one woman who threatened to destroy all he held most dear?

"One day, Jasmine, you will know what it's like to be in my power. I warn you, when that day comes, I will teach you a lesson you will never forget," he breathed, fighting for control, roping in all the wild feelings that wanted only to shake her in anger, kiss her in passion. Bloody hell, what was wrong with him? What was wrong with her?

Thomas turned his back and walked off. One day he would hold her in his power and she'd learn. One day.

Jasmine watched Thomas storm out of the garden, and waited until the door shut firmly behind them. Then she buried her head in her hands.

All the wrong words had tumbled out. She hadn't meant them, but anger had poked her like a stick and she couldn't help herself. And deep down she'd been frightened. She'd had to drive Thomas away because of that letter. No one had known what happened that night in the park with Nigel. But someone did. She longed to confess to someone, but didn't dare entrust anyone with her secret.

I did not kill him. But someone believes what happened was my fault.

If Thomas and his family found out . . . a shudder raked her as she thought of the consequences. Never had she felt so alone in the world.

Jasmine lifted her chin. She was stronger than all of them. She'd prove it as well, and bear the burden alone.

But, someone knew she and Nigel had been in the park that night, and that person wanted her dead. The irony made her laugh. She wished to make Amanda dead to their social circle, and her silent enemy wanted Jasmine dead in reality. Was it someone who had guessed her authorship of the column, as Thomas had?

It mattered not. At all costs, she must avoid seeing Thomas again. It wasn't worth it to her wounded soul. Or her very life.

A little laugh escaped her. "Oh Jasmine, such theatrics!" she whispered, hugging herself. "It's but a prank." Surely whoever penned that note jested—or toyed with her as a cat swatted a mouse.

A bout of riding always cleared her mind. She fled to the stable.

A short while later, Jasmine headed for the park on her mare. She dug her heels into Persephone's sides. Rider and mount galloped like the wind. Jasmine laughed in sheer delight, feeling free at last. Here no social compunctions ruled her. She cared not a whit what others thought of her seat or if they admired her habit; she rode only to break free of everything she wanted, and all she could not have.

As she slowed Persephone to a canter, she glanced to her right and stiffened. Thomas's friends, all of them smartly attired, strolled toward the Serpentine. She recognized the shorter, dapper figure of Oakley. He turned, and his virulent look sent a shudder snaking through her. Jasmine gave a dignified nod, but he turned abruptly away, said something to his friends. They glanced over their shoulders as he pointed at her. Laughter drifted on the wind.

Jasmine sat straighter. They were not worth another thought. Still, she couldn't help the tiny hurt.

Slowing Persephone to a walk, she led her mare off the track and swung one leg over the saddle to dismount. Suddenly a loud whistling sound drew her attention. She turned to see a large stone sailing through the air, followed by a smack as it hit her mare in the flank. The mare squealed, reared and bolted. Crying out, Jasmine wrapped her arms about her mount's neck. Bouncing up and down, she clung with all her might. She bent over Persephone, summoning all her control to hang on. If Persephone threw her, she was good as dead. Her muscles burned with the effort and her breath came in tiny, frightened gasps.

Murmuring reassurances, she soothed the horse, who eventually slowed. Fully in control now, she guided the beast off the sandy track and slid down. Then she checked the horse. A nasty laceration marred the Arabian's side. She put a trembling hand to it and her glove came away red. Oh God.

Vaguely, she was aware of someone running toward her, inquiring if she were all right. If she weren't such an excellent horsewoman, she could have been tossed and perhaps killed. But she had greater problems than that.

Jasmine murmured her thanks to the stranger. She waved aside offers of help and gathered Persephone's reins in her hand to head home. It wasn't safe here anymore.

As she headed back to the area where she'd been hit, Jasmine searched for what had struck her horse. There, on the track, gleaming white in the sunshine: a violent trembling seized her as she lifted the object. The palm-sized stone had paper wrapped about it, and was tied with string. She unbound the note and read the large black letters of hate penned there:

I WARNED YOU, BROWN SCORPION. STAY AWAY FROM LORD THOMAS WALLENFORD. NEXT TIME YOU WILL DIE. YOU DON'T BE-LONG WITH OUR SORT.

Her breath hitched in real fear. Jasmine tried to stop her trembling as she gathered Persephone's reins to lead her home. *You don't belong*. The words in the past had stung, but never had she experienced physical danger from such hatred. She had already received one other warning. The note hadn't been a cruel childish prank; someone did want her dead, after all.

Chapter Eight

The reckoning came later with the publication of another column. Her mother and stepfather summoned her to the upstairs drawing room to talk about her "little writings."

A cool October breeze drifted through the opened windows of the downstairs hall as she paused on the stairs. No other incidents had happened since that day in the park. Jasmine now rode with caution, ensuring she never encountered any of Thomas's set. The note delivered weeks earlier still loomed in her mind, but when no further threats arose, she'd breathed with a little more ease. The stone in the park had been likely tossed by a hateful Oakley. The notes were mere childish pranks sent by Thomas's arrogant friends who thought such threats were jolly good fun, tormenting the brown scorpion. Her parents were her concern now. They had discovered her ruse, it seemed.

She lifted her chin, prepared to sail into battle, unrepentant and ready to defend her actions. She truly hadn't meant to hurt Thomas or his sister. Only his mother.

Or had she? And did it matter?

She stormed toward the gold drawing room that her mother loved. It reminded her of Egypt and the sun. Everyone in her family, it seemed, had a connection to that land. Her uncle Graham, the duke and her stepfather, Kenneth, had a unique one: Two brothers, both very young when accompanying their parents to the desert, they were attacked by tribal warriors, their parents killed. Kenneth was taken in by the Khamsin warriors of the wind, who'd found him hiding in a basket. The Khamsin sheikh had raised him as a son.

The al-Hajid, the Khamsin's enemies who'd attacked the caravan, had taken Graham. They had not treated him as well. Once, when Jasmine asked her mother about it, the countess looked sad and told her it was best forgotten. Just as she refused to say a word about Jasmine's real father.

So many secrets in the past. Jasmine shuddered as she remembered her childhood. In particular, the dark room, the door shutting, her friend's cries. . . .

Her mother and stepfather sat on the couch by the window. Her mother looked troubled, her stepfather severe. "Shut the door and have a seat," the viscount told her.

She did so, feeling a tad shaky as she took the wing chair across from them. Out of all the people she always wanted to please, foremost was her stepfather. He loved her as much as his own children. But Michael, Lydia and Delane were more English-looking than Jasmine, and more acceptable, a fact she was all too aware of now.

His blue eyes focused steadily on her as he held out the newspaper article. "Jasmine, did you write this rubbish?"

Silence remained her best defense.

"Jasmine, it clearly contains details of Hope's birthday party. Details your sister shared with you. Now, answer my question. Are you the author?"

She met his gaze. "Before you launch into a tirade, the publisher, Mr. Myers, said he liked my writing and is giving me a stipend to continue it."

"You will *not*," her stepfather said tightly. "This sort of despicable gossip ends now."

Jasmine's fingers curled on the chair's armrest. "You can't tell me what I can and cannot write, sir." She'd always called him Father. Not today. The disgust and controlled anger on his face equaled her own turbulent emotions.

Her mother leaned forward. "Why, Jasmine, are you doing such a vile thing?"

Jasmine gave a little shrug. "Why not? It's jolly good fun. You must admit, Mother, my sketch is flattering to the subject."

Her mother glanced at the caricature of Lady Claradon,

which Jasmine had also provided, stuffing her thin face with a large slice of birthday cake.

"I'm worried, Jasmine. You've never been this . . . cruel. It reminds me of your—" The viscountess bit back her words, exchanged worried glances with her husband.

Jasmine sat up, sensing the real issue, one that was never addressed. "Reminds you of who, Mother? The man whose name you never mention? My real father? Who was he, this secret man you've never discussed? Truly he cannot be as vile as you think. He was my *father*."

Her real father was a king ruling over the desert, she had always told herself. A king who died bravely, fighting for his people. A worthy king, accepted and loved by his tribe. The fantasy had provided her comfort during many sleepless nights after English children taunted her about her Egyptian heritage.

"Jasmine," the viscount began sternly.

"No, Kenneth. She needs to know. It's time she finally does know." Badra lifted her tear-filled gaze to her daughter as her husband squeezed her hand. "Your real father was a powerful sheikh. Sheikh of the al-Hajid tribe in Egypt, sworn enemies of the Khamsin. Your father, Fareeq, ruled the tribe that kidnapped your Uncle Graham."

A powerful sheikh, just as she'd thought! But the al-Hajid? Confused, Jasmine frowned. "The Khamsin are our friends. And I've heard of Uncle Graham being raised by the al-Hajid, but they aren't wicked."

"Once they were," Kenneth broke in, his face darkening. "Bitter enemies of the Khamsin, because of your father."

The anguish on her mother's face warned Jasmine the story would not be as lovely as she had imagined. Jasmine stood, pacing to the fireplace. "Tell me about the al-Hajid," she said.

Kenneth looked slightly relieved; he clearly did not want to discuss her father specifically.

"The tribe has lived in Egypt's Eastern Desert for decades, but times have changed. Unlike the Khamsin, who expanded their business of raising prime Arabians, they haven't made economic adaptations. Many have left for the city. Graham told me in his last correspondence with the Khamsin sheikh that the rest of the al-Hajid are leaving the desert soon. They're settling in a small town along the Nile."

Her father's people, disbanded and forgotten? *My people. I have a tribe, a way of life*, she realized. "Then their culture will be lost forever!"

An idea sparked and hope filled her. Perhaps there was indeed purpose to her writing.

"I want to meet them before they depart the desert. They were my birth father's people. I can chronicle their history before it disappears. The newspaper publisher likes my writing. Perhaps he'll be equally interested in articles from Egypt."

"I don't know if that's such a good idea," Kenneth said.

"Are you afraid of what I'll find?"

He studied her a minute. "Yes, Jasmine. No matter what you think, I understand—trust me—it's not an easy thing to discover your past. I don't want you to be hurt. I still consider you my little girl."

She swallowed past the thickness in her throat.

"Of course, you're grown now. And if this is something you must do, then go."

The idea of finding out the truth suddenly seemed as threatening and ominous as that dark room into which had disappeared her old friend. But she couldn't back down. Never before had she stood down from a challenge, even one that scared her.

"Your Uncle Graham is visiting there in late December and purchasing the last of their Arabians. That would be a good time for you to go as well, and would put a peaceful end to this 'All-Seeing Eye' persona." Kenneth gave a wry smile. "Though I daresay all of England will be ignoring it by then and paying more attention to Davis's dig in the Valley of the Kings. He's searching for Tutankamun's tomb."

Jasmine's interest rose. "Really?"

"Really. I'm told. Davis is certain to find it—the first intact pharaoh's tomb. Talk of the town, Graham says. Some are already pursuing invitations to attend the excavation."

Egyptology, not Egypt, Jasmine thought. Egyptology was fashionable, unlike Egyptians. Still . . .

"Perhaps I could extend my visit, join the dig and maybe write articles chronicling the activity. That would be splendid. Do you think Uncle Graham can recommend me? Does he have connections? I'd be an apt translator. My Arabic is flawless." For the first time in months, she had direction.

Kenneth studied her calmly. "Is that what you wish, honey?"

She nodded. The thought dangled before her like a tempting peach. Society would covet fresh news of the dig. History in the making! Commentaries on the excavation would be devoured by a greedy public if speculation ran high that Davis was unearthing the find of the century. To be present when such history occurred would also give a person carte blanche, invitations, social acceptance and popularity. Jasmine saw the firmly closed door opening a crack once more: *There goes Miss Jasmine Tristan, who was there when Davis unearthed Tut's tomb! Tell me, Miss Tristan, was it simply spectacular? Do come to tea, Miss Tristan, and tell us once more about how you were there in the tomb with Mr. Davis, recording details for the newspaper about the treasure. And you simply must attend my little fete next month at Patricia's come-out.*

Invitations would pour forth like the Nile flooding. Surely this time, someone would see her worth.

"If Graham secures you a letter of recommendation, will your columns about the Blue Bloods cease?" Kenneth asked.

Jasmine did something else she'd never done. She lied to

her stepfather. "I'm promised to deliver columns until the year's end, but they will stop when I visit Egypt."

Her stepfather sighed. "Jasmine—"

With an innocent look, she spread her hands. "It's a legally binding contract. I cannot cease." Which was the truth, she realized suddenly. But surely Mr. Myers would allow her to cease when she wished.

"Very well. Talk with Graham. He knows a few people, he can get you a letter of recommendation as a translator on the dig site," Kenneth said.

Her mother gave her a beseeching look. "Jasmine—please, honey, don't go to Egypt. Many in the al-Hajid tribe have ill memories of your father and won't wish to talk about him. He was quite cruel. I don't want you to be hurt."

Jasmine felt a sickening twist in her gut as she studied the tension on her mother's face. "Surely he wasn't that bad, Mother."

The blood fled Badra's face. "He was evil. I was his slave—his concubine, sold to him when I was eleven." She drew a deep breath, and her husband slid an arm about her. "He raped and beat me."

"What? That's not possible." Jasmine was outraged.

"Trust me, honey, it's true. Fareeq had many concubines, but they all swore a pact among them never to bear him children. They took fennel seeds to prevent conception. I didn't, hoping that if I gave him a child, he'd stop beating me. I gave birth to you. And when he saw you were a girl, not a son, he sold you into the same brothel where he purchased me. Where I had been sold by my parents."

"Remember, Jasmine? When you were living there and we rescued you?" The viscount's voice was very gentle.

Yes, Jasmine remembered. And she saw: her father had done to her mother what the vile man in the brothel had done to Jasmine's best friend, Nadia. Bile rose in her throat.

"Surely he had . . . some redeeming quality. He must," she whispered. "He was my father."

"The man who sired you. Never a father," Badra insisted. "Kenneth is your father."

Blood will tell, she had once overheard Kenneth saying. And whose blood ran in her veins? A cruel despot's.

"Are there . . . others? Brothers and sisters, other children of his? Is he still alive?" She clung to a desperate hope. Surely she couldn't be like him. And maybe if she could meet siblings . . .

"You were his only child," Badra said gently.

A man with a dark past, whom her mother feared and her stepfather detested. A man who waged war and instilled hatred. A despicable man. This was her father. Jasmine felt even sicker.

"Can't you see, this is why when we heard about that article you wrote—this is the sort of thing your father would do, deliberately hurt someone. You're not him, Jasmine. But your spirits run a bit high at times and . . ." Badra's voice trailed off.

"You say I'm not like him, but you're doubting yourself. You're starting to worry that maybe I am after all." Jasmine stared at her mother, her anger growing. "I'm a cruel tyrant as well."

"Jasmine! That's not true," Kenneth said, but he looked troubled.

"Your temper, Jasmine. You act rashly sometimes, impulsively, letting your emotions rule you. It's at times like those when I worry most. You must learn to control your temper or it will control you." The viscountess knelt at her daughter's feet and took her hands. Confusion and remorse filled Jasmine at her mother's wounded look.

"When I found you living at the brothel—oh, Jasmine! I was absurdly happy and heartbroken at once. I knew I had to get you free and bring you with me to live, no matter what else." Tears brimmed in Badra's beautiful eyes, dark and sloe like Jasmine's own.

"Jasmine, clearly you have a talent for the written word. There is much to explore in Egypt. Other matters are what you had best write about, other than choosing the al-Hajid and stirring up bitter memories," her stepfather suggested gently. "We only want what's best for you."

"Yes, why don't I write about my spectacular origins? How I was raised in a brothel?" Jasmine rejoined. "Wouldn't that shame you? People would talk. Oh, how they would talk!"

"Shame us?" Badra exchanged a meaningful glance with her husband. The viscount's mouth pulled into a flat smile and he said, "You cannot shame us. They already have talked, Jasmine. They talked about us when we first came here and we gave them no reason for conjecture. They continue to talk. Your mother and I are not exactly seen as pillars of society."

"And I could care less about English society," Badra declared, her chin rising into the air. "I don't care about what people say, honey. But I do care about you. This desire you have to wound with your writing. That worries me."

"Maybe blood will tell," Jasmine said darkly. She yanked her hands free of her mother's and watched Badra and Kenneth's reactions with a sinking feeling. They, too, wondered. And that told her more than anything else.

Her mother returned to the sofa, resting against her husband the viscount. She looked at ease, as if she belonged, and Jasmine suddenly realized she didn't belong. All her life she'd tried to adapt to an English lifestyle. It had never worked. Maybe Egypt was where she would fit in. And maybe she would discover things were different there than everyone thought.

"My father, my real father—perhaps he was cruel at times,

but he must have been very noble and proud," she ventured, watching her mother and the viscount's expressions.

Badra looked visibly upset. Her stepfather's face tightened. "Your real father was an utter bastard," he said flatly.

Jasmine stood, unable to stop the raw emotions boiling inside. "You lie," she cried. "My father was a powerful sheikh, and you are merely jealous of his memory."

"Jasmine!" her mother exclaimed.

"He wasn't all that bad; he couldn't be. And if you hate and despise him so much, you must feel the same about me. My behavior upsets you so much, and so you send me back to the same place where you found me," she said bitterly. "That's why you've encouraged me to leave."

The viscount looked troubled. "We would never do that, Jasmine. You're our daughter—my daughter—no matter what person fathered you," he assured her.

But she didn't believe them. She couldn't. Believe them, and she was the daughter of a vile tyrant. She was a vile person herself. She had to make her own way, find her own truth.

"I'm not your daughter," she told her stepfather, trembling inside so violently that she felt ill. "You're denying the facts. You're afraid. You're afraid because I remind you of him."

Her mother burst into sobs. Jasmine felt sicker, but held her ground.

"Jasmine, as long as you remain under this roof you will not upset your mother like this," her stepfather warned.

"Fine. I'll leave. Why should I remain here any longer in the company of those who think I'm as poisonous as my sire. He wasn't as bad as you say he is. You're wrong, and I'll prove it."

I must, she thought desperately.

"I'll stay with Uncle Graham," she decided. "Your plan had merit. And now I see that I must go."

Tears ran down her mother's face. Kenneth slid his arms

about Badra, looking at Jasmine with stinging disapproval. Fresh guilt surfaced; but she was compelled now to follow her course.

"I'll pack my things immediately," she said quietly. "I'm sorry, Mother, that I hurt you, but I must do this."

For she knew her mother was wrong. Someone among the al-Hajid must have respected and admired her father. Fareeq could not have been utterly evil. For if he was, what did that portend for her, his only daughter?

Chapter Nine

Her life slid from bad to worse in a few months. But for the comfort she found in writing, Jasmine found little to enjoy.

Her relationship with her parents remained strained. After a long talk in which they failed to convince her to return home, Uncle Graham and Aunt Jillian had taken her in. Her aunt enjoyed her companionship, and Jasmine adored helping with her nieces. Aunt Jillian had also enlisted Jasmine's support in establishing her newest charitable effort: a school for indigent London street children. But Jasmine herself felt lost and alone.

To her immense shock, Thomas had sent round a note. Polite in tone, the letter had invited her to meet with his sister today at a restaurant to discuss Amanda's possible involvement with Aunt Jillian's new venture. *Perhaps you will see what a charitable heart Mandy possesses, and this will bring a new direction to your columns,* he'd written.

Doubtful, Jasmine was still curious enough to accept. She was willing to give Amanda a chance. Deep down, she worried that attacking Lady Claradon's daughter had indeed been a symptom of paternal wickedness, as her mother and stepfather feared. She was determined to prove herself as her own person, and would judge Lady Amanda on her own merits.

But surely my real father wasn't all that bad, she rationalized again upon entering the restaurant cloakroom and giving the clerk her outerwear.

It was irrelevant. Jasmine was here to ask Lady Amanda to support her aunt's charity. Aunt Jillian's School for the Learning and Advancement was already well-funded, but you could always use more. Her aunt sought to form a social committee to raise money, and Amanda's reputation among her peers would greatly advance Aunt Jillian's cause.

Jasmine paused at the dining room entrance. People turned and looked at her. The ecru walls felt as if they were closing in on her skull. Lady Amanda rose from a quiet table at the window and came forward with a smile.

"Miss Tristan, how nice to see you." Lady Amanda shook her hand politely.

Jasmine greeted the girl with more enthusiasm than she felt. Heads turned, stared, then bent together and murmured. Someone laughed. Was the term "brown scorpion" heard? Faces blended into an unrecognizable blur, and Lady Amanda's smile slipped. She looked troubled.

Gleaming white china and sparkling silver adorned the linen tablecloth as they reached the table. Equally sparkling and shiny were the two young ladies already seated. They wore lacy, pastel-colored dresses and large-brimmed ecru hats trimmed with feathers and beads. Jasmine's stomach clenched. She had expected to meet with Lady Amanda alone, not this brigade. Amanda had brought reinforcements. This was not to be a polite tête-à-tête.

Affixing a polite smile on her face, she greeted them, Miss Avery and Lady Henrietta, then took a seat at the place beside Amanda. Jasmine ordered coffee. Strong coffee. She'd need it.

Lady Amanda remarked how the draft chilled her. Jasmine glanced at the dining room door, at least fifty feet away. Lady Amanda moved, leaving an empty seat between herself and Jasmine. The subtle slight made Jasmine's stomach churn. This meeting would prove a dreadful mistake. But she was caught now, and must make the most of it.

"Surely you are hungry?" inquired Lady Henrietta. "You must have a robust appetite." She gave a pointed glance at Jasmine's curvy waist and hips, and offered a smile that did not reach her eyes.

"Hetty," Lady Amanda said. "Please."

Biting back a caustic reply about how Lady Henrietta's own waist size probably exceeded her intelligence, Jasmine allowed the white-coated waiter to settle a napkin upon her lap.

"I am not, thank you. Coffee will be just fine."

Lady Amanda began talk about the weather and its fineness, then pointedly asked Jasmine about her aunt. Plunging in with wholehearted enthusiasm, Jasmine explained about the duchess's school. Barely had she given details when she saw the looks: The young women had already judged the cause unworthy. Her heart sank with disappointment.

"Amanda told us all about your aunt and her endeavor. Very grand. But surely it is rather queer, isn't it, that she insists on teaching the lower classes *herself?*" Miss Avery sipped her tea.

Jasmine sighed. She'd expected more civility. How silly of her.

"In addition to holding a college degree in education, Aunt Jillian is a philosopher and idealist. She believes in the equality of the classes, and in suffrage."

Three pairs of shocked eyes turned toward her. "Giving women the right to vote? Why, when it's not needed? Why not let the men make the decisions?" Lady Amanda asked. She gave her companions a bewildered look. "My Richard would never hear of it."

"Perhaps his ears require a good cleaning—a cleaning you could well give him if you were so inclined," Jasmine suggested with a little smile. The waiter brought her coffee. She took a bracing sip, noting with disdain that it was cold. And slightly bitter.

"Clean the baron's ears? I never heard such nonsense," Miss Avery said.

No sense of humor. This proposed to be more difficult than she'd ever anticipated.

"Clean ears lead to a clear mind—a mind apt to think for itself," Jasmine continued.

"You see, therein lies the problem." Lady Amanda put

down a forkful of chiffon cake. "Many of our ilk wonder if the duchess is suffering from a temporary ailment of the mind. The very idea of a duchess teaching the lower classes herself? It's quite noble, but impractical." She turned to her friends with an imploring look. "Do you not think so as well?"

This was the real reason for inviting an audience, Jasmine realized. Support. Respect for Amanda disappeared faster than her coffee in her nervous gulps. Clearly the girl lacked the spine to state her true opinions unaided.

"I have heard that the duke is irregular, what with his association with those wild Bedouins he knew from his days in Arabia. The duke and duchess seldom entertain, either," Miss Avery remarked. As if this were reason enough to shun any cause they espoused.

"My aunt and uncle are preoccupied with raising their children, which gives them little time to entertain," Jasmine explained, feeling more tense by the moment. "Which makes my aunt's solicitation for this cause all the more remarkable, for it is dear to her and causes her to take time apart from her family. That is why I offered to help her solicit funds and helpers."

"But, Miss Tristan, do you not see? Your very association with such a cause—well, few would support such a radical venture even with the duchess at the helm. And with you . . . You are quite a kindhearted person, and I applaud the nobility of your intentions, but I must be absolutely honest." Lady Amanda leaned forward with a guileless look. "I doubt any of my set would support the duchess with you as an advocate. You see, those in society . . . well, it would be peculiar."

"Peculiar?"

"Your origins," Lady Amanda explained in a kind tone. "Everyone knows you're foreign. Your real people are quite unknown, except for your mother, and she's Egyptian. Well, to be seen in such company wouldn't be proper."

Miss Avery nodded. "Why, not that *we* believe this way, but you must understand that everyone in our circle *knows* about Egyptians: One simply does not associate with them."

"I see." Jasmine felt her temper almost boil over. "So, you count yourselves among those who would not join the cause. Then, why bother with this meeting? Any of you?"

Lady Amanda gave a gentle smile. "I did so only out of kindness to Thomas, because he asked, and I'd do anything for my dear brother. He's much in favor of the duchess, and friends with the duke. But I shan't be associating with you, Miss Tristan. I'm sure you understand. It wouldn't be in good taste."

"To each her own," Miss Avery put in helpfully.

"Perhaps you could solicit supporters among your own set," Lady Henrietta added.

But I don't have a set, Jasmine thought. She studied the trio and realized they knew that as well. They were laughing inside. And they wanted her gone. Now.

Lady Amanda smiled, a pitying expression that made her look both angelic and beatific. Jasmine's stomach gave a sudden lurch, and while white-clad waiters moved like wraiths to the accompanying clatter of silverware and the genteel swell of strings and flute played discreetly in the corner, she considered taking her cup and flinging the contents into Lady Amanda's face.

After a moment she settled. Her resolve increased. She would continue her column and damn them all. Now, she didn't even care if they discovered her identity. To imply that her beloved aunt and uncle were daft, and that her very society was pulling them down? It was a grievous insult!

Lady Amanda turned away. Jasmine listened as the trio began a new discourse, excluding her in such an obvious manner that Jasmine knew they had dismissed her.

"Thank you for the coffee. I'm afraid I must take my leave," she said.

They nodded, but didn't stop talking as she pulled on her gloves. Suddenly Amanda waved, however, and Jasmine's tension trebled.

"Oh, there's Thomas! I invited him to drop by. Hetty, I told him how you admired the way he won the race last week against your brother on the Row. You should ask him to teach you to improve your seat," Amanda said.

A chill ran up Jasmine's spine. Since the incident in the park she had not seen the man, and being caught in public with him was not wise.

However, leaving as he approached would look odd. Forcing a smile, Jasmine watched him wend his way toward their table. He was greeted quite jovially by several diners who had ignored her. When he arrived, Jasmine kept her sight fixed ahead on one of the splendid Doric columns. But Thomas, damn him, did not choose to accept this. He greeted the other ladies, then went to her side, offering her a polite nod as he put himself directly in her line of sight.

"Hullo," he said, his deep green eyes searching hers. In them she saw the reflection of her own incipient longing. It was madness.

His glance fell to the gloves she'd pulled on. "I thought I'd join you lovely ladies. Miss Tristan, please, stay. You look about to leave."

The anonymous threat loomed large. And even if Jasmine did not fear the cowardly note writer who'd warned her against seeing Thomas—she had taken precautions to avoid riding in the park during hours when the beau monde paraded—she had been through enough with his sister already. She felt dirty, as if she'd been rolling about in the muck.

"Thank you, Lord Thomas, but I'm afraid I've rather had quite enough. Up to here." She tapped her chin and prepared to stand.

She was stalled as Miss Avery and Lady Henrietta gave Thomas worshipful looks. Miss Avery actually tittered. "Lord

Thomas, please have a seat. The three of us were just talking about riding on the Row. Perhaps you would join us for a gallop tomorrow."

Thomas murmured something non-committal, putting a gentle hand on Jasmine's shoulder as he took the seat between her and his sister. Her heart warmed.

"Lord Thomas, I hear you're actively searching for a wife," Miss Avery said. Jasmine stared. Goodness, the woman was brash!

Thomas chuckled. It was the sound of a man at ease in his world and not bothered by such a direct, embarrassing question. "Am I?" he asked. "Or has my sister been telling tales?"

Amanda blushed becomingly. Miss Avery pressed on.

"Of course, you must choose wisely—a woman of good standing, with a good name and able to entertain the friends and associates of an earl. You must consider the future, and your offspring as well."

"Let's see Mandy married off first, shall we?" he said.

"There are many qualities to consider when the time is ripe," Lady Henrietta pressed. "When my brother was ready to marry, mama gave him specific instructions. Marrying a peer demands a certain something of a lady. One must be poised to become the wife of a peer, and equal to the task of running a large household. And one must grace his table with dignity and beauty."

"Of course. When the time is right, I promise you I'll select a lady who is very adept at all of these things." His mouth tilted in an amused half-grin.

Malice shone in Miss Avery's eyes, and she glanced at Jasmine. "Amanda told us you're journeying to Egypt to purchase more horses. So fascinating! I daresay you'll be breeding purebloods. One does not breed a thoroughbred with a nag and dilute the bloodline. There are a great many nags in Egypt, I hear."

Jasmine's heart raced. Had he noticed the oblique insult?

She thought so. His mouth tightening, he ignored the ladies and turned to her.

"Have you had an interesting meeting?" he asked, looking so handsome, so concerned, she could almost believe he cared.

Almost. Her stomach gave another sickening lurch. She fought it down.

"My afternoon has been a rousing success, Lord Thomas," Jasmine said. "I've discovered the apple doesn't fall far from the tree. Thus, my future course of action will not sway. Good day."

A frown creased his forehead as he studied her. "Are you quite all right, Jasmine? Your face . . . you're quite pale."

Pale? What terrible irony. "I'm fine. Good-bye."

"Please stay," he said.

Jasmine rose from her seat, and Lady Amanda seized her brother's arm as he made to stop her. "Oh, do sit and have some of this delicious dessert, and do not delay Miss Tristan. She has important plans, I'm certain."

Past humiliations resurfaced—jeers from classmates at her finishing school, the pot of tea spilled on her at Thomas's birthday party, all the snubs. Nausea boiled in her stomach as Thomas turned to Lady Henrietta. He looked interested in what that simpering cow said. Head high, Jasmine walked away. The hell with them all.

In abject misery, she left the restaurant. Her world and Thomas's had clashed once more, and she had been the loser. She didn't feel comfortable in her own home. She didn't feel comfortable in his circle, either. Where would she fit in? Perhaps in Egypt.

The pungent smells rolling through London's streets swam in her nostrils. Her throat felt dry and achy. Jasmine went to hail a hansom cab when pain struck her so violently she gasped. Hanging on to a light pole, she tried to steady herself. A violent spasm seized her stomach. Jasmine bent over and retched into the street. Oh Lord, she thought in misery, heaving over and over. Pain wracked her insides and she shivered uncontrollably. Tears streamed down her face.

A few people passing by made exclamations of disgust: The Brown Scorpion was humiliating herself in public like a gin-soaked charwoman.

Jasmine managed to straighten, and reached into her reticule for a dainty lace handkerchief. Her hand shook as she wiped her mouth. Oh bother, everyone walking past made remarks. Too miserable to care, she clutched her quivering stomach. Then she retched again.

"Jasmine!"

The deep timbre of Thomas's voice seemed to come from far away. Two strong hands settled on her trembling shoulders. "Easy now," he soothed.

Dimly she became aware of someone making a crude remark about women being drunk in public. Thomas growled at them with the ferocity of a lion. He held her head gently as she emptied the remaining contents of her stomach into the gutter.

She straightened and took the white linen handkerchief he offered. Wiping her mouth, she leaned her feverish cheek against the pole, grateful for the cool metal. "Leave me be. W-what are you doing out here?" The whisper came with tremendous effort. Sandpaper lined her throat and her wobbly legs threatened to give way.

"I was rather worried. You looked beastly ill in the restaurant."

It cheered her a little that he cared. His sister and her friends wouldn't even notice if she dropped dead on the floor. "Thank you, I'll be fine," she mumbled.

His muscled arm slid beneath her arms, propping her up. "I'll see you home."

In a loud, commanding voice, he called out for a cab. As a hansom pulled to the curb he lifted her inside and moved to join her.

With all her strength, she put out a hand and shook her head. "Please, don't," she rasped. "Tell the driver to take me to Uncle Graham's." Then she collapsed against the tattered leather seat. Smells of tobacco, sweat and old whiskey inside the hansom threatened her nausea anew.

Thomas squeezed her hand. "Are you certain you'll be all right?"

She waved him away and turned, unable to face him anymore. The firm click of the door, a rap on the carriage and it lurched forward.

Jasmine groaned and held her stomach, praying she'd not be sick again until she reached her uncle's house. Rarely ill, she couldn't fathom why this had happened now. Right after she'd consumed that vile, weak and cold . . .

Coffee. She licked her lips, remembering the bitter taste.

Once, long ago, before her stepfather married her mother, Kenneth had been poisoned by a man trying to claim Badra. The gruesome story had sent Jasmine's vivid imagination soaring. She'd secretly borrowed a medical textbook and researched poisons, then wrote a story about a handsome, dashing warrior rescuing a fairy princess from an evil troll. Poison was a good way to dispatch someone. The taste could be hidden in strong drink, such as coffee. Had she been poisoned? Remembering the mysterious note delivered to her door, she shivered with dread.

For two hours, she lay on her bed. Sharp pains pierced her like knives. A footman knocked on her door, telling her that Lord Thomas Wallenford had stopped by to inquire about her health. She told the servant to send him away with news she was fine but resting. Finally the aches abated. Weakened, she made her way downstairs to ask Cook to make her a hot cup of tea.

While downstairs in the drawing room, the footman announced Lord Thomas Wallenford again came to call. When she told the footman to send him away, Thomas actually pushed past the startled man and entered the room.

Bowler hat clutched in his right hand, his left arm relaxed at his side, he studied her intently. "Jasmine. I had to see you."

"Persistent, aren't you? As you were told before, I'm fine. Just a bit of a queasy stomach." She waved a hand. "Please leave."

"Are you recovered? What was it?"

Miserable, knowing she was a frightful mess and whoever poisoned her would not like him calling on her, Jasmine glowered at him. "Most likely proximity to your sister. She's as insufferable as your mother."

His mouth twitched. "Is she now?"

"Well, your mother is more so. Our paths shouldn't cross again, and you know it. We simply are not in the same circle, so please leave."

She couldn't risk seeing him again, even if she wanted it. Or being seen with him. What if his friends saw them together? To be honest, the more she saw of Thomas, the more her heart ached. She needed to find her own place, and it was not with him or any of his sort.

He merely regarded her with an odd little smile. "Life has a habit of following patterns, Jasmine. Perhaps I am part of the pattern in your life. Perhaps it's destiny."

"I believe in making my own destiny."

"Indeed you do. But there are some events you simply have no control over. Think of it. I suspect our destinies are interlocked in ways you never imagined, Jasmine. Think about it. I suspect we will cross paths again, and soon. And there is simply nothing you can do to prevent it."

He put his hat on, gave her a little nod and left.

Chapter Ten

In the weeks that followed, Jasmine retargeted Lady Amanda. Finding quiet joy in wielding her pen as a weapon, she castigated the woman. Chatting with the tradespeople whose shops Amanda frequented, she found a treasure trove of information and used it well. From the girl's habit of spending excessive money on fripperies, to her habit of "laughing like a whinnying horse with big teeth," Lady Amanda was ridiculed in print. Often Jasmine would visit these same shops, secretly delighted as tradespeople read aloud her column to the guffaws of their clientele.

Hyde Park provided her with another source of information. Near the Serpentine, she found a quiet spot behind a sprawling tree where she could sit in relative anonymity. The isolated area was a favorite among Thomas's circle. The group often congregated nearby and talked.

With a book open on her lap, she looked absorbed and disinterested. In reality she hid paper and pencil for note-taking. In simple workman's clothing, hair tucked beneath a man's wide-brimmed hat, she could be taken for a working-class man. Or a servant. Servants, like her, were invisible to society. It was here that Thomas's friends walked and gossiped. And Jasmine's ears were ever pricked to glean nuggets of information.

Today, there were no fascinating remarks about how Lady Claradon had quarreled with Baron Ridley's mother about moving up the wedding date for their betrothed children, or comments on how Miss Avery went for a ride with Thomas and he actually held her hand (this last one Jasmine had found disquieting). None of Thomas's friends were about. She'd started to stand when a couple came walking toward her. Jasmine stared at her book to avoid detection. It was Lady Amanda and Lord Ridley.

They paused a few feet away, far enough for supposed privacy but close enough for her to hear. Jasmine stole a glance. The baron's handsome, lean face looked distressed. He stopped and squeezed Amanda's hands. Amanda looked even more upset.

"Please, dearest, try to understand. I love you, and I'm glad you trusted me and told me about this dreadful newspaper column maligning you, but my family cannot risk another scandal. If anyone discovers it's you this columnist writes about . . . The last scandal tore my family apart when they discovered my betrothed had spent the night in another man's townhouse, unchaperoned. My parents were horrified."

Amanda was weeping openly now. The baron proffered a clean white handkerchief.

"I am sorry, pet, but if this awful business in the paper continues . . . I don't know what we should do. This last installment, suggesting you wanted a quick wedding because you had something to hide, perhaps a 'something' that would appear in nine months. By God, the author all but suggested you were increasing!"

"Please, Richard, it's not my fault. This vicious person. I have no idea why he is maligning me—"

The young baron pulled her to him, his face twisted in anguish. "Perhaps we should elope. Gretna Green—it would surprise the gossips, should anyone find out it's you."

Amanda pulled away. "But it wouldn't remove your family's suspiciouns. And elopement would really only give credence to what the paper said. I should never live it down, never! I cannot enter marriage with such a dreadful pall cast over me."

"I will try to defray their worries, dearest. Don't fret, I'll do what I can."

Jasmine's heart sank. She had not written those words, only an amusing remark on how a certain well-known society mama wanted her daughter off her hands quicker than polite society decreed for weddings. But Mr. Myers had severely edited the column to hint said daughter was pregnant. Delighted with the increase in circulation, he wanted to further titillate the public's lurid interest, and each column Jasmine turned in, with hints of gossip, he edited to the point of being viciously scandalous. Jasmine had no choice. She had signed a contract, a legally binding document, and was obligated to deliver. Now, hearing Amanda's pitiful sobs made her feel hollow with regret.

The baron gave his fiancée such a tender kiss that Jasmine instinctively knew he loved Lady Amanda. He squeezed her hands again and walked off, his manner dejected. Amanda buried her hands in her lace gloves and wept.

Regret pierced Jasmine. Despite Lady Amanda's snobbish attitude, she could not bear to see young love turned to ashes. And it was her fault.

Barely had the baron left when she spotted a man striding toward Amanda. Jasmine stifled a gasp as she recognized Thomas. He went to his sister.

"Mandy! There you are. I've been looking for you and Richard. Why did you leave so abruptly?"

With a loud sob, she threw herself into his arms. Thomas murmured to her, his words too low for Jasmine to hear with the wind whispering through the trees, fluttering the autumn leaves. He wiped her tear-stained face tenderly. He let her sob against his shoulder, his face as stricken and anguished as the baron's.

Jasmine heard their steps as they walked off.

Yes, she decided, this must stop. She tucked her book and notepad into her satchel and strode off.

A few minutes later, she sat before the cluttered desk of Mr. Anthony Myers. A thick scent of newpaper ink and the constant clacking of the linotype machine in the back offices once had seemed comforting. Now it grated on her nerves.

"I wish to stop my columns, Mr. Myers. There simply is no more material. I lack access to the inner circles to report their activities. Perhaps we can change it to a report on more noteworthy news, such as the Duchess of Caldwell's admirable success in her charity education of street children."

A fat cigar dangled from his lips. With his round face, bushy waxed mustache and two deep-set eyes, he looked like he'd sunk into himself. A few ashes fell on the shelf of his large belly, dotting his paisley waistcoat.

"Getting squeamish, eh? Too late now, public's hooked. Can't give up on the number one reason our circulation has doubled!" He stood and sifted through stacks of letters on his oak desk, amid the clutter of newspapers, yellowed with stains of old coffee spills. "All these letters in the past month—all for you and your column. Everyone's talking about The Blue Bloods."

"They will cease doing so once the column ends."

"And so will our subscriptions. It's business, Miss Tristan." His voice had gone flat, and Jasmine tensed, knowing she faced a fight.

"As the author of these columns, I have the right to write whatever I wish. That is in my contract."

"And I have, as your editor, the right to change it however I wish. Also in your contract." He sat down, his gaze sharply assessing. Like the beady eyes of a lizard she'd once seen.

"It won't be true," she said, hiding her distress.

"Truth doesn't matter now. Selling papers does."

"I'll report you. People will know you're changing my words, that you are a liar." She stood up, so angry that she trembled.

"And who will you tell without giving away your secret? You'll damage your own reputation more than mine, Miss Tristan. A newspaper runs on scandal. A woman's reputation is dependent on her good name. Will you ruin yours for the sake of saving those you despise?"

Hating the knowing smile on his face, she wanted to slap him. Hating what he was, and what she had become. "I'll fulfill my contractual obligation, Mr. Myers. But I will not write about scandalous gossip. And the secret philanderer I promised at the column's end? It's no longer yours to print. Make up your own, but I will not offer it up."

"No matter," the man said with infuriating calmness. "I know the culprit's identity. Lady Amanda Claradon."

Her jaw dropped. "It's not possible. How can you know—"

"You're not the only one selling scandal, Miss Tristan. Shortly after you arrived with your column, someone else provided me with fodder. A certain servant to a young lady in a very wealthy and titled home, in fact. She told me she knew the person in the scandal you mentioned."

Pain lanced Jasmine's palms. She glanced down to see her hands clenched so tightly her nails dug into the flesh. "Why did you let me proceed if you had all the material you desired?"

He shrugged. "Your idea was brilliant. The columns. The gossip. Stretch out the secret, hook the public like fish and reel them in. Sell more papers. So you see, it doesn't matter. Write whatever you want, and in February, all London will know Lady Amanda's secret."

"Please," Jasmine begged. "Don't do this. She's getting married next June."

"Then she'd better hurry the wedding, eh? Why are you so concerned? You planned the same exact revelation." He grinned around the wet cigar stub. "Only my aim is business, not personal. Always remember, Miss Tristan, money rules all."

"It doesn't rule me," she snapped.

"No. But our contract does. Go home, Miss Tristan, and get me that next column. I hear there's a charwoman who saved a dog from being run over. Write about that. I'll change your words to something more suitable."

"I'll stop you. Know it. There must be a way, and I will find it," Jasmine vowed.

But she left his offices knowing he was right and he would win. Dread filled her, and grief for Thomas and his sister. They were all caught in this sinister spider web, and there was no way out. Lady Amanda would be ruined unless she could find a means to stop the column, and she could not rely on anyone else or reveal herself as the author. There was simply no way around it.

His destiny kept steering him in Jasmine's direction.

Thomas tugged his greatcoat about him as he walked outside. A brisk October chill did not affect him, despite his lack of a hat. He was too worked up to notice. The Duke and Duchess of Caldwell had invited him to tea with Jasmine. The duke, his dark eyes serious as they'd enjoyed brandy at the club last week, had informed him Jasmine was joining them on the Egyptian visit.

Not if I strangle her first, he'd thought grimly.

With each printed news column, hope faded from Mandy's gaze. She had become more withdrawn. Last week the baron had met with Thomas, quietly informing him soon he'd be forced to break off the engagement if any more articles targeted Amanda, and begging him to do something. Quietly working behind the scenes, Thomas had put his best men into finding a means to stop the presses. He'd used funds saved for repairing his family's aging townhouse. Money had influence. He didn't yet attempt direct intervention. One might as well put the gun of social destruction in the hands of the publisher and ask him to pull the trigger. Even a simple visit would solidify thought that his sister was the object of the alluded scandal yet to be revealed.

Yes, other means to protect sweet Mandy must be employed. Her heart was breaking. Discretion, the war cry of his social set, was his best weapon. But he wanted to confront Jasmine. She still affected him in an impossible way: Emotions in a lather, he didn't know if he wanted to shake her, or lock her in his room and keep her trapped in his bed, so busy that she'd never have a spare moment to pick up a pen.

Graham had smiled when Thomas had asked for a little private time in the garden with Jasmine. "Get to know her better," the duke had said when offering the invite. "She's a bit spirited, like a wild horse, but with the proper handling she can be tamed."

Oh, I'd tame you, Jasmine. In my bed, I'd tame you well and proper.

An early promise of winter rippled through the chilled air as he walked to the duke's townhouse. He felt like a warrior marching toward an enemy fortress. *Jasmine, prepare yourself to fight,* he thought grimly. *This is war, and I shall win.*

Blood drained from Jasmine's face as Thomas appeared in the drawing room. He greeted her aunt courteously, had a friendly handshake for her uncle. When he approached her, he clasped her bare hand, lifting it with the grace of a courtier.

"Miss Tristan," he murmured, grazing her knuckles with his lips. The touch ignited her as if she were kindling on a hearth. Why the bloody hell hadn't her uncle told her?

The duchess gestured to the wing chair next to Jasmine's. "Please, Lord Thomas, do have a seat."

Feeling as if her aunt invited a lion to sit, Jasmine watched Thomas warily. No one must know their quarrel. Her mother hadn't told them, and her aunt and uncle mustn't know she was the power behind the pen that mocked Thomas's family.

Every effort had been made to provide the public the gossip they loved without targeting Thomas's family. Jasmine had written columns decrying the upper classes' snobbish attitudes. Mr. Myers had simply rewrote her prose to focus on Lady Amanda. At the end of each column was a sinister warning promising a most delicious scandal yet to be revealed. It was the sword of Damocles dangling above her head.

Deep inside, Jasmine admitted the truth. In some ways, she was torn about ending the column. Her words and caricatures amused readers. Flattering letters of praise poured into the newspaper. For the first time in her life, Jasmine felt respected and admired.

Of course, that was before she witnessed Amanda weeping in the park.

Some news now filled her with hope. Her quest to find a reputable London newspaper to publish stories from Egypt had met with success. They promised a nice stipend for articles on the al-Hajid, as well as reports from Theodore Davis's dig in the Valley of the Kings. So that was something.

A white-capped maid in a crisp black uniform brought tea on a polished silver salver. Jasmine's aunt politely inquired about Thomas's family. Thomas politely inquired about the duchess's school. Straining from the effort to keep a polite smile in place, Jasmine felt like screaming. Uncle Graham and Thomas began a hearty discourse on Arabian mares.

"I trust in your horsemanship, Wallenford, but some fillies can be wild and difficult. How would you handle an Arabian if you had her?" the duke asked.

Busy with the tea tray, Uncle Graham and Aunt Jillian couldn't see the suggestive look Thomas gave Jasmine. "They can be trained. They must know who their master is. I have no doubt my touch can tame the most spirited Arabian filly . . . or mare. If she were mine, I would begin with gentle assurances until she became submissive. Then, when the time was right, I'd mount and ride her until she was weary and spent."

Jasmine nearly choked. Her long-ago remark, "I'm a filly, stupid, not a mare!" had come back to haunt her. The teacup her aunt handed over shook in her trembling hands.

"Perhaps some would rather run wild and free than be corralled by you. You seem to have some overconfidence," Jasmine suggested.

"Arabians need to be kept in line. And there isn't any filly or a mare who wasn't happier after I rode her hard and well. I take very good care of what is mine," he replied.

"I've seen Lord Thomas ride, Jasmine. He's very good with both fillies and mares," her uncle remarked, oblivious to the by-play between them.

"It takes a great deal of skill to control an Arabian," her aunt added.

Frustrated, Jasmine sank back. Why the hell was Thomas here? They were discussing the upcoming visit to Egypt. Thomas had agreed to purchase some horses, but why was . . .

She started, realizing her uncle had addressed her.

"Thomas is joining us in Egypt, Jasmine. He's purchasing mares from the al-Hajid to finance their new farming venture."

Blood drained from her face. "But—"

"We'll both be escorting you. You'll have adequate time to conduct your research and write your stories while we do business."

Thomas slid her a look. "Jasmine writes stories?" he asked in his deep, heavy voice. No one else suspected the irony.

"A newspaper publisher has expressed interest in her reporting on the Egyptian journey." The duke bestowed a fond smile on Jasmine.

She remarked, "You'd be quite surprised to learn of my various talents. I'm visiting the al-Hajid to chronicle their history before the tribe disperses forever. I'm also visiting Mr. Theodore Davis's dig for Tutankamun's tomb. I will write about both visits for the newspaper." His flat look caused her to hasten to add, "The publisher is *The London Daily Forum*, a growing, well-respected newspaper."

Surprised interest flared on Thomas's face. "Fascinating. It sounds quite . . . academic. For a moment, I thought you were referencing distasteful stories as in those printed in magazines and newspapers. That column, for example, that everyone is nattering about. What is it called?"

"The Blue Bloods," Aunt Jillian spoke up. "Very distasteful. I agree."

Jasmine wondered if her face looked as red as it felt.

"I see that the author has made a mockery of Lady Amanda. A bad business. I suppose you'd like to thrash the author," her uncle offered.

"I have several forms of punishment in mind." Thomas's gaze settled squarely on Jasmine. Mortified, she decided to never again accept another tea invitation.

"Makes me wonder about the author's identity. Someone in the know, who has quite a talent for writing. Whoever this person is, you have to admit he or she has skill and an eye for the word," her uncle continued.

Those words made Jasmine's aunt pause in sipping her tea. "Graham, do you really think the author could be a lady?"

"It's possible," he observed.

"Well, I doubt the person is a woman. Women aren't generally that caustic and cruel," her aunt replied.

Shame coursed through Jasmine. She truly wanted her aunt's respect.

"*Most* women," Thomas agreed. "Most are of a gentler nature, and would not inflict such venom on my sister."

Her uncle appeared deep in thought. "Unless, of course, the writer had due reason—or at least justified such actions in her, or his, mind. Sarcasm is an art, but I wonder if there isn't more to these stories than an exercise in literary style." He turned toward Thomas. "What do you say? Your family has been the object of nearly all the author's venom."

Dryness filled Jasmine's mouth as Thomas seemed to consider. "I suspect the writer has real talent, and is capable of greater works than these petty columns. It is my greatest hope he, or she, will cease and explore more valiant opportunities to express such skill."

"Interesting," her uncle murmured. "You sound as if you admire the person but loathe the act."

"I do," Thomas said calmly, and his gaze flicked to Jasmine. "Indeed, I do."

She sat on the needlepoint chair, sipping tea from a bone china cup. Spine erect, dressed in an ivory gown trimmed with pink lace, Jasmine looked lovely. Honey-gold skin shone like polished amber in the dull lamplight. Such civility. Prim pearl earrings dripped from her shell-like ears. Jasmine's mannerisms were as gracious as a respectable English lady's; inside, passion boiled as heated as the burning Egyptian sun. Thomas kept poking at her composure, teasing her, daring her to react.

Sipping her tea with utter composure was getting to her. Fire burned beneath the facade. Glimpses of it erupted and anger flushed her face. She looked ready to scream. Thomas summoned control to avoid thinking about tossing up her muslin skirts and using his skillful hands to give her something to really scream about.

"As I was saying, I do admire the author and detest the works. The author displays a talent for the written word. Then again, I am unimpressed with the target. The public devour such sordid tales with great eagerness. It sells papers. But it is not art," Thomas remarked. He turned his attention to Jasmine, pinning her with his gaze. "I do hope the stories you anticipate writing will be more laudable, Miss Tristan."

"They will be as they are," Jasmine murmured docilely. "Mr. Davis's dig in the Valley of the Kings will be unpredictable. And I cannot make assessments on the desert tribe until I ascertain their history. My remarks may indeed appeal to the lowbrow—should that be appropriate."

A shadow entered her uncle's eyes. "I daresay their history is filled with violence. Many such desert tribes are the same. Even the Khamsin—noble, brave warriors—could be perceived as bloodthirsty savages by the ignorant who are quick to judge what they don't understand."

"What won't they understand, Caldwell?" Thomas asked.

"The laws of the desert are brutal, as life there is brutal. Survival is the goal, and the price of that survival could be construed as barbarism. Still, those who do not adapt do not survive."

Her uncle's cryptic words gave Jasmine pause, but Thomas's next comment nearly made her drop her teacup.

"Such a subject may indeed be appropriate for a newspaper audience, Miss Tristan, and sway readers away from that Blue Bloods column. I'm sure you could outwrite that particular author. In fact, I challenge you to do so."

Jasmine coughed. Quickly, she recovered her composure. Amusement danced in Thomas's eyes, turning to challenge as she glowered at him.

"I'm not afraid of saying what I feel. Nor do I fear what people will think."

He smiled at her double entendre, and saluted her with his teacup. "Then I shall watch very carefully to monitor what you do produce. I may even watch your interviews to ascertain the differences between what is said by the subject and how you record their words. Because, as you well know, one person's perception is not always another's reality."

Thomas would not make the Egypt trip easy. But she had no choice. Back out, and doing so would raise too many questions from her beloved uncle and aunt. Not to mention this was her one chance at finding a place to fit in.

"Do as you must. But know this, my lord, I won't let your presence sway what I write." She locked gazes with him in mute defiance.

Tea ended, and Uncle Graham suggested Jasmine show Thomas the garden. Stammering protests about an appointment, she tried to vanish upstairs. Thomas merely took her elbow, murmuring something about seeing the wildflowers. He all but dragged her down the hallway. Jasmine glared.

"Why don't you just toss me over your shoulder?"

"I would, but the servants would talk," he rejoined.

Anger sparkled in his jade green eyes. Keeping an iron grip on her, he hustled her outside through the French doors. He steered her toward an alcove where a stone bench sat before an array of rose bushes. He spun her round, then practically forced her down.

"I'm giving you an order, Miss Tristan," he drawled in silkly tones. "Stop writing that dreck or I shall do something you will regret."

"Like what? Try to tame me like one of your Arabian horses? I caught your insinuation."

"I could do just that. You would enjoy it. And it would keep you out of trouble." Intensity radiated in his eyes. Jasmine lifted her chin. She had to tell him the truth.

"Listen to me, you've got to give me a chance—"

"You had several."

"It's not that!" Jasmine jumped to her feet and clenched her fists.

Thomas snorted. "Ready to give me another facer like when we were younger? Not a good idea, little Jasmine. Try to punch me and you'll force me to lay a hand on you. And it won't be with my fists," he said tightly. "Sit. Now."

Jasmine sat. She took a long, controlling breath.

"I've got something you must know," she said slowly.

"Well, then. Out with it."

Enough reasoning! Thomas felt on the verge of insanity, Jasmine's scent teasing his nostrils, her nearness teasing his body. He wanted to crush her to him in a bruising kiss. He wanted to roar his frustration to the heavens. How could one small woman cause so much trouble?

He gave her a stern look known to wither the strongest men. "Tell me your plan, Jasmine. My patience has ended. I always protect my own, and I warn you I will stop at nothing."

"I am trying."

Her words gave him pause. Thomas folded his arms across his chest. "Trying?"

"Haven't you noticed the nature of the writings lately? The Blue Bloods stories have maligned your sister, but hasn't the writing changed?"

"So? Your point is?"

She bit her lower lip, looking troubled. "It's not me."

Shocked into silence, he stared as she continued. "I can't . . . fully reveal everything. Give me time, Thomas. I need time. Please believe me. These columns lately, they are not mine. I would not hurt Amanda in that way. Trust me, there are complications—legal ones, binding ones which I cannot ignore. But I will find a way around them."

Something in his chest eased, and his anger evaporated. "You sound as if you've experienced a drastic change of heart. What made you see reason?"

"I saw something. Something which will remain private. *Please.*" She gave him a pleading look that stunned him. Since when had proud Jasmine begged for anything?

"Please, Thomas, give me time. This has gone far beyond what I expected, and I am truly sorry for all the trouble I've caused Amanda. These days, those are not my words."

It is true, he realized as he studied her face.

"No name will be revealed in the paper until February. I have until then to formulate a solution," Jasmine added, looking desperate.

"Let me help you," he insisted. "I know people, I have influence."

"No. The fewer who know, the better. Let it remain a mystery. I have already written several columns the publisher approved. They will run during my sojourn in Egypt until February first. By then I will have arrived at a solution suitable to all." Jasmine heaved a tiny sigh and murmured. "All but me."

Sorrow and dejection laced her words, arousing his suspicions. But he guarded his thoughts, giving only a brief nod. "Tell me, Jasmine. Did you write the column suggesting my sister was increasing?"

"No. I stopped. That's when . . . this person took over the writing and aped my style, took my words and twisted them to give false scandal."

"I see," he said quietly. "But you went back to mocking Amanda right after the meeting in the restaurant, did you not? Because she hurt you by telling you there was no way she could associate openly with you."

At her nod, he did not grow angry. The gap between their worlds yawned like an insurmountable chasm. But if he helped her understand the foundation behind Amanda's actions . . .

Staring into the verdant shrubbery, he spoke slowly. "Let me tell you a little about my family. Do you know what my father did the day Nigel died?"

"It's not my business."

Thomas continued: "He ordered me into his study. He was devoid of emotion. Father reminded me of a stone statue retaining its original form and hardness. The lecture he gave was one I'd heard before—duty and privilege and the importance of keeping one's social inferiors in line. The world was changing too fast.

"He said, 'We must keep the world safe for people like us. Your duty is to honor tradition. Never let your social inferiors rise above their station, especially foreigners like that odd Egyptian woman the viscount married. What would happen if those people thought they were our equals?' My father was very stern in administering that particular thought."

Blood suffused Jasmine's cheeks. "Are you telling me this in order to make excuses for Amanda's snub? That she's justified because I'm your social inferior?"

Thomas clasped her shoulders; he didn't give a damn who witnessed their exchange from the large bank of windows overlooking the garden.

"I'm trying to make a point about my sister, my world, my father, and those who associate in my circle. It's *not* me, but this is how I was raised, Jasmine. It doesn't make it correct, but it is what society believes. Those beliefs will never change, as won't those who hold them dear. One might as well attempt to move the pyramids."

His fingers tightened slightly as he felt the softness of flesh and the firmness of bone beneath his grip. He only wanted to crush her to him, kiss away the past and forget the present. Like a child denied candy in the store window, he must learn to turn his desires elsewhere.

"I don't judge a person based on their birth origins or their skin color. But those I associate with certainly do. Your uncle, the good duke, is the only one who challenges this, and he pays the price by social exile. This is the society we live in and it cannot change. I wish it would, but if I would live in this society, I must accept it."

She rested a palm upon his hand, her touch almost seeming filled with understanding. "And if you choose not to live in that society?"

Thomas swiftly withdrew his hands. "How can I not? I am my father's heir, and carry an enormous duty to my family. I must marry well, and sire a son to carry on the title."

"And your wife, she will be of 'good standing,' as Miss Avery put it? You wouldn't choose someone like Charlotte Harrison?"

Mention of his mistress tightened his mouth. "There are women whose company a man may seek for certain reasons, but they are not for marriage. There are standards required for my bride. I must find a woman with not only an impeccable reputation, but one who is my social equal."

Jasmine's gaze went flat. "That sounds terribly snobbish."

"I suppose it does, but this is my life, Jasmine. It is not possible for me to be otherwise."

"I see," she said. "And you must understand, it is not possible for me to be otherwise. Your world has labeled me The Brown Scorpion. Left undisturbed, a scorpion is happy in the darkness, but once it is poked and angered, it stings. I was only following my nature, as your kind follow theirs."

"That is not your nature," he grated out. "You're not a woman who's afraid to think for herself as my sister is. By God, you've got more spirit and intelligence than any woman I know. Yet you dragged yourself down with that repulsive column."

Anger blazed in her dark eyes. "Don't judge me by what your society made me. We are all, as you aptly point out, servants to that great mistress. Please regard my past columns as a defense, much like a scorpion employing the only protection available to her."

By God, that pride. Thomas softened his tone, trying to reach past the prickly barrier she'd erected. "You do not do scorpions justice, Jas. They're useful creatures who can keep a farmer's field clear of pests who would destroy a bountiful crop. There is beauty and good purpose in them, as there is in you. They do not merely lash out and sting—"

"But the world sees them only as ugly brown creatures known to hurt. So that is the image, and the image overrules all."

"One can change an image. One can do so with a reputable article in a reputable newspaper. You have a chance." Thomas paused, searching her face. "Which do you want most—public respect or notoriety?"

"You make it sound as if I have a choice." Jasmine looked

up at him with a lost look in her dark eyes. "I do not. If I am to save your sister's reputation, I must endure the latter."

A terrible suspicion crested over him. "What are you talking about?"

"Nothing." Jasmine's lower lip wobbled. "I think it's best we part now. Good day. I think you know the way out."

He reached out and cupped her cheek. Jasmine leaned closer, as if she relished his touch.

"Jas, let me help you," he persisted.

She looked so sad his heart lurched. "No, you must not. And we shouldn't be together, Thomas."

He settled his hand around the nape of her neck, drawing her closer. Mindless of who might see, mindless of all but her. "Why is it that all I can think about is your mouth, that mouth capable of uttering venom but possessing such beauty," he murmured, stroking a thumb over it. "All I want to do is kiss you."

"I can't," she whispered. "Not again. Good-bye."

Pulling free, she walked down the garden path. Thomas silently vowed to discover what she planned. There were ways to help. Jasmine did not know the full extent of his power. Never would he let her do anything rash that would make her a public spectacle, and he saw now she wanted to make amends. He wanted to hold her and never let go, shelter her from any storm threatening her life. But, . . . strict social codes prohibited him from doing so.

He'd seen such desperate longing in her eyes. She wanted him as badly as he wanted her, but she would not admit it.

Perhaps in Egypt they'd be free from the conventions keeping them apart. It was possible to find the woman he knew lurked inside the brittle armor of sarcasm and anger, reach past the venomous scorpion to find the beautiful Jasmine flower. He would do this. In Egypt, in the land of heat and burning sand.

Thomas left the garden, thanked the duke and duchess for

their hospitality. He headed home, determination in his every step.

Barely had he removed his outerwear when the footman announced Mrs. Charlotte Harrison was awaiting him in the drawing room. Distaste filled him, and Thomas knew what he must do. Ever since that night at the ball when he'd kissed Jasmine, Charlotte held no appeal. A gift of jewelry, then she'd be free to pursue other protectors who had considerable more assets than he did.

Not the little scorpion charm. With money secured away from his last business deal, he'd purchased a beautiful emerald, large as a robin's egg. That would satisfy her.

Steeling his spine, Thomas proceeded to the drawing room to end the liaison with his mistress.

Two days later, Jasmine sat staring into the looking-glass. Her hand shook slightly as she went to apply rice powder. Suddenly she flung the cosmetic across the dressing table. No more! The Brown Scorpion she'd remain.

A knock on the door drew her attention. The footman stood in the hallway with a note. "Just came, Miss Tristan. Sorry, didn't notice, just slipped under the door, rather queer-like."

Inner dread filled her as she shut the door and tore open the envelope. The words printed in bold block letters made her gasp.

DEATH COMES SWIFTLY TO YOU IN EGYPT IF YOU GO THERE WITH LORD THOMAS. REMAIN HOME AND LIVE, OR JOURNEY THERE AND DIE.

Chapter Eleven

A cool December's ocean breeze caressed tendrils of hair escaping her tightly wound bun. Jasmine had awakened before dawn, too excited and restless to sleep. She wanted to watch the sunrise at sea.

She'd thought her situation over, and nothing would ruin this adventure. The threatening note lay in ashes on the cold hearth at home. Someone, perhaps even in her uncle's household, had kept a close watch on her. Caution was advised, but it was doubtful the note-writer would dare to follow her on this voyage. She would be safe away from those who hated her.

Dawn broke softly on the liquid horizon, with a wash of violet and rose hues. The sun was a distant yellow sphere. Jasmine laughed, lifting her arms heavenward to embrace the dawning day. Each new day brought new possibilities, new promises.

Sunshine warmed her body. She lifted her face and closed her eyes, drinking in the tangy scent of brine. The smell of utter freedom.

She was not quite free, though. She was chaperoned by her uncle, and watched by Thomas.

Days now into the steamship journey to Egypt, an uneasy silence existed between herself and Thomas. The more she ignored him, the more he seemed interested. They dined together with Uncle Graham. Conversation was animated between the two men. Silence was her main offering.

Always she spotted him. Thomas towered over the others. Women buzzed around him, eager for his company. Small wonder, for he was dashingly handsome, charming, and an earl's heir. Yet when his gaze moved, it always landed on her. He almost seemed to be waiting, like a clever predator.

Today, she hovered on the brink of sacrificing herself on the altar of his family's reputation. If she delivered the column that would save Thomas's sister, she'd commit social suicide. Society would talk for weeks. Any dreams Jasmine harbored of gaining respect would vanish with each blathering tongue. Still, it was an option.

Before departing, Jasmine had met with Mr. Myers and extracted a promise: If she would reveal herself as the author of The Blue Bloods and give him a juicy scandal, he would print that instead of Lady Amanda's disgrace. Jasmine had written one that gained his approval. Mr. Myers had chuckled over it with a lurid gleam in his beady eyes. He would not publish the scandal about Lady Amanda, but replace it with Jasmine's story—if that was what she truly wished.

"Do you want to become a social pariah, Miss Tristan? This column will ensure it. I will put it aside. If you change your mind and want to run with it instead of Lady Amanda's story, telegraph me from Cairo," he'd told her.

It was like a tomb door was closing on her life. If published, her very own words would ruin her. They'd make her an object of a scandal more lurid than any of Lady Amanda's indiscretions. She'd told him to set it aside and wait for her telegraph, that either way she would inform him of her decision.

Jasmine shuddered at the prospect of more public humiliation as she'd experienced at Lady Claradon's ball. Yet each time she closed her eyes, she saw Amanda and Richard embracing, heard Amanda's heartwrenching sobs.

One slim hope hung in the balance: Once the Daily Call published her reports about the al-Hajid, it would soften the blow of her scandal. Everything hinged upon her gaining respect as an international correspondent from Egypt before the moment of truth. People might be more accepting then—or at least judicious with their criticism.

One could only hope.

Everything depended upon this Egypt trip. Respectability and acceptance rode on publication of her stories in the paper. She needed this opportunity. It represented her last chance for meaningful direction in her meandering life. Marriage and family were unattainable. She was too intimidating for a match with a tradesman, too foreign to hope for a match with any of the upper crust.

That particular thought dulled her enthusiasm for the delicious promise of morning. Like a pricked balloon, she drifted downward.

"I'm a camel in a herd of Arabians," she muttered, staring at the frothy waves.

"I think not. Camels have a tendency to spit, and you haven't spit once at me since you were nine."

Thomas's deep, assured voice shook her out of her self-examination, and Jasmine colored. Now she must don the armor of indifference. Silence dripped between them. He leaned on the railing, drawing close, eliminating the space between them. Jasmine stiffened but knew drawing away would be perceived as a sign of retreat. She could afford no surrender.

"However, camels are also extremely stubborn. Like you, Jasmine," he said.

Indignation rose as she turned to give him an accusing look. But still she said nothing. He regarded her thoughtfully.

"No, you're incorrect to term yourself a camel. You bathe and you smell quite nice. And you lack the annoying hordes of flies buzzing about, as well as the fellahin eager to sell their services."

Jasmine's temper snapped. "You're an insufferable sod!"

"Got you," he said softly. "At last you've stopped ignoring me. Why *are* you ignoring me, Jasmine?"

Piqued, she turned. Mischief twinkled in his eyes—green today, as the sea below. A smile teased the corners of his full lips. He was bareheaded, the style making him appear roguish and dashing. He looked relaxed. For the first time since the ball, the earl's heir appeared as young and insouciant as when they were children. Free, as if leaving England had unshackled him from some great weight.

All her defenses temporarily lowered, Jasmine wistfully wondered what it would be like to be on the same side. Fighting together . . . against what? Tilting at windmills was a useless occupation. But she should at least be civil to him.

Adjusting her hat to a saucy angle, she ignored his question. "Having never ridden a camel, I would daresay your observations seem correct, except for my obstinate ways. I am not stubborn. And I am much prettier as well."

"No, you more resemble a donkey," he agreed.

Civility was forgotten. Jasmine prepared to attack when Thomas laughed. With one finger he tilted her chin. "You are much, much prettier than any beast. Close your mouth, Jas, though I do adore that lovely shade of rose red your face takes on when I tease you. You are too easy to tease."

"Yes, your friends enjoyed doing so," she muttered. "Of course they'd call me the Brown Scorpion."

"Didn't we talk of you not giving scorpions credit? Brown scorpions bring fortune. So I was told when I bought this years ago." Thomas fished an amulet out of his trouser pocket and cradled it in his palm. "I brought it with me for good luck."

She gave it a cursory glance. "Brown scorpions bring ill fortune according to your mother."

He pocketed the charm. "How I wish that night had never happened for you."

Drawing back, she turned her attention to the sea. Once more, Thomas was reminding her of the chasm between their worlds. "Regrets are like sweets and children. Too easily offered and too easily devoured and forgotten. I regret you have regrets."

Two warm hands settled on her shoulders, turning her toward him. Jasmine refused to meet his gaze.

"Jas, look at me." Thomas tilted her chin up with one finger. His voice was gentle. "I don't harbor regrets about everything that night, just my mother's abhorrent behavior. And I regret the reasons you found necessary to war with my family in print."

Jasmine drew a quivering breath. How crazy her reaction to this man! It was still there, that odd, tingling feeling, as if she were alive from her head to her toes, her blood and cells all thrumming to the surface. Just one touch, and Thomas made her feel achingly alive. She must put distance between them. She stepped away.

"I violated the rules. That's why your mother loathes me. Had I remained in what she regarded as my proper place, perhaps she would have been cordial. Your mother observed the proper conventions, even if her polite whispers were derisive behind my back."

Thomas remained silent.

Society dictated the rules: what china to lay at each place setting, which were the proper words, polite conversation, correct dress. A person's background and social standing. And she had more to hide than he knew. If Thomas discovered her true origins, would he shun her as his friends did? If he knew she'd been raised in a brothel, would he shrink away in horror? Remembering the column she'd written, Jasmine took a deep breath.

"Do you know why I trespassed at your mother's ball?" She asked.

"Tell me."

She leaned against the railing, staring at the flat ocean mirroring the brilliant sky. "I was born in Egypt, but never regarded it as my home. Egypt has . . . memories for me best forgotten. Ever since I came to England I wanted to be as English as those in high society. They're alike in manners and dress and deportment. One could interchange them, like pawns on a chess board, and never glimpse the difference. My greatest desire was to be one of those brilliant, shining pawns. That's why I trespassed. Not to insult or even make a bold statement. Just for myself, to be for just a few moments one of you. Invisible, blending in with everyone else. I would have succeeded, but . . ." Her voice trailed off.

He looked stricken. "If I had not brought attention to you—" he began.

"My intention was only to observe, mingle and then leave. Ten minutes perhaps. I was not hunting for a husband, or even a dance partner. But you persisted." She gave a tiny sigh. "Sometimes I look back on that night and wish it had never happened, and then I remember regrets are foolish. You and I aren't the same chess pieces, Thomas, we're not even on the same board. I can dress as one of you and adapt my mannerisms, the china I use, the theaters I attend, all of that the same. But I will never fit onto your board. At least not on the same side. I'm a black pawn among white ones. I need to follow a new path. I'm weary of pretending to be someone I can never become."

"Then be yourself. It's the real you that drew me the evening of the ball," he pointed out.

"The real me made an enemy of your mother."

"But *I'm* not the enemy, Jas. Can we at least try to be friends?"

"You already have friends," she rejoined, searching his face. Seeing his expression, Jasmine summoned courage. "And a mistress as well."

"Not any longer. Charlotte and I are through." At her perplexed look he added, "I was growing weary of her, and it was for the best. It's been over a long time for me."

"Do you often grow weary of women?" She couldn't help but ask.

"Certain women. But not you. I think I could never grow bored with you. You're too fascinating. So, shall we? Be friends?"

His lips hovered dangerously close, his heated gaze intent.

"Being friends would be pleasant, would it not?" he murmured.

She burned at the warmth of his touch, at the promise of longing in his face. "Yes," she said breathlessly, "perhaps it is."

A frisson of arousal and wonderment filled her as he tenderly cupped her cheek, his fingers a gentle press against her skin. The scrape of a razor this morning had left his skin smooth. She could nearly count every one of the long, thick lashes fringing his eyes. So handsome, her breath caught in her throat. He was everything masculine and urbane, and she could no more resist her own helpless attraction than a flower could stop a honeybee from sipping its sweetness. No one else walked the deck this early hour. They were alone.

His mouth drew closer, and a pulse beat wildly in his neck. Thomas slid his other palm over her cheek, cupping her face.

"Oh, Jas," he murmured.

The single syllable represented all the frustration, longing and yearning she felt. With a sigh holding its own tones of regret, he lowered his mouth to hers.

She'd lost, again.

The kiss was sunrise itself, glowing with soft, dawning warmth after the night's bitter chill, and with the promise of possibilities. Sweet and almost playful, growing deeper and richer like the violet and rose hues in the sky, more intense as his lips pressed against hers, coaxing her mouth open, his tongue leisurely slipping inside to claim and possess. Jasmine gripped his arms for support, drowning in the sensations. She met his passion, returning it equally, pressing herself close to him, wanting to absorb all of him.

A deep groan wrenched from him. Thomas slid his powerful arms about her waist, crushing her to him. Changing the intensity of the kiss, teeth scraping erotically along her mouth, nipping and tasting, each tactile sensation arousing her to a fever pitch. His tongue thrust into her mouth. She tasted him, touching him with her own tongue, a dance of sensuality that sent a thrill racing through her.

Thomas's kiss made Jasmine feel alive, feverish and excited, as if the world were indeed new and fresh and filled with possibilities. A cocoon of warmth wrapped around her. No one else existed at this moment, only him. Truly, he did feel something for her. He must.

He broke the kiss, leaning his forehead against hers. Breathing ragged, he touched her cheek, his fingers trembling slightly. Thomas had felt it as well. Something tender and meaningful, more than a mere kiss.

Heart pounding madly, Jasmine gazed at him in hopeful adoration. Eager for another kiss, she pursed her mouth. Like a jasmine flower opening to the sun, she offered all to him.

Regret flattened his gaze, turning it emotionless. Thomas very gently pulled away. The flower withered on the vine.

Jasmine sucked in a breath, caught between wanting to cry in disappointment and laugh at her foolishness. She felt as silly as a simpering schoolgirl. Summoning all her composure, she offered him an insouciant smile. As if his kiss meant nothing. As if he meant nothing.

"I feel so alive and frightfully awake with this glorious sunrise and refreshing sea air. It was pleasant greeting the dawn, but I think I'll take breakfast now," she said. Then, with a vacant smile that meant nothing and hid everything, Jasmine turned and walked off. Behind her she heard a deep sigh. Or perhaps it was only her imagination.

The kiss was a terrible mistake. One kiss to find the woman hiding behind indifference. A kiss that meant nothing. A kiss that was everything.

Seduction had always been a game to him. He was a gentleman in public, treating his women with courtesy and showering them with attention and gifts. In the privacy of the bedroom, he was a pirate. Thomas planned his seductions slowly, learning each woman's individual sexual needs. Bringing them to one shattering climax after another, he smiled as they begged and clawed and screamed for more. After, when they lay in a stupor of dazed pleasure, he'd quietly preen. And when an affair was over, he broke it off gently, left without a backward glance. His heart had never once been engaged. Thomas protected that particular organ with utmost zeal.

Jasmine's cold indifference aroused the primitive male inside him to the challenge of the chase. Desire made him forget his own good sense. Now, with one kiss, a fire that had been banked glowed once more. If he wasn't careful, it could become an inferno.

Yes, Jasmine touched his heart, the part of him carefully tucked away like buried treasure. And she had been equally affected. Thomas had felt the trembling passion of her mouth beneath his, heard her tiny sighs of surrender, felt her soft body yield against him. Experienced in passion, he knew all the signs of a woman's arousal. She'd exhibited every one.

He'd lost himself in that kiss as if they were two innocent lovers. He was no innocent, and couldn't allow himself such moments again. Such desire was as foolish as wishing on a distant star. Yet when her soft body wrapped around him and her sweet, pliant mouth became his, he forgot all else.

Thomas dragged in a deep breath. He shoved a trembling hand through his wind-tossed hair. Iron-clad control had fled. How utterly presumptuous to assume he could endure forced proximity with Jasmine without it affecting his own turbulent emotions. It was like trying to ignore the burning sun. She was ever-present, in his thoughts, in his vision, everywhere.

He gripped the railing and stared at the glassy water. "Oh,

Jas," he murmured to the uncaring ocean. "Everywhere I go, I see only you. Why do you haunt me so?"

The primitive male in him wanted to stalk after her, toss her over his shoulder, bring her to his cabin and ravish her with mindless pleasure until they were both sated. The reserved aristocrat held these impulses at bay, whipping passion and desire back with the lash of upbringing and reason.

He suspected when he coaxed her into bed and they both surrendered to passion, it would not satisfy. It would be like trying to douse a raging fire with a glass of water. He'd want more. Always would want more.

And he could never have it.

Chapter Twelve

Cairo—noisy, dusty, throbbing like a heartbeat. Dark-eyed children held out a pleading palm, the fellahin were busy hauling items or selling; snake charmers, a man entertaining pedestrians with a trained monkey, the pale-skinned English driven in cabs by dark-skinned drivers—it was a living mass of humanity in the land of the burning yellow sun and the sharp blue skies.

Perched on a settee in her room at the Shepherd's Hotel, Jasmine stopped writing and began eating the dinner delivered by room service. After arriving in the city, she'd recorded observations while her uncle and Thomas searched for the best means to transport the horses they would purchase. Graham had stopped by earlier to ask her if she wished to join them. He was accompanying Thomas to a house in Old Cairo to conduct business with one of the duke's friends. Jasmine declined, explaining she was quite tired.

Truth was, she needed time alone to deal with the past. Memories of Egypt sneaked out of the corner of her mind: the brothel, and the days when she'd felt a thin, childish terror of suffering a fate similar to Nadia's. The fierce, scowling guard who'd threatened to whip her for disobeying his orders. And the pretty, sad-faced lady who turned out to be her real mother, who promised to take her away from all that.

Two days ago, as she, Thomas and Uncle Graham entered the massive lobby of Shepherd's, a cold chill had snaked down her spine. Jasmine had studied the imposing columns, enormous brass containers of flowers and the elegant, wealthy Europeans drifting in and out of the hotel. Memories flooded back. Fear, as she searched the lobby for an Englishman named Kenneth, the kind man who would become her stepfather. Tugging at the hands of pale-faced men, asking in a language they didn't understand if they were her rescuer. The kicks and anger she'd stirred. Some called her names in Arabic: dirty-faced, begging Egyptian girl.

This time, a fawning hotel manager greeted them. An imposing array of stewards hustled their baggage upstairs. Jasmine had managed to hide her ancient fear before Thomas.

Since their shipboard kiss, she'd maintained a cool indifference. Physical distance helped chill the fire in her blood. When she caught him looking at her it was with a banked fire of his own. The intent looks he gave her poked at the glowing coals of her own passion, but Jasmine doused them quickly.

Stretching, she pushed aside the tray and went to run a bath. Jasmine luxuriated in the hot, scented water. After, she shrugged into a clean chemise and donned an ankle-length robe of red Chinese silk. The material felt sensual against her naked arms and shoulders. Masses of heavy hair spilled down her back as she unpinned her topknot. Her reflection in the gilded looking-glass reflected an exotic, enticing woman.

Curling her feet beneath her in a comfortable chair by the lamp, she settled back with a book. Barely had she begun to read when a firm rap on the door interrupted her. She belted the robe tightly about her, thinking it was a steward come to pick up the tray. No.

Thomas stood in the hallway. "Hullo, Jas. Thought I'd check on you and let you know your uncle will be delayed a while longer."

Taken aback, Jasmine clutched her robe closed at her throat. She didn't invite him in, but he advanced. She backed away as he closed the door. He leaned a hip lazily against the doorjamb.

"My first home-cooked meal in Egypt. It was fascinating. Did you know they serve a delightful liqueur named zibib? Ali kept insisting we sample it."

"Most Muslims don't drink alcohol."

"Ali isn't Muslim," he reflected. "And neither am I."

Jasmine bit back a smile. "You're inebriated, Lord Thomas."

"A bit. And I thought nothing could top good English whiskey. Ah, me. How wrong I was."

His cocky half-grin gave him a young and feckless look. Jasmine's heart beat a little faster. Dark stubble shadowed his jaw, giving him a slightly dangerous air. His hair was rumbled and his tie askew. The dishevelment only added to his charm.

"Did you succeed in your business transactions?"

"Quite. They had no choice but to capitulate. I gave them good terms." He leaned lazily against the door.

"You're a pirate," she said, smiling openly now. "You never surrender."

"I do not," he agreed. "But I enjoy making others surrender."

Her smile dropped as his gaze swept over her dishabille. "You look quite comfortable." Now his gaze became frankly appraising, with pure male interest. "I've never seen you with your hair down. It's very becoming."

Her hand went to her curls, and Thomas watched her, his expression intent. The look made her nervous. He stared at her as she imagined a hungry lion would regard hapless prey about to be devoured. There would be no escape.

"I'm a pirate with a heart only for you. Such a mystery you are, little flower. There are layers to you like sands covering the tombs in Egypt. Exotic and enticing."

"I am no mystery."

"But you are," he said softly. "An exotic mystery."

"And you're an inebriated pirate who wishes . . . what?" she asked, backing away.

"To ravish you thoroughly. You're very lovely, Jas, and deserve to be ravished," he murmured, taking a step forward. "So exotic and lovely. I can smell your perfume. Jasmine flowers, isn't it?"

"I–I'm not wearing any."

Suddenly she became all too aware of the lateness of the hour. The fact that they were alone. Very alone, with no Uncle Graham to chaperone, no restrictions between them. His hungry gaze caressed her like a silken stroke.

The shipboard kiss could be but a beginning. This look indicated he wanted more. Much more. And he would take it. Reckless though the decision might be. He wanted her.

Thomas was tempted. And more than a tad inebriated, not only from drink. No liquor could affect him like Jasmine.

He'd spent a pleasant, successful evening with the duke and the duke's very wealthy Egyptian friend. They'd dined and shaken hands. The duke's friend had given Thomas a very large sum of money, transferred to Thomas's private account to partner with him in brokering the al-Hajid Arabians to Europe. The account, which could not be touched by the free-spending earl, would earn interest at a considerable rate.

His money troubles solved, Thomas had left feeling lighthearted and free. Now, seeing Jasmine, desire stirred.

The very sight of the ebony curls spilling down her back, the robe's folds kissing her curves, was more potent than any fiery spirit. He glanced down. From beneath the robe's hem, her toes peeped out. A surge of heat slammed into him. She was naked, or nearly so, beneath the garment.

Dragging his gaze up to her face, he studied her expression. Arousal twined with apprehension. Her huge sloe eyes were wide with expectation. She licked her lips. Lust surged through him like a boiling sandstorm. He took another step forward, staring at her soft, pouting mouth. His groin tightened. Exotic, enticing Jasmine, with her beautiful dark looks, her mouth ripe for kissing.

"What do you want, Lord Thomas?"

"What do *you* want, Jas?" he asked, unsmiling. Advancing further still. "I think I know."

"You shouldn't be here," she said, backing away. "It's not proper."

"No one will see," he rejoined. He crooked a finger at her. "Come here, Jas. Just one kiss."

And perhaps more . . .

One kiss. The thought of Thomas's warm lips against hers made her mouth water as if she'd spotted a juicy peach. "One kiss. Then you must leave," she insisted.

Jasmine stood still, arms at her side as he went to her. She stared at his mouth, firm and inviting. A tiny hairline scar dissected his chin like a cleft. It made her wonder where he'd received it, what hurt he had endured. He gazed down at her through hooded eyes. Something flashed there in those greenish depths, dark, dangerous and predatory.

Thomas slid a hand over the nape of her neck. His touch sent a shiver of arousal darting through her. His mouth hovered over hers, light as the whisper of a butterfly. He brushed his lips gently against hers and pulled away.

Frustrated, Jasmine reached up, pressed her mouth against his. More. She needed more. She licked his lips, tasting him and the tangy liqueur lingering on his mouth. Thomas fisted a hand in her hair, tilted her head back and ravaged her.

It wasn't a kiss, but an invasion. His tongue thrust past her parted lips, plunging and plundering. Taking what he wanted. Helpless in his grip, she closed her eyes and surrendered, sucking on his tongue. Taking him, and giving in return. His hands slid lower, crushing her against him. Jasmine felt a hardness press against the softness of her belly. The empty space between her legs throbbed. Her breasts tingled, the nipples aching for his touch. Jasmine clutched at him as if she drowned.

It was madness, but she didn't care. Whipped by the intensity of her feelings for him, all she held secret in her heart poured out into the kiss. Their mouths melded together, joined as one as their bodies strained against each other. She wanted more of this delicious pleasure. More of the forbidden. Vaguely she became aware of him backing her away from the door. Toward the bed. When the backs of her legs collided with the mattress, she fell back with a little startled cry. Jasmine stared up at him. He loomed over her, large and muscular, intensely masculine. Dangerous, like a beast uncaged at last.

Her lips felt warm, swollen from the possessiveness of his kiss. His body tensed as the cords in his neck tightened with strain. His breathing was ragged, his gaze fierce and intent as he regarded her lying back on the bed.

"What do you want, Jas?" he repeated in a deep, husky voice. "Do you want me?"

Words escaped her. Thoughts tumbled about in her head like a swirling sandstorm. She wanted him, had wanted him for a lifetime. She wanted to keep him forever. But such was impossible. If they only had now, then she would take what tonight offered and content herself with the memories tomorrow.

No speech was necessary. Jasmine reached out, tugged at his lapels to raise herself up and kiss him again. He backed away, the green of his eyes darkening. "Yes," he murmured. "Yes, Jas. I shall give you what you want."

Thomas removed his coat and tossed it aside. He tore off his tie and then his fingers were flying rapidly down to unfasten the waistcoat's pearl buttons. He shrugged it off and then did the same with his shirt. Breath caught in Jasmine's lungs. His chest was hard, with a thick pelt of dark hair that marched into a vanishing line into the waistband of his trousers. Fascinated, her gaze tracked each inch of his naked skin. Muscles lined his stomach, stretched along broad shoulders.

He was so beautiful, raw and masculine. Her nipples felt tight and achy as she stared. She struggled upward to touch him. Her fingers trailed lightly over his hard stomach muscles. Thomas drew in a shuddering breath. He caught her hand in his, kissing the knuckles.

Air brushed against her half-naked breasts as he parted the lapels of her robe. Thomas opened it slowly, an approving smile lingering on his mouth. He traced a line along her collarbone, down to the lacy edge of the chemise barely covering her breasts. His finger circled a tight nipple, teasing it until she writhed and squirmed on the bed. Each touch brought spirals of sensation shooting through her, pooling low in her belly. Never had she experienced this need before, this wanting.

Then he bent his head, feathering kisses everywhere. Thomas nipped the soft flesh of her earlobe, trailed kisses along her neck as her eyes closed. He kissed and licked the hollow beneath her throat, moving downward until he came to her breasts. Sensation exploded as his mouth encased the nipple through the thin material. Jasmine whimpered, clinging to him as his tongue stroked and flicked. His hand slid down her waist, cupped her hip, then delved beneath her chemise. Restlessly she parted her legs, shocked anew as his fingers toyed with her nether curls. Then he caressed her between the legs.

When he slipped a finger between her wet folds, she jerked upwards in shocked astonishment. "Easy," he soothed. "Just let it go, let me give you pleasure."

Jasmine arched and moaned as he caressed the part of her throbbing for his touch. Nothing could be as splendid as this, the fire he created with each skillful stroke. She felt open and wanting, the sweet pleasure he created with each skilled touch bringing her higher and higher. As if she were that bright star he'd said she was, soaring back to her home in the heavens.

Thomas, oh, he was doing something to her, a sweet, slow stroking that made her gasp and squirm and brought all sensation rushing to between her legs. His mouth was flicking slow and steady over her breast. Judging from his satisfied groans, she knew it pleased him as much as he pleasured her.

Dimly, she became aware of a hard knock at the door. A nugget of reason returned as the hard rapping continued. Someone had probably seen Thomas in the hallway. Servants gossiped. She'd be ruined.

Passion fled as Jasmine panicked. Writhing in his arms, she pushed at his chest. "Thomas, no, someone's at the door, they'll hear, it's probably a steward come to pick up my tray . . . People will talk, the hotel staff . . ."

He raised his head, his breathing ragged, looking dangerously close to the edge. "We're in Egypt. We don't know anyone here, and no one will talk." Thomas cut short her protest with his mouth, thrusting his tongue past her lips. Reason and desire battled for control as a moan wrenched from her. She only wanted to give herself over, ride the wave of passion until it brought her higher and higher.

The knocking ceased. Someone said something in Arabic she couldn't quite understand. An amused laugh, then she thought she heard the door creak, as if someone pressed an ear against the wood. Thomas broke the kiss and mounted her. One hand tugged upwards at her chemise, the only barricade between their naked skin. He unfastened the opening of his trousers. Wedging a knee between her legs, he parted them and settled his hips between her opened legs.

He meant to take her. Now. While someone lurked outside in the hallway, listening at the door. Knowing she was inside.

The implication of what this meant sank in. Jasmine struggled frantically. Lust lashed at him like a stallion scenting a mare in heat, turning him senseless with desire. He would take her here and not care a whit about anything else? She must stop him.

"Thomas, my reputation will be ruined! Please, don't let this happen. I'll have no honor and no one will respect me," she whispered, stiffening with the incredible sweet tension as his rigid length rubbed against her wet cleft.

"Who gives a bloody damn about your honor?" he muttered, his breathing frantic as he pinned her hands to the bed. "It's not important. Your reputation doesn't matter to anyone important."

Astonished, she stared. Desire tightened his face, darkened his eyes with merciless arousal. Sweet passion evaporated like summer rain in the desert, replaced by a flood of dawning anger. Jasmine pushed at his chest.

"Would you consider me a whore, then," she whispered, mindful of the person at the door, "to be taken only for your pleasure, since you care nothing for my honor?"

And then he went still, as if her words were a dagger thrust into his chest. Thomas stared down at her, shocked horror flashing across his face. She craned her neck to listen. Footsteps creaked just outside, then faded down the hallway. Whoever had been eavesdropping was gone.

Relieved, she gave full attention to her fury. She gulped down a quivering breath to say what she must.

"You're full of duplicity. You swear to protect your sister's honor, the valiant knight who tilts at scandal with a lance of power and money, but you treat me like a trollop. No, worse. At least a trollop is paid for her services. You lack respect for me just like your mother does, treat me like an inferior whose reputation doesn't matter."

Jasmine struggled with the words. "Because I 'don't matter to anyone important'. Damn you, Thomas!"

Reason slowly returned to Thomas. Like a lash, her words whipped him. Habits of the past charged forth. With the restraint of class, breeding and experience, he pulled away. But his breathing was ragged and the wildness remained inside him.

He'd nearly taken her. Would have, but for her protest.

What the hell had he done? He desired her, certainly; she drove him reckless with passion, mindless with desire, but he respected her far more than this. When had he devolved into such a crass, crude bastard?

Stricken speechless, he could only stare at her, caught up in the dawning of this self-revelation. Thomas became aware of Jasmine sliding out from beneath him, leaving the space beneath empty. Empty as he was.

He had become as despicable as all those he detested. Treating those considered their inferiors with insouciant disregard of their feelings, their concerns. Thomas had vowed never to mimic them. Now he had joined their ranks.

Stricken with shame, he wished he could take back the words he'd uttered. Jasmine was a lady who deserved respect and gentle treatment, not this. He'd forgotten all in his lust to possess her, and had acted as if her reputation mattered for naught.

He dressed, watching Jasmine as she put herself to rights, arranging her clothing in a hurry. *Now. Do something*, his mind screamed. *Save this.*

Thomas summoned all his rigid control to dispel the haze of lust and alcohol. He slid off the bed, gently clasped her wrist. "Jas, wait. I'm sorry. You're right. I'm a cad, the lowest sort for what I said, because I know you're not my inferior. You're no one's inferior. Never will be, either. You're better than the whole sordid lot of us, especially me."

The self-loathing in his tone was clear as a bell on a silent summer night. She raised her gaze to his, expressionless. No emotions. Dead to the world.

"Yes, I am," she said tonelessly. "A shame it took this kind of debasement for you to recognize it. Now, release me."

Instead of letting go, he cupped her chin. Tilting it up, he forced her to meet his gaze. "I would never force you to submit to my caresses, Jas. Ever. I apologize for my actions."

Uncertainty flashed in her dark eyes. "You acted quite unlike the gentlemen of your class."

"I'm not a gentleman. Not around you. I have a tendency . . . to quite forget myself. As do you." His thumb caressed her jaw, slow, lingering strokes that brought a flush to her cheeks.

"You seemed quite content to forget me on the ship after you kissed me, Lord Thomas. And now that you've imbibed, you've changed your mind? Or am I merely a convenient means to exercise your lust? Go find another woman."

"I don't want another woman. I want you."

"Well, you can't have me. This was a mistake." But her hand rested atop his, and her dark eyes were huge as their gazes collided.

"How it happened was a mistake. The words I said, uttered in the heat of the moment, were callous and rude. I'm sorry I said them. But this, what's between us, is not a mistake, and I'm not sorry for it. You want me as much as I want you."

A scowl lined her forehead. "You're an arrogant sod," she muttered.

"Indeed," he agreed with a faint smile. "And you're a beautiful, exotic woman who's like a little cacti, all prickly and sharp, with soft fleshy fruit beneath, Jas. I know the heart of you, the woman inside, is so much more. And I will find a way to her."

His words caused her to back away and hiss like a cat. He knew they stung, because they were true. And she wasn't ready to face that particular truth yet.

"Please release me," she repeated.

Thomas let her go. He hungrily watched her hips sway as she walked to the door. "Get out," she ordered, her eyes flashing.

Thomas turned at the door and lifted her hand to his lips. He grazed the knuckles with a kiss. "Until later, my lady," he murmured. He gave her a long, meaningful look. "And there will be a later. Trust me."

Looking extremely distressed, she shook her head. Long

inky black curls flew back and forth. He ached to fist his hands in her hair, tilt her head back and ravage her mouth once more. He would not. Not tonight.

"No."

"Yes," he said softly.

She didn't withdraw her hand. Her huge brown eyes were wide with disbelief. "You said you wouldn't force me. I am not a lower-class servant girl you can take at your leisure!"

"I told you, you aren't my inferior. And when I take you, it won't be force. We'll be bare of station, culture and country. Just a man and woman, surrendering to passion. When you're ready, it will happen again, and next time I won't stop because you won't want me to stop. You can't deny what's between us, Jasmine."

"I can bloody well try!" She snatched her hand away and muttered something very unladylike in Arabic. He smothered a grin, opened the door and walked into the hallway. The door slammed behind him.

Not now, but soon. There would be another time and place. He'd court her like the lady she was and give her the respect she deserved. Then, afterward, they would both get what they wanted.

Chapter Thirteen

Erotic dreams disturbed her slumber that night. Jasmine tossed on the soft cotton sheets as she dreamed of Thomas. Naked, his muscled body crushed against her, he mounted her and spread her legs wide. Feeling that hard, long length of him pressed against her thigh, she strained against him. Not to fight him and resist, but to pull him closer, eagerly meet him as he poised over her, ready to claim her virginity at last.

Awakening, she found the dreams left her shaken and restless, filled with hot yearning. She ate breakfast in her room, and sent a note to Uncle Graham that she was feeling a tad off but would join him for tea.

Coward. She did not want to see Thomas again. Not until she felt confident enough and chased away the turbulent feelings the dream stirred.

As she waited on the terrace for her uncle to join her for tea, Jasmine tried to relax. Clad in English clothing, her personal suit of armor, she sat stiffly in the wicker chair, pretending casual observation. Inside she was scared as hell. Had anyone seen Thomas come to her room last night?

Yes, appearances mattered. Even here. Jasmine acted as insouciant as before, but despite the mild winter warmth, sweat trickled down her back. Her fingers picked up and set down the silver set out for afternoon tea. On the street below, a flower vendor sang out her wares in a sad, lilting voice. A man with a trained monkey performed tricks to the amusement of tourists stopping to see its antics.

Jasmine looked up to survey the terrace. A mustached man approached. Clad in sparkling white, he resembled an angel, but with a walking stick instead of wings. He leaned on his stick, tipped his hat.

"Jasmine?" he asked.

She offered a polite, bemused smile. "Hullo."

The stranger looked quite jovial. "There you are. Been waiting an age. Shall we go?"

Jasmine's smile turned to confusion.

"I've been told you speak English. Hope they weren't wrong—my Arabic is simply beastly," he continued in a low tone. "Now, let's be off. I paid only for one hour with you, and time is a-wasting. I've booked a room. No one will stop you if you're escorted by me. I've told them you're my niece."

Out of the corner of her eye she saw Thomas approach. Jasmine fervently prayed he hadn't heard. "I beg your pardon?" she asked. "I think you're mistaken—"

"I'm not, am I? I know what you are," the stranger said impatiently. He grabbed her upper arm and she struggled to be free. "I will get what I paid for, damn it. Come on, it's not like you haven't done this before—"

Thomas's fingers tore the man's grip off her, and he snarled like an angry tiger. He looked massive, threatening and protective. "You touch her and I'll thrash you," he said in clipped tones. "How *dare* you?"

Jasmine shrank back, coloring further. Oh bloody hell, he'd heard every single humiliating word.

"I d-do say," the man stammered.

"This is Miss Jasmine Tristan. Her uncle is the Duke of Caldwell," Thomas snapped, standing behind her and placing a possessive hand on her shoulder. "They are both guests at this hotel. I daresay His Grace would be extremely upset to know how you've insulted his niece."

Now the stranger blushed a shade of red deeper than Jasmine. "I do beg your pardon. I thought she was—you were—the girl I was to meet here was named Jasmine. Your coloring is the same, and dark hair and dark skin and eyes, and she was to wear a white skirt and white lace blouse with a cameo . . . A lass worth at least twenty camels, so I was told."

He uttered another apology, then walked off briskly as if fire ate at his heels.

Jasmine colored further. She understood what the man wanted. Glancing at Thomas, his angry gaze told her he understood as well. The stranger thought she was a prostitute.

After the disaster of last night, it had taken all her strength to hold up under those degrading remarks. Buoyant hopefulness became crushed by the uncaring heel of assumptions. In England, she was snubbed for being Egyptian. Now here, where she thought perhaps she'd be treated as an equal, men mistook her for a trollop.

Humiliation poured through her. Scraping together her tattered pride, Jasmine sat straighter, as if a good English spine would erase the insult. But she could not look at Thomas.

"Uncle Graham shall be along shortly for tea. I'm certain you have other business to attend, so you may leave now."

"Jas, look at me," he said softly.

She did. Tenderness filled his gaze.

"He's a nattering dull-wit who doesn't deserve a second thought. You're worth ten of him, Jasmine. Why are you giving him power over you?"

He has no power over me, only you do, she thought dully. *I must cease giving you the power like I did last night.* Better to leap into a Nile filled with hungry crocodiles than subject her heart to Thomas's divided attentions. At the very least the reptiles would dispatch her quickly, unlike this slow agonizing death she felt each time he drew near.

Thomas pulled up a chair and sat beside her, his expression that of a man studying an object of fascination.

"What?" she said in irritation.

"I can see why you're so indignant. You, a beautiful woman, only worth twenty camels? I daresay you're worth more. At least twenty-five."

Jasmine struggled to keep from smiling. His gentle teasing pricked at her bubble of self-protection.

"No, perhaps twenty-five camels and a donkey," he amended.

She stole a look at him. "Are you assessing my worth, Caesar, for perhaps a future exchange if we become stranded in the desert?"

"Splendid idea. Stuck in the desert, you would come in quite handy. If some Bedouin traders offer to purchase you, I might coax your uncle into an excellent deal."

Her mouth curved into a deceptively sweet smile. "Why, I could likely talk him into trading you. I'd say *your* worth would be equivalent to one donkey. An ass traded for an ass."

Mirth filled his gaze. "Calling me a donkey here is worse than calling me an ass, Jas. For such a grave insult, for your lack of tact, I'll have to lower your worth to fifteen camels."

"You drive a hard bargain, Caesar," she mocked. "But my worth is higher than fifteen camels solely because I live in England. Everyone knows English women command a higher price to the fellahin."

"You are wrong, Miss Tristan," he said, surprising her with his softly spoken, perfect Arabic. "A beautiful woman like you, no matter what her nationality, is not just worth more than fifteen camels. No, she is priceless."

He did not want her to be English, with those dainty English movements and the English accent she had perfected. What he truly wanted was her to be her—and naked in his bed, away from everyone else. Keeping her with him like a rare treasure, hoarding her like a jealous excavator who refused to share the priceless treasure which he'd unearthed.

Last night had been a mistake only because of the insensitive words he'd spat out in frustrated desire. He'd wrestled with his feelings for her for too long and finally capitulated. He wanted her to the point of madness. Reason fled whenever he was with her, and here, away from the prying eyes of his friends and family, he felt free at last. Free enough to pursue his interest.

What did he want? He wanted Jasmine to be herself. To discard the façade of her cool English guise and become the fiery, passionate woman who existed within. The Egyptian Jasmine. Thomas longed to discover the girl who had fascinated him in boyhood with her spirit, exotic air and natural grace.

Exasperation filled him as he studied her attire. The prim, white-laced dress with its severe lines and the hat tilted at a saucy angle on her ebony curls barricaded Jasmine from the world. He wanted her to unhook her tresses, let them spill past her waist and flow like the Nile, don a soft gown of brilliant jade or sapphire to highlight her exotic, dark eyes and little triangular face. Adorn her feet with gold sandals, anoint her fingers with henna.

He wanted her to speak Arabic. She had not spoken a single word in his hearing, as if the tongue were foreign.

Oh yes, he wanted to strip away her layers until he could find the real Jasmine again, the woman who'd emerged last night, if only briefly in his arms.

Thomas watched her fall silent, ignoring his compliment. She sat back in languid indifference.

"Do you truly know how beautiful you are?" he persisted in Arabic.

"You are too kind, sir," she replied in the same tongue. Then, realizing her mistake, a becoming blush tinted her cheeks. She excused it with a stammer about studying the language.

"You speak Arabic fluently," he observed. "And yet you refrain from doing so. Why?"

She said nothing, but he caught the direction of her gaze. At a nearby round table, a small cluster of people settled for afternoon tea. Immediately he recognized them. Here for their annual wintering in Egypt were Mr. and Mrs. Percival Darcy and their crop of close friends. Thomas had met them two days ago over tea, for Percival was a friend. His wife's social influence was vast, and many flocked to her side to seek approval. The same friends accompanied them each winter to Cairo, like spaniels obediently trotting at their master's heels.

For the past two afternoons, at the same time and at the very same table, with the ladies' parasols tilted at the exact same angle to shade their fair skin from the burning sun, the little group took tea. The same insipid weak tea served with the same little insipid cucumber sandwiches with the crusts the Shepherd's staff courteously removed at their request. Though they wintered in a foreign land, they packed their habits with them. The Percival Darcys would not stray from their routine any more than they would trudge into the deep desert stark naked.

Thomas turned to Jasmine, feeling propriety tighten about his neck like his cravat. An English noose, he thought suddenly. Damn it, he had not journeyed thousands of miles to take tea on a sunny terrace as if he were in his very home. He wanted adventure and wildness and all that Egypt had to offer.

"Why do you hide your heritage?" he probed. "It is cause for great pride, not shame." When Jasmine gave a tinkling laugh, like little silver bells on a Bedouin's camel harness, he leaned forward, enchanted.

"You make everything here sound glamorous and exciting," she said. "There is great darkness here, dirty little secrets, Lord Thomas. Poverty, crime and utter wretchedness."

He persisted. The boring sameness of his life, the routine dogging his footsteps, had fled. He wanted to coax out Jasmine's inner spirit and see once more the woman hiding behind a wall of proper white muslin and stiff English mannerisms.

"Your perception of Egypt isn't the same as mine. Egypt is

proud and mysterious and fascinating, as complex as the Sphinx and as deep as the Nile. Far from simple, her heritage is like a tomb slowly unearthed, commanding great respect and awe."

"You make her sound like a grand lady, but the fact remains few regard her people as such. They dig at her tombs and gasp with delight at the wealth of her past, but her present citizens are regarded with scorn and indifference. So, why should I desire to be counted among them?" Her head gracefully nodded toward the English who languidly lifted their cups and sipped.

Thomas fell silent, troubled by her words.

"I daresay they know not a word of Arabic," she observed. "And until I hear otherwise from their lips, and for a reason other than to address servants, mine will speak only the tongue of Mother England."

Ignoring the curious looks aimed in his direction, Thomas picked up her hand. "Do not be so eager to be one of them, Jas. The harder you try, the more you lose yourself, as the sand and sun scrape against the Sphinx. Such a terrible loss."

"At least the Sphinx inspires awe and fascination," she said, giving a sigh that tore at his heart.

Suddenly, a flash of the old Jasmine surfaced and an impish light entered her eyes. "Although, I do believe I would command more camels than Mrs. Percival Darcy, if only for the reason that my face doesn't resemble pasty dough. The English upper crust—how appropriate! But how do they stay so pale even in hot climates?"

Thomas pressed her hand. "We do look rather pale. Perhaps it's because many of our sort have ice running through our veins instead of good hot blood. Stand tall and stay cool, and all that. I wonder sometimes if we even lean. I do believe that leaning is expressly forbidden in the House of Lords— except when one is dying, and even then, approval from Parliament is required first."

Jasmine gave a full-bodied, uninhibited laugh. Heads turned, and some people smiled. The Percival Darcy crowd looked disapproving. Red suffused her face. Then Percival spotted Thomas, waved and shouted, "Hullo, Lord Thomas. Don't stay over there alone. Come over. Join us for tea."

The invitation was not extended to Jasmine. She flushed further but gave a gracious smile. "Go, have tea with them. They're your friends. I'll wait for Uncle Graham."

His friends. Not Jasmine's. Thomas did something he'd never done before to a fellow Englishman. Deliberately, he turned his back.

His cut was so obvious that a few in the crowd gasped audibly. Ignoring them, he focused all his attention on Jasmine and took her hand. Surprise flared in her expression. "Where were we? Talking about leaning, tea, I believe, and dough."

She glanced at his friends. "Yes, dough. They look like what they eat. Perhaps they will shock everyone, step out of form and change their diet. What would people say if such a disaster were to occur? I do believe the earth would stop spinning!"

Thomas felt as if he were spinning, holding her hand like this so daringly. Sunlight caressed the rich ebony strands of hair escaping her bun. For a moment he felt as if the world existed solely for them.

Then she withdrew her hand and the old blank expression shuttered her face like a mashrabiya screen closing on a window.

"Here comes Uncle Graham," she observed. "Shall we order tea now?"

Graham greeted them both with a hearty hello. They made small talk while nibbling on cucumber sandwiches and eating small slices of sweet cake laced with honey and almonds. After Thomas's third helping, Jasmine gave him a good-natured pout.

"If you keep eating those, I shall have to order more. I haven't gotten any."

He wiped his sticky fingers on a clean napkin and smiled.

"They're delicious. I must hire a good cook here for my voyage to Luxor when we return to Cairo."

Hearing familiar voices, Thomas spotted two familiar faces: Charles Hodges and Edward Morrow, former business associates. Morrow had given him good stock tips in return for one of Thomas's Arabian foals, and Hodges had joined with him in a short but successful stint in stock speculation. The men, escorting women in large white hats, parasols and white frocks, were glancing about the terrace. One saw him and hailed him with a boisterous shout that turned heads.

Thomas stood and politely greeted the couples as they approached. He made introductions. The men sat down at the table and their wives opened their parasols. Thomas conversed but keenly observed Jasmine. She seemed eager to join in the conversation, and did so, making several witty remarks, that caused Morrow to burst into another round of laughter. Both the Morrows and the Hodges were open and animated around her, and curious about her journey, when Matty Hodges very bluntly asked Jasmine.

"Pardon me, but are you a native?"

Jasmine drew herself up with dignity. "I was born in Egypt, and my mother is Egyptian. My mother and stepfather live in London now."

Instead of the sneer his other friends would have tendered, Mattie Hodges looked intrigued. "Oh, how splendid!" she cried, clapping her hands. "Charles, we simply must invite this intriguing young lady to dine with us tonight. I find the Egyptian people so fascinating, and their culture equally so."

Jasmine looked so desperately hopeful that Thomas felt a twist of sharp pity. "Do you, Mrs. Hodges? Why is that?"

"Why not? They're from an ancient line, very proud and dignified, and they're very friendly and clever."

A shadow fell over Jasmine's face. "Some people say Egyptians are sly, filthy beggars who are morally and intellectually deficient."

"Stuff and nonsense," declared Mr. Morrow, twirling the waxed ends of his mustache. "Rather would judge a person on his merits, not nationality. Else we'd all be in trouble—eh, Lord Thomas? Just like a book, it's what's inside that counts most."

"Indeed," Thomas said softly, deeply moved by the relief on Jasmine's face. "You said it best, Morrow. I only wish all could believe it."

Jasmine lifted her shining gaze to his. "Perhaps one of us can. Yes, perhaps one can."

Chapter Fourteen

Two days later, they boarded one of Mr. Cook's famous steamboats to journey up the Nile to their destination at al-Minya. From there, a member of the Khamsin warriors of the wind would escort them to the al-Hajid camp in the deep desert.

Jasmine confided in Thomas that she wished they'd booked a private sailing vessel where no strangers would inquire about "purchasing" her. The incident was fresh in her mind. He told her the steamboat was faster. In only seven days, they would make the 450-mile journey from Cairo, with the added boon of stops along the way to see ruins.

"If anyone propositions you, tell me and I'll thrash him," he insisted, earning a grateful smile.

They went to the salon to take tea and mingle with passengers. The pine-paneled walls showcased elaborate tapestries. Large floral settees were arranged before small tables with lace coverings. Magazines were stacked neatly on a table, along with some novels. Leafy ferns were scattered about on several tables. The room had a bar at one end, its inlaid rich mahogany wood shelves holding an assortment of spirits in glass bottles.

Two hours later they docked at the small town of Bedrachin to explore the ruins at Memphis. Thomas watched in fascination as Jasmine relaxed, as if she felt at home among the high mudbrick buildings, towering palm trees and curious peasants. When an eager peasant named Abdul asked her for baksheesh to act as tour guide, she replied in Arabic that she had no need of a guide, as she desired to wander aimlessly and let her heart guide her.

Thomas smiled, and Abdul laughed in apparent delight. As a courtesy, he directed them to a donkey boy who could take them to Memphis. Rabi was a very good guide, the man insisted.

"Let me guess," Thomas said dryly in Arabic. "He's also your grandson."

The man gave his high-pitched laugh again. "Of course."

The Cook tour guide had already arranged for donkey boys, and Rabi was among them. He secured three small donkeys and they set out for the ruins. Thomas rode a gray donkey named King Edward, a private joke that amused both him and the grinning donkey boy.

His long legs dangled over the little donkey's sides, his boots nearly scraping the rocky earth. Jasmine remained oddly quiet. He wondered if her silence was due to awe at this towering ravine of ancient rock and sand. The shimmering expanse beckoned to him in a mirage. Thomas tilted his broad-brimmed hat to shade his eyes.

They plodded along a road rising above verdant, fertile fields, passed through groves of towering date palms. Jasmine clung to the saddle, looking elegant despite the warm afternoon sun. Desire and something deeper filled him as he studied her. She was as regal and beautiful as an ancient Egyptian queen.

When they reached Memphis, his throat clogged with emotion. Towering date palms stood like silent sentinel over the sands. A wood building sheltered the statue of Ramses, Rabi told them. He slid off his donkey and walked forward in rapt awe. They went inside, ignoring the stream of other tourists chattering and pointing at the colossal statue of Ramses the Great. The red granite statue greeted them with a secret smile. Overcome with silent wonder, words failed Thomas. Here was the Egypt of his dreams, the ancient mystery and myth come to life.

After exploring the grounds, they broke out the baskets of sandwiches. On a checked cloth spread out on the sands beneath a shady palm, they ate. Jasmine tilted her head up, exposing the long line of her lovely throat. Thomas swallowed his mouthful with difficulty.

"The sky is amazingly blue here, so sharp it could slice through metal. In London one never does see such a pretty sky."

"Because of the coal smoke and fog," her uncle remarked, drinking a glass of mint tea.

After lunch, they rode on to Saqqara and the step pyramid, passing through fields of golden wheat. Tourists milled about the structure, admiring and pointing. Two boys played nearby, throwing stones up the pyramid in a test of skill, scolded by the scowling guard. Each time the guard left, the boys continued their game.

Jasmine looked up at the pyramid with an impish smile. "Shall we?" She lifted her skirts and set a dainty foot on a lower stone.

"It's too dangerous Jas. Stop," Thomas ordered.

"Just a little. I want to return to England and tell my family I climbed the famous step pyramid." She ignored his warning and climbed.

Thomas fumed. Damn it, would she ever listen? He had a good mind to spank her bottom. Taking a look at her bottom as she leaned over and climbed another step, he changed his mind. Spanking her bottom might lead to other, much more dangerous but pleasant activities.

"Jasmine, get down please," her uncle called.

She ignored him, her brow furrowed in stubborn lines. Thomas waited no more. He strode forward, climbed up and grabbed her about the waist.

Mindless of her incensed protests, he carried her back and let her drop onto the sand. From her undignified position on the ground, Jasmine glared up at him. Thomas laughed, and even Graham chuckled.

"Next time, mind your elders," he admonished with a grin. They left her there, pouting.

"Jas, are you joining us, or shall I have the stewards wait dinner for you?" he drawled after a few steps. Glancing over his shoulder, he saw her stand and brush off her skirts. Suddenly something sailed through the air. Jasmine yelped and recoiled.

Thomas ran to her side. Her huge sloe eyes stared up at him, and she clutched her arm. He gently pried her fingers loose, then rolled up her sleeve. Her worried uncle came over and studied the ugly bruise forming on her dark skin.

"No blood, but you'll have a nasty mark for awhile." He picked up a rock and examined it with a speculative look.

Furious, Thomas looked around, searching for the stone thrower. Several boys. Seeing them, he advanced, yelling in Arabic.

"But we didn't throw a stone at the pretty lady," one protested.

Tempted to shake them for hurting her, Thomas ordered them away from the pyramid, watching with narrowed eyes as they left.

Returning to Jasmine, he frowned at the mark on her arm. Blood had drained from her face. She looked distraught as she gazed in the direction where the boys had been.

"Bloody irresponsible of them, throwing stones where people could get hurt," Thomas muttered.

Her large, dark eyes were huge in her face. "But Thomas, they weren't throwing in my direction. I saw them. They were tossing stones up the pyramid, and they were too far off."

"Probably someone else then, causing mischief, and you got in the way. Good thing they didn't do worse. That stone could have done a bit of damage if it had hit you in the head," her uncle said. He patted her shoulder. "Are all you right?"

She nodded.

"Well, then, let's return to the ship. I'll tell the steward to find you some ice for that bruise," he suggested.

But as they left, heading for their donkeys, Thomas saw the look of trepidation did not leave her face. She was terribly ashen, as if someone had indeed tried to do far worse.

Jasmine did not sleep well that night. In the morning, she woke and went to the shady deck at the boat's stern. Cane chairs with pretty blue-and-white striped cushions were arranged around small tables perfect for serving tea. A smiling steward brought a steaming pot and a china cup. Steam curled into the air as he poured her coffee.

As she watched a felluca drift lazily northward past their docked steamer, she heard footsteps on the deck.

"Good morning, Jas."

She glanced at Thomas. "Hullo, Caesar. Why are you up at this hour? It's dawn."

"I couldn't sleep well. Too preoccupied with thoughts of those dastardly fellows hitting you with stones in a far more sensitive place."

Thomas took the seat next to her, a hank of dark hair hanging onto his forehead. In his ecru suit, chocolate brown tie and stiff white collar, he looked wonderfully polished, even at this hour. Of course dark stubble shadowed his jaw, contrasting the elegance of his attire. Jasmine's heart beat a little faster at his nearness and the searching look he gave her.

"A sensitive place? Do you mean my bottom? That certainly *would* have hurt," she said.

"I meant your head, Jasmine. It's quite odd that it happened. The more I thought about it, the more I realized those boys couldn't have done it. They lacked sufficient strength to throw a rock that hard, as you said. You were too far away."

Precisely her feeling, but she didn't want to add to his disquiet. Voicing her fears might give her uncle pause, too, and reason to send her home.

"You're thinking too much for such a pretty morning. The

boys probably ran up, tossed the stone and thought it a merry prank. I wasn't hurt much," she said.

"You could have been seriously hurt."

He became quiet. The steward returned, but Jasmine waved him off, not wishing to disturb Thomas's pensive mood. Silence stretched between them as he stared at passing sailboats. When she looked at him again, his mouth was set.

"What are you thinking of, Thomas?"

A haunted look in his eyes twisted her heart. For a moment she thought he would not answer. A shadow chased over his features.

"I was thinking of how brief life is."

He seemed so tormented and lost, she wished she could offer comfort. Insight struck her. "Are you speaking of Nigel?"

His eyes closed briefly. "Yes, quite."

"You were very close?"

"Actually, yes and no. We were close in childhood, then he became an utter bas—sorry, rude boor. That changed again—the day you hit me, remember?"

Despite his somber tone, she smiled. "Of course."

"We weren't good mates, but became close in an odd way. Rivals, you might say. He was always trying to best me. I think, when I look back, that Nigel brought out my best. Forced me to strive harder, be more diligent—the competitive edge. He once told me I'd let him down too many times because I thought more of my horses than my family."

He studied his hands. Such strong, square hands. Not the elegant, smooth hands of an aristocrat, but sturdy hands accustomed to physical activity. A long, ugly pink scar ran the length of the back of his left hand. Jasmine had never noticed it before.

"I thought he was jesting, but he took my new mare that night. Then I lost him all over again, the night in the park. He should never have ridden there. They brought him back to the house, he was a terrible mess, bloodied and in pain, but I insisted on seeing him. He apologized. God, he told me he was sorry for stealing my horse. I told him to sod off, why the hell was he riding at that hour?"

Jasmine held very still. "What did he say?"

"He told me he'd been there seeing a woman."

Her heart raced. Oh, dear God, did Thomas suspect anything of her?

"I see. Did he say anything else?"

"No. He fell unconscious, and that was the last I saw him. The doctor told me they could not control the infection, and it killed him."

Thomas stared at the water. "He could be a right boor at times, but he was my brother. My only brother. I miss him. I try remembering all those times we fought, but it does no good. I still miss him dreadfully. Sometimes, when I'm alone in the house I can almost hear his laughter. And then I catch myself and realize I'll never see him again." Bitter grief laced his tone.

The breath caught in Jasmine's throat. *I'm sorry,* she cried out silently. *Oh God, Thomas, I'm so very sorry. You were nothing like him. How I wish I'd known!*

"I promised myself when he died that I'd do everything to protect my family from harm, see Mandy happy. I let Nigel down; I wasn't about to do the same to anyone else in my family." Thomas dragged a hand through his hair, ruffling the dark waves. "So you see, Jas, my family comes first. They always will. Family is everything."

"I see," she said, the awful ache in her chest increasing.

She'd abandoned her family, her mother and stepfather. Her half brother and sisters were left behind. Here she was, sailing toward another family, her origins. Thomas's intense loyalty left her feeling bereft.

Desperate to divert the conversation, she turned to Egypt. Somehow she managed to distract him by asking his impressions of the sights they'd taken in so far. Thomas gradually relaxed, and even became animated.

The steward interrupted. "Lord Thomas is joining me for breakfast," she informed the man, who nodded and silently vanished. Thomas looked at her, the anguish gone from his face.

"I am?" He sounded amused.

"Now you are."

"Ah, the lovely Jasmine giving me orders. Like a Nile queen, commanding all in her presence."

"Cleopatra breakfasts with Caesar on the Nile. I thought it fitting."

They laughed, and Jasmine distracted him further, asking about his initial impressions of Egypt. She listened in fascination as he talked with animation about the ruins they'd seen and the history of the step pyramid.

"You know far more than I do about the place of my birth," she mused, sitting up as a bevy of stewards set a table before them with a white linen cloth and began laying dishes down.

They chatted as they enjoyed fresh oranges, eggs, toast and coffee. A hint of evening chill lingered in the outside air. Thomas spread orange marmalade on his toast and ate a slice. She gave him an impish smile.

"What a terrible sweet tooth you have. I suppose it was you who ate all the dates our steward left out for us after dinner."

"Guilty," he said, winking. Jasmine watched his tongue slowly lick stray marmalade off his lower lip. Drawn to his mouth, she studied it with growing arousal. Oh, how she knew the taste and texture of that full lower lip, and the skill employed with every caress of his tongue as he'd kissed her. To feel his mouth pressed upon hers once more, the warm authority of his lips claiming hers . . .

"Jas? You're staring."

Flustered, she returned her attention to her eggs, spearing them with vigor to hide her embarrassment. When she looked up, she saw him studying her with equal intensity. Then he caught himself and looked out at the Nile.

As the rising sun nudged aside the violent pink streaking the sky, sounds of the boat engines started, the incessant churning disturbing the harmony of the quiet morning. The ship's bell clanged rudely as the whistle blew. Paddlewheels churned the Nile into white, lacy froth.

Passengers drifted onto deck and glanced at them. A handsome young man she'd seen at the hotel pointed at Jasmine, waved and smiled. Jasmine smiled and waved back.

Thomas gave her a disapproving look, and the youth a scathing one. The young man hastily walked away, and Thomas tracked him with his gaze like a lion defending his pride. The sight amused her. He was very territorial.

"It's very rude to point in an Arabic land," Thomas noted, sipping his coffee. "But of course most Europeans and Britons wouldn't know it, or respect other cultures' dictates. They'd merely consider it societal eccentricity."

Jasmine stopped buttering her toast. "You sound disdainful of your own people."

"Disdainful? I adore Mother England. But seeing how some of her children behave while abroad makes me cringe. Respect is courtesy in any land. Have you noticed how the English treated the Egyptians in Cairo? Don't you remember that incident with the flower vendor?"

She did, and it troubled her, although she had expected nothing less. The pretty, slender flower vendor selling roses and jasmine on the street below the hotel always had a bright smile for passers-by. When Jasmine, Thomas and Uncle Graham were departing the hotel for the cab that would take them to the quay, they saw the girl try to press a rose upon an Englishman for his wife. The man had blustered and told the girl, "Get away from me, you filthy, ignorant beggar."

Crimson-faced, her uncle had bought the flower vendor's entire stock. It now perfumed their staterooms, the delicate roses and jasmine scattered throughout their chambers in makeshift vases.

"Not all English treat Egyptians so vilely. The Morrows are quite fascinated by them, and so are the Hodges. They've fit nicely into the life here. The Morrows are even discussing moving here permanently." Jasmine had taken an instant liking to the couples. Their hearty laughter and undiscriminating natures attracted her, as did their willingness to include anyone else in their circle, regardless of race or class. They based entrance on personality, not peerage.

"True. They've benefited from years of wintering abroad and are more broad-minded than most. A decent sort, even if socially they don't quite fit into the top tier."

Curiosity consumed her at his casual remark. "What do you mean? Are you indicating the Morrows and the Hodges are not . . . acceptable among your social circle?"

Coffee cup halfway raised to his mouth, Thomas paused. He looked thoughtful. "I've always viewed them more as business acquaintances, and I seriously doubt they would be welcomed among my friends and family. The Morrows are relatively nouveau riche. Edward came into money when he married Marian, and her father employed him as vice president of his insurance firm. Edward's father worked on the docks. He doesn't have any family of note. The Hodges are more bourgeois, but Mattie Hodges was divorced from some German, I believe."

Laughter brittle as glass fled her. "And here I thought you were becoming less of a snob."

He looked startled.

"Among Egyptians, you're not, but to your own countrymen you are. You treat all Egyptians fairly, but divide your fellow Britons into classes like a cook slices a roast. Are they all round or square, slotted neatly into categories according to your perceptions of class?" Jasmine softened her tone. "You keep proclaiming to me that you are not like your friends. But you are when it comes to class distinctions and family background. The brush you use for painting takes on increasingly darker strokes."

His dark brows knit, as if he didn't like this conversational thread, but she persisted. "Should you transplant Edward Morrow permanently to Egypt, bundle him into a *galabiyah* and paint his face darker, I daresay you would be more accepting of his lack of background than you are now."

Thomas's face reddened and his jaw tightened. He set down his coffee cup so hard it rattled the silverware. "You certainly are quite opinionated about my opinions, Jasmine."

"Only because I care, and I see in you the ability to shatter preconceived ideas about English class distinction." She had taken a leap of faith mentioning it.

His jaw continued to work, and he appeared to struggle for words. Then he merely stood and gave her a curt nod.

"The coffee is too strong for me, and I promised Amanda a letter. Good-day, Jasmine."

Not the coffee, which tasted delightfully rich and hot, but her tongue. Jasmine sighed. His firm tread indicated his displeasure. She hadn't meant to strike at the heart of his prejudices with a such a sharp dart, but had seen no way around it. Criticism, even if intended kindly, was not easy to digest for such a proud man. Especially a proud heir to the peerage.

Could he ever change and see reason? Or, for that matter, could she ever learn to live comfortably inside her own skin, dark as it was? Jasmine winced at that thought. Time enough to ponder it later. At the very least, she could relax here, knowing no one would mistake her for a trollop. Or worse, try to kill her with more thrown stones.

The day passed in a disquieting blur. Jasmine spent most of it writing an article about her first impressions of Egypt.

Thomas avoided her, except when they shared tea with Uncle Graham. The duke filled that empty silence with observations of the Khamsin tribe. He wisely avoided asking why Thomas and Jasmine weren't speaking.

Dinner that night was strained. Jasmine concentrated on observing the occupants sitting at the round dining tables, noting which ones would add to her article. The dining room was opulent, as were its richly-dressed guests. Gold tasseled cords pulled back crimson velvet drapes. Brass gas lamps added a soft glow to the room. Waiters in red fezzes and red sashes around their white *galabiyahs* efficiently wended their way about as they served. On the room's far side, men in turbans played soft music.

Much later, when the boat docked for the night after dinner, Jasmine worked up sufficient courage to quietly ask Thomas for a private word. Giving her a guarded look, he followed her to the upper deck. Lanterns swung on hooks attached to the posts, casting the deck with a soft golden glow. Moonlight splashed over the striped chairs and cast a silvery glint on his gray suit. The cheep of crickets on the nearby bank and the cry of birds overhead added to the Nile's exotic romance. Jasmine did not feel romantic.

"I wanted to apologize for my bluntness."

If her words surprised him, he gave no indication. Thomas folded his arms across his chest and said nothing.

Jasmine inhaled sharply. "I don't apologize for what I said, because I meant it, but the way I said it was too sharp. Like my tongue, which I have trouble guarding at times. I didn't mean to castrate you."

His brows furrowed. "I think you meant castigate," he pointed out. "A reprimand, not what the Bedu do to male horses not suited for breeding."

Oh, dear. Red suffused her cheekbones. Jasmine put a hand to her face. "Er, I am sorry. Sometimes I mix my metaphors."

"It's quite all right. I assure you, I'm not in the least danger of either."

A twinkle lit his green eyes. Relief filled her as she realized he felt more amused than insulted. He laced his hands behind his back and began to pace.

"Indeed, I've given much thought to what you said, Jasmine. There is some truth to it, and sometimes the truth is difficult to look square in the face."

So, he did take her words to heart. And that meant, just maybe, he could change. *If you will, I will,* she promised silently. *I will accept whatever I find at the al-Hajid camp about my real father, and embrace the truth, as hard as it may be.*

"It takes courage to admit that," she told him.

"Not so much courage as shucking one's preconceptions," he said ruefully. "I suppose it is far easier for me to treat other cultures with equality than my own. The standards I was raised with still lurk beneath the surface. Like crocodiles, they can prove quite difficult to stop."

"Then pray to Sobek, the Egyptian crocodile god," she suggested, wanting to lighten the somberness of his expression.

"A pragmatic action, indeed," Thomas agreed. "What I'm trying to say, Jas, is that I shall try harder in the future to look at everyone with the same eye, no matter where they hail from."

Giddy with happiness at his very real smile, Jasmine felt like dancing. She actually twirled, her skirts flowing out. "Use the eye of Horus, for it is all-seeing and protective."

"I will try, Jas—if you will try as well."

She halted, searching his face. "Try what?"

"Try to run to your heritage instead of from it. Speak Arabic, not just to the servants, but to Graham and me. Change your dress." He gave her violet skirt a pointed look. "See what it's like to be an Egyptian instead of striving to be English. You might find you like it."

His request disturbed her, for he'd somehow seen her inner turmoil. She longed to explore her culture, but felt restricted and shy before the English and Europeans. The challenge felt like new territory, and she had no map to guide her. But Jasmine never backed down from a challenge.

A compromise, then: "I will try, but only when we arrive at the al-Hajid camp. Then I will speak Arabic and perhaps even dress as the women do. And you will do what you promise. Agreed?"

"It's a start. I agree. Let's seal the promise," he suggested.

She stuck out her palm, but Thomas did not shake it. He took her hand and pulled her into his arms. "I didn't mean a handshake," he said softly, and kissed her.

Madness and moonlight. His lips were warm and firm on hers, and she trembled in his arms. One kiss swept her on a tide of growing passion. Tunneling his hands through her hair, he cupped her head. His mouth claimed hers fiercely, like a warrior staking a prize.

You are mine, the kiss declared.

Her knees felt wobbly as erotic pleasure shot through her. This was dangerous, out in the open, anyone seeing them. Remembering what transpired in the hotel, she murmured a protest against his mouth. Thomas released her, his eyes dark and a pulse racing in his neck.

"I think I'll retire to the salon for that game of chess your uncle promised."

"And I think I need fresh air, a stroll about the boat."

He drew in a deep breath and touched her cheek. "Be careful. The captain informed me crocodiles abound in this section of the river. They'd make quite a nice meal of you."

"Don't worry. I made a special petition to Sobek. I'm protected."

"Sobek is highly overrated when it comes to modern-day reptiles. Do be careful, Jas." He kissed her cheek, a mere whisper of a kiss, and left.

She remained still a moment, struggling to regain her composure. After a minute, she strolled on the deck, staring at the stars blanketing the night sky. A wild sense of daring filled her, a desire for adventure. Thomas's kiss made her giddy with anticipation of possibilities.

She peered over the railing into the water slapping against the boat as it floated up the Nile. Moonlight mirrored the silvery waters. Sighing, she pondered the Nile and its deep mysteries. Egypt provided her with a long-evaded peace, far from the worries and frets of home.

Climbing the railing, she half hung over the side, peering into the inky depths. She tried seeing the history of the mighty river. Had her real father once sailed these waters? Had he ever stared at them in awe of their majesty and mystery? What had her real father been like, truly? Soon she would discover the truth. The truth might not be as pretty as she hoped.

Jasmine shivered, staring into the water. Peering over the side, she climbed the first railing, balanced herself, relishing the wind caressing her cheeks. Letting her imagination soar, she opened her arms wide, pretending she was a falcon majestically riding currents high above the Nile, free to explore unknown territories. Unburdened, unbound and uncaring whether she was a white falcon or a dark one. Color did not matter. Only the air and its currents did.

Wind teased her hair, lifting it and wrapping it around her face. She was just fully into her fantasy when someone pushed her from behind. Jasmine teetered for a minute, arms flailing wildly. Then, with a shrill scream she toppled over the side.

"Did you hear a scream?"

In the salon, Graham looked up from his book on Egyptology.

Sharp worry pricked Thomas. "Jasmine," he breathed. "I left her on the upper deck."

Wasting no words, he sprang up and dashed for the stairs. He ran up to the second deck, peering about for Jasmine. He scanned everywhere. No sight of her. Dread filled him as he glanced at the river. He called her name, his heart beating frantically.

"Help me!" The cry came from below.

He ran to the railing and peered down. Blood froze in his veins as he spotted a figure wildly thrashing about in the water. Jasmine. And her damnable heavy English clothing was pulling her down.

"She can't swim!" her uncle roared behind him.

"Hold on, Jas, I'm coming," Thomas yelled, tearing off his jacket and waistcoat and kicking off his shoes.

He grabbed a nearby life ring and vaulted over the railing. Warm water embraced him. He swam in strong strokes toward her. Thomas reached her and grabbed her about the waist. She coughed, clinging to him as he fastened her hands to the life ring.

"I've got you," he gasped, as his powerful kicks kept them both afloat. "Calm now, Jas, I've got you. Can you kick off your shoes?"

"T-trying," she said through chattering teeth.

"Hang on to the life ring and kick your legs in the water, it'll keep you up."

A sputtering cough answered him, but she did as he directed. Relief filled him as the boat's engines churned to a halt and the steam whistle blew. Men appeared like magic on the deck, pointing and shouting.

With powerful strokes of his legs, he kept them afloat as he fumbled for the waistband of her skirts.

"W-what are you doing?" she gasped.

"Getting rid of this damn skirt. It's weighing you down." But his fingers were clumsy as he fumbled with the fastening.

"I-I'll d-do it," she stammered. Jasmine reached around, undid her skirt and struggled to get it off. She wriggled free.

Keeping an arm about on her waist, Thomas began swimming in sidestrokes toward the boat. He grimly concentrated on the lights like a beacon cutting the inky blackness. He was still yards away when a terrified shout from the boat turned his blood into ice.

"Crocodile!"

Chapter Fifteen

Thomas stared, stupefied, at the long cigar shape silently gliding in their direction. His heart dropped to his stomach but he kept a cool head. Calm, he said silently. Stay calm. He kicked furiously, dragged back by Jasmine clinging to him. They'd never make it.

"I need your help. Kick your legs out behind you. Like scissors. Hard as you can," he told her.

On deck, he saw Graham point a rifle. Shots splintered the water, one hitting near the crocodile. Thomas began a series of long, sure strokes. Jasmine aided with fast, furious kicks of her legs.

Men appeared at the boat's lower deck with a rope. They tied one end to the railing and tossed the other into the river. Thomas handed the rope to Jasmine, giving the order to hoist her up first. As she reached the deck, two burly men lifted her over. Thomas followed, collapsing on deck beside her.

Though the river had been warm, a chill dropped over the night and she trembled violently. Droplets clung to her dark hair. White cotton stockings rolled down from the force of her kicking showed slender, shapely calves below her soaked chemise. Fear clouded her large dark eyes, then it vanished as a brave smile touched her mouth.

"For someone purportedly so ex-experienced in removing w-women's clothing, you were t-terribly inept," she said in Arabic.

"Only in water when Cleopatra herself has fallen from her barge," he answered softly, brushing back a strand of wet hair from her cheek.

He became uncomfortably aware at her state of undress, the thin blouse plastered to her body, barely concealing the generous round breasts. Her hardened nipples were clearly demarcated. Thomas swallowed hard. Men nearby looked at her with avid interest.

"Stop staring and get her a bloody blanket for God's sake, before she freezes," Thomas barked at the curious bystanders.

Someone tossed over two thick, warm blankets. He pulled one across her shoulders, then took the other and wrapped it about himself.

"I suppose a prayer to Sobek, the crocodile god, did help after all," she said, huddled under the blanket.

He studied her. "What were you doing that you ended in the river? Didn't you hear me warn you?"

He didn't care for the guarded look shuttering her expression. "I was a-admiring the water, and I g-guess I fell in."

"You guess you fell in? You, the woman who never gets tossed by a horse, even the wildest Arabian?"

Her large wide eyes regarded him. "Maybe . . . I think someone might have bumped me."

Suspicion flowered inside him as he gently hauled her to her feet. Her uncle slid an arm about her, rubbing her briskly.

"Let's get you into a hot bath, sweetheart," Graham said, giving Thomas a thoughtful look. "I think you need to warm up first."

But Thomas wasn't about to let it go. Not until she answered his question.

"Jasmine, did someone *push* you overboard?"

Droplets clung to her long lashes as she peered up at him. "Why would anyone hurt me? I'm of no consequence. None at all."

No further incidents marred their voyage. Jasmine kept quiet about the incident, excusing it as an accident. But she knew better. Someone had pushed her overboard. She didn't dare think about what might have occurred had not Thomas saved her. In every shadow she saw possible enemies. The English who languidly sat on lounge chairs on deck, observing her with lazy gazes. The Egyptian servants with their polite smiles. Anything was possible.

She breathed a sigh of vast relief when they finally reached al-Minya. On the docks, as their trunks were unloaded, two indigo-draped men stood waiting. They wore long coats reaching their thighs, loose indigo trousers tucked into soft leather boats and indigo turbans. A vague memory tugged at her as she studied the taller man, with his handsome, black-bearded face.

"Khamsin warriors," remarked Thomas quietly. "I believe the tall fellow is Jabari, their sheikh. Quite an honor."

With a wide smile, Uncle Graham descended the ramp. He hugged the men, who hugged him back with equal affection. The duke introduced the pair to Thomas, who shook their hands. Jabari, the Khamsin sheikh, and his Guardian of the Ages, Ramses. The guardian was the sheikh's bodyguard, Jasmine dimly remembered.

"Jasmine, look at you." Ramses spoke in English with a thick desert accent. The warrior's friendly grin did not put her at ease. He swept her an elegant bow and kissed her hand in a courtly gesture. "All grown up. You were such a little thing, with a fondness for lemon drops."

Her smile felt stiff. Dignity was necessary. She did not want Thomas to know her origins, or where her mother had found her. Living in a brothel!

"I prefer my lemon with tea now," she said with a digni-fied smile.

The Khamsin sheikh kissed her cheek and lightly clasped her hands. "Jasmine, you look exactly like your beautiful mother. How is Badra, and your father?"

My father is dead, she wanted to say, but she murmured politely that both were well.

"Do you remember me, Jasmine?" he asked in perfect, ac-cented English. "You were but a small girl when you stayed with us. You were so fond of the horses and clamored to ride them, you said living in the desert was like heaven if you could only be among the horses."

Oh God, this would be harder than she'd imagined. All her English dignity and dress and efforts crumbled to the ground like dust. She didn't dare glance at Thomas, knowing he must conjure the image of a small, brown-skinned girl running wild among Arabian horses.

"Yes, of course." She tilted up her chin.

Jabari gave her a long, thoughtful look, glanced at the very English Thomas in his wide-brimmed hat, khaki suit and brown silk tie, and smiled. "And so the girl has become a very beautiful woman, a mirror of her mother and the England you now call home."

She flashed the sheikh a grateful smile. He winked at her, so quickly and furtively one might think it was dust in his eye. Small wonder his people adored him so; he was powerful and kind, and quick to assess a difficult situation and smooth it over.

The sheikh escorted them to a nearby home of one of Ramses' relatives. Sitting on comfortable chairs, they refreshed themselves with cool glasses of tea and a meal of sandwiches while awaiting the arrival of several porters and camels to escort them into the desert. Uncle Graham and Thomas went to freshen up.

When they returned, Jasmine recoiled in delighted surprise at her uncle. Instead of his English khaki suit and white, broad-brimmed hat, the duke wore an outfit exactly matching that of Jabari and Ramses. A lethal steel scimitar and a curved dagger hung from his belt. He still looked as distinguished as if he wore a suit.

"Uncle Graham, you're Khamsin again!"

"Part of me always will be," he replied in Arabic. "There's a reason for this. I'll be more readily accepted and respected for my judgment in horseflesh like this than as an English duke. Jabari warned me that the newly-elected sheikh of the al-Hajid does not trust Englishmen, who are infidels and foreigners. While Thomas here will make the sheikh think he's getting the best of the 'infidel,' I'll be the one bargaining him down."

Thomas smiled lazily and fingered a rifle slung over a broad shoulder. "Saves the Bedouins' honor while not costing me dearly. While my trusty English rifle helps keep away the scavengers."

Jasmine traced a line of condensation on the glass. "Uncle Graham, do the al-Hajid know who I am?"

"They only know you as Miss Jasmine Tristan, daughter of Viscount Arndale. I thought it best and told Jabari and Ramses as well. If you wish to inform the tribe otherwise, then by all means, do so."

Sensing Thomas's keen gaze, she murmured, "No, it's quite all right. It's for the best."

They left the house's cool clay interior as trunks were loaded carefully onto the camels. Uncle Graham gave a quick lesson in mounting the dromedaries. Jasmine hung on as her beast rose to its feet. It felt familiar, as if she'd finally come home.

Yet, this was her home no longer. Where did she belong?

Jabari told them the journey would take a few hours, but they would take rest stops. Bobbing with the camel's rollicking gait, Jasmine stole a glance at Thomas. Gone was the distinguished nobleman. He'd shed his jacket and waistcoat, now looking shockingly improper. In white shirt with the sleeves rolled past his muscular forearms, and khaki trousers and sturdy leather boots, he resembled an explorer. The rifle tucked firmly into a leather holster on his back fit the severity of his watchful expression.

His protectiveness warmed her, and yet the reason for it frightened her. Whoever had pushed her over the railing must be those notes' author. The threat had somehow followed her to Egypt.

Enormous sandstone and limestone cliffs surrounded them. Boulders washed down from the mountainsides from past floods scattered throughout the canyon. Signs of animal life cropped up infrequently; a gazelle shyly grazing at a green brush, a hyena loping off in the distance, a quail roosting in a stubby tree.

They rode through deep limestone canyons for a long while then stopped to rest. Uncle Graham, Jabari, Ramses and Thomas talked of the horse-breeding business, the European market and bloodlines, as they sat on boulders and sipped from generous goatskins of water.

Jasmine turned to Thomas, his handsome face serious and searching beneath the shade of his broad-brimmed hat as they started off again. "Have you read anything of the desert people of Egypt?"

He flicked a fly off his camel's neck. "Quite a bit. Some of it seems rather biased, so I am curious to see for myself." Thomas nodded toward Jabari and Ramses, who were leading the way. "They seem dignified, fierce chaps, unlike the Bedu described in some travel brochures."

"Such as *Cook's Tourist Handbook for Egypt, the Nile and the Desert*?" Jasmine searched her memory. "Oh yes, the Reverend T.W. Chambers, quoted in the book, described the Bedouins as—how did he put it? 'Rude, ignorant, lazy and greedy.'"

Thomas's mouth flattened. "Such comments are made by individuals who think themselves superior to all other cultures. They arrive with pre-conceived notions and don't care to change their assumptions. I daresay if they saw a colony of industrious, well-educated Bedu they would think the same. From what I've heard of the Khamsin and other desert tribes, they're the ones who value what is most important in life, and they have great honor and pride."

Warmth filled her. She wanted desperately for him to like the desert and its people. It meant possible real acceptance of her culture and heritage.

They neared the camp as the sun began setting, blanketing

the mountains with deep violet and saffron hues. Purple shadows deepened on the distant cliffs. At last they reached a clearing in the deep desert. Tall date palms scattered about the dusty sands, along with acacia trees. Sparse outcroppings of yellow and green vegetation showed life in the desert. The camp was entrenched on a long stretch of flat plain nestled between rough ridges of mountains.

A scattering of black goats'-hair tents enticed her. Jasmine dismounted and stared at a woman weaving colorful fabric on wooden looms. Older men sat smoking cigarettes, lounging lazily before their tents. In the distance, a boy herded a flock of sheep. The boy's sharp cries to the sheep, the clatter of the wood looms and the men talking filled her senses.

All the inhabitants glanced up and let loose what sounded like a war call, but she instinctively knew was a welcoming greeting. The desert also called to her, sang with its sweet music of searing heat, sun and sand. *This is my father's land, my father's people.*

Hot sun warmed her skin, and a gentle breeze billowed her skirts. She felt a sudden urge to release an ululating yell back. *It must be in my blood*, she realized with delight. *Here I belong, at last.*

"Once the al-Hajid numbered over one thousand," Jabari, the Khamsin sheikh, said softly as he dismounted and stood beside her. "But now they are reduced to little more than four hundred. This camp holds the last—less than one hundred. Most have already departed for villages along the Nile. Ever since Nahid died, they have lost heart. Nahid was Elizabeth's uncle, and their last sheikh powerful enough to keep the people united."

"How did he become sheikh?" she asked.

"He was elected after Fareeq . . . died." Jabari's face tightened as he stared into the distance. Ramses put a hand on the hilt of his sword. Jasmine immediately sensed this was sensitive territory.

And yet, she would find out more, such as how her father died. The fact they did not call Fareeq her father, but referred to Kenneth as her father, said enough.

Hiding her thoughts behind a smile, Jasmine gestured to the pack of writing papers and pencils she'd brought. "It's good I'm here to record their history. I'm eager to write about their nomadic lifestyle. I'm certain the battles they fought were fierce and many brave men died fighting them."

"And I'm certain no one else will die—not while I keep watch."

Thomas said this as he shouldered his rifle and removed his hat. Sunlight glinted in chestnut highlights in his dark hair. His strong jaw looked as determined and harsh as the rock mountains surrounding them. Ramses rested a hand on the scimitar at his belt.

"There is no need for you to arm yourself, Lord Thomas. The people here are at peace and have no enemies. They have few possessions for desert raiders to covet, and we will see to your safety."

"I thank you, but I'll keep my rifle close at hand. I'm certain you understand I have a need to keep certain valuables protected at all times." His gaze flicked to Jasmine.

A slight smile quirked the sheikh's mouth upward. Uncle Graham and Ramses exchanged knowing glances.

Jabari introduced them to the newly appointed sheikh of the camp. Yusef Rasmussen was a short, lean man in his late sixties. His gray-bearded face held dignity, despite the shabbiness of his red and black robes. He barked a sharp order to a middle-aged woman in a black robe and with a black scarf covering her dark hair. She sat on the ground, rocking a goatskin bag back and forth on a small wood stand, but rose at his command.

Like an obedient doll, she came to his side. Yusef introduced her as his wife, Warda. She was a silent, careworn woman. She barely addressed the men, but her sharp gaze assessed Jasmine's English dress and large, lacy white hat.

"My wife has been with the tribe since birth. She will be most happy to tell you any information you desire, English lady," Yusef told Jasmine. And with that, he dismissed her presence and walked toward Jabari, Ramses and her uncle. The irony of Yusef calling her "English lady" amused Jasmine.

Thomas raised an eyebrow. "Yusef thinks you are a lowly woman who fails to understand the quality of fine Arabians, and I am too white and foreign to appreciate anything other than a donkey. Your uncle, on the other hand, is a true Bedu who can judge fine horseflesh."

"We'll simply have to prove him wrong. You and Uncle Graham were quite right in assessing how tailoring makes the man. He makes a dashing warrior, doesn't he?"

"Perhaps. But I'd rather spend my time admiring someone else much more lovely," Thomas murmured in Arabic.

Warmth filled her at his compliment. His heated gaze swept over her like a lingering caress. Jasmine reminded herself to keep a distance; she was here to work.

As the porters unpacked their belongings, the sheikh escorted them to three large canvas tents. Colorful, soft carpets covered the ground, and the interiors were furnished with tables, chairs and low beds. Ramses explained the furniture had been brought from the Khamsin camp to make the visitors comfortable. The Khamsin would assist the al-Hajid with negotiations and use the profits from the horse purchases to begin their new life on the Nile Valley.

"Why are you being so good to them when they were your enemies?" Jasmine asked. "Why not buy their horses and sell them yourself at a greater profit to my uncle?"

"Our code of honor honors their people," Jabari said qui-

etly. "It is my wish they retain their dignity as they leave the
land of their ancestors. Such a move is difficult enough for
them."

"And for you as well, I imagine. The disbanding of a great
Bedouin tribe leaving only their memories behind is a great
loss of culture and custom." Thomas surveyed the camp.

"Indeed." Jabari nodded. "Jasmine, you serve an important
purpose here in taking their oral histories. It will be the only
record of their people."

"Jasmine, if you wish I can help you with the translations
from Arabic to English. I can easily divide my time between
that and cataloging their stock of Arabians," Thomas volun-
teered.

"Let me assess the situation first," she demurred.

She didn't want Thomas's involvement. What if her worst
fears were realized and her father was indeed the beast her
stepfather and mother claimed? Jasmine could not bear him
discovering her ugly past, for the present could turn ugly
enough.

Dinner was served beneath a carpet of brilliant stars. Sparks
from crackling campfires rose and danced on the air. Though
Yusef had tried to make Jasmine eat with the women,
Thomas insisted she sit with the men. Yusef gave grudging
acceptance to "the white man with the big rifle," much to
Jasmine's secret amusement.

A large round platter filled with lamb, rice and tomato
sauce and wedges of flatbread sat before them. The old customs came back with alarming familiarity. Dipping a wedge
of flatbread into the pan, she scooped up the lamb and rice,
eating with her fingers.

Sitting nearby, Thomas did the same. He seemed as comfortable here, among these desert people, as he did in the ballroom waltzing.

"Surely many in society back in London would be horrified

to see you dining thus, Lord Thomas. What, no silver knife and fork? Heavens, I'd rather starve!"

He wiped his mouth with the back of one hand and grinned. "They would indeed, sitting straight as arrows, their wasting skeletons an outcry of defiance. They would warble a dying cry as defiant as a warrior's call to war: 'Hetty forgot the tablewear, and I shan't eat one bite until I have my linen napkin and my silver!'"

Jasmine laughed, feeling happier and more relaxed than she'd been since the Nile accident. No threats had followed her here. Thomas's protectiveness made her feel cherished. His constant awareness, the way he held himself with a quiet, confident manner, made her very aware of the muscle rippling beneath the white linen shirt, the very masculinity of him. He did not need the scimitar or the warrior's garb of the desert Khamsin; the steely green in his eyes and his air of natural authority sufficed.

A cool breeze caressed her cheeks. Jasmine shifted, restrained by the heavy English skirt as she sat on her knees. Her glance flicked over to the al-Hajid women and Warda. In their loose, billowy kuftans, they looked far more comfortable.

She was not changing into desert attire. Not yet.

Dinner ended with honeyed dates. As Yusef and the men talked quietly, the women rose to clear the meal. Jasmine studied the silent Warda. When in Rome . . .

Fit in. If she continued congregating with the men, Warda might not be as accepting or forthcoming. Jasmine turned to the al-Hajid sheikh.

"With your permission, sir, I'll leave you men to talk while I help the women clear the table. Perhaps your wife could use my assistance," she said in Arabic.

Yusef looked shocked, either at her request or her command of the tongue. Thomas grinned in apparent understanding. "Good show," he murmured in English.

The sheikh gave a dignified nod and rapidly informed his wife. Warda only nodded.

As Jasmine went to follow Warda to where the women were scrubbing dishes with sand, Ramses followed her. The handsome warrior seemed very serious as he called for her to wait. She studied him, suddenly very uncomfortable.

"You are not merely offering help, but wish to strike a bond among the women to begin your questions, am I not correct?"

At her nod, Ramses' voice dropped to a whisper in English. "Jasmine, you need to know something before you begin your questions. I assume you are also curious about your father, and want to glean information about him. What he was like, how he ruled."

Her mouth went dry. Jasmine nodded, a little sickened by his uneasy expression.

"My mother . . . told me things. I wish to discover the truth for myself."

"You need to know this. What I tell you is not easy for any daughter to hear, but you must understand . . . Jabari once threatened to kill any offspring of Fareeq's, for he was so evil he did not wish any of his children to live," Ramses said quietly. "He did not mean you, Jasmine, for he loved your mother like his own sister. But ask questions hoping to find a good man beneath the surface of the bad one and you will be grievously disappointed."

"My father—surely he had some goodness in him," she whispered. "You did not live among these people, you were their enemy when he ruled."

"True, I was their worst enemy. Worse than Jabari—and better-looking, of course." Ramses grinned crookedly, a charming smile that did not quite dispel his previous words. His grin faded. "Be careful, Jasmine. The truth is not always what we wish."

His words echoed those of Mr. Myers, the publisher who

wanted only to sell papers. In her case, she wondered if it would hurt worse than any conjecture her vivid imagination could conceive. With assurances to Ramses that she could handle whatever truth she discovered, she set out to find Warda.

The campfires before the black tents had died to glowing embers. By a kerosene lantern, Jasmine scribbled madly in her notebook. Warda and other women had welcomed Jasmine's offer to share chores, and she gained their trust through easy chatter in Arabic. Dressed in a brilliant rose kuftan, her long hair unbound, she listened as they talked.

The women shared the rich history of the al-Hajid. They were known to possess the finest Arabians, the fiercest warriors. Jasmine listened and wrote, hiding a smile. The Khamsin would dispute Warda's extravagant claims.

Yusef's wife sketched the air with her hands, illustrating great battles of the past and the history of a proud desert people. How her husband became elected as sheikh and made the difficult decision to shepherd his people to live along the Nile in greater prosperity.

"Our people once ruled the desert, always raiding the Khamsin. Now we are reduced to few, and must seek a different path for our children. Our way of life will vanish forever. But we were once strong and mighty and powerful."

"Led once in the past by a mighty sheikh? I have heard of Fareeq and how powerful he was."

Warda's sad expression became hard as granite. A shiver snaked down Jasmine's spine. The other women rose and murmured excuses about retiring for the night. Jasmine saw she had touched upon a very sore subject.

"He was powerful," Warda said; then she looked about and arranged her fingers in a gesture Jasmine recognized. A sign to ward off the Evil Eye.

"He was well-respected," Jasmine hinted. "A mighty, powerful sheikh who led his people to victory."

"I have nothing more to say." Warda rose gracefully, the folds of her black abbaya flowing about her. "If you wish to know of that one, you may ask my husband."

Jasmine bid her good-night, and Warda left as silently as she had entered the tent. She tapped the pen against her chin. Gathering her notebooks, lantern and pen, she went to find the al-Hajid sheikh.

Yusef sat before his tent, smoking a hand-rolled cigarette. Smoke wended upwards in delicate blue swirls. The red tip glowed in the darkness. He ignored her until she spoke in low, perfect Arabic.

"I am here to record the history of your people, and publish what I am told in great newspapers in England. What I know is only this: Fareeq was the most powerful sheikh to rule the al-Hajid. If you wish to dispute that claim, you will talk with me. Otherwise, I'll print exactly that."

The elderly man sputtered and coughed. Jasmine smiled serenely, and hung the lantern on a tent pole hook. "I'll take that as a yes." She sat on the carpet, arranging her clothing about her, and opened her notebook. The sheikh made a sound of disgust and crushed out his cigarette.

"Your words are wrong, English lady. Fareeq was a vile, cruel man who delighted in crushing both his enemies and his own people. Every day I thank Allah he lives no more. Nor do any of his sons. They would be cursed." Hatred sparked his gaze. "I would curse them."

Her heart dropped to her stomach; Jasmine bent her head over the pages, her long hair hiding the shock on her face.

"Do you really believe his . . . offspring would be like him? Is that a reason to hate them?"

"A man that evil is like a rotten pomegranate. He passes evil on in his every seed. Such seeds must be destroyed to prevent more ill fruit from being sowed. It is why his concubines and wives vowed never to bear his children, or so it was said after his death." Yusef fell silent for a moment. "My wife was one of his concubines. He longed for a son, and she and the others rejoiced in denying his greatest wish."

Her heart went still as Yusef's voice dropped to an ominous note. "Except for one woman, who defied the pact. She delivered a child. A small, delicate girl child who looked too weak to live."

A violent trembling shook her hand. Jasmine hid it by gnawing on her pencil as if in thought. "Do you know what happened . . . to the girl?"

"She was sold, thankfully removed from our sight. I do not know if she still lives. I pray she does not. Her mother left. I thanked Allah the day she did. She delivered evil into our midst."

"Evil?" Jasmine echoed.

"Any offspring of Fareeq's is destined to become evil." Yusef again made the sign against the Evil Eye. Lamplight flickered in the aging, rheumy eyes. "Nothing can save that child from being like her father. If she still lives, in time she will turn as foul and vile as he. This I know. Such a child would be better off dead. Indeed, such a child is better off not born at all."

Jasmine retired to her tent, kicking off her little gold sandals. Leaving the thick black goatskin entrance rolled up, she shuffled across the thick, richly colored Oriental carpet. Wind billowed the silk curtain guarding the entrance. Moonlight glinted upon a silver salver upon a low round table. The quarters were lush, exotic and fascinating as Egypt herself.

Egypt. Her birthplace. And her birth father . . . Jasmine sat on the bed and buried her face in her hands. Cursed. Evil. Vile. How glad she was Uncle Graham had not informed anyone of her real origins! For if Yusef felt this way, and the women feared to mention her father's name, what would the others say?

"Jas?"

Recovering her composure, Jasmine pasted a smile on her face and pulled aside the silk curtain. Thomas stood outside, hands jammed into the pockets of his khaki trousers. Silver moonlight gilded the chestnut highlights in his hair. His tall body looked powerful, a quiet and assured presence. The top two buttons of his shirt were undone, allowing an enticing view of the dark thatch of hair on his chest. Fascinated, she stared.

"I stopped by to say good-night and check on you. Is everything well? How did your interviews fare?"

Terrible. The sheikh here thinks I'm the very devil. Perhaps I am. "Just fine. I'm fine. Thank you. Good-night."

Those terse words uttered curtly changed his mood. He stiffened. "Very well. I'm in the next tent, if you need me for any reason. Good-night."

He started to turn when she suddenly didn't want him to go. She hastened to add, "It's frightfully . . . quiet isn't it? After London, I mean."

White teeth flashed at her in a charming grin. "Quiet? With the dogs barking, the horses snorting, the wind rustling through the mountains and various assorted other night sounds far more distracting? I can't sleep."

All those but the last she ignored as easily as if she lived here. Jasmine wrinkled her brow. "What other night sounds?"

"Sounds I would not mention in polite company, especially to a lady. A young, unmarried lady. The music of the night."

Jasmine frowned at him and cocked her head. "Just because I'm not married . . . oh!"

A tell-tale blush raced across her face at the same time she heard the sounds. Rustling cotton sheets. Bodies moving. Quiet sighs and little whimpers. A man's deep moan and a woman's shrill cry.

"It's beautiful, is it not? The language of love, the melodious music of the night. In any culture, the words may not be the same, but the sweetness remains," Thomas said quietly, his gaze affixed to her face.

"I wouldn't know," she muttered, her emotions all in a jumble at his intense look.

"No, you would not. Not yet. Trust me, Jas, when the time comes, you will know. And know it well."

His statement created such emotional pain for something she wanted so dearly, but could never have, that it was better to deny such longings. She was the bad seed, as Yusef had darkly alluded to when he talked of Fareeq. Who would want to marry the daughter of an evil man?

"It will never come for me. It's not natural. It's animalistic," she declared, hating how she sounded so priggish.

Thomas arched one dark brow. "Trust me, little flower, it's quite natural and normal for men and women. If not, why would the instinct be so overpowering? You've seen your uncle's prize stud being bred. Did it not seem pleasurable to the stallion?"

"I daresay the mare might argue," she muttered. "At least the ones I've seen . . . Oh good gracious, will you stop smiling at me like that?"

"Like what?" he asked in a teasing voice.

"We're not discussing horses, but people. And I think we'd better stop discussing this. Matings are not for polite company or gentlemen. . . ."

"When it comes to this particular topic, I'm no gentleman."

The words were there in the open, bold and assured. Jasmine drew in a deep breath.

His meaningful smile made her blush as he touched the tip of her nose. "Good night Jas. Sleep well. You look lovely in that kuftan. Very feminine."

Muttering a hasty good-night, she hurried back to her bed. Jasmine climbed between the cool, smooth sheets, but tossed and turned. Sleep seemed impossible. Sounds she'd easily dismissed before now haunted her. The naughty images he'd placed in her mind, naked bodies writhing against each other.

I'm no gentleman.

And I'm no lady, she thought, putting her palms to her hot face. Goodness, what will become of us both? And, he's in the very next tent? A thought she was afraid to explore.

Jasmine closed her eyes and drifted to sleep, dreaming of stallions and mares, desert moonlight and magic.

Chapter Sixteen

The next few days Jasmine saw little of Thomas, her uncle and the Khamsin men as they inspected horses. Her time evolved into a regular routine with the women. She took meals with them, helped with chores and sought out Warda. Learning the culture, how to make yogurt from goat's milk, how to weave bright fabrics on the wooden looms, she eased herself into the al-Hajid life like a swimmer testing cold waters. Her patience was rewarded when Warda began smiling and even briefly mentioned Jasmine's mother.

"She was a sweet child, quiet and brave. I looked upon her fondly, and was happy when she left our camp for a more peaceful, happier life with the Khamsin."

But when pressed further, Warda changed the subject.

Jasmine planned to coax answers from other men. Her father's warriors might voice a different opinion, once she convinced them to talk.

The opportunity came when Alimah, a shy younger woman, asked if Jasmine wanted to meet her grandfather, Halim. Alimah brought her to a tent where a gray-haired man wearing a black turban and distinguished black and red robes sat whittling a piece of wood. He smiled fondly as Alimah approached.

After introductions were made and Jasmine accepted the usual polite offering of sweet tea, she casually mentioned the tribe's past. She took copious notes on the elderly man's animated discourse on fierce battles fought over grazing rights and desert raids, and when Alimah excused herself to prepare the evening meal, Jasmine addressed the burning issue.

"You served under Sheikh Fareeq, the last sheikh before Nahid?"

Halim fell silent. His gaze dropped to the wood he'd abandoned. The elderly man picked up the carving with a tremor not previously seen.

"What was he like, Fareeq? I've heard a few talk of him, but I need a noble warrior's opinion," she pressed.

Wood chips sprayed as he guided his sharp steel knife across the olive wood. Jasmine waited, watching him chip away at the intricate grain like water wearing down stone. Like water, she had patience. She would wear him down.

At last he spoke, his voice filled with such bitterness that she drew back as if he were about to strike her.

"Fareeq was a jackal, a devourer of rotting flesh. His own men knew him as a coward, never a noble warrior. He had no respect for any man, nor had any respect for him."

Wetting her lips, Jasmine recalled tribal law. "But he was sheikh. The sheikh of such a great tribe surely was admired by his people—or some of them—for he was elected into power."

"He stole power. Threatened those who opposed him, and any who challenged him for the position disappeared into the night like rain into sand." Halim's lined face looked pained. "Do not ask me any more questions of the past, honored lady from England. Fareeq is dead and has met his destiny."

Still, she could not help but ask, "Are there other men who served under him? Perhaps they remember differently."

"Those who would were as corrupt and vile, and they are long dead. Allah be praised, we have long had peace since Fareeq died. Perhaps we should have rested in it sooner had he not kept us fighting with the Khamsin."

"Fareeq may have been a tyrant, but he kept the people together. What can you say now, all of you scattering like dust in the wind to the Nile? Your history lost, your culture gone?"

"Allah wills all things must change, and so as he wills it, we go. But we go with peace in our hearts, and our history and our memories will live on in our children's children. For

Fareeq I express gratitude, for upon his death we received a new life, and will not die here in the desert, our bones bleached by the sun, our children sold into slavery. Our friendship with the Khamsin has sealed our fate, and with the money we receive from selling our horses, we will forge a new path and make a new history."

Our children sold into slavery? Jasmine shivered. The philosophic words offered no comfort. No one remembered her father with any kindness or respect. He lay somewhere in the desert, his bleached bones forgotten, his memory despised. The thought sent such sadness through her that she choked back a sob.

But I am not as evil. Or am I?

Tormented by the thought, Jasmine managed to thank the elderly man for his time. She left, deeply troubled. Her stepfather had warned what she sought might not be as appealing as she'd wanted. How she wished he were wrong!

As she walked to her tent, Jasmine glanced up to see a group of women studying her with dark eyes. Expressionless and unemotional. Did any of them guess she was the daughter of the sheikh they despised?

Deep in the desert, at the secret breeding grounds where the tribe kept their horses, Thomas became absorbed in the fascinating history of the Majd al Din line. He read over the notes he'd copied from the al-Hajid's breeding book. With these, he'd maintain the purebred's history, a history certain to become lost when the al-Hajid scattered along the Nile. The breeding book not only contained the record of the Arabian's descendents, but anecdotes about each sire and dam. Thomas found the stories far more revealing than the statistical bloodlines.

Nibbling on his pen, he lifted his gaze skyward. The desert was harsh and unforgiving but there was great beauty here, and clean simplicity in the starkness. Jasmine was descended from this tribe. He'd overheard her uncle talking quietly with Jabari in English so as to not alert the al-Hajid.

Purebred in her own right, Jasmine was a thoroughbred as much as the horses. Yet she would not claim her heritage, the duke had grimly informed Jabari. To do so meant admitting a legacy she requested remain private. The knowledge saddened him. She must believe people in England would find out, and it would become more fodder for mockery.

This camp put them physically closer than ever. From his own tent, he could hear her restlessly tossing in sleep, making small whimpering noises. Her distress ripped him apart, yet he didn't dare comfort her. Doing so would stir the passion he kept in check.

Nearby, mares descended from the great line cropped yellow patches of grass in a wadi. A stone well and a wood trench were nearby. Jabari, Ramses, Yusef and several men were tending to the horses. Al Safi, the great stallion, was guarded zealously by two men armed with rifles and scimitars. The black stallion's coat gleamed in the sun. Mares already in heat were kept in a separate area, ready to be mated.

Despite his English manner and dress, these desert men had accepted him. His command of Arabic was impressive, and his knowledge of horses had earned him respect. Here in the simple life of the Bedu, he found an easy peace lacking in England.

A shadow fell over the page he'd just copied. Shading his eyes, Thomas glanced up to find the duke. "Come on, Thomas. We're leaving. You need to take a rest from that work."

Thomas stood and stretched, carefully tucked away the breeding book into his rucksack. "I suppose I've managed to while away a bit of time. Fascinating history, this breed. The pedigree is astounding. Al Safi is descended from the finest stock in Arabia. Did you realize his great-grandfather was a champion racer? Small wonder Nahid guarded him with such care. I first doubted reports where he housed Al Safi in his very own quarters during the harsh winter nights, but it's all recorded all here. I suppose he treated his wife with far less consideration."

"Nahid loved his wife, but she was not as fiscally important to the survival of the tribe as Al Safi." Graham smiled as they mounted their horses, joining Jabari, Ramses and a handful of al-Hajid warriors.

Thomas checked his compass as they rode north. When he asked their destination, Graham only offered a smile. Finally, after an hour's ride, they reached a flat plain that looked no more notable than the land they'd left behind. A few scattered trees offered slim shade, but the small bubbling spring hidden behind a cache of large rocks promised refreshment.

"It's the warrior initiation grounds for the al-Hajid," the duke explained as he dismounted. "A tribal secret, soon it will lie abandoned. The Khamsin and the al-Hajid are gathering to mark the last time the al-Hajid will use this land for battle. I thought you'd like a real taste of desert life."

Other warriors dressed in Khamsin indigo greeted them. Dismay filled Thomas as he watched Jabari, Ramses and the duke strip to the waist. Clad only in trousers and boots, Graham was bare-headed and bare-chested. The duke picked up two steel scimitars. Sharp steel flashed ominously in the brilliant sunlight.

Thomas looked around and realized all the men were bare-chested. With a sinking feeling, he managed a smile.

"A scimitar requires a different skill than the foil you're used to, but I'm sure you'll do fine. You can work with me," Graham told him, handing him a blade.

Steel clinked against steel as warriors began dueling with each other. Jagged towers of limestone cliffs surrounded them like giant's teeth, solid, ancient and menacing as the men fighting with scimitars.

The steel held no fear for him. Taking off his shirt did.

Thomas tensed, unwilling to bare his scars before these warriors he admired. In the dark of night when he felt the erotic caress of a lover's touch across his back, and questions arose, Thomas always held a ready excuse for his scars. Inflicted during a fight with a callow bully during his youth who wielded a horsewhip, he would say. His lover would cry out in abject horror, and he would weave more lies: His opponent bore scars from Thomas's equally skilled fists.

In truth, his father had not one single mark on him.

Here, among these men of the desert, who valued honor and whose lips told only the truth, he didn't want to lie. Shame poured through him. *My father horsewhipped me.*

"I'd rather not," he said, handing the scimitar back to the duke.

Graham did not take it. "Well then, strip to the waist, sit on the sand and watch. One rule exists here, we are all equal on the battlefield."

Thomas shook his head. "I should return to camp. I must skin those hares I caught for dinner."

Graham gave him a long, searching look that seemed to penetrate his very soul. Thomas felt uncomfortable.

The duke swept a hand over the men fighting with swords. "You see all of them? Ramses, there, fighting with Jabari. He has battle wounds more than any other, and he boasts of them. But do you know his deepest scar that he refused to admit for a long time?"

Despite his apprehension, Thomas was intrigued.

"He's part English," the duke continued. "Admitted to me himself how he hid his heritage for the longest time. He was ashamed because he wanted to be as Arabian as the others."

Shock filled Thomas. As he studied the warrior with interest, the man's long dark hair flew out as he dueled with his sheikh.

"Even Jabari has scars. I have many. I daresay each man here has scars in some form or another. Some scars are deep and internal. They are invisible to the eye. But with time, and the love of a good woman . . . they do heal. Trust me," the duke said quietly.

A brief flash of haunted pain entered Graham's eyes. Thomas understood then: some were harder, but all wounds could heal.

He drew in a deep breath, slowly unbuttoned his white shirt. Sweat plastered the cotton fabric to his skin. Thomas drew it off his shoulders, tension tightening his muscles.

The shirt fell to the sand. Bare-chested, he faced the duke as he summoned all his courage and picked up a scimitar. Deliberately he turned, so the nobleman would have no choice but to see the fat, ugly stripes marring his flesh.

"Let's have it, then," he said in a strong voice.

Graham circled around, facing him. "I think you will make a worthy opponent, Lord Thomas."

With a swift, graceful move, Thomas whipped the scimitar out, slicing through the air. "Splendid weapon. Very lightweight steel, yet an efficient blade, I'm sure. Shall we?"

He engaged the duke with far more ferocity than anticipated. After several minutes, his footwork becoming surer on the rocky, pebbled sand, Thomas began to enjoy himself. Other men ceased their swordplay and watched him. He felt the heat of their critical gazes.

And didn't give a damn.

"The white-bellied English has war wounds of his own," he overheard one warrior say.

"He is not an English. A *samak*, a white-bellied fish," Ramses shot back. "He is one of us now, an honored warrior."

Thomas felt a quiet sense of pride. He was one of them. Even scarred, with war wounds from a different kind of battle.

Dear Readers: Today I awoke to a stunning sunrise peeking over a cascade of tall, jagged black mountains.

Soft murmurs of mothers crooning to their babies, the sounds of cooking pots rattling, indicated the start of a new day. The life here is simple, yet the people have a deep communion with the land and its harshness. They almost have become part of the desert as much as the sand, rock and wind. Like the desert, the Bedu can be fierce as the heat or gentle as the soft sigh of a breeze brushing against your face.

In the shade of her tent canopy, Jasmine sat on a folding chair writing her article. Her heritage. Her people. Yet she did not feel at one with them. Especially since the people had loathed and feared her very own father.

Her mother's people were lost, for they had sold Badra when she was eleven. Then they vanished like the wind, following ancient caravan routes. For all she knew, her grandparents were dead. Part of her felt grateful, for what could she say to people who sold their own flesh and blood into slavery?

She wondered about the upcoming visit to Davis's excavation with the Andersons, about the articles she would write. How much easier it was to make an historical dig come to life for readers with minute details of everything from what the diggers wore to Mr. Davis's own observations, than recording her own people's history. Emotions cluttered her mind here, making it much harder to be impartial.

Familiar voices sounded nearby. Jasmine glanced up to see the Khamsin sheikh and his bodyguard. They washed their faces at a basin on a table outside the sheikh's opulent, many-poled tent. Laughter rippled from the pair. Bitterness encased her. They laughed, while inside she wanted to die a little.

She had to ask the question plaguing her, so Jasmine went to the sheikh, who dried his face on a clean towel. Ramses silently nudged his friend, giving her a guarded look.

"Jabari, I would speak with you. Alone."

The sheikh nodded at Ramses, who walked away. Wind

flapped at the silks billowing at the tent's entrance. Jabari gestured to fat silk cushions on the carpet set beneath the tent's shady canopy. Nodding her thanks, Jasmine sat as he joined her.

She wasted no words. "I need to know how my father died." She gave him a meaningful look. "My real father, Fareeq."

Jabari stared into the distance, his long fingers resting on his sword hilt. Finally he turned, and looked at her with his deep, penetrating gaze.

"Jasmine, why do you ask? Is it not enough that you know he is gone? That your mother has found happiness at last with Kenneth, her true love, the man who has raised you and is more your father than the one who sired you?

"No. It is not."

Tension tightened his jaw line. Jabari tilted his head back and sighed, a sound like the desert wind whispering over the shifting sands.

"Then I will tell you. But you will not like the truth."

Too many had told her the truth was ugly. She folded her arms across her chest. "I will be the judge of that."

Jabari nodded. "Very well then. Fareeq and I were sworn enemies, vowing to shed each other's blood. One night he kidnapped my wife, Elizabeth, in a desert raid. With a loyal band of warriors, I pursued him. There was a battle, and Fareeq and I fought." The sheikh drew in a deep breath. "He lost."

Jasmine stared. "*You* killed him?"

"Yes. And it was a merciful death. More than he deserved."

Ignoring the sickening feeling that warned the sheikh was being diplomatic, she pressed on. "How can you say that? Warriors fight in battle and die, and deserve to do so with honor for their bravery."

"He was not an honorable man." Jabari's dark eyes narrowed. "When I rode into the camp, I found my beloved tied to a stake, Fareeq with a whip in his hand. He was flogging her." The sheikh's lips pressed together in a flat line. "He was horsewhipping my beautiful Elizabeth, and for no other reason than he enjoyed beating women. Just as he did to your mother."

"Maybe, maybe . . ." Her father could not have been that despicable. "Perhaps my mother did something to deserve it. And Elizabeth was your wife, the wife of his enemy."

Fury filled the sheikh's brown eyes. He seemed to struggle for control. "Do you dare insult your mother? Badra was a sweet, innocent girl whom he stripped of innocence and whipped for his own pleasure. She escaped and begged me to take her as a concubine. When she came to me, she was terrified of men. All men but Kenneth. Through his love, she learned to trust again. Fareeq had stripped away more than her flesh. He stripped away her spirit."

Jasmine's mouth worked as she struggled for words. "But . . . he was . . ." The words finally tumbled out, in shaky syllables. "My f-father."

The fire died from the sheikh's gaze and his expression softened. "Not in the true sense. He only sired you; he did not give you love and was not your true father. Not like our Kenneth."

But his blood runs in my veins. She lifted her chin. "I heard you threatened to kill any of his offspring, should they live, because you vowed his seed would not flourish."

Jabari reached over and lifted her chin with his calloused palm, his smile sad. "Men say things they later regret, little Jasmine. I said it to Kenneth before I discovered your existence, and I will state it now for your ears alone: Your dear mother is like my very own sister, for I took her into my family as one. Therefore, you are my niece. How could I do harm to my own flesh and blood, my family?"

Her tremulous smile did not reach her heart. *Your words offer no comfort, Jabari,* she thought. *Every family has its black sheep*

and I am far blacker than any you have known. I am his daughter.
Fareeq, your greatest enemy. The one all deem wicked.

Am I equally so?

"You are my niece, Jasmine, and under the protection of my tent, always."

"Thank you, sir," she said with a dull smile.

Jasmine left, shoulders straight and proud, despite her anguish. She concentrated so on looking forward that she didn't notice Thomas until he gave a gentle nudge. Contentment radiated from him. With shirt sleeves rolled up to reveal strong, tanned forearms and his khaki trousers, he appeared more at ease than she did in her Bedouin attire.

"Hullo Jas. Lovely evening. Why the glum face?"

"Glum? What gives you the right to say that? I'm happy, damn it."

Emotions tumbled out of her like water spilling from a dam. She bit her lip and looked away. "Please excuse me. I should rest."

As she went to pass, he reached out and very gently grabbed her arm. "Jas, what's wrong. Come now, tell me. Is someone ill treating you? Tell me the culprit's name and I shall thrash him."

Thomas looked grim, as if he wished to punch the person. She nearly laughed, imagining him engaging in fistfights with the great Khamsin sheikh.

"I thank you for being so gallant. But it's nothing."

She could not let him know the truth. Her father was despised by everyone, even those in his own tribe. The daughter of a vile despot. Stained by her father's despicable actions.

Jasmine changed subjects. "Tell me of the horses. Have you had much success recording the breeding book?"

He gave her a long, thoughtful look, as if ascertaining her reasons for diverting the conversation. "The pedigree is pure, and I've ascertained small anecdotes that will illustrate each horse's personality and traits as well as the Bedouin lifestyle.

Those are the facts I've sought, in both oral histories among the tribe, and records kept by former sheikhs. When I breed the mares with Al-Safi and then sell the foals, I'll include the pedigree and that information for the buyer."

Pedigrees. Thoroughbreds. While she was the daughter of a despot. *My own bloodlines are tainted.* "And as an Englishman, what do you think of the Bedu's own pedigree? Jabari and Ramses, as well as the al-Hajid."

"Jabari seems a good sort, a chap I'd gladly fight alongside, as is Ramses. They are as noble as any titled Englishman."

Could he really mean it? If he did, perhaps there was hope for her as well. The thought anguished her so much that she squelched it. His sort in England would never regard the desert people as noble. Thomas could not change that.

"Your peers would find such a remark quite insulting. The barbaric savages are noble? Heavens no, they're bloodthirsty and heartless, and will never be as civilized anyone from Mother England."

He sighed at her sarcasm. "Stop it, Jas."

"I'm only pointing out the obvious. Desert people will never be considered as anything but savages by the English peers. Their heritage is lower than the dust on their sandals."

"Their heritage is proud, just as your own ancestry is a noble one. Your true heritage, Jasmine. You should acknowledge it instead of running away from the truth."

My true heritage belongs in a grave with an evil man while yours is that of a titled peer respected by all.

She bit her lip. "Acknowledge I belong to people seen as barbaric savages by your set? I give an easy enough excuse for society to mock me again. Jasmine, the Egyptian, all nicely catalogued then shelved and forgotten. Your kind slaps a marker on me, just as they do with everything in Egypt. The pyramids, the Nile, the Bedu, Jasmine the Egyptian. We're all down there, and you look at us as if viewing us through one of Mr. Breasted's stereoscopes. Fascinating! Absorbing! But foreign, and then you tuck us away carefully into a box, left to gather dust in a forgotten corner of some attic."

Her voice dropped. "Even you, Thomas. Would you dare to be seen with me openly in England with your friends? I think you would ignore me because I lack breeding. You said in the hotel, when we—you didn't care about my reputation. Why? I know why. Because I'm not in your class, and not the sort you should marry."

Fury snapped in his eyes. Thomas pressed forward, forcing her to step backward until they were sandwiched between the lee of two tents. Gone was the urban civilized gentleman. Replacing him was a savage, ruthless man as primitive as her own ancestors releasing wild cries while galloping into battle.

In this more private area, he unleashed his anger.

"Damn it, Jas, what must I do to prove I'm not like them! You cluster everyone together as if each Englishman were the same. In truth you are as damnably prejudiced as those you disdain. Even me. Instead of seeing me for who I am, you label me as neatly as my friends have done with you. You assume, and that is the heart of all prejudice."

Jasmine put up a protesting hand, shaken by the depth of his feeling. But he was far too incensed to stop.

"I've tried, by God. I've tried to erase the damage I did to you in the hotel. I'm only a man, a man who was carried away by his feelings. God! I've never, ever felt that way about a woman before. You take me and spin me about like a bloody top. I apologized. I didn't mean to insult you, but I would have said anything to keep going, to have you in my arms. Do you understand? I would have charged a bloody brigade of armed warriors."

He dragged in a breath and continued pressing toward her until she backed against a tent wall. "You frighten me, Jas. You scare the bloody hell out of me because outwardly we're so different, and yes, you're not the sort I should marry. But all I can think about is you. When I'm with you I want to toss aside everything that matters to me—the title, my family, my own damn heritage—and throw it to the winds. I'd do anything to keep you with me. It's madness, sheer madness, but I can't stop, and I will not run from it or you. Not anymore."

A violent trembling shook his hands as he clenched them into fists. "When I'm with you, I feel set free for the first time in my life," he said hoarsely. "And I want you with me, but you still mistrust me and doubt me. Why, Jas?"

The brutal honesty of his confession undid her. Her lower lip wobbled precariously. She felt dangerously close to sobbing. Something dawned in the depths of his eyes. Thomas cupped her face with his hands. His touch was absolutely gentle, as if he cherished her. His thumbs brushed the edge of her eyes where tears threatened to spill over.

"Ah, I think I see now. Jas, it's something else, isn't it? It's not just me or my kind you're railing against . . . it's your father, isn't it? Your real father, the former sheikh of this tribe. He's the reason you're upset."

Shock held her immobile. Jasmine struggled to regain her lost composure. Oh, bloody hell, he knew despite her silence. Jerking free from his touch, she wrapped her arms about herself.

"I'd make a horrid actress, wouldn't I?" The shaky laugh did little to disguise her distress. "How long have you known?"

"Only since yesterday, when I overheard Jabari and your uncle talking—in English, so I doubt many others know."

"Then know this. I've yet to find one damn person in this tribe who remembers him with a degree of fondness, let alone respect. They all praise the heavens that he is buried." She looked away, trembling with rage and pain. "He was my father. Condemning him, and his memory, condemns me as well."

"Jasmine, you are not your father," Thomas said softly. "Who you are is not defined by who sired you."

"It is in England. Your sire defines you, for you're his heir."

His gaze grew distant. "But I am not my father, and will never behave as he did."

"And I am not my father. Yet his blood flows in my veins. And—" She halted, unable to give voice to the deepest fears inside her.

Thomas did it for her. "You fear that he was as despicable as they claim, and that you will be as well? Little flower, any fool can sire a child. It takes a real father to raise one. I daresay the viscount is more your father. Didn't he teach you kindness and respect? You wouldn't have learned those attributes from the sheikh."

Dropping his hands, he looked weary and resigned. "I never learned kindness nor respect from my father. He beat into me all that he valued, but fortunately he did not rule my life."

"We are products of our upbringing, our parents," she whispered. "We cannot change that."

"We can, if we wish. We're capable of change, Jas. If you want it enough. Do you?"

Filled with grief, she closed her eyes. She'd thought finding a smidgen of respect for her long-dead father would give credence to her recent actions. Her behavior was a hallmark of a strong, powerful individual who brooked no insults, just like Sheikh Fareeq. Her deepest fear had surfaced. Her father had been a vile beast and her actions mimicked him in writing the Blue Bloods column. Even justifying her behavior as revenge did no good. Instead of rising above her hurt, she'd sunk into the mire.

But she did not want to be like him. Ever.

"Where do I begin?" she asked.

"You may begin with me. Will you not give me merits to stand on my own, see me for who I truly am instead of judging me along with my peers?"

Jasmine wrinkled her brow. "And who are you?"

"Someone who sees you for who you truly are, Jas—a beautiful, intelligent woman. Not of any culture, ethnic origins or class. You are the rarest, brightest shining star in a dark Egyptian night, who outshines them all. The whole bloody lot of them. I should be proud to be seen in public with you, be it Egypt or England."

His intent gaze focused on her as if she were the only woman in the whole world. "Shall I dress in Arabian robes and strap a sharp sword to my side, I should still remain the same man. In Arabian dress or an English suit, I am Thomas, no matter what the culture, custom or manner of garb. In the end, isn't that what matters most? For that is how I see you. You are uniquely Jasmine, exotic, fascinating and charming, regardless of who sired you. I see inside you, the woman who is bright, shining and fierce as a thousand Roman candles, dimming all else in its brilliance. I would no more turn away from you than I am doing now."

"Oh, Thomas. T-truly?" she asked on a choking sob.

"Truly, little flower," he said solemnly. "You and I come from different worlds, but we can overcome them. My friends might like you if they got to know you better. But your acerbic tongue keeps at bay those who might change their mind. It's more lethal than Khamsin steel."

Rapidly she blinked away her tears. "I do often speak before I can think. It's as if the words escape my mouth and I wish to grab them all back and stuff them all in. I wish sometimes I lacked a mouth merely so I could better guard my words."

"Mouths are not only for speaking, but for other . . . enjoyable pursuits." Tenderness filled his gaze as he fixated on her mouth. Clasping her lightly by the upper arms, he drew her closer.

Her mouth watered in anticipation of his kiss. "I suppose it seems tremendously stupid of me to be agitated over what I can't control."

"There are many things in life beyond our control, and all

we can control is our reaction to them. We must master our emotions or they will master us. Anger, joy, guilt, regrets, sorrow . . . and passion."

He touched her cheek, his warm, calloused fingers a mere whisper of a touch that sent awareness through her like a firestorm. "Mastering passion may be most difficult of all. Perhaps, at times, even impossible."

Thomas felt as if they'd crossed a new, dangerous threshold leading to unknown territory. Understanding sparked between them, and with it, mutual acceptance of their differences. With acceptance all his feelings poured forth.

Her voice speaking Arabic was sultry, low and exotic. The language sounded musical and enchanting as it flowed from her perfect, rosebud mouth. Thomas found himself intoxicated. It *was* Jasmine. With the peacock blue kuftan billowing about her ankles, her dark tresses flowing past her rounded hips, and the henna-painted toes peeking out from fine gold sandals, she embodied mystery and allure.

Desire overcame him, a fierce longing as fiery as the bright yellow sun. He wanted to take her by the hand, lead her inside one of the billowing tents with its silk curtains, and lay her down on the soft Egyptian cotton sheets. He would love her with his mouth, his passion, until she cried out his name and he'd branded her soul with his possession.

It felt as if they were alone on an island surrounded by a sea of people. The sounds of cooking and laughter, conversation and life, dimmed in his ears. He focused solely on Jasmine, her exquisite beauty. The large, sloe eyes as dark as the Egyptian night. Her delicate cheekbones and finely tilted nose, the little chin and the smoothness of her honey-gold skin. His mouth watered to taste hers; as if she were a succulent date, he craved the sweetness.

Kissing her here would prove more foolhardy than kissing her in Hyde Park, however. Her uncle and the Khamsin were nearby. Yet, that didn't cease the restless yearning, the wild need to let the lusty beast out from inside him. And though he was an earl's heir not a savage, for a moment his hand trembled with the fierceness of his need.

Then he bent his head and took her mouth.

The kiss felt like the sealing of a promise and dawning of new possibilities. He poured everything into it: his turbulent feelings, the joy of being with her. Thomas drank her in, elated like a weary traveler coming home at last. Sunlight beat upon them, and the wind whispered around them. His arms tightened around her, crushing her to him. He only wanted to keep her close, safe from all harm, all taunts, and cherish her for the wonderful, beautiful woman she was.

His heart thundered as he deepened the kiss, thrusting his tongue inside her mouth. He wanted her in his bed, fleeting moments of pleasure where he could lose himself in her. Buried in her tight, wet heat, he'd feel free at last from social restrictions and conventions. He'd be himself, truly, as he slid his body over hers, losing himself and able to fill a little of the lonely emptiness inside.

Voices nearby broke them apart. He groaned in frustration and released Jasmine. Thomas straightened, reassuming control. His once rigid control.

"It's nearly mealtime. Yusef has invited us to his tent for dinner. All of us."

A shadow chased away the languid desire on her face. "Yusef and his wife? Must I? I believe I'll choke first."

He tapped her mouth with his index finger. "Manners, Jas. Remember that tongue of yours. You need not worry. The meal is shared at his tent, but I cooked it," he said, wondering why she seemed so reluctant.

Making a face, she stuck her tongue out playfully and bit it. He laughed, sorely tempted to do much more, his imagination conjuring erotic images of much more pleasurable pursuits.

"Very well. I'll see you at dinner. I do hope we have something much more appetizing than the tough mutton I've eaten," she said.

"Desert hares in a rich stew. I caught a few this morning," he said absently.

I know exactly what I would like to dine upon, he thought, gazing hungrily at her lush mouth. *But I suppose I shall settle for the hares.*

A soft, silly smile played about her lips as Jasmine went to her tent to freshen up before dinner. Inside her quarters, she washed her face and hands. Patting her face dry, she twirled about the tent. Thomas cared. He cared!

She wanted to shout the news to anyone within hearing, ride it on the winds like a wild Arabian mare. The kiss, oh, she'd felt it. His feelings could not be denied.

Was it even possible he loved her? One could only hope.

Dreamily, she looked at her reflection in the mirror hanging on a pole. A kiss-swollen mouth, a flush in her cheeks—it all betrayed her.

You're falling in love with him.

Jasmine pressed her hands to her burning face. *Yes, I suppose I am. What am I going to do about it?*

She went to sit a moment and ponder the thought.

But as she approached the snowy white bed, a folded note on her pillow caught her eye. Curious, Jasmine opened the crisp white paper. Shock reeled through her at the bold English words whose author had indeed followed her all the way to Egypt.

THE BROWN SCORPION WILL MEET ITS DESTINY IN DEATH.

Chapter Seventeen

"Jasmine, if you don't eat this excellent meal I've prepared, I shall take it as a personal affront." Thomas waved a hand before her face. "Jas? Hullo? Are you listening? Are you here?"

She blinked, managed a wan smile. "Yes, thanks. It's quite good, I just haven't the appetite right now."

"It fled when she saw you were the chef this evening, Thomas," joked Ramses.

"Faster than the hare itself," added her uncle. Jabari joined in the laughter.

No, my appetite is back in the tent, along with the note hidden in my trunk, she thought. *Who wrote it? Did the person trying to hurt me follow me here?*

Thomas did not laugh with the men. His gaze grew critically assessing. It felt as if he could see through her. He mustn't know. His protective nature would insist on sending her away to the safety of the village. But Jasmine could not leave. Someone here in this camp wanted her dead. If she ran, and kept running, she'd never find out who had left the note. She would never truly be safe.

To allay Thomas's suspicions, she took several scoops of the meat, sauce and rice. It smelled delicious but tasted like dry paper. Dry paper . . . with damning, threatening words.

Jasmine sipped her sweet tea. Inside Sheikh Yusef's enormous tent, they sat on the carpet upon lush pillows. A circular silver platter, big as a carriage wheel, was heaped with a stew Thomas had prepared from the desert hares he'd killed that morning. They sat around that.

Someone in the camp had threatened her. That made no sense. No one among the al-Hajid spoke perfect English. Had her enemy truly followed her into the deep desert? If so, how could he hide here, in the open? Fear filled her as she stared at the dinner. It could be poisoned.

Silly. Her imagination was running amok again. The note, though, was real. Too real.

Drinking her tea, she glanced around the circle. All seemed absorbed in conversation and eating. Except one. Yusef stared at her. Venom dripped from his gaze.

Startled, she nearly dropped her glass. When she looked up again, the sheikh was looking elsewhere. But there had been no mistaking the hatred in his eyes.

Thankfully, the meal finished. She lingered a few minutes while the men talked, and Warda cleaned up. Jasmine did not offer to help, but listened to the men discuss breeding the stallion. Then she politely excused herself and stood. After bidding them all good-night, her gaze remained on Thomas.

"Will you escort me to my tent?" she asked him.

Thomas stood, nodding good-night to the others. The ever-present rifle slung over his shoulder, he walked with her. The sight of the weapon provided a small comfort.

At her tent, Thomas paused. "Jas, whatever is the matter? You've acted so distracted tonight." His green eyes, filled with seriousness, seemed understanding. Jasmine capitulated.

"Caesar, please stay close by. I haven't slept well." Jasmine hugged herself. "I'm . . . afraid. Someone may be playing tricks on me. My real father . . . well, you've heard, I'm certain. He was not well liked, and I fear the feeling has spread to me."

"Who is it? Do you know?" Thomas's jaw clenched as he glanced about.

"No, I don't. And it could just be my silly imagination."

"Do you wish someone to spend the night with you? I can ask one of the women."

She laughed to dismiss her fears. "No thank you, Caesar. You're so kind, but it's the night and my too wild imagination, I'm sure."

He started to protest when she clapped a hand over his mouth. "Good night, and thank you for caring." Then Jasmine reached up and gave his cheek a light kiss. As she ducked inside her tent, she was quivering with emotion. That kiss meant more than he would ever know.

Inside, she blew out the lamp on the low table, shrugged into a white lawn nightgown. Barefoot, she went to the bed and tossed back the covers, then slid into bed, leaving the top sheet down, for it was too warm.

Many in this camp would hate her if they knew she was Fareeq's only surviving daughter. Labeled evil, condemned as such because of her sire. Just as English society labeled her as an outcast. She'd come here to find a home, or some connection, but even that had failed. Did she fit in anywhere? Was the person leaving the note warning her of an impending fate, or had it been meant simply to frighten her? She had to take it seriously. The peculiar and ominous reference to the Brown Scorpion was too coincidental.

Staring at the tent ceiling, she'd begun to drift to sleep when she heard a rustling noise. Jasmine blinked, too weary to lift her head. Probably a curious child, or merely the desert wind.

Something—so quiet it could be her imagination— seemed to move across the carpet. She heard a soft shaking sound, felt something on the top sheet. Instinct urged her to light the lamp at her bedside. Struggling against exhaustion, Jasmine sat up and did so.

Golden light filled the tent, chasing away darkness and revealing shadows in the corner. Shadows drifted across the bottom of her bed. They moved. It was a mass of scorpions, brown against the white sheet, and they crawled toward her.

Chapter Eighteen

Immobilized by fear, Jasmine stared. The scorpions sluggishly crawled up the bed toward her exposed legs. One reached her bare skin and skittered up her ankle. She stuffed a fist into her mouth as it crawled across her calf. Resisting the urge to flinch, she watched it pause; then the scorpion headed for her knee. Another navigated the top sheet and landed on her ankle.

Brown scorpions?

The irony was too much. Her assassin had followed her here, to this isolated place, to this haven where she had hoped to be free and safe from the outside world. Safe no longer.

Other scorpions followed in a dance up the sheet, waltzing north toward her body. A sting from one, she might survive. But surely not this many. Jasmine drew in a deep breath. She screamed for Thomas. Screamed his name with all her might.

Alarmed shouts followed and then the blessed, strong figure of Thomas. He tore aside the frail silk curtain, his dark hair rumpled, his green eyes sharp. Bare-chested and clad in trousers, he clutched his rifle.

"Don't come near. But Thomas . . . help," she rasped. "Scorpions. Many. On the bed."

"Oh God," he rasped. With brisk, blessed efficiency, he set down his rifle very carefully, and walked toward her with the grace of a panther. "Jas, sweet, I'm here, try not to move."

"As if I would," she choked out.

Noiseless as an assassin, he slid toward her and held out a strong palm. His assured, dear features were as comforting as a beacon in the dark night.

The tent door drew aside and her uncle and Jabari entered. Thomas held up a hand with natural authority. "Stop. Any movement may cause them to strike. I shall handle this. Be ready on my word."

Her uncle swore quietly as the sheikh nodded. Jasmine's muscles ached and burned with the effort not to move.

Reaching her, Thomas held out his hand. "Jas, dearheart, I know how frightened you are. I'm scared as well. Trust me. I'm going to take the scorpions off you on the count of three, and when I do, you jump and roll to the ground."

"You'll get stung!"

"I'm far larger than you. The venom won't affect me as much. My body can absorb it better."

Jasmine drew in a calming breath. "All right. I trust you. Please, Thomas, be careful."

His voice softened. "I will, dearheart. Now, one, two . . ."

At "three," his hands shot down, plucked the scorpions away. The tails lashed out, stung at Thomas. Bringing her knees to her chest, Jasmine dove off the bed and rolled on the floor. But her motion knocked Thomas backward, onto the bed, and the scorpions bounced upward. Three more landed on his bare chest and left arm. He yelled as they stung but rolled onto the floor.

Graham and Jabari pulled Thomas to safety. Ramses killed the scorpions, then took the sheet and balled it up, encasing the monsters in a makeshift bag.

Jasmine sprang to her feet, her body trembling, and she stared down at Thomas. On the carpet, he writhed, moaning in pain. He'd saved her. And he had paid the price.

Drifting in and out of a haze of pain, Thomas tossed and turned on the bed. Sweat dampened the sheets beneath his naked torso. His entire body burned. He writhed, wishing for a lake of ice, any damn thing to cool the stinging. Anything. Bloody hell, anything . . .

"Thomas, I'm so very sorry." Teardrops splashed upon his heated skin, cooling it. Thomas opened his eyes to see Jasmine crying over him. "It's my fault."

She bathed his brow with a cool cloth. He heard Jabari

murmur as more cloths were pressed to where the scorpions had stung. Thomas gritted his teeth and fought back the pain, but it washed over him in great waves.

"Is he going to die? We can't let that happen!"

"No, little Jasmine," Jabari's soothing voice sounded. The sheikh peered down at Thomas. "You are lucky, my English friend," he said, as if from a great distance. "The brown scorpion's stings burn, but they do not kill. You are young and your body is strong. The pain will pass, eventually, perhaps in a few hours."

As would pass the pain of not having Jasmine, though that pain would remain with him far longer, he thought hazily. How unfair life was.

"Thank you for the encouraging news," he muttered, wincing.

"Can't you do anything else for him? He's in agony!" Thomas felt Jasmine lace her slim fingers through his. He relished the contact, concentrated on it like a distant oasis in the burning sand.

"We are doing all we can," Jabari said.

Thomas's eyes unfocused, and he concentrated on the blur of Jasmine's lovely face hovering above like a mirage in the heated desert. He wasn't going to die; he'd just suffer like hell for a few hours. But seeing her care so much made him smile, for that was all he truly wanted.

Chapter Nineteen

A few days later, Thomas was on his feet and all seemed well, but no progress had been made on finding who'd put the scorpions on Jasmine's bed. She had shown the note to her uncle. His angry countenance and abrupt manner in dealing with the situation convinced her she was right in telling him. Yusef denied any of his people would want to hurt her, but he did admit that there had been other "English buyers" at the camp before their arrival. They had expressed interest in purchasing the al-Hajid stallion and vowed to have him, no matter what.

Jasmine did not tell anyone of her suspicions about Yusef. The elderly sheikh was far too powerful, and she had no proof. None at all.

Jabari offered to send his most trusted warriors to guard her. Jasmine refused. She didn't care if one hundred men guarded her tent, only for the only one who had saved her, the one who slept mere footsteps away.

In need of a diversion, she sneaked over to watch the breeding of Al Safi. Already purchased by Thomas, the mare would be shipped afterward to England, every precaution taken to ensure care for her and the foals she would carry.

The breeding was not for polite company, her uncle had told her, but when Jasmine joined the clustered group, no one said anything. She stood apart a little, watching, and Thomas joined her.

She looked at him anxiously. "Are you well enough? You should be in bed."

"Any more time confined to my tent and I'll grow very cranky."

"Thank you, Thomas, for what you did," she whispered. As an answer, he offered a grave smile. Then he turned his attention back to the horses.

Her uncle, Jabari and Ramses drifted over. They watched the stallion prancing as he whinnied to the mare. Jasmine flushed as she watched the stallion's penis grow erect. This was not as purely scientific as she'd intended. Not while Thomas stood alongside her, his big body radiating heat, his keen gaze riveted.

Naughty thoughts invaded her mind, but Jasmine pushed them aside, striving for solemn indifference. Still, the raw, wild beauty of the horses pulled at her, the eagerness of the stallion and the prancing mare, their coats gleaming in the sunshine.

"He's quite a stud," Thomas said calmly, as if discussing the weather. "Small wonder his pedigree has been revered from generation to generation."

"Small is not a word I would use in this matter, for Al Safi's most notable asset is far from small," Ramses said cheerfully, then he glanced at Jasmine and a charming flush filled his face. When the man muttered something about tending to the other mares and stalked off, Thomas chuckled.

Nervous as the mare about to be covered, Jasmine strove for dignity. It had been so much simpler when she was a young girl spying on the proceedings in the stables and didn't quite understand what transpired.

A warm hand squeezed her palm. Thomas. "Are you quite all right now, Jas?" he asked softly.

Was *she?* When he had been the one weathering the scorpions' burning stings? Filled with emotion, Jasmine could only squeeze back, grateful for his concern. *I am if you are,* she thought.

Thomas nodded, and turned his attention back to the stallion. The beast thrust violently into the mare, then dropped from her. Thomas said, "You know, it would make a fascinating tale, documenting the purebred bloodlines of Arabians who, in a sense, carry their tribe's history with them." He gave her a meaningful look. "Perhaps that's a topic you'd care to write about for your paper."

Seeing his point, Jasmine smiled. "I'll go fetch my note-books."

Inside her tent, she searched her trunk. Footsteps sounded behind her.

"I've got them here somewhere, just give me a minute—"

"You have not another minute," a raspy female voice said in Arabic.

Jasmine stood and turned, confronting the figure of Warda. The woman held a lethally sharp dagger and advanced. Cold sweat broke out on Jasmine's forehead.

"You're the one! You left that note on my pillow! And put the scorpions in my tent. I thought it was your husband."

"Men are too weak to do what must be done. I can see him in your face," Warda said calmly. "The mark of stubbornness, the firmness of your brow. You are *his* daughter—the one Badra bore, breaking our vow."

"And you tried to kill me!" Jasmine backed away, her gaze not leaving the curved dagger clenched in Warda's hand.

"The English paid me to place the scorpions. He gave me the note as well. They were to kill you, daughter of the evil one. I agreed to do so because your soul is black." Hatred twisted the woman's face as she spit at Jasmine, who leapt back in alarm. The spittle burned her cheek.

"I spit upon you, seed of evil. No good will come of you, for you are the living issue of wickedness."

Jasmine wiped her cheek with a shaking hand. "You liked my mother and was glad she found happiness with the Khamsin!"

"I rejoiced when she left our tent, the weak one. I was among the evil one's concubines. No sons or daughters would live to carry on his name. I hated your mother for birthing you. I hated her when she escaped Fareeq, for in his anger at her birthing a girl, he punished me as well, for it was my hands that delivered you. He sold me to a passing caravan. I returned to my people years later."

Warda birthed her, Jasmine realized with a sickening jolt. The very woman who'd brought her into the world now sought to end her life.

"You. Was it you all along? You hired someone to push me over the railing on the steamer. It was you."

Warda frowned and waved her knife. "No. But there are others who hate you equally."

The fear and misery gathering in her breast flowered until it mushroomed into a great cloud of haze, which Jasmine released. How she tired of people labeling her, ridiculing her, all without even knowing her. She'd had enough. And she also realized, suddenly, in a blinding flash of insight, that who her father was no longer mattered.

Tired of being judged and labeled by prejudice, she drew herself up. "You're ignorant and ruled by desert superstition," she breathed. "I am not my father. Nor my mother. I'm Jasmine, my own person. And I spit on *you,* you stupid woman who insults my mother. You won't get rid of me quite so easily."

Jasmine lunged for the knife. Her attack caught Warda off guard and she caught the woman's wrist, struggling for the blade. Warda expelled a stream of obscenities in Arabic, kicking Jasmine in the shins. Jasmine grimly hung on to her wrist, ignoring the pain.

With the heel of her hand, she delivered a hard blow to Warda's nose. The woman screamed and dropped the knife. Blood gushed from her nostrils. Jasmine grabbed the knife, dancing out of her reach.

"That was for my mother, you silly cow. She taught me that move, after my father taught it to her to protect herself from cowards like you who would hurt her."

"Your real father, Jas," a quiet voice said behind her. Jabari.

In back of Warda, the Khamsin sheikh, several of his indigo-draped warriors and a very grim Ramses surrounded Yusef's wife. The al-Hajid sheikh came forward, looking pale and very old. Anguish filled his face.

"I apologize for my wife," he said in halting English. "She has dishonored my name and my house. I did not know . . . She will be punished."

Jasmine's stomach gave another sickening twist as she imagined the type of punishment awaiting Warda. "No, don't. She's not right in her head. Please."

"All will be well, Jasmine," Jabari said softly, his gaze fixed on Warda. "I will see to it. Go now with Thomas."

Thomas appeared. He gently grasped her wrist and eased the knife from her shaking hand. "Come now, Jas." He tossed the knife down as they left the tent.

Jasmine found herself shaking. If Warda had not tried to kill her on the steamer, it meant someone else had. And that person was still out there. Who was this "English man" Warda had mentioned?

She still shivered, and Thomas slid an arm about her, escorting her to his tent. He lit the lamp, remained at her side as she collapsed onto a chair. A few minutes later, her uncle came, looking distressed. He hugged her tightly.

"Good God, Jasmine . . . that woman." The duke kissed her cheek and set her back, searching her face. "Are you all right? Did she hurt you?"

"Not as much as I hurt her, uncle." Her shaky laugh cloaked her distress.

"That's my girl," Thomas said softly.

"Did you get anything out of Warda about the Englishman who paid her to put the brown scorpions in my bed?"

Graham frowned. "All she said was that it was dark when she met him. He dressed like an Arab, but spoke with a foreign accent in English, and he was short. He arrived with the party of people from England who wanted to purchase the al-Hajid's mares and stallions."

Disappointment filled Jasmine. No answers then. No more than before.

The duke ran a hand around his collar. "I'm afraid I must leave you. Jabari and Ramses want me to escort Warda tonight, out of camp to Cairo and a special institution where she may receive help. I've offered to pay for her treatment, and they require my influence."

"It's very generous of you, Caldwell."

The duke shook his head. "No, Thomas, it's merely my way of making peace with the past, and healing any damage that bastard Fareeq inflicted. It comes with a price, of course. I've bargained Yusef down on the hefty price he had for Al Safi. Yusef is a sly one. Through Warda I discovered he'd been arranging to sell him twice, once to me and then would steal him away to give to the English people who'd been here before we arrived. In return, I'll keep the matter quiet and not press charges. When Warda is released, she'll stay in Cairo."

Jasmine's uncle gave Thomas a long look. "Thomas, will you look after my niece during my absence? I trust you will keep her safe."

"You need not worry about Jasmine, Caldwell. She'll stay safe, upon my life."

"I trust you will," her uncle said somberly. "You already have risked much for her." Kissing her forehead, he said, "Stay safe, sweetheart. I'll return soon as possible."

When night arrived, Jasmine remained unable to shake her anxiety. The idea of sleeping in her tent again made her ill.

After a tense dinner at Yusef's tent, in which the sheikh kept apologizing profusely, Thomas stood up. "If you're ready to retire, Jas, come with me."

Curious, she followed him to the far reaches of the camp. An enormous, many-poled tent was set there. Apprehension filled her as Thomas opened the flap with a flourish. "After you, Cleopatra. You won't sleep in your tent, so this is a preferable alternative. It's far enough away from the others that I can keep it well-guarded."

Guarded? "You mean, you're staying here with me?"

Thomas's expression softened as he touched her cheek. "Did you think I'd allow you back to your tent after what happened there? Caldwell gave me the task of protecting you, and I shall not fail him."

Jasmine hugged herself, her dark eyes wide. "But where will you sleep?"

She went inside. Not only had her trunk been moved, but his things as well. A modest silk curtain divided the tent in half. Two large beds sat on either side. "His and hers." Jasmine gave a shaky laugh. "I'll retire to my half now. Good night, Thomas."

She went to her quarters, lit the lamp, filled with awareness of the man on the other side of the curtain. The rustling of clothing alerted her to his undressing. A furious flush ignited her cheeks. Did he sleep nude?

Someone had thoughtfully set a small hip bath with warm water at her bedside. Jasmine bathed quickly, relishing the feel of the water cooling her flushed skin. She dried off and dug her nightgown from the trunk. The fine lawn fabric clasped loosely in her fingers felt thicker than a sheepskin blanket.

What did it feel like to sleep without clothing? It must be deliciously naughty. With a sigh of fabric, the nightgown fell to the carpet. Then Jasmine went back to her bed and sat down, waiting for Thomas to fall asleep.

Naked in his bed, Thomas did not sleep. He lay awake in abject torment, listening to the soft sounds of Jasmine moving about across the partition. She was so close he could touch her. He wanted her, badly.

Yes, sleep proved elusive. Restless, he sat up. Against the silk curtain he saw Jasmine backlit by the lantern's soft glow. She was undressing, drawing the kuftan over her head, dragging down the loose trousers past her hips.

His pulse raced as he watched the innocent yet erotic movements silhouetted by the light. The outline of her young, lush body showed in stark relief. The fullness of her breasts, the curve of hip and delicate slender legs. Thomas felt his sex harden.

It was a foolhardy move, sleeping in here. He knew what would happen eventually. They could not resist the passion between them. It was not good for either of them, for Thomas had finally realized that bedding her would engage his heart at last. He could not walk away from Jasmine as he had with the others; he had wanted her too much and too long.

Yet, he could not deny his feelings, his urgent desire. After spending time with her, laughing with her, admiring her spirit, her individuality, her intelligence and gentle compassion, he was no longer content. He wanted her. And if she dared cross the room, lift the curtain and enter his chamber, he knew what he would do.

No one could stop him then from having her. He would have her tonight.

Instinct made Jasmine turn.

Thomas was watching her. Shy and embarrassed, she put her clothing back on, but the secret hollow between her legs throbbed with need. What would it feel like to be naked, Thomas's hands stroking her bare flesh? Her body hummed with awareness.

There could never be any physical passion between them. Their worlds were too separate, the hatred his friends harbored for her too strong. But her heart sang a different story. She wanted him. She was tired of pretending.

Jasmine made up her mind. She went to the curtain, lifted

it and stepped into his chamber. Thomas sat up, a snowy sheet pulled up to his waist. His broad chest was exposed, showing a dark thatch of hair. Desire darkened his eyes. He held out a hand.

"Come to bed with me," he said, his deep voice husky.

"We can't do this," she protested, hugging herself. "As much as I want to . . . we're too different, Caesar. Your friends and family detest me. Face it, we're as different as night and day. I'm the dark night"—she gave a nervous laugh—"and you're the shining day. People will talk when they find out, they'll bend their heads together and look at you differently for daring to be with someone . . . like me. The Egyptian girl. The Brown Scorpion."

His jaw worked violently, as if he wrestled for control. For a moment the only sounds were his harsh breaths and the frantic fluttering of Jasmine's own heart.

"Do you want me, Jas?"

"With all my heart," she replied softly.

"Then forget all else, what anyone else thinks. If we're ever to be together, it must be as if we are only a man and woman, each desiring the other. There is no English nobleman here tonight, nor an Egyptian girl, just us. Tonight belongs to us.

You're my brilliant star descended to earth, Jas, and if I can only have you tonight, then I'll love you tonight and damn the morning sun. I'm going to love you all over, kiss every inch of your lovely body and hold you against me as if tomorrow will never come. I will make you mine so no one will ever come between us again. You can't deny that you want me as well, so take off your clothing and get into my bed. Now."

He was only offering tonight, but she would not deny herself. Jasmine swallowed hard.

"Undress for me," he commanded.

Slowly she shrugged out of her silk kuftan, letting it fall to the floor. As she undid the drawstring of the blousy trousers

and wriggled her hips, a harsh intake of breath alerted her to
his feelings. Jasmine stepped out of the trousers and stood before him naked. Suddenly shy, she wrapped her arms about
herself and looked down. A shiver wracked her.

"You're more beautiful than dawn over the pyramids."

The husky admiration in Thomas's voice gave her confidence. Jasmine lifted her chin, let her arms drop to her sides.

He held out a hand. "Come to me, Jas."

This was it then: No turning back. One more step and she
crossed a threshold for both of them. Jasmine hesitated a moment, feeling as if she were about to embark on a wonderful,
exciting yet fearsome journey.

Making love with him meant she'd never be pure for a future husband. Giving herself to him meant handing over her
heart as well, for she could not love with her body alone.

If she turned away, it meant turning away from everything
her heart longed for. Turning away from him forever. She
could never dare risk this emotional intimacy again, not outside this exotic arena of moonlight and desert magic.

She hesitated one heartbeat more, then went to his side.

Chapter Twenty

Jasmine tried to put the light out, but he stayed her hand.

"I want to see you," he said, his gaze so hot she felt as if her very skin were on fire. "I've waited so long for this, Jas. Don't deny me. You are my shining star descended to earth," he said hoarsely.

Thomas swung his legs over the bedside, the sheet hugging his lean hips. He held out a hand as she took it, and pulled her to his side. Jasmine shivered with anticipation as he slid his hands gently up her waist. Admiration shone in his gaze. "I would worship at your feet, my queen, if I were indeed Caesar."

The soft praise dissolved her. She felt as beautiful as Cleopatra, exotic and adored. Spanning his hands across her waist, he pressed a single, delicate kiss to her navel. Warmth suffused her. Jasmine ran her hands through his thick hair.

Suddenly he pulled her back with him, tumbling them both on the bed. Thomas cupped her face in his strong hands and kissed her. The kiss was gentle, filled with tenderness.

"Please, Thomas. Show me how to love," she whispered.

He had her in his arms at last.

"So beautiful," he muttered, running his hands over her tawny, supple skin. "You are like a star in the sky, burning me with your brilliant fire."

He bent his head and nuzzled the hollow of her slender shoulder, inhaling her delicate fragrance. Exclusively feminine, floral and musky. Exclusively Jasmine. Thomas nipped the flesh there, tasting her. He wanted to absorb her, penetrate her so deeply they joined together, not knowing where one began and the other ended.

This was madness, he foresaw; a dream realized, and such

dreams could never last. Desire had never ruled him before. It lashed at him now with primitive male possessiveness, an ancient call to make her his own. To be her first lover, the first to claim her sweetness. Brand her with his passion so she could never, never forget him. Never.

He raised his head to regard her tenderly. Her dark skin flushed as she lifted her shy gaze to him. Thomas laced his fingers through hers, and raised them. The Egyptian sun had darkened him to a tawny hue like hers. Her fingers were slim and delicate, contrasting sharply to his strength.

"No regrets," he whispered. "Not tonight. Tonight is for us."

"Only us," she echoed dreamily.

Thomas kissed her again, feathering light, tiny presses over her dark skin, tasting her sweetness. Her skin was satiny smooth, not the tough leather his mother had declared "all those brown-skinned women have." He traced a pattern over the full roundness of one breast, letting his fingers drift over to the rosy nipple. Teasing it to a taut peak, he raised his head to watch her reaction.

Her eyes closed, her lips parting on a moan. Thomas smiled. Good, but he wanted more. Would have much more. Before tonight was over, he'd wring a cry of his name on her lips as she climaxed. He replaced his hand with his mouth and fastened his lips over the taut crest, suckling her. Jasmine arched higher and clung to him. his tongue expertly flicked over the bud, teasing her mercilessly.

This was a dream—her dream—and Jasmine wanted to cherish every moment it lasted. Fear of the unknown twined with joy and growing excitement. With each stroke of Thomas's tongue, arousal shot through her. The space between her legs pulsed with need. Jasmine tunneled her fingers through his thick hair, whimpering with pleasure.

When he raised his head, she pushed him back on the bed playfully. "I want to touch you, see you," she said.

With a smile, he obliged. His face and forearms, exposed to the sun, had tanned, but the rest of his rock-hard body was pale. So unlike her own. Jasmine's trembling hand stroked his broad chest, ran downward in fascinated exploration as she touched his skin. Light against dark. Their skin, like their worlds, was so different.

She touched him, marveling at the hard muscles under velvet skin. His forearms were strong, and a deep V at his throat showed the clear demarcation of skin darkened by the sun. His body was so much whiter. Jasmine trembled as she ran a dark hand over his broad chest, the ivory skin clearly contrasting with the honeyed darkness of her own.

Her hands slipped past his shoulders, wandered down his back to feel the hard muscles. Then she stopped.

Jasmine arched over him to look. Thomas tensed, holding perfectly still. Shock filled her as she gazed at the ugly silver scars marring perfect flesh. Deep, ancient gouges were carved there. Jasmine trailed a gentle hand over the marks and he flinched.

"Oh, Caesar, who did this to you?" she asked.

Thomas drew her hand away and pulled her roughly into his arms. "No one of any importance. It was a fight, a long time ago."

As he silenced her protests with a deep kiss, she gave herself over to him. *Scars of the past, go away,* she said silently as she tried to vanquish everything he'd ever suffered. With each kiss of her mouth, she showed him everything hidden away for so long. Everything she'd tucked away, afraid to show the world. Jasmine's newly awoken passion swept aside everything as if they two existed only for the moment and each other. No regrets, ever.

Feathering gentle kisses over her skin, he created a trail of fire. Jasmine arched and squeaked as he parted her thighs with his strong hands. She tried to cover herself, but he pushed her hands away.

"You're beautiful here as well, my queen. As lovely as a Jasmine flower. Open yourself for me."

Erotic pleasure spilled through her as he parted the petals of her sex. Very gently he slid a finger back and forth across her cleft. Tension mounted and she felt moisture seeping from her. Like dew on a flower.

"Yes, that's it," he murmured. "So sweet, so very sweet—"

Pleasure turned to shock as he bent his head and kissed her there. His tongue delved into her cleft, slid back and forth. He was kissing her, tasting her, and the sensations his tongue caused with each long, slow flick—Oh!

She keened softly, fisting her hands in his hair as his tongue pressed against her most sensitive spot. Each whirl and slow stroke sent her spiraling upwards, higher, until the tension in her loins felt enough for her to explode.

And then she did explode, sobbing his name and arching upward as she shattered.

Gentle, tender kisses feathered over her wet sex as she shuddered, gradually returning to earth. Thomas sat back on his heels, wiping his mouth with the back of his hand. His gaze was hot, intense.

He mounted her then, settling his powerful body atop her more fragile one. She felt his rigid length probe her feminine opening, and Jasmine stiffened, knowing what was coming. Her fingers curled around the hard muscles of his broad shoulders.

"I suppose this is the part where I should lie back, look at the ceiling and think of England," she joked weakly.

A small smile diminished his hard look of arousal. "Look at me, Jas. Concentrate on me," he said softly.

Cradling her head in his warm hands, Thomas kissed her, coaxing her response. Her body lost its rigid tension as he broke the kiss and his cock nudged her softness. A little more . . . Determination flared on his face as he pushed harder. The burning, stretching feeling increased.

"Easy," he soothed. "Just relax, yes, that's it, relax, open for me, sweet Jas . . . yes—"

With a hard thrust, he breached her. At her startled cry of pain he murmured soothing assurances. A feeling of fullness took over as the pain ceased. Thomas raised himself up, lacing his fingers through hers, pinning her to the bed with his heated gaze. The conqueror.

"Cleopatra surrenders to her lord Cæsar," she whispered.

Tenderness filled his gaze. "The lord Caesar is honored by his queen's sweet surrender, and promises her his heart in return."

Awed, she watched him as he began to move inside her. This was making love, that mysterious dance she'd heard of, the ultimate union between a man and woman. He was part of her now, deep inside her body and her heart. England and Egypt were melding together, two bodies joined as one. Like dazzling colors spilled and splashed over on a palette, no telling where one color began and the other ended.

His shaft eased out then he pushed himself back inside. Awash of awed emotions, she instinctively opened her legs wider. Thomas groaned. A bead of sweat from his forehead dropped on the curve of her breast. He thrust, angling himself so he pressed against that delicious part of her where all sensation centered. Jasmine flattened herself against the mattress as pleasure filled her and pain became a distant memory. Silently she watched him, his features harsh in the lamps' soft glow, a warrior claiming his prize. His sex slid in and out of her and he clasped her thighs, holding her open for him.

Claiming her, marking her for his own. Jasmine arched into each thrust, screaming as the tension inside her burst again. The hot splash of his seed filled her as he threw back his head and uttered a harsh groan.

Thomas collapsed atop her, his head pillowed next to hers, his breathing ragged in her ear. She felt the rapid pounding of his heart and hers, and she stroked his silky hair. Sweat molded their bodies together.

Gradually he rolled off her and eased carefully out. She winced as his cock slid against sensitive tissues.

He pulled her to his side. "My beautiful star," he said thickly. "You are heaven to me."

Cuddling against him, she tunneled her fingers through the sweat-dampened hair on his chest. They had tonight. Nothing more could she ask for. Nothing more would she dare.

She awoke to the lamp burning low. Jasmine reached over to extinguish it and paused, staring at her lover. Dark stubble shadowed his jaw. Long black lashes feathered against his tanned cheeks. His mouth parted slightly in sleep, and he looked roughly masculine and yet vulnerable, all his defenses lowered.

Enchanted, as if she'd chanced upon a sleeping prince, Jasmine pressed a kiss on his forehead. Then she inched away to steal back to her own bed.

His eyes flew open. The irises were green as fiery emeralds. His chin was chiseled; his mouth—those full, firm lips had kissed each inch of her skin.

"You're not going anywhere." His voice was deep and sleep-roughened. He reached out with one muscled arm, rolled over and pulled her against him. Jasmine snuggled against his hard body. If someone found them, so be it.

Thomas's hand skimmed up, cupped her breast. He began a slow, lazy exploration of her body. Fully awake now, she wriggled against him, feeling his erection dig into her hip.

He flipped her over and slid a palm over her stomach. Stomach muscles jumped beneath his touch and she quivered as his hand tunneled through her dark curls and slid lower.

"Are you too sore for this?" he asked, testing her, gently sliding a finger inside.

"No, I don't think—oh!" Jasmine arched as he skimmed over a sensitive area, the friction so wonderful she gasped.

"There?" he murmured, doing it again.

"Oh yes, please," she begged.

He obliged her, then teased some more. Thomas withdrew his hand and spread her legs with his knees. He settled on top of her and gently pushed his hard shaft inside. Jasmine wanted to weep with frustration. Close, she'd been so close. Then he angled his thrust so that he hit the very spot that had given her such pleasure. Biting back a startled cry she stared up at him.

His gaze was intent, possessive and fierce. "Go on, scream. No one can hear you. I want to hear you, Jas. I want to hear every single lovely cry."

He pumped into her again, and she did cry out this time as he began thrusting harder and faster. She met his thrusts, her hips rocking upward, and screamed his name as the orgasm seized her. Thomas threw his head back and released a warbling cry, then fell atop her.

Trembling together, they lay in each other's arms, Jasmine reluctant to part. Soon enough, they'd have to part for good.

Chapter Twenty-one

They ate breakfast together the next morning, Jasmine's bashfulness vanished under Thomas's easy conversation. It felt as if they'd been together forever. Later that morning, he packed a basket filled with food, took a goatskin of water and told her they were riding into the desert.

"It's a surprise," he said simply.

Delighted, she saddled a sturdy Arabian mare and joined him as they rode north. The sun burned brightly in the sky. A gentle wind lifted the scarf about her head, teased her hair. Thomas consulted the compass once in a while. In his khaki trousers, scuffed leather boots and white shirt rolled to the elbows, he looked like an adventurous explorer. She stole a look at his sharp profile, the stubble darkening his strong jaw.

"And where exactly are you taking me?" she asked.

"Your uncle let me in on a little secret. The training grounds where the al-Hajid once initiated new warriors. He took me there when the al-Hajid and the Khamsin engaged in one last practice session to honor the ground's memories."

"That was your little trip that I was banned from?" Jasmine shot him a mocking stern look. "He told me it was to assess horses."

His look was somber. "A different type of assessment."

Thomas was lost in thought as they reached a wide, flat plain. They dismounted. Jasmine looked around with interest. He led their horses over to a shady tree, letting them drink from a long, shallow stone trench filled with water.

Wind swept across the sand. Suddenly sensitive, Jasmine rubbed her arms. The place had an eerie feel, as if she could sense the ghosts of warriors who once fought here. "What will the al-Hajid do with the land?"

"They will not use this ground again. It's sacred, but it will lie abandoned and forgotten."

"It's so sad," she said, feeling haunted as she gazed upon the tawny, pebbled sands, the shadows of purple mountains looming nearby. Her father had learned to become a warrior here. Had he turned into a cruel tyrant here as well? Had the seeds been inside him all along?

Enough maudlin thoughts. She undid the scarf from her head and smiled. "Are we picnicking? I am hungry."

His gaze was steady and intent. "I brought you here for a reason, Jasmine. To tell you the truth."

Her heart sank. Had he doubts about last night? Would he politely inform her that *Yes, it was splendid making love to you, but there will never be anything more between us.*

To her astonishment, he began removing his jacket, then his shirt. Naked to the waist he faced her with proud dignity. "I lied to you last night. I didn't get my scars from a fight. I got them from . . ." Torment filled his gaze. "I got them from my father."

Her sharp intake of breath made him wince. Slowly he turned, exposing his back.

"Look at me, Jas," he said quietly. "I couldn't bear to tell you and ruin what was between us, but I must show you now because you deserve to know the truth. I will never lie to you again. When I was twelve, he horsewhipped me."

Trembling, she reached out to the ugly, marred flesh. He flinched beneath her gentle probe.

"Are you ashamed? I was for a long time, but no longer. Not the punishment but its reason. It happened after you punched me in the park. He did it to teach me a lesson, to never let an inferior best me."

Dread coiled tightly in her stomach. "It was my fault," she whispered, clenching her fists as if she would punch again, but his father this time.

Thomas turned, gazing at her. "Yes," he said softly. "He beat me because of you, but he also did it because I defied him. I stood up to him because of you. Remembering your toughness gave me the strength."

Emotion clogged her throat. "I'm sorry. Oh, Thomas, I never would have punched you—"

He caught her hand in his. "I'm not sorry," he said roughly. "Not for that, or for anything else. These don't matter to me anymore, Jasmine. But you do."

Pressing her palm against his cheek, he closed his eyes. His full, sensual lips flattened to a tight line as if he fought a war within himself. Jasmine brought his hand to her lips and kissed it.

"So do you. And if I had it to do all over again, I'd kiss you instead of punching you. And I'd punch your father instead."

His eyes flying open, Thomas sputtered with laughter and pulled her to him. He brushed back a stray lock of hair escaping her scarf. "My beautiful Cleopatra, my fierce warrior. I do believe my father would run from you in fear."

"Good. Because I'm most inclined to punch him when we return."

His grin widened. "I've got much more interesting activities in mind. Come, let me show you around."

He escorted her to a small pool in an alcove of large boulders. Warriors used the waters, which they believed were sacred, he explained, to cleanse themselves before battle.

Thomas cupped her cheek, his warm gaze sending ripples of anticipation through her. "Care for a swim, Jas?"

Minutes later, Jasmine waded in the warm water, still wearing her chemise. Naked, Thomas descended the stone steps. Her breath caught in her throat as she stared. He was such beautiful, masculine perfection. Muscle rippled along his flat stomach; his arms and legs were long and sturdy. Her fascinated gaze roved to the hard length of his member jutting out proudly from a nest of black hair. She went to him, feeling shy in the stark daylight, but deeply curious.

"I feel like an explorer in a new land filled with adventure," she confessed.

He sat on a low step, arms splayed, thighs opened. "Go ahead then, sweet," he said softly, his gaze upon her. "Explore."

She did. Her hands stroked, lingered, then touched his lengthening penis. It felt like satin over steel. The knob was purple, rounded, and she stroked a gentle finger across it, evoking a shudder from him. Thomas closed his eyes and groaned. Seeing his reaction gave her a sense of utter feminine power. Lightly she traced a line down his shaft, watching his jaw tighten. Growing bolder, she explored further, cupping his ballocks, testing their weight.

His hand shot out, stayed hers. Desire etched his expression as he opened his eyes. "My turn to explore," he said in a husky voice.

Before she could protest, he tugged her soaked chemise off, tossed it aside. Thomas drew her to him. His palms made small circles on her breasts, making them feel aching and full. Jasmine shuddered as he teased the nipples, drawing them to tight little buds. He bent his head and he suckled one, drawing it in, hard. Over and over his tongue stroked her, sending hot ripples of pleasure through her. The space between her legs ached for him to fill her.

She arched in pleasure as he massaged between her thighs, drawing fire there. Her entire body felt bathed in heat, as if the very water around them boiled. Suddenly he ceased his ministrations and led her over to the stone steps, turning her around so her back faced him.

"Kneel," he told her.

With faint trepidation, she did so, bracing her hands on the top step. In this position, she felt vulnerable and exposed, but his soft murmurs of reassurance eased her tension. She felt his hard body behind her, his warm hands skimming her hips, pulling her against him.

"There is a certain wild eloquence to how horses mate," he murmured.

She felt his hard length probing her softness, his chest hair scrape against her back as he drew her against him. His hips pushed forward and he sank into her, meeting with some resistance as she tightened around him. She tensed. Surely he was too large and she was too sore, too new at this . . .

"Easy," he soothed, ceasing his attempts at penetration.

He leaned down, his hands caressing her skin in gentle strokes, arousing her. He reached down to her feminine flesh, and flicked. Jasmine whimpered as he stroked. She felt herself ease around him.

Thomas pushed again, a satisfied grunt escaping him as he entered her deeper than ever before. His hands slipped to her hips, clasping them, and he began to thrust.

Water sluiced around them as his flesh slapped against hers. Jasmine grated her teeth, her muscles tensing as she poised on the edge. More; she needed more. Now.

"Please," she begged. "Oh please."

He seemed to understand her plea, and reached down with a hand to play with her sex once more.

"This is how horses mate, little flower," he whispered. "Wild and free, uncaring of anything but the moment. Feel the wind against your body, Jas. Feel me inside you. I'm one with you now, sweet. I will always be part of you, no matter where you go. You're mine, forever."

She arched against him as he grasped her hips again, hammering into her in a rhythm that built the pleasure higher and higher. Jasmine reached for it as he thrust. She screamed to the heavens, her cries echoing over the empty canyons as the pleasure burst into thousands of stars. He gripped her hips tightly, his own cry echoing hers.

Wild and free. They were one. And no one would part them.

Ever.

Graham and the Khamsin returned six days later with Jabari and Ramses' families, who wanted to meet the English visitors before they departed for Cairo. The week-long visit with the Khamsin families went fast, and Thomas became aware of how time was slipping away.

He'd been discreet since her uncle's return. Stealing kisses in the lee of tents, brushing a hand against the softness of her cheek. Now, as the day drew near for their departure, he found himself as if at a great distance from Jasmine. It was as if chains of their destinies draped about them both, tugging them in separate directions.

Thomas rubbed his forehead wearily. Nearby, a cloud of dust arose as two beautiful Arabian horses thundered past. Ridden by black-haired, green-eyed youths he'd seen earlier, the horses galloped through the camp. The youths hooted the eerie Khamsin war call.

Ramses yelled something to the riders, then shook his head. "They are out of control," he said, but Thomas sensed a father's pride.

"I met them earlier. Your children are twins?"

"Asad and Fatima are inseparable."

Thomas studied the teenagers as they dismounted. The girl hugged her brother, who hugged her back. The sight welled unexpected emotion in him. "They get along so famously," he mused.

"It has always been so. They are fourteen, and Fatima is becoming a woman, but she still prefers Asad's company and that of our sheikh's heir over her female friends." Ramses released such a deep sigh Thomas instinctively knew this admission was a sore spot.

"Fatima has agreed to belly dance for us. Perhaps Jasmine would care to join her."

Remembering how Jasmine denied all things Egyptian, Thomas doubted it. "I'm not certain Jasmine knows how to dance," he remarked.

Ramses winked at him. "She does. Trust me, it is in her blood."

Ululating shrieks filled the air as the drummers beat upon their small round drums.

In the center of a small circle sat her uncle and Thomas. Jasmine swirled her hips, teasing the air with her hands. The delicate, feminine costume made her feel exotic and alluring. The wide emerald trousers drawn at the waist were tied at the knees. Over these she wore a loose silk emerald shirt. A diaphanous scarf adorned her head.

Fatima had assured her during practice that Jasmine's moves were skilled. Jasmine felt alive, free and as exotic as this land. Her people and heritage. Sitting beside his father, the blond, handsome Tarik watched Fatima. He seemed transfixed.

Jasmine's gaze landed on Thomas, watching him watch her with avid interest.

The dance finished, and to enthusiastic applause Jasmine and Fatima took their seats. Flushed with pride, Jasmine accepted a cool glass of sweet tea. Thomas studied her with a slight smile.

Apprehension filled her. Their cherished, sweet time in the desert was ending. In Cairo, she'd have to send a telegraph to Mr. Myers, informing him which column to run. Did she ruin his sister or ruin herself?

Laughter surrounded her; Jabari and Ramses' children were teasing Fatima. The sheikh's blond son did not join in, merely assessed Fatima quietly with a look far more mature than his fifteen years. Elizabeth exchanged a loving glance with her husband Jabari. Clearly, they had breached a difficult gap in culture and custom. But Thomas was an earl's heir, and belonged to a more aristocratic set than Elizabeth.

Thomas belonged in England.

Jasmine belonged in Egypt, she now saw.

I fit in perfectly, she thought with sudden awareness. Stylish fashions, wealth, parading on Rotten Row and entrance into high society no longer mattered. Here, Jasmine no longer felt the need to prove herself. Judged on her own merits, she finally found acceptance. No one thought her Egyptian heritage or the color of her skin was cause to label her ignorant, filthy, or morally and intellectually deficient.

This was the land of her origins. The desert burned in her blood and called to her more than London's cold mist. She'd spent so many years trying to adapt to England's culture and customs without success. In a few short weeks, Jasmine had taken to the desert as easily as . . . as a scorpion. I *am* a brown scorpion, she thought ruefully. And yet, it does not feel bad. Thomas was right. There are advantages to scorpions.

She saw him watching her with quiet tenderness, and her heart turned over. Emotions expressed in his gaze made her tremble inside. Surely he did care for her. But how could anything more exist between them? Marriage? How could she, daughter of desert people, marry a wealthy earl's heir whose loyalty remained in England with his family and title? Their relationship was doomed to be buried beneath a sandstorm of differences. Jasmine did not see how it could survive.

Chapter Twenty-two

They returned to Cairo by train. Thomas had been quiet, conversing only briefly. Clearly something was on his mind. Jasmine wondered if it was the same thing holding her attention: the deadline for The Blue Bloods column.

At the Shepherd's Hotel, he went to finalize arrangements for his journey up the Nile to Luxor. Jasmine would travel there by train with friends of her uncle's.

She joined her uncle in the hotel's Moorish Room. In his sand-colored suit with white waistcoat and white tie, Graham looked very distinguished and English. Unlike her.

"You look lovely. I must confess I had hoped you wouldn't change your dress now that we've left the desert," he remarked, kissing her cheek.

Jasmine settled on an ottoman near the divan where he sat. "Egyptian dress suits me, and the colors are more flattering to my complexion."

He regarded her with his thoughtful, dark gaze. "I'm afraid I've some bad news. The Andersons have been delayed in Europe. They won't arrive here for another two weeks. I would remain with you, but I wish to return to my wife and daughters. I'm booking passage for the day after tomorrow. Do you wish me to book passage for you?"

She didn't want to return to England. Jasmine yearned to remain in warm, friendly Egypt.

"I could stay here alone. It's safe and I'm very capable, Uncle Graham. Two weeks on my own will be fine. Or do you worry Cairo cannot handle your niece?" she joked.

Graham leaned forward, looking somber. "Jasmine, I love you like my own daughter. I sense you're lost and trying to find yourself. Spend time here in Cairo, get to know Egypt as I know her, until the Andersons come. Egypt is your heritage and your birthright."

She gave a light laugh. "I can write an article, if nothing else, and perhaps this journey will make for good reading." Her smile faded as she remembered the cold hatred directed toward her real father. "It's been a painful one, thus far. It wasn't easy, finding out the truth about Fareeq."

"Sweetheart, I learned long ago that you cannot put off painful and necessary journeys. The truth can hurt. But it is less painful with a helpmate at your side." His glance flicked off to the entrance, then came back to her. "Do you think Thomas could be the one?"

Startled, she drew back. "You mean . . . marriage? Don't be absurd, Uncle Graham. I'm not interested."

"I think you are," he said. "And I've seen how he looks at you, Jasmine."

Her lower lip trembled dangerously. She had considered the idea, in her most private thoughts, but it was a dream and nothing more.

"Lord Thomas will marry for breeding and money. We're from two different worlds, he and I, and we do not match."

"What I see before me does match. What your heart says, and what your lips tell me, are more contrary than you and Thomas. Follow your heart, Jasmine, not your mind. That's the journey most of all worth taking." He nodded toward the doorway, where Thomas entered, his stride brisk. With shining eyes, Jasmine watched him take a seat.

"Well, Caldwell, will you return to England now?"

As her uncle explained his arrangements and the plans made to ship Thomas's mares to London, Jasmine studied her lover. With his classic, chiseled features, face tanned by the Egyptian sun and his natural air of authority, he looked very distinguished and every inch the earl's heir. Thomas belonged to the aristocratic set. She did not. Marriage to him was simply impossible, even if he wanted her.

Yes, he'd wanted her in his bed. He'd proclaimed his affections; not his love, but his desire. It wasn't the same. Had she made a terrible mistake? Remembering the passion in his arms, she knew she had not. No matter what else, they'd shared something beautiful and special.

Thomas turned his attention to her. Jasmine's heart turned over at his smile.

"And you, Jas? Are you remaining here to wait for the Andersons? I'm not pushing off for another few days. I thought we'd do some shopping together in the Khan el Khali. I'm quite interested in the goldsmiths."

"That would be lovely," she said, warmed at his attention.

Bloody hell, she was as besotted with him as a schoolgirl. Dismay filled her. How would she feel once he sailed away, up the Nile and out of her life?

Such thoughts depressed her, so she pushed them out of her mind. Jasmine began discussing Cairo's bazaar and its delights, but a uniformed clerk in a red fez approached.

"Lord Thomas, telegram for you."

Thomas's smile dropped. She and Uncle Graham fell silent as he read the wire. He crumpled it with one hand as his expression went perfectly blank. But his eyes darkened, the green growing sharper.

"Excuse me," he said politely, his gaze distant, as if affixed on a distant shore.

Jasmine chatted with her uncle. When Thomas returned, he was so brisk that instinct warned he'd received dreadful news. He did not look at her. Jasmine's heart sank. What was in that telegram?

"I ordered tea and cakes for all of us," she said, searching his face.

"Thank you, but I'm not hungry," he said curtly. "I came back to tell you business calls me away for a while. Caldwell, if I don't see you before you depart, thank you for your hospitality."

Her uncle glanced at her, then nodded at Thomas. Thomas did not look at her as he left.

The wonderful closeness they'd shared had completely vanished, the sweet passion dried. Jasmine knew then that she'd lost him. She hadn't telegraphed Mr. Myers yet about her decision on the column. His cold disregard of her indicated she was at fault.

But what had she done?

Thomas walked through the lobby with its elegant façade and milling guests. Some greeted him and he answered absently. Oh for fresh air, warm sunshine and the stark barrenness of the Egyptian desert! Here was too crowded. He needed a moment to think, and went to the terrace. Leaning on the railing, he stared at the street below.

Dreams had shattered like fragile Egyptian faience. As Thomas remembered the terse telegram sent from England, his heart hardened.

Your sister's joy, not yours, his conscience grimly reminded him.

He stared into the street, debating his next action. The trip to visit the al-Hajid had merely been a respite. Trouble awaited him back in England, and it had grown worse. He must deal with the situation at hand or risk his sister's reputation.

Bedding Jasmine had been a sweet dream. This was the reality.

Two days later, Jasmine sat on the terrace in the late afternoon sun. In her brilliant saffron kuftan, gold sandals and a turquoise scarf about her head, she looked exactly as she felt: like an ordinary Egyptian girl. The dress suited her. Until she returned to England, Jasmine planned to continue wearing it.

She sipped mint tea in an agony of indecision. Today she must telegraph London. Doing so sealed her fate. Flexing her hands, she stared at the fingers that had wielded such vicious words—fingers that penned equally apologetic ones. She could save Thomas's sister from disgrace and ruination.

At her own peril. Ruining her own reputation? How silly. I have no reputation, she thought a little sadly. I am no one in England.

Surely the publisher had stuck to his word and awaited her wire. Yet Thomas's odd behavior warned her something dire had happened. For days she hadn't seen him. It might be he had been preoccupied with business as he'd said. Or he simply chose to avoid her.

Voices at a nearby table caught her attention.

"Mama, look at the pretty Egyptian lady!"

"Hush, Susan, it's not polite to stare."

Jasmine turned and smiled at the little girl in her bright white frock, her hair tied back in a wide pink ribbon. The daughter beamed at Jasmine, earning a slap on the wrist from her frowning mother. A mustached man gave Jasmine a disdainful look. He didn't bother to lower his voice.

"Egyptians. Sly beggars, the lot of them. What's become of decent hotels like the Shepherd's that they allow them here?"

For the first time, the prejudice did not bother her. She merely offered a smile and turned her back. Years ago she'd asked Uncle Graham if the English children would ever accept her if she dressed as they did. He'd offered a noncommittal answer. She knew the answer now. Either in English dress or Egyptian, she was still different. But today the difference did not bother her.

Of course, her origins did, because of the hate her real father had evoked. Jasmine closed her eyes, remembering the stream of anger directed at her birth father. Not one person had a single kind word in remembrance. Her mother and Kenneth had not lied, after all. *I am my father's daughter. Or am I?*

She had the opportunity to prove otherwise. With one telegram, she could prove to the world, and herself, the blood of Fareeq might run in her veins but had not tainted her.

Jasmine stood with determination and headed to the lobby.

Chapter Twenty-three

With a spring in her step, Jasmine set out for the bazaar. She had wired Mr. Myers and felt at peace. Returning to England was no longer an option, not until her articles were published in the other paper. But at least Lady Amanda's reputation would be spared.

The Khan el Khali offered a veritable feast for shoppers as well as theatrics performed daily by shopkeepers determined to sell their wares. The warren of alleyways was a world of its own. China, glassware, teas, striped bags of fava beans, clothing, trinkets and jewelry were displayed to catch the eye. She strolled among woven baskets offering plump, shiny dates, small, squat bottles of spice, wicker baskets filled with oranges, pomegranates and other fruit. Scents tickled her nose and sunshine warmed her skin.

Jasmine halted a minute to admire the domed archway of the narrow alley where sellers lounged in low stools before their intricately fashioned crafts. An alert shopkeeper bounded to his feet. Waving a gleaming silver coffee urn, he began singing out words to lure her into a purchase much as a lover wooed a shy woman to his bed.

Familiar with this dance, she admired the handiwork. A small Eye of Horus adorned the side, and an elaborately carved handle resembling a pharoanic boat. Thomas would like its whimsy. Jasmine began hard bargaining in Arabic. A gleam entered the man's eyes as he sang back a counter offer. Their duet continued, finally concluding with a price satisfactory to both.

"I have no idea when he'll use it, but I do like the Wedjat." Jasmine opened her purse to remove her money.

Someone jostled her and, suddenly, rough hands grabbed her purse. Thrown to the ground, she yelled out, then sprang to her feet to pursue the thief. The shopkeeper, frantic at losing his sale, tried plucking at her sleeve, but she ignored him.

Zigging and zagging through the bazaar, she lost him quickly in the crowd. Jasmine panted and halted, angry at her foolishness.

Oh well. She had money back in her room. At least she'd been clever enough not to bring it all, knowing the reputation of Cairo's thieves.

Jasmine headed back for the Shepherd's. She sprang up the stairs, wondering why the doorman frowned at her.

As she walked to the desk to retrieve her key, she spotted the manager. Jasmine scurried over to him. Instead of his usual friendly smile, the man looked cold, almost forbidding.

"Oh, hello. I must speak with you. I've been robbed of my purse in the Khan el Khali, and I'm afraid the thief took my room key as well. Will you please tell the porter to let me in."

"Your room is no longer available," the manager said coldly. "You will leave now, before I call the authorities."

Her jaw dropped. "What—I'm not due to check out for another two weeks! I have an account here. Jasmine Tristan, remember?"

"I have been told exactly who you are, and you are forbidden in this hotel." The man gave a disdainful sniff. "If you do not leave now, I shall have you escorted out. Please refrain from creating a scene."

"I'm the Duke of Caldwell's niece," she cried.

"The duke is no longer here, and other guests have complained about your soliciting them. You were also seen on your previous visit conducting business with a male guest who had arranged to engage your 'services.' Go somewhere else and find another 'uncle.'"

"This is a dreadful mistake."

The manager sniffed. "If you have identification to prove your identity . . ."

"It was stolen from me."

"How convenient." The man looked up, signaled a porter.

"My clothing, then, and the money that was in my room. Give them to me," she insisted.

"There was nothing in your room," the manager insisted.

Whoever stole her room key had acted quickly and stolen her belongings as well. Suddenly, she thought of Thomas. Surely he could straighten this ridiculous problem out. "I must send a message to Lord Thomas Wallenford's room. He'll sort this out and tell you who I am."

"Lord Thomas is not here. And you must leave. Now." Two uniformed porters appeared. "Please see this *lady* out," the manager ordered, sneering the word.

Jasmine shook off their hands. "Leave me be," she said in her haughtiest tone.

She left, pausing on the terrace. Her predicament sank home. In her Egyptian dress, without money or credentials, she did resemble just another girl. Her only means of proving her identity lay with finding someone who had met her. But the Morrows and the Hodges had departed for Luxor. There was no sign of Thomas. . . .

A familiar laugh on the street below filled her with relief. There!

Thomas was talking with a flower vendor. She hurried down the stairs. The pretty vendor looked annoyed as Jasmine approached and beckoned him away, but he followed her to a quieter area.

"I must talk with you, Thomas. I'm in a terrible fix. I was robbed in the Khan el Khali, and now for some odd reason the hotel staff has escorted me out. They think I was with Uncle Graham because I was his . . . um . . . they say I don't belong. I keep telling them I'm the duke's niece and they won't believe me!"

Staring at her, he twirled the bowler hat in his hand. He said nothing, but smiled an odd little smile, as if he were privy to some secret information.

Suddenly she knew. "Did you know about this?"

Please, say it's not true, please . . .

"Did I?" he drawled.

He looked so unconcerned, so cool that she felt ill.

"I'm in a dire situation, Thomas, and this isn't funny, so if it's some prank you pulled, then stop it now. The hotel manager said I've been seen 'soliciting other male guests,' for heaven's sake. He even mentioned that man who asked if I were a trollop."

She gulped down a calming breath. "I can't go up to my room to change into my English dress. I have no credentials to prove my identity because my purse was stolen. I have nothing, and I'm on the street. Now will you please escort me back to my room so they won't toss me out like I'm some Egyptian beggar girl?"

"It is a pity, is it not? Being an Egyptian beggar girl?"

Her heart sank. Jasmine stared as if seeing him for the first time. How could he? After the tenderness they'd shared, his protectiveness? It was as if he were another person. A person she did not want to know. How could he be so vicious and callous?

"Don't you care?" she asked in a broken voice. "Thomas, can't you see I'm serious?"

"You should have taken more care, Jasmine," he said calmly. "You, above all people, should be more careful. A lesson I daresay you'll not soon forget."

No help from him. She racked her brain for another solution. "I'll tell the authorities. I'll go to Sir Eldon. Uncle Graham's met him before, he'll believe my story—"

"Will he?" He began circling her. "Another story from a desperate, penniless woman who claims to have connections. An Egyptian woman, regarded as lowly and invisible. You wanted to become Egyptian, and here you are—no better off than that poor flower girl, except at least she has the promise of income." The earl's heir dropped his voice. "She's agreed to share my bed tonight, Jasmine. A pretty little thing, is she not? I think I will enjoy . . . plucking her flower. There is something immensely satisfying about bedding virgins."

The stark cruelty of his words sank into her like a dagger. She wanted to kick him. Jasmine clung to her dignity, refusing to surrender to the impulse to behave like a whining child. There were other options.

"Why are you doing this?" she asked.

"I think you know the answer."

"But I—the column—it's not as you believe. I changed the words—"

A blank look slid over his face, and he waved a hand in dismissal. "None of that matters now. It's far too late to make amends, Jasmine. Though I did enjoy our time together, I must be off to attend far more important matters."

He had used then abandoned her after having his pleasure. Just like his friends, he did not care.

"You're a bastard, Lord Thomas," she breathed, fighting the urge to slap the smug smile from his face. "And here I thought you were the last decent man in England."

His smile widened, carrying a hint of malice. "But we're not in England, are we?"

Jasmine turned and ran down the street, ignoring his mocking laugh. He did not follow her.

After a few minutes, she slowed, hugging herself. No money. Not even a change of clothing. What horrible quandary, and all because of Thomas. Shaking inside, she sagged against a doorway. Never could she have expected such vicious revenge, yet his stormy expression the other day when he'd received the telegram hinted at fury.

I probably deserve it, she thought miserably. *And much worse.*

Well, she would get worse. With no money, nowhere to go . . . Except the local brothels.

She nearly laughed at the irony as she looked around. Close she was to the ruins of the brothel where she'd spent part of her childhood. It burned down when Kenneth torched it after rescuing Mother.

Her parents! She could wire home for money. They would aid her. Yet she had no coins to even pay for a wire. Jasmine ran a hand down her face, laughing. Laughter was better than tears.

In her flowing yellow kuftan, leather sandals on her feet and the delicate gauze scarf around her head, she resembled an ordinary Egyptian girl. Begging for money was her only hope.

Jasmine swallowed her pride. *Just enough to wire home for money.* Pasting a bright smile on her face, she headed to the Khan el Khali where most of the tourists flocked. In the doorway of a busy street, Jasmine held out a palm to a passing English gentleman.

After an hour, she grew desperate. No one gave her a pence, and she'd received five lewd offers from Englishmen who were not gentlemen. Her plea had changed from a woman asking for two pounds to see her home to a young mother needing food for her starving child. The world passed by, uncaring and oblivious.

A lone man dressed in a khaki suit strolled toward her from a distance. Jasmine draped the scarf about her lower face and steeled her spine. One last time. Her gaze cast modestly downward, she thrust out her open palm.

"Please, sir, I beg you, I need a few shillings to buy food for my dying mother."

"Good God, Jasmine, what are you doing?"

Jasmine froze, recognizing that familiar, deep voice. She turned her head. "Go away, Lord Thomas. Haven't you more important business, such as finding flower girls to deflower?"

Anger tinged her words as she turned from him, but he took her elbow. "Come with me."

It was an order she must obey, for his grip was tight and he all but dragged her off. Lord Thomas escorted her to a quiet residential alley nearby, away from the sellers and the tourists.

Trash lined either side, the stench making her gag. Movement down the narrow alley caught her eyes. A medium-sized dog, more gray than white, trotted eagerly toward them. A woman on a balcony yelled something to the dog and tossed a bucket of dirty water at it. The dog yelped, slunk into the shadows.

I know how you feel, Jasmine thought.

"Are you quite mad, lurking in this area? It's far too dangerous. What sort of nonsense is this?" he demanded.

Doffing her scarf, she raised her head and gave him a cold look. "I'm asking strangers for money since you refuse to help me. What else am I to do? I've been robbed and the hotel staff thinks I'm a prostitute. I have no choice in the matter."

His dark brows furrowed as he stared at her. "What?"

"Oh, don't be such a dolt. I need money, kind sir, and if you don't give me enough I shall have to go elsewhere."

"What are you talking about? You make no sense."

"Are you trying to change your tune? What you said back to me at the hotel, when you practically admitted you were the one who'd had me tossed out of the hotel, to teach me a lesson about the column I wrote. Don't deny you were the one, Thomas."

To her immense surprise, he actually looked guilty. Thomas closed his eyes. "Oh, dear God . . . so that is what happened. Jasmine, I didn't realize the extent of this—"

"So, sir, I only ask you for enough money so I may telegram my parents and inform them of my situation. Once they wire the money to me for my passage home, I'll return it to you." Pride evaporated under his severe frown. "Please," she whispered. "I've begged enough strangers today. Just pretend you don't know me, then you can walk away."

His mouth worked as Thomas looked away. Oh God, his jaw tightened as if he were trying to control a temper that threatened to erupt. Jasmine remained silent, hoping in vain.

"I'll give you money. If that is truly what you desire."

Relief made her knees weak. Or perhaps it was hunger, for she'd only sipped a cup of weak tea that morning. "Thank you. When I return to England, I will pay you back, I promise. You certainly are acting strange though, Thomas. I'd almost say you were two different people—the man I know and the horrid one back at the hotel. What has gotten into you?"

Thomas looked down the alley, clearly lost in thought. He looked at her again, his gaze sharp and assessing. She didn't care for that look. It was calculating, the same one she'd seen him exhibit while bargaining for the Arabian mares.

"No, I won't wait," he said slowly. "I require more immediate payment."

Her heart sank.

"I have a proposition for you—one better than returning home. Go back home, where no one need know of your failure, your one chance to achieve greatness by witnessing the unearthing of Tut's tomb? Is that what you truly want? I think not."

He knew her all too well.

"Perhaps I will anyway," she challenged. "Why should I care about digging in the sand?"

The look he gave her made her even more miserable.

"You know why," she whispered. "You would see my dream destroyed. Thomas, why are you doing this to me? What do you want?"

He laced his hands behind his back. Pedestrians streamed past them like water, some casting curious glances into the alleyway. Out of the corner of her eye she saw the dog peek hopefully back out from behind stacks of trash.

"I require a personal servant during my stay in the Valley of the Kings. I failed to arrange for one before who is fluent in English and Arabic. I'll pay your fare back to England, and a handsome salary as well. You'll have access to the dig site and the opportunity to write your observations and wire them to London to your editor. In exchange, you'll work for me as my servant. Launder my clothing, serve my meals, keep my quarters tidy, clean and do anything I ask. Do you quite understand, Jasmine? *Anything*."

She stepped back, filled with fury and tempted to slap him. "I will not be your whore."

"Of course not," he said. "But you shall become my servant and obey me in everything. I think learning a little humility will prove beneficial for you."

"You are acting as horrid as you did at the hotel. Why? Why this?"

His gaze whipped up and down the alley again. Thomas reached into his coat pocket, unfolded a paper and handed it to her. "This is the column that will run in Myers's newspaper next week."

She scanned it in shocked disbelief. It was not the column she'd instructed Mr. Myers to publish, the one that would malign her. Neither was it any other she'd written.

Jasmine lifted her troubled gaze to his calm one. "It's a lie! You didn't seduce Amanda's maid in the garden!"

"Of course it is. But the world doesn't know it as such. And now my sister is saved. Your column created far worse gossip. Richard's family was horrified at our family being dragged through the mire and was pressuring him to break Mandy's engagement. I warned you off my family. You nearly ruined her, Jasmine. Her good name—all a woman truly has in this world—would be gone. So I prohibited it from happening."

"Mr. Myers never would have approved this dreck."

"No, for the real scandal whetted his sensationalistic appetite for puerile gossip. The tidy little sum I gave him to print that guaranteed his approval. I would have quashed the article entirely, but the gossip had already started, some suspecting poor Mandy, and I knew only a column saying I was the one caught in the garden would stop tongues from wagging."

Blood drained from her face as he named the sum he'd paid.

This was why he had acted as he had back at the Shepherd's before the flower girl, she realized. His anger had been far too great to assist her. Jasmine felt ashamed.

"I never intended for this to happen," she cried.

"It doesn't matter, does it?" he said, almost gently. "It happened. I've been called a good businessman, and a good businessman always ensures a debt is paid back. You owe me, Jasmine. My mother was horrific to you, but it was your choice to trespass on the ball that night. You did not give Mandy a choice when you wrote your columns. You attacked her without provocation."

He advanced, looming over her, large and vaguely threatening, powerful and making her feel as helpless as a fly caught in a spider web. "I warned you that I protect my own, Jasmine. You failed to pay attention. But it's still your choice—come work for me, or remain begging on the streets. I daresay I'll be a more understanding and gentler master than anyone else."

"No one is my master," she shot back.

"Every man, and woman, has a master. For some, it is what society thinks," he said, and she caught the note of bitterness in his voice.

"I will not be your mistress, Lord Thomas."

"Understand this, Jasmine: I am furious, but I want you in my bed again. I will not lie to you about it. I won't even try."

Her breath hitched as his heated gaze swept her. He did not lie.

"You would take me against my will?" she asked. Like another once tried, she thought bitterly, her heart twisting.

Thomas shook his head. "Never. When you come, it will be of your own free will—and trust me, Jas, you will come to me again. You cannot resist it any more than I can."

"Then damn us both," she whispered, stricken.

"Yes, damn us both," he said.

"Why do you want me when you can have your little

flower girl?" Jasmine asked. "She's already sharing your bed tonight. And I'm no virgin." Emotion clogged her throat. *You saw to that, didn't you?*

His dark brows knitted. "I see. No, she isn't coming, though I'll see she is . . . compensated. Forget the flower girl. In the meantime, from this moment on, you shall stick to my side as if you were part of me. Understood? You will not leave my sight."

Swallowing her pride, she agreed.

Thomas considered a moment more; then, to her amazement, he called in Arabic to the dog, who skulked out of the shadows. "He's been waiting for me," he said.

He bent down and withdrew a stained white packet from his pocket. Jasmine's eyes widened as Thomas unwrapped the packet and put a large offering of scraps on the ground. The dog gulped down the meat, then licked Thomas's hand.

A real smile touched Thomas's mouth. "I found him two days ago when I came here. Since then, I've been feeding him and looking for a good home. I do believe I found one. One of the waiters has a little boy who wants a white dog. He believes a white dog brings good luck."

"He looks rather lost," Jasmine said absently, bemused by Thomas's abrupt mood change.

"Aren't we all?" He straightened and brushed off his hands. "Let's go."

Allowing him to take her elbow, she walked with him. But as they left the alleyway, a thought struck: What had he been doing here two days ago?

Thomas went out into the night, his leather sandals making little sound. He wended his way through the streets, his steps determined. A snowy turban sat atop his head, his silk *galabiyah* indicating wealth. Tonight, he dressed to blend. Discretion was best.

Upstairs, Jasmine slept. He'd escorted her boldly inside the hotel, silencing the stammering manager with one look. The hotel was far safer than his boat, and he'd paid the night porter handsomely to guard her room. The dull, listless look in her eyes stabbed him. Part of him longed to comfort her with assurances, but he had more important business at end: Finding the identity of her would-be assassin.

Into the Islamic section of Cairo he went, treading toward the enormous labyrinth of the Khan el Khali. Few tourists were about at this late hour, for the city had a sinister slant to it after most shops had closed, and thieves were known to abound. Or much worse.

Thomas's hand went to the silver hilt of the curved *jambiyah* strapped to his belt. Jabari the Khamsin sheikh had given him lessons in the dagger's use: It was more discreet than the rifle he'd begun carrying after the first attempt on Jasmine's life. Thoughts of her made him smile. Here he was, cloaking his identity with Egyptian dress, much as she had disguised herself at the ball by donning an English costume. Each worked to not stand out. Blending into the crowd was imperative.

The information he sought would ease his mind from the suspicion niggling there since the first attack on Jasmine's life. He had not told her, but that night on board the steamer he had caught a glimpse of someone familiar, someone familiar who should not have been aboard the steamer. Or in Egypt at all. Thomas had dismissed it as an overly active imagination. Tonight, he would discover the truth.

Entering a narrow alley off El-Hussein Square, he hurried his steps. A soft glow of lamplight spilled out into the alleyway from the opened shutters of the coffee shop. Thomas lingered a moment to allow his eyes to adjust to the light, then went inside.

Glass lamps set on low, round tables emitted a soft light amid the blue smoke lazily drifting upwards. Spiderweb cracks ran through mirrors on the wall and the ceiling was yellowed from years of nicotine. Four men clad in white *gal-abiyahs* and wearing skullcaps sat on hassocks, clustered around a *narguileh*. They smoked the water pipe and conversed in low tones.

At a quiet corner table, a bearded man in a blue galabiyah and a dark turban lounged on a pillow, a small china cup before him. Thomas drifted through the shop, murmuring polite greetings in Arabic to the others. He settled on a tattered cushion opposite the coffee drinker. Their table was far enough away to allow for a measure of privacy.

A grim waiter brought a thimble-sized cup and another urn of thick, dark Turkish coffee. Thomas poured a little and sipped, savoring the rich taste.

"What do you have for me?" he asked.

The bearded man looked about covertly. He fished a paper out of his bag and slid it across the scarred tabletop.

Tension gripped Thomas as he scanned the report. He crumpled it beneath his fist, quivering with incredulity. "This cannot be true. There must be a mistake."

"There is no mistake, *saiyid*. The person giving this information had no reason to lie, for he was well paid to discover the truth," his companion said quietly in Arabic.

Disbelief coursed through him, followed by growing rage. His instincts had proved correct, and his parents, his mother most of all, had lied to him. All the more reason to suspect the identity of Jasmine's assassin.

Thomas took a deep breath to calm himself. In each shadow, he had seen danger lurking as a wraith ready to strike. Now the wraith had a face, and the knowledge stabbed him with such anguish it felt like a dagger thrust into his chest. He must return to the hotel now, before anything else happened. Every moment he left Jasmine alone put her in extreme danger. Even if he had to strap her to his side, he'd keep her in sight at all times. Above all, she mustn't suspect what he knew, for Jasmine might be tempted to take matters into her own hands, endangering her further. He had defrayed suspicion by forcing her into accompanying him to the dig as his servant. He must continue the ruse a while longer.

"Thank you," he said quietly in Arabic. "*Allah yisallimak.*"

"And may God protect you as well, my friend," came the reply in perfect English. The bearded man looked Egyptian, but in fact he was British to the core, having served with His Majesty's army for some time in Cairo.

Fishing money from the small purse on his belt, Thomas tossed it down. The clink of coins hitting the table thundered in his ears. He nodded to the smoking patrons as he wended his way through the tables, then left as silently as he'd entered, more troubled than ever.

Chapter Twenty-four

Jasmine spent most of the day alone, a virtual prisoner, except for the seamstress who came to measure for new clothing. A tray of breakfast and lunch was brought to her, along with a curt note from Lord Thomas instructing her to not leave her room.

I cannot ensure you will be allowed back inside if I am not there to accompany you, he'd written.

Towards evening, an array of new English clothing arrived for her: dresses, large floppy hats, silky chemises that she fingered dubiously. How odd that he wanted her now to dress as an Englishwoman, when previously he'd urged her otherwise.

He summoned Jasmine at last to his sitting room, displaying the arrogance of a pasha. Inwardly fuming, she stood before him as stewards scurried to pack his clothing. Lord Thomas sat on a comfortable chair by the window. A cup of tea and several papers were on the inlaid table before him. He did not invite her to sit.

"I wish to discuss your duties. We set sail tomorrow morning. I've hired a dragoman, Hamid el-Hussein, who will act as tour guide. My captain assures me the winds are right to depart. The journey will take approximately two weeks. I plan to stop along the way to explore ruins."

She brightened at the thought of scrambling over the hills, happily investigating ancient tombs. But dismay flowered with his increasing list of requirements. She was not to leave the boat without him escorting her. Thomas expected her to keep busy while on board, helping the stewards keep everything tidy and clean, arranging his clothing at night and ensuring the champagne he'd stocked was well iced. Her eyes glazed over at the thought.

"Must I report to you each time I wish to take a drink? Or do you wish me to sip from the Nile?"

The cold glint of his stare warned her she pressed too far. Jasmine bit her tongue.

"When we reach Luxor, I will not remain on board the *Nile Queen*. I have a suite at the Winter Palace." Thomas looked at Jasmine through his hooded eyes. "Each morning, when I wish to visit the valley, the captain will sail the boat across the river to the quay, dock there and await my return."

"Avoiding the ferry fees," Jasmine said with sarcasm. "You're very economical. Will you use the savings to order more champagne, sir?"

Anger flashed in his eyes, then vanished.

"When I visit the valley, you will accompany me at all times. You may bring your notebooks and conduct interviews as you please, as long as I'm with you. You will be allowed freedom to explore the dig, as long as I remain with you. Is that clear?"

Delight twined with anxiety. At least she'd accomplish her goal of exploring the site; but what about at night? With Thomas staying at the hotel, and her quarters on the boat, it meant she would remain with the servants. She preferred the safety of the hotel; there'd be less opportunity for an assassin to creep on board, dagger in mouth, and stab her as she slept.

But one must have courage. "You wish your staff to report to you each morning?"

"All but you will remain on the boat. You'll have the room next to my suite. It was occupied, but I gave the manager a generous tip to escort the occupants to other quarters."

Relieved, she muttered a low thanks.

"And of course, there are times I shall require your company in the middle of the night."

She gave him a blank stare.

"If I wish for a cool drink, I shall expect you to fetch one for me. If I take a long stroll by the banks of the Nile in the moonlight, you will be ready to dust off my boots and polish them. Each morning I expect you to have my suit neatly laid out and ready, my collars sparkling white, and my ties pressed." Thomas paused, steepling his fingers, a man of authority expected to be obeyed without question. "I'll need my dinner dress pressed and ready, as I am dining tonight with the director of antiquities and several others."

"I see," she shot back with irritation. "Do you wish me to draw your bath as well, sir?"

"If you wish, you may assist me with bathing."

A blush raced across her cheeks like sunrise. Jasmine put her hands to her heated cheeks and turned, hoping to hide her reaction. Behind her, Thomas laughed.

"Er, no, I'll . . . er, I'll go see to your evening wear now." Jasmine fled, and Thomas continued to chuckle in her wake.

They departed without incident. The *Nile Queen* was a fine dahabiya. He'd given Jasmine a stateroom so she didn't have to sleep with the crew. The comfort of the quarters surprised her. It featured a sinfully large four-poster bed, mahogany dressing table with a beveled mirror and armoire and a small secretary—even a marble bath, complete with a gold-veined, pink marble sunken tub big enough for two.

The bath, she realized with dismay, was connected to his room by adjoining doors. He occupied the very next room.

The deck offered red and white striped chairs as well as a dining table. The salon had a faded Oriental carpet, rectangular windows shaded by crimson drapes pulled back with ornate gold ropes, and red and white floral settees lining either side of the chamber. A dining table sat in the middle.

The salon had a maplewood desk for writing correspondence. Between chores, Jasmine penned her articles there, nibbling on her pen as she dreamily gazed at the passing banks of the Nile. She'd barely write a paragraph when the cook would interrupt her for help preparing the evening meal, or the housekeeper asked her to scrub the floors.

Jasmine spoke little to Thomas. The long journey against the current proved agonizingly slow. Catching the wind as the sails allowed, the vessel labored along. Several times the crew disembarked to use tow ropes to pull the boat along when the wind died. She reported to the dragoman, who actually enjoyed talking with her in fluent English. She took the orders of the servants silently. In silence she served Thomas his meals. In silence she scrubbed the dishes, cleaned up after meals. Tidied his cabin. Thomas, whose tent had been so neat in the desert, now had clothing tossed about as if caught in a sandstorm.

That afternoon as she cleaned his suite, Jasmine picked up a shirt from the floor. She inhaled, smelling him, remembering the masculine scent of leather, spicy cologne and man as his body had covered hers and she'd clung to him. She had been his for those precious nights.

No longer. Now she was his servant.

"What are you doing?"

Guilty, she dropped the shirt. Thomas stood in the doorway, his dark brows drawn together in a severe frown.

"I told you to tidy my quarters before we arrived. You'd best be quick, you have shirts to launder. Sniffing them won't make them clean."

"I was merely marveling at how one man who insists on others doing everything for him could get so dirty," she shot back. "And smell like a camel after a ten-day sojourn across the Sahara."

She tossed the shirt into the hallway with a pile of dirty laundry then went to dust his dresser. His small brown scorpion charm caught her eye. She picked it up.

"It's protection against those who would harm me." Hands thrust into his pockets, Thomas leaned against the wall. "Do you recall the myth of Isis and the seven scorpions?"

"I prefer novels."

He prowled toward her with lazy grace, his fingers trailing over the amulet, brushing over her fingers. She sucked in a trembling breath.

"Isis was traveling with her infant son and, as protection, had seven scorpions as escorts. One day she stopped at a rich woman's house to ask for shelter. The woman slammed the door in the goddess's face, and later, the scorpions returned to sting the woman's child."

"That's a dreadful tale!"

"Oh, it has a happy ending." Thomas gave her a level look. "Isis refused to let an innocent child die. She uttered magic words, calling each of the seven scorpions by name, giving her power over them. Then she ordered the scorpion poison to leave the child, who lived."

"A very happy tale," she shot back. "And the moral is—"

Thomas took the charm. "Isis was refused hospitality by the rich woman, and later given shelter by a poor woman who shared all she had. I myself use the amulet as a reminder never to judge a person by their status, for it is one's heart that matters most—and one's generous spirit." He gave her a meaningful look. "Just as a scorpion cannot be dismissed as evil. They can be protectors of goddesses."

Jasmine fell silent, not knowing what to say.

Thomas set the scorpion charm down. "There is a spell for exorcising a scorpion. It's inscribed on a stela found on a wall of a Franciscan monastery in 1828. It's on display at an art museum in New York."

"A real spell? Do you recall the words?"

It is all ancient mumblings, if almost musical and poetic. I won't repeat them. One does not casually mutter magic words unless they desire the spell to actually work."

Jasmine edged closer, clutching her dustrag. "Do you then, not wish the spell to work, the scorpion to lose its power?"

His breath hitched as he stared down at her. He brushed a

thumb over her cheek. "You have dirt on your face," he said softly. "Like a chimneysweep."

"Do I now?" she breathed, their mouths close, nearly touching.

His lips parted. Then he dropped his hand and turned, jamming his hands into his pockets.

"Get out of my room, Jasmine," he said thickly. "I desire to be alone."

She dropped the dustrag on the bureau and left.

Get out of my room, scorpion. And out of my heart. I exorcise you from my yearnings, my deepest desires. Bending his head, Thomas gripped the bureau edge. Good God, this was far more difficult than he'd imagined. He'd meant to teach her a lesson while keeping her close and protected from harm. Instead, he was punishing himself.

How the hell could he endure this—her nearness, the faint fragrance of the woman, the very essence of her, teasing him?

But she was here, where he could watch over her. If she'd returned to England, quite possibly anything could have happened. A shudder raced through him as he envisioned Jasmine pushed overboard and lost to the cold blue ocean.

Yet, such a move was unlikely. Instinct told him the person causing this series of accidents did not want her dead—yet. Each had allowed for escape: Pushing her off the steamer. The stolen purse in the bazaar. That had been the final clue. It would be easy enough for an assassin to walk up to her and thrust a knife into her back.

A chill fell over him. Jasmine's would-be assassin toyed with her as surely as a cat swatted a trapped mouse before devouring it. That person wanted to torment her. And perhaps he would try to kill her in the end.

Thomas now had good reason to suspect who it was. He

lacked proof. For now he must ensure she didn't stray far from him. All his staff was hand-selected by a trusted friend in Cairo. Thomas paid them handsomely, and gave each one strict instructions to see that Jasmine was not harmed in any fashion. The true test would come if Jasmine was attacked again. Here on the boat she was safe, but on shore, anything could happen.

Thomas went to his dresser, unlocked the bottom drawer and withdrew his pistol. He loaded it and tucked it securely into his belt, along with the silver dagger Jabari had given him. Armed now, it was time to put his theory to the test. An upcoming, popular stop on the Cook's Steamer deserved further exploration. Beni-Hassan swarmed with tourists. They would stop there, and Thomas would take Jasmine with him. The barren rock tombs would make Jasmine a clear target, if someone was following them.

Mid-morning they reached Beni-Hassan. The Doric and lotus columns did not interest Thomas, nor did the ruins of the ancient Arab village destroyed by Mohammed Ali. He planned to explore the tombs, taking Jasmine. And his pistol and knife.

Jasmine glowed with pleasure when he'd mentioned the outing. Her obvious excitement made him determined nothing should happen.

Children shouted and ran barefoot through the village streets. Jasmine smiled and waved at them. The mud brick homes of the town built over the ruins of the ancient village gave way to the pathway to the tombs.

Thinking how life in the Middle Kingdom was portrayed in the array of rock tombs in the limestone cliffs high above the town, Jasmine's eyes shone with bright enthusiasm as they rode up the cliffs. Thomas remained tight-lipped, scanning the barren terrain for enemies. Other tourists streamed about the area. Easy enough for someone to blend in and be anonymous.

The group's little donkeys trudged gainfully up the steadily rising mountain slope. Below the tawny sands lay fertile fields and the serene waters of the Nile. Heat shimmered in the scimitar-sharp blue sky.

They dismounted. The dry, stony mountains were as impassive as the regally-carved tombs they had reached. Whirlwinds of sand blew upward as they walked the paved pathway. Thomas remained behind Jasmine as they toured the tombs without incident. No one seemed to follow them, as she scribbled notes and exclaimed over the finely-preserved murals.

As they approached Kheti's tomb, Thomas tensed. Gooseflesh broke out on his arms. He knew this feeling, and had not experienced it in a very long time. He put a hand on the butt of his pistol as he followed Jasmine into the tomb.

Kheti's tomb—Number 17—was a large unoccupied chamber. Two slim, lotus-shaped columns hung from the ceiling. Lights placed in the tomb showed scenes of men involved in daily life. On the rear wall, paintings showed men making wine and harvesting grapes.

Jasmine was rapt. "Look, isn't it spectacular, Caesar? I feel as if I've been transported back thousands of years. Imagine if the wine they fermented still existed today."

Despite his apprehension, he smiled at her enthusiasm, even more so at her use of his pet name. Flushed with excitement, her cheeks took on a delicate rose tint, and her dark eyes sparkled.

"I daresay it wouldn't taste very good."

"Here's Kheti and his queen." Jasmine pointed out a painting of the ruler and his wife. "Oh, she's so lovely!"

You are more beautiful than any ancient painting, he thought, her beauty intoxicating him once more. He watched her nibble on her rosy lower lip, an adorable frown of concentration furrowing her brow.

"Breathtaking," he muttered, dropping his hands to prevent from reaching for her. "Come, now, let's leave. I want to be underway soon."

"Just another minute." She scribbled something on her pad.

Another minute in this musty, hot tomb alone with her, and he wouldn't be able to contain himself. Thomas gritted his teeth and took her wrist in his hand. *"Now."*

He led her outside, blinking at the brilliant sunshine. A few people milled about, but he saw no one suspicious. Perhaps it had been merely his imagination. Thomas dropped her wrist, and Jasmine closed her notepad with a snap.

Oh, how he had desperately wanted to back her against that tomb wall, spread her legs and lift her skirts and plunge into her wet, welcoming heat. Thrust into her until she screamed, the sound echoing in the ancient chamber like the distant cries once echoed in the palace walls where Kheti pleasured his wife. Thomas ran a finger around his too-tight collar. He turned toward the rock wall, pretending to examine it as he waited for his arousal to fade.

How could he continue like this, Jasmine around him at all times? A delightful distraction, she made him lose concentration on what was most important. Keeping her safe.

Jasmine made a small exclamation. "My word, is it . . . No, it simply can't be."

Dread crawled down his spine. "What is it?"

"I thought I saw someone . . . impossible." She shrugged. "It must be my imagination."

But Thomas knew exactly whom she'd seen. Tension tightened his body as he glanced around.

"Let's go," he ordered, herding her toward the pathway. His right hand remained securely on his pistol.

As Thomas hurried her down the dusky slope leading to

the riverbank, he resisted the urge to look over his shoulder. He knew they were being watched.

Days later, their elegant dahabiya docked at the quay in Luxor just outside the Winter Palace. Jasmine's room was comfortable and had a small balcony. Next door, the Luxor temple shimmered in the early morning sunlight. Golden shadows touched the ancient stone walls as light played over the ruins. Jasmine longed to explore, but Thomas planned to visit the Valley of the Kings this morning. Her pulse beat faster at the very idea.

A knock came at her door. Jasmine ran and flung it open. A scowl on his handsome face, Thomas stood in the hallway.

"You shouldn't open the door for every single person who knocks."

Piqued, she glowered at him. "You're right, I shouldn't." With that, she slammed the door.

After a moment, Jasmine collapsed against it, dissolving into laughter. Outside, Thomas called out he was leaving and she'd best get ready to go. She continued to chuckle.

Mere minutes later came another loud knock. She called out, "Who is it?"

"Maid service," a high-pitched voice said.

Throwing open the door, Jasmine peered out. No one. Puzzled, she stepped into the hallway.

A hand seized her roughly about the waist at the same time a calloused palm slapped over her mouth. Terrified, Jasmine struggled. Her screams were muffled as her captor dragged her inside the room. Jasmine opened her mouth and bit down hard. Her captor muttered something in Arabic, kicked the door shut with his foot. Instinct took over. Jasmine went limp, forcing him to bear her dead weight; then, as she sensed he relaxed, aimed backward with her elbow. Her elbow met rock hard stomach muscles. Her captor barely flinched but released her.

Jasmine whirled, set to knee him in the groin. Two hands blocked the move.

"Please, for the sake of my future heirs, don't," a familiar voice said.

Shock filled her as she stared at Thomas. Her heart continued its erratic racing. Carefully, he detached himself from leaning against the door.

"I want to impress upon you—never open the door to anyone but me. Maid service, room service, I don't care. Anyone could pretend to be the help. This is a dangerous city. I made arrangements for the hotel staff to enter your room only when one of my personal staff is present. You're only to open it if you hear my voice. If you need something, you ask me. Is that clear?"

She nodded slowly, gulping down deep breaths to slow her racing heart. Thomas jammed a hand through his hair.

"Now, get ready. We're visiting the dig. I'll be calling for you in one hour."

"Why are you being so protective, Thomas? Is there something you know?"

For a moment he said nothing. Then his gaze flicked away. "All in good time. Now, go and get ready."

They rode small gray donkeys to the Valley of the Kings. Jasmine breathed in the hot air, but her floppy white English hat shaded her eyes from the burning sun.

Thomas rode behind her. Ahead, rode the dragoman. She was flanked only by the high cliff walls.

When they finally reached the dig site, the dragoman held her reins as she dismounted. Porters scurried to set up a small canvas canopy and a table and chairs beneath it. With brisk efficiency, they unpacked hampers, bringing out a cool pitcher of lemonade, glasses and a tin of biscuits.

The dig site was a hive of activity. Men clad in ankle-length *galabiyahs* and light-colored turbans chanted in singsong rhythms; picks whistled through the air as they worked barefoot among the sharp rocks and small pebbles. Some had removed their outer garments and worked in shorter under robes. A small boy carrying a bulging goatskin over his shoulders and a cup dangling from a string wended his way through the men, handing out water.

There were other visitors, including a German couple with their daughter. The blond daughter looked about sixteen.

Pad in hand, Jasmine sat and began sketching. Thomas went off to greet a tall young man who was supervising, but the dragoman protectively hovered by.

Jasmine glanced at him. "I'm quite all right. You can go about your business now."

"*You* are my business, miss," he said courteously. "The young lord instructed me not to leave your side."

Perplexed, she nibbled at her pencil. Thomas nodded to the man he chatted with, and the two walked off. Jasmine busied herself with observing.

The workers bent over, scraping and digging at the earth, coaxing it to yield long-dead treasure. Debris and rocks were dumped into large woven baskets. Small boys standing patiently took these baskets. They trudged off, forming a long, white caterpillar of basket boys moving toward a dumping ground.

Jasmine frowned at several men standing about, carrying switches and herding the white caterpillar when it moved too slowly. She asked Ali about them.

"Each group has a *reis*, a foreman," came the reply.

Heat poured down on the valley, mingling with the dust rising in the wind. One *reis* barked orders and work halted. Thomas joined Jasmine. He poured himself a glass of lemonade and sipped, glancing at her.

"Enjoying yourself?"

Too many questions swirled in her mind. She contented herself with asking about the dig's particulars.

The workers now sat in small circles and untied cloth-wrapped lunches. Tomatoes, onions and simple brown bread were devoured as they talked and laughed. The bundles were tied to long sticks called *naboots*, Thomas explained.

"Don't let its simple form deceive you. The *naboot* is a weapon. Those sticks are employed in a rather vigorous form of fencing called *tahtib*. Ancient Egyptians performed these fights to honor their pharaoh. These days, it's also used in dance."

"Dance? Does your opponent beat at your ankles if you step on his toes?" she asked.

He laughed. "Only if your partner cannot waltz—and you waltz most divinely," he said, looking at her with sudden warmth. Then he looked away and became business-like once more.

"Excavations are hard work, long hours and rather tedious, Edward tells me. But the excitement lies in the find, and in the potential for the find. Every scrap of earth must be removed carefully, lest the worker miss a small antiquity in the debris."

"It's a huge hunt for buried treasure."

Lunch ended and the diggers returned to work. Other visitors came to observe. Thomas remained by Jasmine, watching warily.

"Davis is a master showman. He likes mingling with the wealthy and important, which is one reason I was granted access," he said absently, studying the German couple's daughter.

"And here I thought he invited you because of your impeccable good taste in hats." She gave his battered chapeau a pointed look.

Thomas glanced down at the wide-brimmed hat and grinned. "It *is* a tad worse for wear since the desert."

"It looks like something ready for the rag man. Haven't you another? What about the bowler you wore in England?"

"Bowler?" He shot her a quizzical look.

"The one you wore when you called on me after I fell ill outside the restaurant."

His mouth flattened. "Not suitable for the heat," he muttered.

Jasmine watched an Egyptian youth carrying a basket stare at the blond German girl. She gave a shy smile, filled with promise and hope. The young man stumbled, nearly spilling his basket.

Thomas followed Jasmine's gaze. "They're in love, you know. Edward told me. He's been watching them."

Jasmine scowled. "Pity them. It will never go anywhere. He's Egyptian, and she's so—" Pale. Rich. Acceptable. "Young," she continued. "She'll just ignore him."

"I think not," Thomas said softly. "It's quite sweet, how much he adores her. How she looks at him. They're both so young, and innocent of the world."

The basket boy walked off, trailed by the blond girl. Thomas grabbed Jasmine's hand. "Come on, then. I'll show you not to be quite so cynical."

They went behind a canvas tent. The Egyptian boy had dumped his dirt and was looking at the German girl, who had escaped her parents' watchful gaze. Very shyly, he took her hand. He stole a quick, tender kiss on the girl's pale palm.

Emotion brought a lump to Jasmine's throat. The reverent, worshipful look in the boy's eyes and enchantment in the girl's nearly made her believe in such impossibilities.

When they returned to their seats, Thomas seemed deeply pensive. "I envy their hope. Nothing matters but their feelings for each other. They consider not propriety, nor the future, but live for the joy of the moment, and steal away each one."

"It's so sad. Because soon they will both discover life doesn't reward such tender feelings, but crushes them like glass beneath a hammer. The digger is only destined for heartache." Jasmine gave an indifferent shrug to hide her wistfulness.

Thomas gave her an odd look. "And the girl is not?"

"Oh, I suspect she'll forget and move on, after her parents return to Europe and tennis meets and horse races. She's from a higher class. She'll lose sight of her first love, and he will be a distant memory. She'll remember at night, perhaps when she brushes her hair, and then sigh at the silver moonlight reflected in the window, and think of the grand pyramids and how an Egyptian boy stole a kiss. And that will be it."

"Is that it, Jas?" he asked quietly. "I think not." Stark longing etched his expression. His feelings were not gone. Just hidden well.

"Is it not? I'd like to . . . to think not, too," she breathed.

Thomas traced her cheek with a finger. Reflected in the turbulent depths of his green eyes was her own incipient longing. She parted her lips, craving his kiss.

He started to bend his head toward hers when a loud shout broke them apart. Thomas jerked back, excitement flaring on his face.

"Good God. They've found it. Tutankamun's tomb."

Chapter Twenty-five

Amazing, how quickly everything changed. In a heartbeat, Thomas's cold attitude had changed to heated passion once more. In a heartbeat, a young girl surrendered to a shy boy's trembling touch. In a heartbeat, a tomb was found and would change history.

Surely it was Tutankamun's tomb, Davis had declared as he stormed to the site. Blustering and short, with bushy sideburns and an arrogant air, the dig's sponsor was now in a fever of excitement. He was sure he was right.

In the next week, the dig site swarmed with people. It took a few days to clear debris from the ancient burial place. Disappointment filled Jasmine as she heard the news; the tomb was not only empty, but deteriorated from rainfall dripping inside over thousands of years.

Caught up in the excitement, she and Thomas visited the site often. Days after the initial discovery, Davis came over to Thomas and shook his hand. Thomas politely introduced Jasmine, but Davis paid no attention. He chatted with Thomas and invited him to dinner.

Theodore Davis only invited elite and noteworthy. He barely glanced at her. Jasmine felt invisible. Ignored. Again.

But Thomas shocked her. Putting a hand at the small of her back, he gently propelled her forward. "Thanks, Teddy, but I'm dining with Miss Tristan tonight."

Davis took a second, quick glance at her. "Busy, eh? You'll miss a treat, a real treat."

Dazed, she watched him leave. "We're dining tonight? Since when?" she said to Thomas.

"Since I decided."

"And when were you going to ask me to this distinguished event?"

"Jas, I'm your employer. I told you, you must do everything I say. And that includes dining on the most exquisite beef, drinking the finest French wine and indulging in every culinary delight my cook has to offer." A teasing light ignited his gaze, making him look boyish.

"And putting up with your company. I suppose I must," she said, giving a deep sigh, as if he'd proposed shutting her inside the musty tomb.

He playfully tapped her nose. "You must. Now, come. Let's explore."

As they approached the tomb, the guard posted there nodded courteously. No one else was below, he informed them.

Jasmine peered dubiously at the steps leading to darkness. "Is it safe?"

"Perfectly. I'd never lead you into danger." Thomas offered her a lantern. He held another.

Summoning her courage, Jasmine followed him. Light played over the gloom as they descended into the tomb's inky depths. Shadows cast by their lamps danced on the rock walls, Thomas's most lighting the way. The stone stair ended in a hallway that had a second set of steps. Jasmine licked her lips. A musty and dank odor filled her nostrils: air that had been sealed for thousands of years.

Summoning all her courage, she followed Thomas. Self-confidence and excitement flowed from him, reassuring her.

When they reached the first room, her own enthusiasm bubbled up. This was her heritage, her birthright, her country of proud and ancient people. Flipping open her pad, she began sketching the gods standing in proud relief on the walls. Isis in queenly splendor. Horus; Hathor, the cow goddess; and Osiris, king of the underworld.

Thomas studied the painting of the pharaoh standing with Anubis, guide to the underworld. "Teddy brags this is Tutankamun's tomb, yet I wonder. From what I know of hieroglyphs . . . it doesn't look like his cartouche." At her bemused expression, he added, "Cartouches are the symbol indicating a king. Rather like a personal mark."

His extensive knowledge humbled Jasmine. Together they explored the tomb. When they finally reached the burial chamber, Jasmine reeled back.

"My word," she said in awe.

Six towering pillars decorated the room. The red granite sarcophagus stood empty. For a king's burial chamber, it was rather simple, albeit emptied: Davis had already removed several jars, models of boats, chairs, faience beads and a couch in the shape of a lioness.

An enormous painting of Osiris, lord of the Egyptian underworld, dominated the far wall. They advanced toward it as Thomas began talking of ancient Egyptian mythology. A thought struck Jasmine. The painting was impressive, but the coffin was equally so. She closed her eyes, seeing the dead king laid there, robbers stealing away his mummy. Yes, readers would be impressed with the king's empty tomb. There was something sad about an empty coffin, its owner forever lost.

"I daresay this tomb isn't quite finished," Thomas mused aloud. "I doubt the king was ever laid to rest here."

There went her theory. Well, she could improvise. And imagine.

He glanced at her. "I want to go back to the first chamber and take a good look at those wall paintings. Coming?"

"I'd like to sketch this room so I can recall details later when I write my piece."

The approving smile he gave filled her with warmth. There can't be anything more between us, she sternly reminded herself.

"You shouldn't be alone."

"It's perfectly safe. No one else is here and the guard is watching the entrance."

"Do be careful, and don't stay long," he advised, and walked away.

Alone here, in the burial chamber, her claustrophobia kicked up a notch. Jasmine dragged in a deep breath, coughed as dust filled her lungs. Better sketch everything quickly, then join him.

I do loathe dark, enclosed spaces, but oh! This is simply spectacular! What my readers will say when I describe to them the tomb, the unearthing of ancient ruins not seen in thousands of years.

Jasmine made her way to the coffin, picking over old rock. As she peered down into its empty depths, a noise sounded behind her.

"Thomas?" she said.

Rough, cold hands seized her about the neck. Squeezed. She gasped for breath and struggled. Darkness swam before her eyes. She was going to die. But, bloody hell, not without a fight! Jasmine lashed backward, sending a sharp elbow into a soft stomach. Angry mutters sounded. As the pressure around her neck eased, opening her mouth, she released a terrified scream.

Thomas studied the tomb walls, and marveled at the paintings of the Egyptian deities. The golds of these kilts, brilliant whites, vermillion and browns had been preserved for thousands of years. The ancient gods and goddesses presided over the empty chamber in silent splendor.

Pity the pharaoh wasn't found, but still, this was magnificent. He bent over and picked up a small stone. Even the rocks: here for thousands of years. Thomas imagined the workmen singing and struggling to carve out the tomb, sweating in the heat much as the diggers had labored to find it.

A scream echoed through the tomb. Thomas dropped the rock. He tore toward Jasmine, entering the burial chamber. She sat on the ground, gasping. Even in the dim lamplight, he could see ugly red marks around her neck. His stomach gave a sickening twist.

Setting down his lamp, he gently touched her shoulder. "Jas, what happened?"

"Someone tried to strangle me," she rasped. "I, I was studying the coffin, and heard a sound behind me. I thought it was you. And then these hands came around my neck— oh, God!"

"It's all right now," he soothed, squeezing her shoulder. Damnation. Bad business. Thomas suddenly realized how vulnerable they were. Alone, in this dark tomb, encased in rock. And someone was trying to kill Jasmine.

He heard quick, light footsteps in the corridor.

Thomas lowered his voice. "I've got to get you out of here."

He helped her to her feet, grabbed the lantern. A familiar yet odd scent for these surroundings teased his nostrils. Thomas sniffed. "Are you wearing perfume?"

"I never wear—" Her voice trailed off as she inhaled the air.

They both recognized it: a woman's perfume, heavy and cloying.

"Come on," Thomas whispered, tugging her hand.

Jasmine's chest felt hollow with panic. The tomb walls seemed to march toward her, enclosing her in rock. *This could very well be* my *tomb*, she realized. The walk down the corridors was agonizingly slow. She tried to avoid looking over her shoulder. Whoever was responsible for the prior attacks still trailed her.

Finally, they reached the outside stairs and climbed. Fresh air surrounded them. Jasmine took several deep breaths. Standing at the top of the steps, the guard greeted them.

"Has anyone come from the tomb in the past few minutes?" Thomas demanded in Arabic.

"No, sahib. No one but you and the pretty miss have entered or left."

Diligently he questioned the guard, but the man denied it. Then the guard slyly suggested a few pounds of baksheesh would loosen his tongue.

Wide-eyed, he stared as Thomas withdrew a pistol, cocked it and pointed it at him, saying, "This is all the baksheesh you'll get, my friend."

Stammering, the guard admitted he had been given money to walk away for a while and leave the tomb unguarded just before they entered. When pressed at gunpoint, the man pleaded and said he only knew the person had been an Englishman. He'd been wearing a black robe, but spoke with a foreign accent.

With a few choice words for the guard, Thomas put the pistol away. He slid a hand on the small of Jasmine's back as they walked to their donkeys.

They rode in relative silence through the Valley. She felt grateful he was armed. Finally they reached the donkey stand, giving the donkeys over to the attendant. As their boat sailed across the Nile, Jasmine thought about the attack.

"Thomas, a woman couldn't have attacked me. The person had rough hands, like that of a laborer. Man's hands. But why try to strangle me?"

He touched the bruises on her neck. "Try? He almost succeeded."

"But he didn't. I wonder. Wouldn't a knife in my side be quicker and more efficient? There are many efficient ways of dispatching a person. I've read about them in all the novels. A knife, a bullet in the head—very loud but quick. Poison."

Thomas pressed a finger to her lips. "Hush. This is becoming far too morbid, talking about your potential death. I'm only interested in keeping you alive, Jas. Whoever did this probably failed because they knew I was close by. And I very well intend to keep you very close should they try again. From this moment on, you will not be alone."

And then it clicked, as if a curtain in a dark room were flung aside to reveal harsh sunlight.

"You never intended for me to sail back to England, did you? You wanted to keep me here with you."

Even before he nodded, she knew Thomas conspired to make her his servant to watch over her. Because he suspected something dreadful.

"Thomas, what do you know? What's going on?"

"I'm not certain." He frowned. "I believe some things, but have no proof. It's not something I'm at liberty to talk about—not now."

An odd expression crossed his face. It almost looked like shame. His Adam's apple moved as he swallowed. "Jasmine, I've something to tell you. My behavior . . . back at the Shepherd's, that whole dastardly exchange and what I told you about the flower girl. I apologize for my crudeness. I wasn't . . . being myself."

"I suppose you had the right to be angry with me," she responded, sighing. "I knew something dreadful happened that spurred your anger."

"Not at you, Jas," he said very gently. "There are things I will tell you, but I can't now. Trust me. Will you trust me?"

A faint smile touched his mouth as she nodded. "I do trust you, Caesar. You're one of the few I can. Your friends, on the other hand—I think, desire to get rid of me. It occurred to me that the person wishing me harm is one of your friends. The notes back in England were quite blunt."

He went very still. "What notes in England? You mean, this didn't start with the incident on the steamboat?"

"I thought it best to keep silent on the matter. It seemed . . . unimportant at the time."

Anger tightened his expression. "Jasmine, someone has been trying to kill you since before we left England and you thought it unimportant?"

A flush ignited her cheeks. "Oh, bother, there I go again,

saying the wrong thing. Not 'unimportant.' But . . . I was too ashamed to tell you and Uncle Graham. And I was afraid he would insist on sending me home, and I just could not face going home yet. Besides, all these things that happened, they've been rather clumsy. If someone wanted to kill me, wouldn't they use more efficient means?"

His hands rested on her shoulders, comforting and secure. Thomas gentled his voice. "Jas—out with it, sweet. Tell me about the notes."

She did, leaving out the part about the writer accusing her of killing Nigel. As he listened, his expression grew furious.

"You should have told me sooner, damn it."

"I couldn't. I didn't want anyone to know."

"Did you think I wouldn't understand? Or care? Because I do care. More than you know."

Jasmine's heart thundered. A low sweep of wind brushed through the foothills, billowing her skirts and teasing the hank of brown hair hanging over his brow. Green in his eyes blazed as if lit by the very sun.

"Do you, Thomas?" She could barely whisper the words.

He slid a hand up to cup her cheek. "Yes, Jas. I love you. I have for a very long time now. I can't deny it any longer."

"Nor can I. I love you, Thomas." She wanted to leap for joy.

"You know it's impossible," she said after a pause.

"The only thing I know is that we have this moment and everything in it. And I'll seize it and do all I can to cherish it . . . just as I cherish you," he said. His kiss was brief, tender and gentle as the wind brushing against them. He rested his forehead against hers a moment.

When he pulled back, his smile faded. "Let's go," he said abruptly. "The sooner I have you safe in the hotel, the better."

Chapter Twenty-six

The balcony outside Thomas's suite commanded a stunning view of the Nile. Fellucas drifted northward, white against the blue sky. Heat shimmered across the Nile in the Valley. To his right, the setting sun cast intricate shadows across the Temple of Luxor.

Too overwrought to appreciate the scenery, Thomas paced back and forth. Until he could confirm all his suspicions, how could he risk sharing such drastic information with Jasmine? It was too fantastic even for him to believe. Too dreadful. Thomas fisted his hands, grief raging through him.

With his usual meticulous care, he pondered over the identity of her attacker. The stone in the park could have been Oakley. Oakley hated Jasmine.

The person Thomas had seen at the rock tombs had not been Oakley, however, but someone who shouldn't have been there. He dragged a hand through his hair. What the hell could he do?

A servant set a silver bowl of grapes, pomegranates and oranges on the table outside. Another poured ruby wine into a sparkling crystal glass and set the decanter down. Two china plates and heavy silver completed the place settings.

Thomas tipped and dismissed the servants. He watched the play of light on palm trees below, the striking contrast between the valley in the distance and the verdant rice paddies and lush fields hugging the river. Tranquility flowed here like the Nile. Contrasted to Jasmine's gruesome experience in the tomb, it felt safe.

He studied the encroaching darkness. One could not see all the stars at night because of the city lights, but in the valley they would shine like brilliant diamonds cast against black velvet. In England, covered by yellow fog in winter, their brilliance faded.

Jasmine came to his room. They dined as the sun sank below the horizon. The beef was tasty, the French wine exquisite, but Jasmine barely touched her food. He questioned her lack of appetite.

She pushed back from the table and stood. "It was lovely, but I can't stop thinking of what happened in the tomb. I wish . . . I wish—" Her voice trailed off.

Thomas went to her, placing his hands gently on her shoulders. "What, sweet? Tell me what I may do."

Doubt shadowed her eyes as she glanced at him. "Did you mean what you said, Caesar? About me? Loving me? Is this something you wish to keep secret from others?"

He touched her cheek. "Watch me."

With purpose he strode to the edge of the balcony. Thomas leaned on it and cupped his hands to his mouth. "Do you hear me, world? Everyone! I love this woman! Thomas Wallenford loves Jasmine Tristan!"

Jasmine laughed as he turned to her with a grin. "There, I said it in English. Would you prefer Arabic?"

Erotic heat filled him as her tongue traced her rosy mouth. "I need you, Caesar. Make me forget everything awful. Love me as you did before," she whispered.

Clasping her hand, he pulled her into the room.

"Damn it, *I* need *you*," he muttered. "Seeing you isn't enough. I need to touch you, taste you. I need to have you, Jas. I can't help this, you're rainwater to my desert."

Thomas touched Jasmine's cheek, a smile playing about his lips as he pulled her into his arms. His kiss was warm, inviting and deeply drugging. A shiver raced through her as she stared in rapt fascination at the prominent bulge in his trousers. For her, all for her, was this crazy, raging desire. She felt a wild sense of feminine power. Raw hunger and promises of hot sex glistened in his piercing jade eyes. The startling contrast between the cool, arrogant and reserved earl and this sexually aggressive, virile male aroused her. Jasmine felt as if Thomas had stripped off an outer layer allowing her to glimpse the passionate man hiding deep inside.

Buttons snapped off with loud violence. Breathing heavily she stared, then her own eager hands fumbled with his clothing. Thomas cupped the back of her head, tunneling his fingers through her thick ebony curls, and kissed her. It was a kiss of passion, ownership, and she thrilled in it. Backing her against the wall, he pushed up her skirts, passion twisting his face into a mask of agonized need. Jasmine arched against him. He unbuttoned his trousers. His hard, raging erection sprang out.

Nudging her legs open, he stood between them and lifted her skirts then cupped her naked bottom with his hands. He lifted her up, sliding her bottom against the wall.

Jasmine bit back a moan as he positioned himself strategically. He took her with one upward thrust. The hot, hard length of him pushed inside her, nearly to her womb. Jasmine cried out and arched upward in shock and slight discomfort. He rained tiny kisses over her face, her eyelids, her mouth. This was what she'd missed in her life: real undiluted passion, two bodies melding as one, merging together, chasing away the loneliness inside her. Here was where she belonged.

Her arms slid about his neck as she drew him closer, seeking his mouth. He kissed her and began moving again, pounding into her, his naked flesh slapping against hers. Never had she felt anything this primitive, the warm smoothness of his member sliding in and out of her, her leaden limbs trembling as she wrapped them about his moving hips. Raw and elemental, the passion felt as earthy and heated as the desert.

Shifting, he angled his thrusts, sliding against the most sensitive part of her. Jasmine's fingers dug into his shoulders.

Feeling her climax approach, she bent her head and bit him on the shoulder, teeth sinking into the hard muscles past his shirt. Thomas pushed into her so hard she gasped. She flew apart, convulsing around him. Thomas looked at her, veins bulging in his neck, his nostrils flared as ragged breaths filled the air. He groaned as his body convulsed and he pumped his seed deep within her.

Trembling, their breathing ragged, they remained motionless a minute. Then he let her down. She slid down the wall in a boneless, shaking heap, her skirts falling about her like rumpled flower petals. With a hungry look she watched him smooth back his disheveled hair.

Removing their clothing, they went to the bed. Stretching out, they held each other, listening to their hearts beat rapidly then resume a more normal rhythm.

Peace filled him as Thomas held Jasmine close. She felt warm, soft and utterly feminine. His hand cupped her breast possessively. Through the partly open window, brilliant stripes of twilight streaked the sky. Nothing could be more perfect than night in Egypt and Jasmine in his arms. He felt as if everything in his life had suddenly made sense and fell into place, the last piece of a mosaic fitted to create a stunning masterpiece. She had stolen his heart, the part of him he'd tucked away and hidden like a scorpion hiding beneath a rock.

Yes, they had created a tiny oasis in this luxurious suite. Here, they loved in a world isolated. He knew it could not last. This was a lovely dream, and all dreams must end. But for now, he would greedily lap up all he could, relish each single moment with her in their little oasis.

Thomas lifted the dark curtain of her hair and studied the nasty bluish bruises marking her perfect skin. Gently, he pressed his lips there, as if to erase the pain. She stirred in his arms, her rounded bottom rubbing in delicious friction against his groin. Instantly he hardened. He ran a hand down her spine, and began kissing her. One gentle press of his lips after another, awakening her with loving kisses.

With a flutter of long, dark eyelashes, she awoke, a sleepy smile on her face. He lightly bit her neck, then chased it with a tender kiss. Thomas kissed his way down her body, his mouth fastening on the rising crest of one nipple. Very lightly, he teased her with his tongue, watching with pride as she moved restlessly. He put a hand between her legs and tested her. Wet. Very wet. Aroused, nearly painfully now, he could not wait. Mounting her, he parted her trembling thighs with his knee, and pushed his hard cock inside her.

He groaned with the exquisite feeling of her body squeezing him tightly, caressing as he thrust inside. She was silky heat, gripping him as he slid inside her. Thomas raised himself on his hands, watching her passion-drenched face, the lovely color flushing her cheeks. She arched beneath him, and gripped his arms as he went deeper, deeper than ever before.

"Come for me, Jas," he breathed, "Come for me, my beautiful shining star—yes, that's it, that's it, let it go, love, let it go."

A scream tore from her throat. He watched with loving tenderness as she climaxed. Masculine satisfaction filled him. God, she was so damn beautiful, so responsive to his caresses. She was his. All his.

Thomas felt her convulsing around him, and gave one last thrust. With a shudder and a groan spilling from his throat, he climaxed.

Shaking, his heart thundering, he rolled to his side, still inside her as he pulled her into his arms. He stroked her hair as she rested against him.

"I don't want to let you go," he said thickly.

"Let's just stay like this," she replied, her voice languid, her body relaxed against him.

He kept stroking her hair, holding her, guilt and sorrow rising up. For he'd meant letting her go when they left Egypt.

Could he keep her in his life? Could he convince his set to see her as he did?

He couldn't bear to think about that now. Time enough to ponder it later.

Steam misted the air from the bath chamber as Jasmine emerged. Dressed in a flowing silk robe of peacock blue, she went to the open balcony door. She began brushing the thick mass of her ebony hair in long, luxurious strokes. Sounds of the muezzin calling the faithful to prayer greeted the dawn in a lyrical chant. A dreamy smile on her face, Jasmine began singing a haunting melody.

It was an Arabic love song about a woman pining for her lover. Thomas raised himself up on his elbows and watched Jasmine sing, the rhythmic movements of her brush keeping time to the enchanting lushness of her sultry voice. Utterly transfixed, as if held in a spell woven by her siren voice, he could not move; Thomas could only watch and listen. Jasmine, his beautiful Jasmine, held him in her power. Her voice wept for the lost lover, each note rising and falling like sand tumbling from the dunes. Like a bird taking flight then falling to earth, her delicate hand dropped, the brush dangling loosely from her fingers. Her eyes closed as she sang to the open window a mournful plea for the lover she could not have, the sweetness of an embrace forever lost.

His throat closed. Thomas swung his legs over the bed's edge. Naked, he went to her, sliding his arms about her waist. She leaned back against his chest.

"Not lost, Jas, but here. Always here."

A tiny sigh wafted from her, musical and sad as her song. "Will you be? I feel as if we are living a sweet dream. And now the ordinary world has rushed in and we have to awaken, and face it, and live as ordinary people do. Our troubles haven't left. They're waiting for us. Like desert jackals waiting to pounce."

"Not yet. I'll take what I can, for the moment. Forget everyone else. They can wait, the whole bloody lot can wait." He kissed her shining hair.

She turned, smiling a little. "You're not very practical, but you are quite a romantic."

"A practical romantic, sweet. With you here in my arms, no one will dare harm you," he said, unable to keep the tightness from his voice. Thomas rested his cheek against her head, relishing the silkiness.

"Oh, right. I had forgotten, somehow. You made the world go away so brilliantly, and all my woes. I feel safe with you, Thomas."

"I'll keep you locked here, forever, if it means keeping you safe."

"Until we must leave," she pointed out practically. "And someone is still out there, wishing me dead. Do you think it's one of your friends? A rather drastic measure for not liking me, Caesar, knowing he would rather see me in a coffin than with you. It does make our liaison a bit challenging."

"It's not a liaison," he muttered, touching her cheek. "A liaison is something you hide, a discreet affair."

"And this is not? Thomas, let's be honest. For both of us, well . . . we won't ever have anything more than this room and this moment."

"A thousand moments more are not enough."

"Such poetry. Eloquent, but wasted. Like in the park." Her smile faded.

"What is it, sweet?"

"There's something I must tell you. About the notes, and their threat. And the real reason your brother died."

Thomas went very still. "Nigel was thrown from his horse and died of injuries caused by the fall."

"Why he was tossed." She detached herself from him. "It was because of me. You see, it's all my fault. I killed your brother."

Chapter Twenty-seven

Impossible. A sickening jolt slammed into him. Thomas struggled to talk.

"Tell me," he demanded.

"It's my fault. That night in the park. I think one of your friends must have been there. Whoever it was blames me for Nigel's death—as he should."

Thomas stared at Jasmine's drooped shoulders, her dispirited air.

"It was two days after you bought the Arabian from Uncle Graham. You sent me a note, daring me to meet you in the park at midnight for a gallop, teasing that you had the better horse. I couldn't resist. So I went."

"I wrote no such note."

"No, I realized afterward. Your brother did."

"I'd told him not to ride that night," Thomas said hoarsely. "He could not handle Sheba. He was intoxicated."

Jasmine laid a hand upon the sill. He barely heard her words through the thickness of her voice.

"He called to me. I ran to him, he was quoting poetry and it was so very romantic. The moonlight. The words. Romance and moonlight. What a fool I was. I thought perhaps his compliments were sincere. I was wrong."

Jealousy consumed Thomas. Nigel? Jasmine? He remained silent, waiting.

"He took me into his arms and kissed me. But it was wrong. All wrong. I saw who he really was. I saw he was Nigel. Quite drunk. He told me Egypt fascinated him, like I did. He said, 'My mother calls you a brown scorpion, but the brown scorpion hides the key to a rare treasure on her belly. I want those riches.' Then he laughed and we had words. He became quite . . . ugly. I've never seen anyone so angry."

"What did you say that riled him?"

"I told him . . . that I'd never go to the park to meet with him. He simply wasn't you, and could never be so. You were perfect."

The word sent a chill racing along his spine.

Jasmine continued: "Nigel said only trollops were out at that hour and so I must be one as well. A pretty brown Egyptian trollop. And everyone knew what happened to trollops."

"Jas," Thomas said thickly.

She turned, and light streaming through the window caught the sheen of tears glimmering in her eyes. Tears she refused to shed.

"He ripped my gown. Ironic, isn't it? Just as his mother, your mother, did at the ball. Is that a habit your family has— ripping my clothing? Only, Nigel's purpose was different. All that riding I did . . . I was strong, but he was much stronger. He insisted on another kiss." Her large dark eyes looked haunted. "I had no recourse. My uncle is a duke, but everyone knows we have little social influence and we're regarded as oddities. Unlike Nigel and your family. He told me he just wanted a little fun and what was the harm? That's when I kicked him."

Jasmine lifted her head, anger shining in her eyes. Brilliant anger, shiny as a sparkling star.

"I had never been with a man . . . as you well know." She gave a humorless laugh. "But I knew exactly how to hurt him. Right in the ballocks."

"Good girl," Thomas said softly, his own fury gathering like a thunderhead. He wanted to take her into his arms, but didn't dare distract her. "What happened?"

She gave a bitter laugh. "He released an ungodly howl. I got away, but he shouted at me. I told him to sod off. He staggered away to get on his horse. And I knew, he couldn't ride. He could barely walk. I told him to stop, but he paid no attention. He rode off and I heard . . . I heard . . ." Jasmine gulped down a breath. "I heard the horse fall and Nigel scream. Oh God, how he screamed. He was in so much pain. I ran to the street, where there was someone walking. I shouted for help. Then I left, relieved no one recognized me. But someone obviously did."

Thomas fisted his hands, fury and grief twisting him inside.

"That's the reason for the notes," Jasmine said. "It's my fault he was so reckless when he rode off. If I hadn't gone to him that night, thinking it was you . . . he might still be alive." She went still, staring at the glass. "What happened should have tempered my resolve to fit into your little circle. Incredibly, it strengthened it. I thought—silly, really, but I thought—that if I was accepted and one of you, something like that would never happen again. I could walk in the park when I wished, and would have respect at last, just like your sister."

"Jas," Thomas said thickly. "Oh, sweet . . . how wronged you've been. I could kill him for what he did."

She raised her tear-filled gaze to him. "You're too late," she choked out. "He died, anyway. Don't you see, Thomas? I never would have gone to the park to meet anyone but you. I've had the silliest schoolgirl crush on you for ages." Her voice dropped to the barest whisper. "You're not like him, Thomas. Not at all. But he certainly did look like you that night. You are—well, were—identical twins."

Thomas dropped his hands. Oh, God. She'd thought it had been him that night. And she had gone to him, eagerly, hoping for sweet words and an innocent kiss.

Instead, Nigel had deceived and tried to assault her. Rage consumed him, white-hot rage. Nigel had nearly ruined her.

"Goddamn you, Nigel," he muttered, soothing her as he stroked her hair.

"I just wanted a kiss," she sobbed into his shoulder.

He let her cry, holding her as the maelstrom of emotions poured from her. Thomas found a handkerchief. Jasmine blew her nose and went to dry her eyes as he took the cloth from her, tossed it aside.

Cupping her face in his hands, he gently kissed away her tears. Feathered tiny, soothing kisses over her cheeks, her lips, her chin, down to her neck and the little hollow at her throat. Jasmine clung to him, her head thrown back as he kept kissing her. Giving her the kiss she'd longed for that night in the park, and many more.

Thomas eased the robe off her slender shoulders, letting it fall to the floor. Lifting her into his arms, he laid her on the bed and continued kissing her. His mouth landed on the taut crest of her nipple and he suckled gently.

Lacing his fingers through hers, he entered her slowly, almost reverently. He pushed inside her swollen sheath with absolute gentleness, as if to banish that night from her mind. Thomas gazed down at her as his body joined to hers. He wanted her to remember him, only him. No other.

He was not Nigel, no matter how many times women in the past had made comparisons. Jasmine would never remember Nigel after today. He'd put his mark on her so deeply, all nightmares of his twin would vanish.

Thomas kissed her as he continued thrusting. Jasmine moaned, lifting her hips to meet him.

"Say my name, Jas," he commanded softly. "Say it. Say it."

"Oh, Thomas, Thomas," she sobbed, clinging to him as she arched upward and shook, the force of her climax causing exquisite joy. Thomas threw back his head and shuddered, and his seed spilled from him.

Much later, Jasmine dozed as Thomas stole over to the window, lost in thought. Something wasn't adding up.

Nigel had told Jasmine Egypt fascinated him—a falsehood, for Nigel seemed bored after that one trip to Egypt the winter before he died. And the brown scorpion being the key to a rare treasure? Certainly Jasmine was a rare treasure, but . . .

Sudden insight came to him. Thomas swore softly. He dug through the pocket of his trousers lying on the floor of his room and picked up the brown scorpion amulet. Impossible. Still . . .

Weighing it in his hand, he studied it in the light. A knife and a bowl of oranges lay on a nearby table. Thomas picked up the knife and scratched the top of the amulet. To his immense shock, the stone began peeling. Paint. The stone was painted.

Scratching some more, he saw green beneath the surface and markings. His breath hitched as he saw the ancient marks.

His fake relic was genuine.

A light brush against her cheek awoke Jasmine from her nap. Blinking, she smiled sleepily at her lover. His expression was somber.

"Jas, I have to leave you for a while, but I'm making arrangements to have your room guarded. Stay here, where it's safe."

She listened as he explained about the amulet's authenticity. "Edward is with Davis in the Valley of the Kings, and I don't want Davis to hear of this. There's another archaeologist working at the Temple of Hatshepsut I've arranged to meet. I need information on its origin."

"I'm going with you."

"No. It's safe for you here."

"And I'm as much a part of this as you are, Thomas. Please."

He raked a hand through his hair and sighed. "Very well. But stick close."

Hours later, they were at the temple. Jasmine felt relieved that Thomas finally knew about her part in Nigel's fall. He still didn't know about her birth, though. He'd find out soon enough. The past haunted her no longer. She must tell him, before he returned to England and read the shocking news for himself.

Stark and impressive, the three-tiered temple was set at the head of a deep valley. Today it was closed to visitors because of the archeologist's work. He was to meet them at exactly three P.M. As they climbed the stone steps, Jasmine drew in a deep breath.

"Before he arrives, there's something else I want to tell you," she began.

Thomas gave her a steady look. Oh God, this was going to be far more difficult than she'd ever imagined. But she must do it, before she lost courage. Before she lost heart. If he condemned her for it, then so be it.

"I gave Mr. Myers a scandal guaranteed to be more scintillating than any indiscretion your sister could commit. I sacrificed myself on the altar of public opinion in my next column." She looked away, unable to bear his scrutiny. "It was written to draw suspicion from your sister, saying it was a false trail to delay revealing the real scandal. I revealed myself as the author of The Blue Bloods, and also my past.

"I wrote the column in a way that would not shame my mother. I told readers how my mother was informed after my birth that I . . . that I died soon after. In truth, an evil man stole me away and sold me to a . . ." Her voice dropped with shame. "Sold me to a brothel. My mother had no idea I still lived until I was seven. Seven years old and being trained as a prostitute. My best friend, an older girl, had already been sold to another man, and I never saw her again." Emotion thickened her voice. "So you see, I gave your set fodder to ruin me forever. Your mother once called me an Egyptian trollop. The truth is, I was raised as one until my stepfather and mother rescued me."

"Jas, look at me," Thomas said. His voice was very gentle. She could not—did not want to see the repulsion on his face, the disgust, that his sort had been right all along in their estimation of her origins.

Two warm hands settled softly on her shoulders, forcing her to turn. Thomas raised her chin so she met his tender gaze. "I know. I know all about it, sweet."

Tears blurred her eyes. Blinking them away, she stared as he wiped one with the corner of his thumb. "And that article will never see the light of day. I had it destroyed."

"I don't understand."

A grim smile touched his features. "I told you I was a ruthless pirate in business and enjoy watching others surrender. I'm a very patient man. From the moment I first encountered you and this ridiculous column, I set out to stop it on my own."

"You couldn't. Mr. Myers owns the paper. He can print whatever he wants—"

"He doesn't own the paper anymore. I do."

Shock caused her jaw to drop. Thomas gently kissed away her tears. "I hired investigators to track *The Daily Call*'s debts. Myers mortgaged his business heavily. It took time, and considerable money I had secured away, but I bought the note." His expression hardened to granite. "And I called it in, giving him a deadline to raise the capital. When he failed, the paper became mine. I hired reputable newspapermen, and told Myers he could stay on under the supervision of the editor I hired. He was quite grateful, and in my debt. Grateful men seldom take revenge."

Realization dawned. "The telegram . . . that's what it was about?"

"No one bests me." Thomas's expression hardened, and she saw in him a reflection of the pirate.

"And you then found out about my column, what I had written. Why didn't you simply publish it? It is nothing more than I deserve. All this . . . I started it," she whispered.

He brushed a lock of hair from her face, his touch so soft

and assured it sent shivers through her. "I destroyed it, and the copies as well. It will never be published. I told you before, Jas, I always protect my own."

"Oh!" Sheer wonder filled her. "I suppose . . . I see."

"Do you now?" His fingers trailed down her neck, sending a shiver of arousal coursing through her. "When I want something, I become quite determined. I pursue it until it is mine."

"Horses? Newspapers run by shady publishers? Or something more?"

"Everything. Including an Egyptian woman whose intelligence is matched by her beauty and compassion," he murmured. His hand cupped the nape of her neck as he drew her close.

Suddenly, Thomas went very still. "It's not safe here," he whispered. He pressed his mouth close to her ear. "We are being watched. Someone over there, hiding among the pillars."

"Is it your friend?" she whispered back.

"Definitely not. Whoever it is has a pistol. I saw the sun strike the barrel. Let's go." Thomas shouldered his rifle more firmly and tugged her hand.

Blinking furiously at the blinding sand, they slowly emerged from the temple. He glanced up at the mountain. "That path. Ayrton told me it leads to the Valley of the Kings," he said.

The day seemed far too bright and sunny for such a menacing threat. As they reached the narrow mountain pathway, a shot rang out, hit the ground a few feet away. Jasmine stifled a scream as Thomas tugged her up the mountain. Below she saw a shadowy figure dart behind a rock.

"At this range, he'll miss with that pistol. We can outrun him. Come on!"

Sand stung their cheeks as they climbed. Jasmine's breathing became labored and her heels slipped on the rocky path.

Thomas did not slow, but firmly laced his fingers through hers, feeling their sweating palms lock together. Relentlessly, he tugged her up the mountain.

Wind whipped the pretty scarf around her neck. In the distance she thought she saw the cool Nile, and the safety of the Winter Palace. How she longed to be there and safe! Dignified servants were hovering over ladies languidly sipping tea and complaining of luxurious boredom. Her mouth felt drier than the gritty sand, but Thomas pushed on.

As they reached the top of the mountain, another sharp crack echoed through the valley. A bullet kissed the air near her cheek. Jasmine shrieked. Thomas pushed her downward. Withdrawing his own rifle, he scanned the sands.

"Bloody hell, there must be two of them," he muttered.

Jasmine lifted her head, saw movement below. "There, Thomas," she whispered.

He went to shoot. Then a female voice behind him chilled him to the bone.

"Drop it, Thomas. Or would you wish to kill your own brother?"

Chapter Twenty-eight

Nigel, his twin, was alive.

Shock filled Thomas as he watched Nigel climb toward them. Charlotte Harrison, his former mistress, laughed and pointed her pistol at them.

"Miss me, Thomas? And you abandoned me for this brown whore?"

"Charlotte, leave Jas alone," Thomas said tightly. "Your business is with me."

"Our business is with her," the woman said. "It was all Nigel's idea. But he only wanted to scare her, and I wanted her dead. Nigel was too cowardly. All those threats in England were childish. When I came to Egypt, I knew he'd fail."

"You did everything." Jasmine stared at her lover's former mistress.

"Yes—pushing you off the steamer, throwing that rock, hiring that silly Bedouin woman to put scorpions in your bed. All me. It's astounding how easily one can be masked in this country. I did it all—except the market. Nigel arranged to have you robbed. I wanted you stabbed. When he told me what he'd done, I knew I had to step in. I hired someone to strangle you in the tomb. Easy enough for me to hide and wait for him to do it. Stupid peasant was supposed to stab you, but he was too cowardly, and got scared when you fought back."

"You bitch," Thomas growled. "I suspected it was you when I smelled your perfume."

Nigel reached them. An arrogant sneer twisted his lips. "It's me, sweet," he said in perfect imitation of his twin's voice. "I do hope you didn't suffer too badly after I poisoned your tea. Easy enough to slip into a disguise and do it when the chef's back was turned. I'm a master of disguise. And I look exactly like Thomas."

"You're nothing like him," Jasmine retorted.

"Nigel. Nigel, why?" Thomas said, anguish twisting his guts.

"Long story, brother. It's been fun, this masque, hasn't it, Char? Too bad the fun's over."

"Over for good. The little brown scorpion will die here in the desert, just as she deserves," Charlotte said, her eyes bright.

"I never meant for them to die, Char. You know that. I just wanted her to suffer a good fright. Put the gun down," Nigel said.

Instead, Thomas's former mistress cocked the trigger. "The hell I will. You ruined everything, Nigel. It's my turn now."

As she swung the gun at Jasmine, Thomas sprang in front of her. He pressed her against the rock, shielding her with his big, solid body. Her finger was on the trigger, but Nigel sprang forward and pushed her. Pinwheeling her arms, Charlotte staggered dangerously close to the edge of the cliff.

"'Bye, Char. You were a bore," Nigel said softly. Then he delivered a well-placed kick to her back.

A high-pitched scream followed. Nigel watched in silence as the woman disappeared.

Thomas's heart thundered as he stared in disbelief at his twin. "I suspected it was true, but didn't want to believe it," he said quietly. "I'd rather believe Oakley was behind all this."

"That fool? He could no more pull this off than he could piss in a pot. It was a grand plan. You never guessed it was me."

"I knew it was you the moment Jasmine said I stole her purse and she was accused of openly soliciting as a prostitute at the Shepherd's." Thomas clenched his fists, resisting the urge to pummel Nigel's face. "You made one mistake, in addition to acting like a bastard. Your hat. Jasmine asked where my bowler was. I never wear one."

Jasmine's eyes widened. "Oh, God. And I never thought—"

"You never did because you had no reason, Jas. I suspected

as much when odd things started happening in Cairo. People telling me of my appearance in places I hadn't frequented, places that made them shun me. Certain brothels, for example."

"A man must have his pleasures," Nigel drawled.

"I hired someone to find the truth. He investigated and discovered you were alive. All this time I thought you died. Why? And why did you do this to Jasmine?" Grief and fury tore at Thomas.

Nigel looked darkly amused, and he glanced at Jasmine. "I had to keep her from you, Tommy, should she recall what I said in my drunken rant that night in the park. You'd have guessed what the scorpion charm really hid."

"You told me, 'The brown scorpion hides the key to a rare treasure on her belly. I want those riches,'" Jasmine recalled. "You were talking about me."

A frown darkened his brow, then Nigel laughed. "Oh, this is simply too bloody brilliant. All this time you thought I was talking of you! Because my mother called you the brown scorpion! I was talking about the charm."

"It's jade," Thomas said tightly. "I was meeting here with an expert to discern the age and value. And this is why you tried to kill Jasmine—over a small piece of jade?"

"Not kill her. That was Char." A shadow briefly crossed Nigel's face. "I told her we would only scare her away from you, Tommy. That night at the ball I was in masque and saw you kiss Jasmine. I instructed Char to ask you for the scorpion charm."

"That's why Charlotte wanted it," Thomas realized.

"Char told me it was in your treasure room, but when I broke in, it had vanished. Oh, it was bloody fun, hiding so you wouldn't see me as I was trying to deduce a way to steal it. Give me the scorpion, Tommy. You gave it to me as a gift, remember?"

"It wasn't worth Jasmine's life. Nothing is," he said, infuriated. He removed the scorpion and threw it. Nigel caught it one-handed.

"Didn't you always think it odd the tail lacked a stinger, Tommy?" Nigel removed a knife from his pocket and scraped the charm's underside. Markings appeared. A soft smile touched his mouth. "The ankh and the jackal."

Realization slammed into Thomas. "A pharaoh's cartouche."

"Not quite. Remember the old man who sold you this, Tommy? I met his son on that trip to Egypt. That trip you offered to me when you couldn't go. I decided to explore for treasure. In the eastern desert, I found a cave with an ankh and a jackal on a rock wall. The digger I hired told me the cave was cursed. I got Malik drunk and he confessed the wall I found is a door leading to a room hiding a treasure map. For generations, his family robbed tombs and dumped the booty inside a vault hidden in the desert. The key to opening the door and getting the map is a scorpion amulet and a ruby that was the tip of the scorpion's stinger. But the ruby was missing.

"Malik's father thought the pharaohs had cursed him because he had lost the ruby, so he painted the scorpion to hide the markings and sold it to a pale-faced English boy whose eyes matched the stone's true color."

Thomas stared at his twin. "All this time, the worthless amulet I bought as whimsy—"

"Is quite valuable. I know where the ruby went, and now I have the main part of the key." Nigel gave him a sly look. "I knew if you discovered the markings, you'd be your usual honorable self. You'd make inquiries. Tell officials and they'd search for the lost treasure. Since my 'death,' I've made a nice life selling antiquities, but I've always longed to get my hands on that hidden treasure. I won't let anyone else have it."

Thomas's guts twisted violently. "Is that what you've gotten into, Nigel? Smuggling rare objects out of Egypt?"

"What does it matter?"

"You're a thief," he realized.

A crooked grin touched Nigel's mouth. "I prefer the term pirate. Sounds more dashing, eh, Jasmine?"

Jasmine looked troubled. "You're planning to rob that vault of ancient treasure that belongs in museums."

"Stealing treasure from Egypt is despicable, Nigel," Thomas added tightly.

Nigel gave him a flat look. "Then I'm despicable. Unlike you, the perfect twin. I could never be as perfect as you, perfect in our dear father's eyes. I was deformed, a curse to his line."

"Good God, what the hell are you blathering about? You were the perfect twin, not me."

His twin's lip curled in a grimace. "Do you know why our dear parents refrained from telling us who was firstborn? We thought it a game to test us. It was no game to Father. He was waiting, Tommy. Waiting to see who was best."

Thomas's heart gave a sickening lurch. "Father told me I was his heir. But only after I returned from Egypt—"

"When I was sick and they thought I would die. But I didn't."

Dawning realization kicked him in the teeth. Damn their father. Damn him to hell.

"Odd, isn't it, how Father chose to tell us you were the heir after I recovered from measles. They thought they'd lose me. I survived." Nigel gave a flippant shrug. "The doctor said my ability to father children didn't survive. He doubted I'd ever make a woman pregnant."

Jasmine made a small noise. Nigel glanced at her and snorted.

"That's right. My precious ballocks were useless to father. That's when he suddenly announced you were firstborn, Tommy. But he lied. They all did."

"They couldn't have deceived the doctor." Thomas's fury

and rage howled within him as he struggled to recover his lost composure.

"They bribed the doctor. I overheard Father and Mother when they thought I was unconscious from the fever. I was the heir, but no one knew. You were perfect, Tommy." Nigel paused and his gaze went flat. "Little brother. Born only 10 minutes after me, but born after me."

"You should have told me," Thomas grated out.

"It was all Father. I spent the rest of my life trying to please the bastard. Being perfect in every way to get him to acknowledge the truth. But I wasn't perfect enough." A shadow passed across his face, then he gave an indifferent shrug.

"But after you fell . . . I saw you lying in the bed, you were so bloody pale . . . then I stood at your graveside, watching mother weep, feeling as if part of me had been ripped away. Damn you, how could you deceive us, Nigel?"

"Deceived only you and Mandy." Nigel shot Jasmine a grin. "I wrote in the first note that it was your fault, Jasmine, just to poke at you. It wasn't, and I do apologize for being such a rutting bastard that night we shared in the park. That lovely, romantic night." He heaved an extravagant sigh.

"You nearly raped her," Thomas said tightly. "I should kick your bloody ass for that."

His twin gave a bitter laugh. "I suppose I deserve it. Oh, I'd never have gone through with it, Jasmine. All I wanted was a kiss, because I knew you wanted Tommy here. I thought I'd steal a kiss before he did."

"You shouldn't have gone riding," she cried out. "I told you to stop."

Anger drew his mouth down. "That damn horse fell on me, broke my arm in so many places the doctor said it would be useless. I was better off dead. I was dead already to our parents. I threatened to parade myself around London making a scandal unless our dear mother and father did as I asked.

"Dead to them, why not make me truly dead? There were

doctors in America who might save my arm. For the price of a steamer ticket and money to line my pocket, I died that day. I never wanted to see them again. And they were glad to get rid of me." Torment filled his eyes as he gazed at his twin. "You. You were the only one who truly grieved, Tommy. Even Mandy, she didn't care."

"Did . . . did you find doctors?" Thomas could barely speak.

"I got lucky for once. In New York, I had surgery. They saved my arm, but it was bloody painful." Darkness filled his eyes as he rolled up his left sleeve. Thomas felt repulsed by the ugly twist of pink scars wending down Nigel's arm. Jasmine put a hand to her mouth.

"You could say we're even now, little brother. Both of us with scars." Nigel looked away, his jaw moving. "And so I'll quietly vanish again. Don't worry, Tommy. You'll never see me."

Choked with emotion, Thomas could barely speak. His brother. His only brother. He could have killed Jasmine, but had saved her from Charlotte.

And Nigel had been dreadfully wronged. They all had.

"Come back to England. You're the rightful heir. I'll talk to Father, do anything, pound sense into that bastard. Strip away the finances. They will not deny you your birthright."

Hope flickered in Nigel's gaze and then died like an extinguished candle. "It's too late, little brother. Even if I wanted the title, and I don't, you can't bring the dead back to life."

"Yes, you can," Jasmine blurted out. Thomas slid his hand down to grasp hers.

"You can, because my uncle did," she continued. "Everyone thought Graham died in the attack that killed his parents. When Kenneth, my stepfather, was duke, he found Uncle Graham living in the desert. He brought him back to England and he assumed the title. Everyone believed the story how he was raised by an English couple in Egypt. It worked out splendidly."

"Did it?" Nigel's gaze was cold and flat. "Your uncle is eccentric. Few want to associate with him. Your stepfather is even more so for marrying your mother, the dark-skinned heathen. Your family is odd, Jasmine. They don't fit in, just like you."

Thomas stepped forward. "Watch what you say. Don't you dare insult her."

Nigel threw up his hands. "Just stating a fact, as stated before by others of our rank and class. My past, it's rather tainted. Black as pitch, one might say. I can't change. The documentation is there for you to assume the title, Tommy. It can't be changed, either."

"The title is rightfully yours, Nigel."

For a moment he looked lost; in his eyes Thomas saw a flash of vulnerability. "I suppose maybe Mother and Father might want me back—" Then he snorted with derision, and Thomas knew the truth: Neither of their parents would welcome him back.

"You'll be the next earl, Tommy. It's too late for me. No regrets," he said crisply.

"Never," Thomas echoed, remembering their boyhood pledge. Never regret, never look back. But this time, he would look back and remember. And look forward. "When I return to England, I'll tell everyone you are alive. I'm leaving the door wide open for your return. Whether you kick it shut or fall down on your ass again is up to you." He gave his brother a long, meaningful look.

"I'll be staying in Cairo . . . if you want to get in touch." A reckless grin touched his mouth. "At the Shepherd's, under the name Nigel Smith." He jerked a thumb down the ravine to where Charlotte lay. "Sorry to dash off and leave you with that mess. But I can't risk running into trouble with the law, as delightful as that encounter may be. Might land me in jail this time."

A crooked grin touched Nigel's mouth.

How easy it had been for him to deceive Jasmine, but Thomas knew his smile was merely an image; deep inside, Nigel was far more scarred than the telling marks on his arm.

Nigel went to turn, then he looked back. The anguish in his eyes reflected Thomas's own. Suddenly he rushed forward and enveloped Thomas in a hug. A lump clogged Thomas's throat. His twin stepped back, looking embarrassed. He glanced at Jasmine.

"Good-bye, pretty little Jasmine, little brother. Have a splendid life together, if you must. Marriage, babies, happiness, all that rubbish." Nigel touched his forelock in a mocking salute.

"Go sod yourself," Thomas shot back, his own crooked grin faltering.

Nigel looked somber. "Sorry it couldn't be different." Then he shrugged again and shoved his hands into his trousers, walking off with a jaunty stride. A stride Thomas believed he'd never see again except in a mirror.

They returned to the hotel in silence. Thomas alerted authorities about a woman meeting with an accident near the temple, then retired to his room. When Jasmine came to him, he put out a hand. "Please, Jas, I'm not a good person for company right now."

"I'm not company," she said softly. "Oh, Caesar, why did he do it? You loved him so. He's your family, and you'd have done anything for him."

"Anything," he agreed brokenly. "But sometimes anything simply isn't enough.'

Closing his eyes, he accepted her embrace as she slid her arms about his waist. Deep inside he felt like screaming out for everything he'd lost. Instead he simply clung to her, losing himself in the comfort she offered.

When her lips pressed against his neck, Thomas yanked her close. He kissed her with desperate fury to hold back the grief raging through him. His lips feathered her closed eyes, her cheeks, her hair. He trailed his long fingers over the rise of her breast. He gently cupped her breast, drifting his thumb over her nipple.

She turned toward him as he captured her mouth, his tongue swirling and mapping the inside of hers. Their tongues mated in heated frenzy as his restless hands roved over her body, cupping and molding. Panting, he tore his lips from hers.

"I need you, Jas. Oh God, I need you."

It was a soulful plea from his heart. An admission that shook him to the core. Jasmine took his face in her hands kissed him. They removed their clothing and fell into bed. With her body she loved him, giving him all the reassurance he needed. Her kisses feathered over his face, his body; then she went lower, taking him into her mouth.

Thomas arched upward in startled pleasure. A groan wrenched from his lips as she encased his rigid length, licking and tasting him. He fisted his hands into her hair, awash with erotic torment. What she lacked in experience Jasmine made up for with eagerness. With a grunt, he pushed her away.

"Not like this. With you, atop me," he said thickly.

He showed her how as she climbed atop him, and he guided her to sink down upon his thick, hard cock. Jasmine did so with a look of dazed pleasure. She rode him—up, down—as his hands gripped her hips. His hands touched her, pleasured her.

When his own release came, he threw his head back and shouted. His cry echoed through the room, raging with grief and anger.

Spent, he trembled as she rested against him. They remained like that for a time, as he simply held her. And tried to forget his pain.

Jasmine caressed his chest, looking troubled. "Caesar, all these times we've made love . . . what if, what if I'm—"

He raised his head and looked at her. "If you have my child?"

Anxiety filled her large, dark eyes. "Yes," she whispered.

The possibility had occurred to him. Indeed, secretly he relished the idea, for it sealed an unbreakable bond between them and would force his hand. Thomas settled a palm on her belly.

"If you did carry my child, I would marry you, Jas. No further questions."

Relief filled her expression. "But marry me because of the child, or because you wanted to? Would such a marriage work?"

He kissed her forehead. "We could make it work."

Seemingly reassured, she snuggled against him and closed her eyes. The evenness of her breathing told him she'd fallen asleep. But for a long while he lay awake, pondering the question.

If they did marry, could they make it work?

The following day, they ate breakfast on his terrace. Fleeting peace settled over him. Surely, somehow he could see Nigel again. His brother could be found. Amends must be made and their father must answer for all he'd done to Thomas's twin.

A knock at the door interrupted his thoughts. Impatiently, he called out for the person to enter. A servant handed him an envelope. Dread spilled through him. Thomas ripped open the telegram. His face went blank with shock as the paper fluttered to the ground.

"I have to go back . . . My father had a heart attack and died. I'm now the Earl of Claradon."

Chapter Twenty-nine

Jasmine remained at his side on the journey back, offering what little comfort she could. When Thomas expressed desire to be alone, she walked the deck. When he took her into his arms and made love with a desperate fury, she took all he gave and gave back all her love.

Amends must be made as well. Encouraged by Thomas, she penned a letter to Amanda, asking forgiveness for what she had done. When the London docks loomed, gray and dreary, her heart plummeted. Rustling up hope, Jasmine forced a brave smile.

Things were not the same, she reasoned. Her stories in the paper had garnered respect and the publishers even asked if she could write a book. Thomas loved her. She loved him. It could all work out, she reasoned. Even if he was earl now.

But changes were already apparent. As they hurried down the gangplank Thomas became swept up in a flurry of friends and acquaintances. He turned to Jasmine, but she waved him off with a smile. The entourage enclosed the new earl of Claradon like a sarcophagus shutting upon a mummy, and he was out of sight.

Spotting her uncle, she felt relieved. His hug made her resolve crumble a little.

Upon her request, Graham instructed the driver to go to her parents' house. The prodigal daughter needed to apologize to her mother.

Badra sat in the gold drawing room, her face worried. Kenneth was with her. They both looked up expectantly as she entered.

"Are you all right? Graham told us what happened in Luxor," Kenneth said.

Jasmine ran to her mother, who held out her arms.

"Oh Jasmine, honey." Badra's voice quavered.

"You were right, so right. I'm sorry." She broke out in a sob, and buried her head in her mother's shoulder. They clung together, crying, as her father, her real father, hugged them both.

In the days that followed, Jasmine tried to piece her life back together. She wrote furiously, ignoring the gnawing worries that Thomas had forgotten all about her. He had many pressing matters requiring his attention.

She held long, poignant talks with her parents. Her columns from Egypt had garnered enthusiastic reader response. The publisher was interested in much more of her writing. When she told her parents her plans, Badra became upset but understanding.

"If Thomas doesn't follow through, you must do what you deem best, honey. And it isn't as if we will never see you again."

Her heart belonged to Thomas, but could she fit into his world? She'd posted her letter to Amanda, and received a reply. Amanda not only forgave her, but begged forgiveness for her own actions in treating Jasmine so horribly. Desperate hope rose within Jasmine. If Amanda could forgive, and accept, why could not others in his circle?

Four weeks passed. She had her monthly courses, with a feeling of relief and disappointment. Not carrying his baby. No more ties to him now. Except of the heart.

Then she heard from her aunt that shocking news reverberated around London: Thomas's brother, Nigel, was actually alive and living in America. Their father had driven him away. The taint of scandal evaporated under speculation the new earl would soon seek a bride, and father children of his own.

That morning, she received a note from Thomas. He had been at the family's ancestral home near Manchester, taking care of business, and had just arrived back in London. He invited her to the house and then a ride in the park. Her spirits lifted. Jasmine dressed carefully in her bottle-green habit and rode Persephone to his townhouse. Surely Lady Claradon must now acknowledge her. But when the footman admitted her into the drawing room, he informed her Lady Claradon was visiting friends. Only the new earl was home.

Delight soared through her as Thomas entered the drawing room. His soft smile evaporated all previous fears.

Her voice dropped to a whisper, should servants eavesdrop. "Thomas, I've something to tell you. I had my monthly courses."

Was that relief flashing in his green eyes? She couldn't be certain. Thomas took her hand, squeezed it. "I have something to show you, Jasmine. In my room."

Upstairs, he opened a door at the end of a long hallway, then closed and locked it, leaning against it. Jasmine turned, started to tug off her gloves. Thomas took her hand, lifted the glove and pressed his lips to her wrist.

"Take off your hat," he told her.

She did so, placing it on a small table beside the door. "What did you want to show me?"

His two arms slid about her waist, pulling her against him. Thomas swiftly undid her hair, combing through the heavy masses. He rested his cheek against the top of her head. "Ah Jas, Jas, I've missed you so, my darling Jas," he said huskily. Swiftly he turned her around.

Kissing, they tore at each other's clothing, fumbling to get undressed. Jasmine was desperate to feel his naked skin next to hers. She felt starved for his touch, his passion. Thomas went to the tall mahogany bureau and fished something out of the top drawer. Wide-eyed, she studied the object in his palm as he rolled it onto his stiff cock.

"It's a French letter. No chances taken now."

Before she could question him, he went to her, raked his fingers through her long curls, pulling her toward him. His hand dropped to the apex of her thighs, stroking and culling moisture. She lifted her thigh, wrapping her leg around his with a moan as his finger slipped into her wet cleft, sliding back and forth, coaxing her arousal.

"I'm going to take you now," he murmured, crushing his lips against hers. His tongue thrust into her mouth, warm and wet and she sucked on it, clinging to him. They lowered to the floor, clinging to each other. Thomas kissed her neck, nipped at her shoulder, then lowered his mouth to her breast. He suckled hard, his tongue lapping over her peaking nipple. The soft scrape of his warm tongue against her overly sensitive flesh was more than she could stand. Jasmine cradled him to her, writhing.

She wanted him inside her.

In desperation, she opened her thighs and arched her hips upward in nameless pleading, hooking her legs around his firm buttocks. Panting, he mounted her, his erection pressing against the inside of her thigh. He gathered her to him and pushed inside. Sobbing with relief, she drew him closer, kissing him.

This was heaven: Thomas in her arms, inside her body, inside her very soul. It would work. They'd make it work, she vowed silently as he pumped into her. Each long, steady thrust of his shaft matched the rhythm of her hips pumping up eagerly to meet him. His naked body slid against hers, creating an exquisite friction. Jasmine opened her mouth to scream out her pleasure, but he kissed her, muttering against her mouth.

"The servants . . . will hear."

Instead, she stifled her whimpers. Jasmine fisted her hands in his thick locks and as she felt her orgasm approach, buried her head against his shoulder and bit his collarbone. With a long shudder and a low grunt, he climaxed.

He lay atop her a bit, his head beside hers as he panted heavily against her ear, her own heartbeat thundering. Thomas raised himself off her with a rueful smile. He sat up, and she leaned on an elbow, peering at him as he removed the sheath and discarded it in the fireplace.

"What does that do?"

"It prevents me from making you pregnant. I can't afford to take chances," he said, crouching by the fireplace and jamming the object into the coals with the metal poker.

Disquiet filled her. In Egypt they'd been skin to skin, abandoning all caution. He had promised to marry her if she carried his child. Now, here in England, he was the earl, and he guarded his seed against impregnating her.

Because he would only do so with his chosen bride, and conceive an heir. Things had changed, as she'd feared.

They dressed and as she buttoned her riding habit with hands that shook slightly, he rested his hands on her shoulders. Understanding filled his gaze.

"It's not that I wouldn't be proud for you to bear my children, Jas. But now is not the time," he said softly, helping her with the pins.

Pushing aside gnawing concerns, she concentrated on dressing. In Egypt, they'd made love without inhibition, not caring who overheard. Now Thomas insisted on discretion, and that worried servants would overhear. She felt as if a veil dropped between them.

He tiled her chin up, nodding toward the fireplace. "Have you seen my Egyptian Girl? I bought it because she's exotic and beautiful, just like you."

Jasmine gasped with wonder. She shot him an impish look. "So, Lord Claradon, this is how you saw me? Without a stitch of clothing?"

"Beautiful, touchingly innocent and unique," he said huskily. "It's you, Jasmine. I've dreamed of you, longed with all my heart. And now I have you at last. I will not let you go."

She reached up and kissed him. "As have I. I thought it would never happen, but only in my dreams."

"Let's ride in the park," he said with a smile. "I've arranged to meet my friends there."

Doubts filled her. Would they accept her? Would they see her as any different? She felt different. No longer trying to fit in, but a woman of purpose who felt secure in Thomas's love and approval.

They rode to the park, galloping down the sandy track. Laughter spilled from Jasmine as Thomas gleefully took the lead. When they finished and dismounted, he swung her off her horse into his arms.

"My beautiful Cleopatra. You are an exotic wonder," he murmured.

She slid her hands about his neck and went to kiss him. Shocked sounds of disapproval followed. She glanced over to see his friends gathered nearby. Thomas very gently removed her hands. A stiff smile touched his mouth.

Gone was the passionate, uninhibited man who loved her passionately in the bedroom, shouted his love to the wind in Egypt. Replacing him was the formal, reserved Earl of Claradon. Her heart dropped. It was as if the true masque had begun, and he was in his mother's ballroom putting on a show.

He placed a hand on her shoulder as he greeted his six friends, each who stared at her with loathing. Thomas formally introduced her as his sweetheart. Flat, censurious looks touched their faces. Oakley muttered something and looked away.

"I thought we could have tea at the house, and you could become better acquainted with Miss Tristan," Thomas said quietly.

One by one, excuses were made. All friends drifted away. Sharp anxiety speared Jasmine as she glanced anxiously at Thomas. Sadness flashed in his eyes, then vanished.

"Let's have tea at the house," he suggested, but his smile was strained.

When they returned to his house, Lady Claradon was in the drawing room. Draped in black bombazine, she saw Jasmine and turned her back.

"Get that thing out of my house, Thomas. I will not speak to her."

"Jasmine and I are in love, Mother. And you will accept that fact."

"Then you must accept I will never acknowledge her. She is as dead to me as your brother." The woman gripped a lace handkerchief tightly in one fist.

Fury darkened Thomas's face. Jasmine pressed her hand against his arm. "Please, Thomas, let's leave."

"No," he said tightly. "Mother, Jasmine is in my life now, and you can go to hell. For what you did to her, and to Nigel."

Lady Claradon's shoulders tensed. "I will not hear that name spoken again in this house. Leave me be, Thomas."

Jasmine tugged him away, out of the room. He followed her outside to the garden. A damp mist touched her cheeks, sending a shiver down her spine. England in March was dreadfully dreary, unlike Egypt. Her beloved Egypt.

Jasmine knew what she must do. Dryness filled her mouth. She could scarcely speak.

Her heart was breaking in two. She felt the pain, as if large stones pressed against her chest. It could never work out. Egypt had been a beautiful adventure—one that had passed.

Droplets clung to his jacket, looking like tears. He watched her, a hank of dark hair hanging over his forehead. How she longed to brush it back. But touching him might weaken her resolve.

"I'm sorry for how they treated you, Jas. And my mother, I thought things would be different."

Jasmine felt her heart turn over at his agonized expression. "I'm sorry as well, Caesar. But is that to be our life? Apologizing always?"

His jaw tightened. "What are you saying?"

"Your friends detest me still, perhaps even more now. They look at me sideways and whisper I ensnared you somehow. And your mother—you saw what happened. They're worse than ever. England is the same." She made a derisive sound.

His expression went flat. He drew himself up, and she saw the dignified, urbane Earl of Claradon, the air of authority on his broad shoulders. "England is my home, Jasmine. My home is here, my family and my duty. Life is different for me now. I have the funds at last to begin repairs on my home, and the ancestral lands. I have tenants who rely upon me, and pressing obligations."

"I know," she said softly. "And those obligations don't include me. It simply will not work out."

Thomas looked deeply troubled. "Jas," he said thickly.

"Hush, please, this is difficult enough. I must say this now. I love you, Caesar. I love you so much it feels as if I'm losing part of me. But you're the earl now. You need—"

Words clogged her throat. She struggled against the rising tears, the emotion threatening to spill over. Jasmine summoned all her strength and self-control.

"You need a w-wife who will be all you need, all they expect. A perfect wife who fits in, who can accompany you to parties and balls, entertain and socialize. I'm not . . . her. How I wish it were otherwise! But I simply cannot be her. I must be Jasmine."

"But . . . leave? Jasmine, stay. We can work out something, I'm certain—" His voice trailed off as he realized the futility of such a quest.

"How?" she asked, her voice gentle and understanding. "You're an earl who requires a wife of fine breeding, not one who causes whispers and rude conjecture. An acceptable wife, not a 'foreigner' who rouses all manner of suspicion. I will never live down what your set has labeled me. In their eyes, I'll always be the despicable Brown Scorpion."

Deep inside, she hoped he would declare himself, toss aside all his concerns. Hope died at his expression.

"How I wish it were not so," he said quietly, and she knew she'd lost him forever. But Jasmine forced a brave smile.

"What will you do?" He looked at her with such tenderness a sob rose in her throat. Ruthlessly she quashed it.

"I'm returning to Egypt. She is my home, in my blood. I realize now." Because she wanted to reassure him all would be well, she added, "My parents fully approve and understand. I've made arrangements with my publisher to pen articles from Cairo. A book as well. He's offered a handsome advance, enough to live upon. Uncle Graham has purchased a home in Cairo and I'll reside there."

"Jas . . . living alone in that city. Please, don't go."

"I'll be fine. Truly," she choked out. She reached up and brushed the softest kiss against his cheek. "Good-bye, Caesar. I'll . . . miss you. Nothing in your life has been perfect, but truly, I hope you find the perfect woman."

She turned and picked up the English skirts that weighed on her legs like lead. As she fled down the dark hallway, she thought she heard him say softly,

"But I already have."

They were gone for good: Nigel, his brother. And now Jasmine. His only love. His shining star.

Thomas braced his hands on the mantel, remembering the sweetness of their first kiss. That night only a few stars glittered. Now, they were forever extinguished. Jasmine was gone from his life.

Earl of Claradon. Wealthier and more powerful than Julius Caesar himself! Master of all he surveyed! Master of . . . nothing.

Thomas sagged against the mantel, staring up at the Egyptian Girl. "Jas," he said hoarsely. Hanging his head, he wept for the first time. For everything he'd stood to gain. And lost instead.

After a while, Thomas shouldered his resolve. He was the new earl and had many responsibilities. Finally he could make the changes his father never implemented.

Downstairs, as he headed into the drawing room, a footman brought him a letter. Seeing it was from his sister, Thomas eagerly ripped it open.

Still in Scotland, in her husband's ancestral home, she hadn't been able to return for the funeral, but planned a visit at a happier time. "When the baby arrives," Amanda had written. "Thomas I'm so happy. I'm blissfully in love and wish you could find the same. The world changes when you are with someone who loves you with all his heart. Nothing else matters."

The letter fluttered from his loosened fingers. Thomas went to the fireplace, lost in thought. *Nothing else matters.*

He had spent his entire life trying to be as perfect as his brother, living up to the family responsibility to shoulder the title. And then he'd found so much was lies. Now that he had his goal, he felt . . . empty.

He had everything. The title. Wealth. Friends. He enjoyed his very English lifestyle, loved England. It was part of him.

Yet, Egypt . . . it still called to him. Like a woman who made his blood burn.

England or Egypt. He felt torn. Thomas stared into the proud portrait hung above the fireplace. Hundreds of years of ancestry, proud lineage dating back that he could claim. "I am now Earl of Claradon," he whispered. "I have a duty to my family."

And what of your own joy? the voice inside him whispered.

What was more important, the title and England, or his heart?

In silence, Thomas pondered the question.

"Well, is she gone?"

He glanced at his mother as she walked into the room. He said, "Jasmine is gone. For good."

She sighed and shook her head. "You're an intelligent, well-meaning person. I understand how you could have had an adventure in Egypt and be indiscreet with a woman like that, but you must put such things aside now. You'll be a fine earl, the man your father never was. Why bother with her?"

The man his father never was. Man enough to make his own path, carve his own way.

"You were blinded by the false charms of a brown scorpion," his mother added. She sniffed. "You always were."

Brown scorpion. Thomas looked at his mother as if she stood at a distance. It would be painful, but if it were the price he must pay, so be it. Nothing worthwhile in life came without cost. Your own joy.

"I'm not blinded, Mother," he said slowly. "You call her the Brown Scorpion because all you see is a color. But not me. For the first time in my life, I can see clearly, and the only color I see is love."

Her brow wrinkled. "What are you talking about?"

"You shall see." Regret filled him. Thomas pushed it aside. No regrets. None at all.

He walked out of the room, leaving her staring after him with a bemused look.

Chapter Thirty

Cairo. City of pyramids, wonders, and now her new home. Jasmine hummed as she walked back to the house in the fashionable district. The book she'd promised her publisher was coming along nicely. She'd also received work writing articles for other publications. The Morrows and the Hodges, delighted to see her again, had taken her under their wings and introduced her around. At last, she had her own set, new friends who accepted her for who she was. A new life. A new career.

But no Thomas. Nights were hardest. She'd walk to the window, listen to the haunting sounds of the city, and remember making love to him. Then she'd cry for a while.

Tears cleansed, but the pain still lingered like a sharp wound. It would get better, she assured herself. Someday she might even allow herself to forget.

Jasmine approached her house and unlocked the front door. She went in, crossing the courtyard. Beneath the shade of a sprawling fig tree, a man sat on a cane chair at the little table where she liked to write.

Her heart raced. Surely it must be her imagination. . . .

Jasmine dropped her purse and ran forward. He sprang out of the chair. Laughing, he caught her up in a tight embrace. She laid her head on his shoulder and wept.

Finally she raised her tear-streaked gaze to his. "Please tell me this isn't a dream. For so long I've dreamed this, now I fear I may awaken and you'll be gone."

"This is no dream."

His handsome face, now burnished by sun, smiled at her. Jasmine touched Thomas's cheek in disbelief. Clad in casual trousers, and a white shirt, he looked far different than the distinguished earl.

"But Thomas—" The enormity of his sacrifice struck her. "I can't be with you. Our worlds are too different."

He leaned close, his eyes so filled with love she found it difficult to speak. "Then I shall make them the same. I need you, Jasmine. I need you like I need my next breath. I can live without my title, England and my family. I can't live without you. One doesn't reject a shining star when it comes to earth and graces your presence. You embrace it with all your heart and follow it wherever it goes. Just as I will follow you, Jas."

Tears blurred her eyes as he continued. "I want you at my side, with me. In my bed, making love each day. Beside me as we go through life, having children, growing old together. I shall not promise it will be easy, but I love you and I shall do my best."

Desperate hope filled her. Could he actually be saying what her heart so longed to hear?

"You can't. Your home is in England—the title, your family!"

"I've given it all up, sweet." He smiled tenderly. "I had to make arrangements first. I cabled Nigel and arranged to meet him here in Cairo. Told him the title is his and unless he comes to assume his rightful place, the entitled lands will pass to our cousin upon my death. Nigel was horrified by the idea of priggish cousin Sterling inheriting. He's gone back in my place—as me." Mischief twinkled in Thomas's eyes. "He did play the part rather well and no one will suspect the ruse. At least until Nigel tracks down the doctor who birthed us, and forces him to admit the truth so he can legally inherit. He's promised to make the changes I want. Land, title—that life means nothing next to you. I love you and I want to be with you the rest of my life."

"Caesar, what do you want with me?" she asked on a sob.

Thomas gathered her trembling hands in his. He pressed a gentle kiss on the knuckles of each. "Jasmine Tristan, will you be my wife? To have and to hold, to cherish and love for all time? Here in Egypt. Or wherever your heart desires. My heart desires it as well, my darling, for I desire only you."

He kissed her, his lips urgent and warm. Jasmine clung to him, wildly hoping it was not a dream. When they broke apart, she held him, fearing to let go.

Filled with loving tenderness, she gave him a tremulous smile. "You are such an incurable romantic, and I'm the luckiest woman in the world. I love you so much. But Thomas, how can you make a life here? You said once before you are English to the bone, and England is your only home."

"I warned you. I stop at nothing to gain what I want. And I want you. Besides——" His green eyes twinkled. "I still know how to make money. And I did manage to tuck away a very healthy amount for us. I've set up a business, and I'll continue brokering Arabian horses."

Emotion clogged her throat. She wanted to pinch herself, to see if it were real.

"So, will you marry me, though I'm nothing more than a lowly commoner?" he murmured.

"Yes," she said, touching his cheek. "I do like commoners."

Thomas kissed her, and he crushed her to him as if he never wanted to let her go. He never would, she thought in a daze of joy. They would be together now, no matter what people said or did. No matter what names they called her, or that his skin was fair and hers was dark.

She had spent her life searching for a place to truly call home, feeling lost and lonely because she did not belong.

She finally did realize where she belonged. In his arms, forever.

Jasmine was home at last.